*First Love Never Dies*

*Heart-Glow Volume II*

*First Love Never Dies*

*Heart-Glow Volume II*

SHEILAH R CRAFT

STARLIGHT BOOKS

**STARLIGHT** BOOKS



Cover photograph and front piece photograph taken by Sheilah R Craft.  The dolls in the photographs represent the main characters Angilia and Matthew.  The dolls were manufactured by the Tonner Doll Company.  Based on the author's descriptions of the two characters, Laurie Lenz customized the two dolls to resemble the characters.  Angilia's one-of-a-kind wedding ensemble was created by Sherry Isenbarger.  The author does not have any business affiliations with either Tonner Doll Company or ANGELS Doll Studio.





This novel is registered with the United States Library of Congress.

First Starlight Books edition June 2013

ISBN-13: 978-0615779829

ISBN-10: 0615779824

# ACKNOWLEDGMENTS

My greatest inspiration and encouragement come from God. More than anyone, God provides the foundation for these characters and what will ultimately become their epic story. The novel series began with <u>Heart-Glow</u> in 2012 and will take the DeBruce Martineau family through more than one century spanning four linear novels and two supplemental novels. This family's story began in January 2012 in <u>Heart-Glow</u> and concludes in August 2112 in the fourth linear novel. The two supplemental novels move into the family's past, and in that sense are prequels to <u>Heart-Glow</u>. God allowed me to see into their past, present, and future. The cycle of life, therefore, is confronted in each novel as characters age, die, and are born. The encouragement to confront my emotions as I write comes from God. Angilia is correct: life never ends.

The characters who populate the novels are gifts from God—friends, actually. I know them so well, deeply and intimately, and I truly love them. They sprang to life in me and took root in my heart. They remain part of me. I am, in many ways, part of them, as well. For the characters to resonate and to live for readers, they must reflect truth and life as I do. I could never bond and live with characters through more than one intense century if they and I shared nothing in common. My favorite poet—and Angilia's—Shelley wrote that all art must authentically spring from the heart and soul of the artist; otherwise the art contains no life or merit. <u>Heart-Glow</u> and <u>First Love Never Dies</u> show my belief in Shelley's philosophy. Neither I nor readers would care about these characters were they not forged in my heart and soul.

The readers of <u>Heart-Glow</u> continue to respond enthusiastically to the characters and that tumultuous, near-tragic one year through with Eric, Angilia, and their family and friends live, endure, and triumph.  Without the readers, my characters' lives would exist only within me, not in the world.  Books are meant to be read, and I remain eternally grateful to my wonderfully encouraging readers.

Two of those readers played important roles in bringing <u>First Love Never Dies</u> to publication as I envisioned.  Because I insist on the characters looking as I see them, I continue the trend of having one-of-a-kind custom dolls made for each of the characters in the novel series.  Eric and Angilia appeared on the cover of <u>Heart-Glow</u>.  One of the key moments in the lives of Angilia and Matthew graces the cover of <u>First Love Never Dies</u>: their Royal Wedding.  Matthew was created, as were Angilia and Eric, by the talented Laurie Lenz of ANGELS Doll Studio, whose web site is at http://laurielenzdollstudio.com.  Those amber eyes of Matthew's, which light up when he looks at "his Angilia," are perfectly lifelike.  Angilia's one-of-a-kind wedding gown was designed and made by Sherry Isenbarger, who made me feel like Angilia the bride-to-be during our e-mail conversations and planning.  She created the gown which both Angilia and I wanted for the fairy-tale wedding.

My family, present and past, deserves tremendous gratitude.  The patience, understanding, and time which my family accords me cannot be taken for granted.  They know that writing a novel is exhausting (yet joyous) work, and they give me the time and space needed.  My ancestors loom large over this series, as well, as I have placed several of them in Angilia's genealogy and life.  Robert the Bruce, Joan Plantagenet and her father King Edward I, William Wallace, and Abraham Lincoln teach, inspire, and contribute to who I am.  Angilia's passion for history and genealogy mirror my own.  I honor these magnificent ancestors by placing them in my fictional family's lives.  I also feel a deep debt to those ancestors who overflow my DNA by gifting me the writing gene: F. Scott Fitzgerald; Zelda Sayre; Thomas Lanier "Tennessee" Williams; William Sydney Porter (O. Henry); Percy Bysshe Shelley; Martin Luther; Faltonia Betitia Proba; John Milton; Richard Lovelace; and Gloria Jahoda among them.  Thank you for the inspiration and encouragement to fulfill my life's work.

vi

DEDICATED TO MY NEPHEWS


TROY DEVIN CRAFT


AND


NATHAN MICHAEL CRAFT

THIS IS MY BELOVED, AND THIS IS MY FRIEND.


--SONG OF SOLOMON 5:16

# CHAPTER 1

Angilia stood on her sitting room balcony watching the sunrise, its hues reminding her of Monet's paintings. Nine days earlier, on Christmas Day 2015, her best friend Matthew had requested her to accompany him to the palace chapel, where he took her hands in his and asked her to marry him and become his eternal partner. She knew that God had destined their union, and she had replied that she was honored to be Matthew's wife. He replaced the promise ring he had given her three years to the day earlier with a ring that filled her heart with love and peace. The round emerald surrounded by round-cut citrines was the engagement ring her father Eric had placed on Marisol's left ring finger on May 21, 1990, her mother's 39th birthday.

More than 25 years later, Angilia looked down at the same ring, a symbol of her parents' eternal love, now a symbol of her and Matthew's eternal bond and love. Her happiness overflowed her heart as she watched the gemstones sparkle in the early morning sunbeams. Eric stood in his daughter's door, smiling as he watched her, knowing how full of love and happiness she was. Eric's own soul radiated true peace and happiness, as well, for he, too, knew— he had long known—that God had predestined the union of Angilia and Matthew. God had reunited them on earth nearly four years earlier, on the worst day of Eric's life, the day his beloved daughter had nearly died for him.  Eric thanked God for Angilia, his most treasured and precious gift.

"Happy birthday, my beautiful daughter Angilia."

Angilia turned, smiling at him, bathed in the sun's halo and looking like the angel he had first seen almost 39 years earlier on the day his brother Patrick had died.  That familiar look of love in her eyes brought tears to Eric's eyes as he met her in a hug.  "I love you, Daddy," she said against him.

"I love you, Angel.  Today is a very special and important day, a very happy day," Eric smiled at her as he handed her a velvet jewel case.  "Happy birthday."

Angilia recognized the tiara.  Her mother had worn it with her wedding gown and veil when she and Eric married on June 26, 1991.  Tears filled her eyes, and she hugged her father tight.  "Thank you, Daddy.  I will wear this with love and honor on my wedding day, too," she said and stood on her left toes to kiss his cheek.  A lone tear slid down Eric's cheek, and she smiled at him, knowing it was a happy tear.  "I am so very happy.  My life is just as God destined it to be, with you and Matthew, and all our family and friends.  Everything is perfect and blessed."

"Yes, it is, Angel.  Absolutely perfect and blessed."  He smiled and handed her an envelope.  "I love you," he repeated as he kissed her forehead and left her suite.

Angilia ran her finger over the diamond tiara, tracing the central heart motif.  She bowed her head and offered a silent prayer of thanksgiving to God for blessing her life so tremendously.  She smiled before she closed the jewel case and placed it on her desk.  She took a deep breath and looked at the envelope he had handed her, her name written on the front in her father's elegant handwriting.  A birthday letter from him to her, continuing what was now an annual tradition early on her birthday morning.  Like she had done three years earlier, she sat on her window seat and carefully opened the envelope, reading his heartfelt words through her tears:

*3 January 2016*

*My Beautiful Daughter Angilia:*

*I love you. Happy 20th Birthday, Angel. I thank God daily for the gift of you, my light, my heart, my love. Whatever I did to deserve you, I know not, but I am so grateful that you are mine—eternally mine.*

*Today we share your engagement to Matthew with the world, and my little girl begins the next journey in her remarkable life. Watching you grow and mature into the awesome, courageous, compassionate young woman you are today has been my life's honor and joy. Every moment with you has been and will continue to be a breathtaking blessing. You really do amaze and awe me, Angilia. Everything you do is stunning and ordained.*

*At times I feel a hint of what I am sure Joseph must have felt, knowing he was the father in Jesus' life. What a great miracle and privilege for Joseph to be chosen by God above all other men to be the earthly father of Jesus Christ. What Joseph witnessed, heard, felt, and learned from Jesus! Angilia, I feel such reverence to be the one chosen by God as your father.*

*You are my angel, my soul, my daughter. My heart feels such peace, happiness, and love today as you—and the world—celebrate your 20th birthday and your engagement. When I walk with you down the aisle of the church on your wedding day, I know that I fulfill God's will. I love you so much more than I did yesterday, yet so much less than I will tomorrow.*

*Eternal Love,*

*Daddy*

Angilia reread his letter as tears fell down her cheeks, and then held the letter close to her heart. *Thank you, dear God, for blessing me with my father*, she silently prayed. Smiling, she walked to her desk and placed the letter in a drawer where she kept his letters and cards, as well as the letter from her mother that he had given her on Christmas Day 2012. She treasured each and would keep them always, leaving them behind for her child and grandchildren to read, so they, too, would know how much love flowed from Eric and Marisol to Angilia. Love created them and bound them eternally, just as it now bound Matthew and Angilia. That love was their legacy, the greatest gift Angilia would give to her own child.

§§§§

As if on cue, Matthew appeared in her doorway and handed her another envelope. He smiled at her, his amber eyes glowing, and softly said, "Happy birthday, my Angilia." Before she could respond, he brushed a tear from his face and walked away. The day had barely begun and it was already highly emotional. She looked at the envelope, her name inscribed on the front in Matthew's bold handwriting. Angilia smiled, returned to the window seat, and carefully opened the flap to find a letter from her fiancé:

*Angilia, my love!*

*You are the most beautiful, wise, loving, and compassionate woman I have ever known or imagined. Since the moment I first saw you nearly four years ago, my heart has known and loved only you. All that I am is yours eternally. You have not only my heart, but my soul. I believe, as you do, that our love is divine and destined to exist for eternity. I promise to cherish you now and always. You will never be without my love.*

*Happy Birthday, my love, my Angel.*

*Your Matthew*

Angilia bowed her head, still smiling, still radiating happiness, and prayed, yet again thanking God for his blessings and grace. He had brought Matthew and Angilia together long ago in the Unborn Children Sphere and had reunited them on March 7, 2012 after Gregor Jamieson's hired gunman had shot Eric and Angilia, nearly killing her. Matthew and her mother, under God's protective embrace, had preserved her life that day, despite her dying twice. Now, nearly four years later, Matthew and Angilia prepared to announce their impending wedding and to share their love and joy with the world.

§§§§

*It is with the greatest love and honor that HM King Eric de Valdavia announces the betrothal of his beloved daughter HRH Princess Consort Angilia,*

*Duchesse de Valmondois to her best friend Dr. Matthew Taylor, son of Dr. and Mrs. Mitchell Taylor. The King's happiness is unparalleled, and he welcomes the Taylors to his family with love and joy.*

Roger posted the official announcement on the palace gate at exactly 9:00 that morning, knowing the reaction it would elicit when he read it aloud. The crowds who had gathered for Angilia's birthday screamed, cheered, cried, and applauded immediately. Eric and Mitchell smiled broadly as they watched from the music room windows. Katherine, Juanita, and Alejandro watched from the Martínez' sitting room window, ecstatic and elated. Eduardo bounded in, as well, and hugged his parents as he joined them to watch the reactions below.

Simultaneously, Eric's Press Secretary, Carol, released the announcement and the engagement portraits, which Royal Photographer Bonnie Glaser had taken on New Year's Day. The formal portrait showed Angilia in a typically romantic, feminine vintage-style dress, Matthew in a suit, her left hand on his right arm and her head against his left shoulder. His arms were protectively around her. The informal portrait showed them attired in blue jeans and matching white shirts, Matthew seated in a chair as Angilia leaned behind him, her arms around his shoulders and her head resting against his. Their love shone forth, evident to even the most unromantic and cynical of people. Susan and Roger glimpsed the breaking news alert as they rushed to make sure all was ready for the press photo call, television interview, and balcony appearance.

Two dozen selected press photographers waited on the back lawn for the photo call. Angilia and Matthew would step outside at 9:15 and allow the photographers 15 minutes to take pictures while they walked slowly across the lawn, stopping occasionally. Angilia wore a gold silk dress and the green agate cameo of her mother, an outfit that not only mirrored her heirloom engagement ring but paid tribute to her beloved parents. Matthew wore a black suit, his tie emerald green in honor of Angilia's mother. The moment the couple walked through the double doors onto the patio, the sound of 24 cameras frantically whirring filled the air. Angilia's left arm was linked through Matthew's right arm, and she felt his nervous trembling.

Angilia gently squeezed his arm and smiled up at him in reassurance. He looked down at her, the full impact of the moment washing over him. He and Angilia were engaged and now the world knew. His smile broadened as he looked into those incredible turquoise eyes that had snared his heart nearly four years earlier. She stood on the toes of her left foot and whispered in his ear. "Are you as happy as I am?"

"Happier, I think," he smiled in reply. He lifted her left hand and kissed it, and the photographers all but walked over each other to get their pictures of the romantic gesture. Angilia leaned her head against his arm as he kissed her hand, and then they began slowly walking across the lawn toward a flower bed. Spontaneously, they stopped in front of rose bushes, the red, white, and pink buds and blossoms creating the perfect backdrop for the engagement day pictures. Five minutes later, the photo call ended and Roger thanked the photographers for their participation and respect. Angilia waved at them as she and Matthew returned to the palace to prepare for the live television interview.

Eric, Mitchell, Katherine, Juanita, Alejandro, and Eduardo had watched from the second floor windows, their hearts collectively filling the palace with almost-palpable love. "Mi hijo Eric, this is a most happy day for me. I prayed to live long enough to see mi nieta marry her true love, and I am so grateful," Juanita said as she hugged her son-in-law. Eric kissed her cheek and hugged her reverently. On May 21, 1990 she and Alejandro had watched a similar scene when King Gerard IV announced Eric's engagement to Marisol. More than one quarter of a century later, Eric wrote the announcement of his precious daughter's engagement. Eric was truly grateful, as well, as were Mitchell and Katherine, he knew.

Eric smiled, hearing the elevator carrying Angilia and Matthew, who came to him and the others with smiles and entwined hands. Angilia walked straight to her father and hugged him. "That went well, thank goodness. Be prepared to see those pictures everywhere," Eric said with a smile and a giggle. "Tea towels, tea sets, t-shirts, posters, post cards, bell pulls, flags, plates, thimbles. You name it, and someone will put one of the pictures on it." Eric had noticed Matthew's touch of nervousness earlier, although he also noticed—as did everyone else—how well Angilia had charmed him over that. "Are you both ready for the interview? Is everything set, Roger?"

"Yes. The cameras are set up and ready to go. Laurie and Franklin are waiting in the office with Carol. They want you there in about 10 minutes for the light check," Roger told Angilia and Matthew. "The large screens are set up on the mall, too, for those who are gathered outside. The feed is set up in the media room for all of you, too," he said to the family members. Katherine kissed Angilia and Matthew, as did Juanita, and Mitchell and Eduardo hugged them. Alejandro hugged Matthew and held his beloved granddaughter close as tears filled his eyes. He kissed the top of her head and went with the others to the media room so they could watch the engagement interview live.

Eric smiled at his daughter and future son-in-law and walked with them to the elevator. Angilia still limped and still used the elevator rather than the hundreds of stairs in the palace. It was the one daily reminder of what had happened in March 2012. Matthew and Eric held her hands as they entered the office she shared with her father, and greeted Laurie and Franklin, the most-trusted broadcast journalists in Valdavia. The two were selected by Eric and Angilia for the honor of conducting the coveted engagement interview. Franklin bowed and Laurie curtseyed, both of them elated for the Princess Consort and His Majesty.

Eric thanked them both, and then turned to his daughter. "I love you, Angilia." He kissed her forehead, and then turned to Matthew and hugged him, winked at him, and left the office to join the others in the media room. Angilia and Matthew settled on the sofa, while Laurie and Franklin sat in the matching chairs facing them. The four cameras were in place and adjusted, as were the lights, moments before they went on air live to the country and the world. Angilia smiled at Matthew, seated to her left, and squeezed his hand as if to tell him that the interview would be fine. He smiled and nodded at her, just as the countdown indicated they were live.

"Welcome to a very special edition of the news from the Palais Royale de Valdavia. I am Franklin Sydney."

"I am Laurie Dougray.  Franklin and I are honored to bring you this exclusive interview with Her Royal Highness Princess Consort Angilia, Duchesse de Valmondois and Dr. Matthew Taylor on this very special and exciting day."

"We are, indeed, Laurie.  Your Royal Highness, Dr. Taylor, congratulations on your engagement," Franklin said.

Angilia and Matthew smiled, still holding hands.  "Thank you, Franklin and Laurie," Angilia said with her smile still wide.

"Thank you," Matthew said, still nervous.  Other than the infrequent statement or comment, Matthew had never appeared on live television before.  Angilia gently squeezed his hand in encouragement.

Laurie smiled, as well, and added, "Congratulations.  And happy birthday, Your Royal Highness."

Angilia slightly blushed.  "Thank you, Laurie."

"Your Royal Highness, we have all watched you from a distance your entire life," Franklin commented, which heightened Angilia's blush.  "We—everyone in Valdavia—watched over the past nearly four years as you and Dr. Taylor began working together. We are all joyous and elated today, seeing you celebrate not only your 20th birthday, but your engagement."

"Thank you," Angilia again replied, and Matthew smiled at her as he had done almost constantly for four years.

"Your Royal Highness, may we ask what you feel today?" Laurie asked.

"I feel so very happy and loved, Laurie.  I have always proclaimed that my life is blessed, and today only reconfirms this."

"And you, Dr. Taylor?  How do you feel today?"

"Also happy and loved.  Every dream that I ever had or even dared not dream has come true a hundredfold.  My best friend and I will share all of eternity together," Matthew said as he looked at his Angilia, tears shining in his luminous amber eyes.

Laurie asked him, "Dr. Taylor, as you prepare to assume your royal duties, what are your immediate thoughts?  What do you see as your primary role as the Princess Consort's husband?"

"My number one priority is and always will be Angilia.  I want to do whatever I can to assist her and support her.  I want to get more involved with organizations and charities, as well, and do all I can for our neighbors and our country."  Matthew glanced at Angilia.  "I have the best teacher beside me, so I cannot go wrong if I follow Angilia's example."

"Dr. Taylor, when did you propose?  What can you share with us about the proposal?" Franklin asked.

"On Christmas Day, just a few days ago, I asked Angilia to go to the palace chapel with me.  I asked her there, she said yes, and I replaced our promise ring with the engagement ring," Matthew shared.

"How utterly romantic," Laurie sighed.  "Speaking of the engagement ring, may we see it, please?"

Since Angilia and Matthew were already holding hands, Matthew lifted her left hand for a better view of the very beautiful and symbolic ring.  Angilia looked at it with obvious love on her face, and in the media room, Eric felt even more tears fill his eyes.  Everyone in the media room knew the ring's history, and that Matthew had specifically asked Eric if he could give that same ring to Angilia.  Many Valdavians caught their breath at the sight of the same ring they had seen on the left hand of then-Prince Eric's fiancée in 1990.

Laurie and Franklin, of course, recognized the ring, though no details of the proposal or engagement had been provided to them prior to the interview.  Franklin swallowed his tears and echoed everyone's thoughts.  "Your Royal Highness, we all recognize that ring as the one His Majesty gave to your mother on the day they became engaged.  Had you known in advance that this would be your engagement ring, too?"

"No, Franklin.  My father kept the ring in a porcelain jewel case on his night stand.  I often looked at it with love.  To me, it represents the eternal, true love my parents share," Angilia softly said as she looked at the ring. She felt Matthew gently squeeze her hand.

"I asked His Majesty about the ring on Christmas Eve, actually. There is no more perfect or beautiful engagement ring for Angilia than her mother's. Her father designed and had the ring made for his one love, and it just seems right that their daughter wear it as a symbol of not just their eternal love, but now of ours," Matthew confessed to the world.

In the media room and around the world, peoples' emotions and tears overflowed. Laurie struggled to contain and control her own tears as the interview progressed. "If anyone ever doubted that this is a royal marriage of love, they no longer can. I dare say, Laurie, this is the most heart-felt, romantic, and emotional interview we have witnessed," Franklin commented as Laurie regained her composure.

"I agree, Franklin. Your Royal Highness and Dr. Taylor, are there other details you can reveal? Have you selected a wedding date yet?" Laurie asked.

Angilia and Matthew beamed at one another, realizing the question would likely be asked. They had decided, while they stood in the chapel on Christmas Day, although they had not yet shared their chosen date with anyone. Angilia knew her father was watching, and she looked straight into the camera, at him, and revealed, "We have: June 26, 2016." Gasps filled the media room as Eric placed his hands over his chest and looked into his daughter's eyes. Tears slid down his cheeks, and the others sitting there with him also cried.

"Your parents' wedding anniversary," Laurie declared. "Twenty-five years to the day that your parents married, you and Dr. Taylor will marry."

"That's right, Laurie, and in the same church," Angilia smiled.

"That was the only date for us, really," Matthew added. "That was an easy and quick decision for us."

"What was His Majesty's reaction, if I may ask?" Franklin inquired.

At that exact second, Eric appeared in the office doorway, his smile and glowing eyes displaying his happiness. Without any delay, Angilia smiled and truthfully answered, "My father is elated, Franklin. Matthew is correct. There is no other wedding date for us. We both knew that instantly. We never even discussed dates, because we both knew in our hearts."

Matthew smiled and nodded his agreement. Angilia had wanted to surprise her father with the news of the wedding date, and she had succeeded. Matthew was still awed by the love that shone forth from Eric and Angilia, love stronger than and unlike any other love. Eric joined Carol and Roger near his desk and watched the remainder of the engagement interview with them.

Eric saw the love that flowed between and around Angilia and Matthew, tenderly embracing them. Eric's memories showed him that look of love in Matthew's eyes that tragic day in the ambulance as he prepared Angilia for emergency surgery. For Matthew, this truly had been love at first sight. Angilia had written about that in her 2012 diary, and she had been right. God had placed Matthew in the proper time and place to be the cardiac surgeon on call that day. God had brought them back together.

Roger felt tears stinging his eyes, too, as he watched Angilia, her love and happiness so evident. Roger had stood beside his best friend Eric when Angilia was born. He had watched her grow up and do things very few people her age did. Roger had witnessed the incredible love between father and daughter from the first moment of her life. Now he shared this beautiful moment with them.

Roger put his hand on Eric's shoulder, and the two men smiled at one another. As the interview concluded, they saw Matthew's hand slide to Angilia's back, as if to support and protect her, as the young couple thanked Franklin and Laurie. Finally, the lights and cameras were turned off, and the crew began quickly packing their equipment.

Franklin, Laurie, Angilia, and Matthew all stood, thanking one another for a joyous and emotional interview. The journalists turned and finally noticed Eric, surprised and unaware he had entered earlier. Eric shook their hands and thanked them for their respect and professionalism. Carol escorted them to the garage, where the crew loaded the news van and prepared to leave the palace grounds. Once they exited the gate, Carol rushed back to the office, stopping suddenly in the doorway.

Inside, Matthew and Roger stood smiling, their arms around one another's shoulders, while Eric and Angilia shared a hug. "I am so happy and proud today, Angel. We have one more public event before we can enjoy our private time with your birthday and engagement party." He turned to Matthew with a smile. "Let's get ready for the balcony appearance." Roger clapped Matthew's shoulder, hugged Angilia, and left to ensure all was ready on the fifth floor.

Matthew and Eric went with Angilia in the elevator to the third floor to freshen up before what Eric knew would be a lengthy balcony appearance. Juanita came into Angilia's bedroom with Susan, and both dabbed tears from their eyes. "Mi nieta, my heart is so very full of love today. You are so beautiful, more beautiful than ever with your love for Dr. Matthew shining in your eyes."

"Yo amor tú, Abuela. Yo amor tú," Angilia said as tears of joy filled her eyes yet again that day. She hugged her grandmother, grateful that she was still with them in this life to share the day.

The crowd had grown substantially outside the palace, and the three women heard the shouts and cheers from Angilia's suite. Susan went with Juanita to help her freshen up while Angilia washed her tear-stained face and reapplied her makeup. She looked in her vanity mirror and smiled when she saw her uncle's image reflected there. "Uncle Patrick! I am so happy you came today!" She stood and smiled up at him, and he pulled her into a hug.

"Happy birthday, Little One. And happy engagement. I have no words for how I feel," Patrick softly said. "Heaven rejoices today for you and your happiness."

They heard someone enter her suite, and Patrick began to fade until Angilia squeezed his arm and said, "Don't worry. It's Daddy." Sure enough, they heard him call for her, and she responded, "We're in here, Daddy. Please come here." Eric stepped to her dressing room door expecting to see Angilia and Susan. He gasped when he saw his brother instead.

"Eric! Our little girl is a woman now, engaged to marry her friend. I swear, though, she hasn't changed at all." Patrick smiled at his niece. "You still look exactly the same as you did that first day. How long ago?"

Eric giggled. "She does, doesn't she? She seems as ageless as you do, Patrick. It was 38 and a half years ago. It doesn't seem possible, does it? In some ways, time stands still while it marches forward."

"Almost 40 years? So I would be 58 in a few days if I were still on earth? Time is so hard to wrap my head around now, you know."

"I know. It took me a while to get used to it after I was born. It seems so strange to be so bound to time here. Everything is so scheduled and run by the clock. I much prefer the way it is in Heaven, with no time," Angilia admitted.

Eric's cell phone beeped, and he read a text message from Roger that everything was ready for the balcony appearances. "Speaking of time, we best get everyone to the fifth floor." He looked at Patrick, but before Eric could say anything more, Patrick hugged him.

"I'll be back later today. I want some quality time with both of you on this most special day." Patrick kissed Angilia, hugged Eric, and waved as he disappeared. Angilia beamed at her father as they gathered everyone to head upstairs. They all exited the elevator, hearing the screams, shouts, and cheers quite clearly through the open double doors to the balcony.

"Angilia and Matthew, you two go out first, and then your parents will join you. Then your grandparents and uncle will come out to join you," Roger explained.

Matthew nervously adjusted his tie, took a deep breath, and looked at Angilia. He offered her his arm and they walked onto the balcony to the most thunderous cheers and applause Matthew had ever heard. Several thousand people crammed the mall in front of the palace, waving signs, jumping, taking pictures with long-lens cameras, and screaming, their fervor unrelenting. Angilia waved, as did Matthew—albeit timidly at first—inciting more cheers.

Matthew looked at her and leaned close to say, "This is scary. I've seen this happen before, but not to me." Angilia took his left hand and squeezed it reassuringly, as she had already done several times that morning. He held her hand tightly, relying on her to get him through his nervousness during his first day in the public spotlight. Eric had warned him about the public scrutiny and pressures during their talk in October 2012, and Matthew still believed this interest in him would subside after the Royal wedding hysteria. Angilia was their much-beloved Princess and a world-renowned performer and writer. He was her fiancé, soon to be her husband, and he wanted to support and help her as much as possible. She would become the first hereditary Queen de Valdavia, so there had never been a—what?—King Consort before. Matthew would have to create and forge his role as he saw fit, something he and Angilia had discussed over the past three years. Matthew did not care about whatever title he held; he wanted to support his wife and do his own charity work.

Suddenly, the crowd's cheers escalated, and Angilia knew why. Eric joined them, standing beside Matthew. He put his arm around the young man's shoulders, knowing how unnerving the day's events were for Matthew. Eric smiled at his daughter, and then waved at the crowds, which thrilled the people, who loved and respected their King tremendously.

Angilia turned and motioned for Dr. and Mrs. Taylor to join them. They both took deep breaths and walked out together, standing next to Angilia. Katherine put her arm around Angilia, and looked out at the thousands of people in pure amazement. Angilia encouraged them to wave, so Mitchell shrugged his shoulders and did so. Katherine did likewise. They were even less accustomed to this than was Matthew. At least he had accompanied Angilia on public engagements. They had rarely received any public attention. Angilia squeezed Katherine's hand, reassuring her that everything was going well. "I hope so," Katherine said into Angilia's ear.

A moment later, Eduardo escorted his parents onto the balcony.  Alejandro and Juanita were well known and loved.  They were cheered as they walked to stand beside their beloved son-in-law.  Eduardo stood next to Mitchell.  He, too, found the public attention rather alien still, despite becoming more visible during public events such as this.  He knew that people were not there to see him, and that Angilia and Matthew were the focus of attention.  Still, he was always fascinated to observe such events from the inside, a rarity he knew.  Most people watched the balcony appearance via television or computer and not from their vantage point on the balcony.  How fantastic to look down at so very many screaming people.  Eric and Angilia had lived with this since birth, born into the Royal Family and to this life.  Eduardo sensed how Matthew felt, stepping into this life of not only privilege but duty, scrutiny, and examination.

After 45 minutes, Eduardo, Alejandro, and Juanita waved and blew kisses to the crowd below, then went indoors.  Katherine kissed Angilia's cheek just before she and Mitchell followed the Martínezes inside.  Eric waved at everyone and motioned that he and the engaged couple would go indoors, too.  People voiced their disappointment, and pleas for them to come down to the courtyard were clearly heard.  Eric leaned close to Matthew and asked if he and Angilia wanted to go down for a meet-and-greet.  Matthew's wide eyes betrayed his discomfort, but he repeated the question to Angilia, who smiled and nodded.  Matthew shrugged his shoulders, knowing he had to get used to this.  Eric motioned to the crowd that they would all be down soon, and thousands of people screamed in delight.

Inside, Eric asked the others if they wanted to join him, Angilia, and Matthew outside, so they took a quick refresher on the third floor prior to going out onto the courtyard.  Angilia and Matthew, still arm-in-arm, walked out the front door, followed by Eric, the Taylors, and finally the Martínezes.  The screams were deafening as they approached the gate.  Angilia asked the guard to unlock the gate, and she took Matthew's hand and pulled him out beside her.  They were instantly surrounded by well-wishers, many of whom had come to wish her a happy birthday never anticipating a Royal engagement.  Flowers, cards, and gifts were thrust into her arms, as well as into Matthew's, as people hugged, kissed, and congratulated them.

Mitchell and Katherine were wide-eyed and amazed to experience the outpouring of public emotions first-hand. They had watched this happen to Eric and Angilia practically every day, but they had never been directly involved in such excitement. People reached to shake their hands, offer congratulations to them, and welcome them to the Royal Family. They glanced at Angilia, at ease and comfortable talking to everyone, as she continued holding Matthew's hand and helping him to feel more relaxed as he, too, talked with people. Mitchell and Katherine took their cues from their future daughter-in-law and their son, and soon they chatted with people who were, essentially, their neighbors.

Eric and Angilia had been asked to autograph copies of the <u>Heart-Glow</u> CD, which still sold millions of copies each year, as well as pictures and magazines. Angilia and Matthew were asked to sign copies of the two engagement portraits, which at first took Matthew by complete surprise. Her slanted script alongside his straight bold signature brought a smile to his lips, and he was struck once again by the reality in front of him. He and Angilia were engaged to marry! Matthew felt happier than he ever imagined he could feel.

Roger forced his way through the crowd and reminded Eric of the time. The party guests would arrive soon, and they had to prepare for the combination birthday-engagement party. Eric smiled at his best friend and nodded. He stepped to Angilia and Matthew and put his arms around them. "Ladies and gentlemen, thank you all for coming today to wish my daughter a happy birthday. I know I surprised you with the announcement this morning. Thank you for sharing our happiness and for wishing Angilia and Matthew a happy engagement. I know I speak for all of us that we are happier than ever. Thank you each for making this day even more special for us. We love you," Eric said, his voice loudly carrying over the now-hushed throng of people.

Angilia smiled up at her father and added, "I do love you all. Thank you for taking time to think of me today and to come. Thank you for sharing my joy, happiness, and love today as I begin the next chapter in my life as Matthew's wife." She blew them a kiss as she, Eric, and Matthew waved before they turned to follow Mitchell, Katherine, Alejandro, Juanita, and Eduardo into the palace foyer. Angilia and Matthew turned for a final wave to their fellow Valdavians before they stepped inside and closed the door.

§§§§§

After a quick refresher, Angilia, Matthew, and Eric greeted the guests who began to arrive at 2:00 that afternoon. Everyone had expected a birthday party. Like the rest of the world's population, they had heard the news of the engagement earlier that day, not necessarily surprised but nonetheless exited and unprepared. They had received no hint that the engagement had actually occurred just days earlier. No one knew except one very special guest, that is, who was the first to arrive for the party.

"Mr. Brennan! I am so happy you are here with us today," Angilia smiled as she bent to kiss her friend on his cheek.

"I would not miss today for anything, Princess. Isn't that so, Ginny?" he smiled up at his loyal nurse. "I am still on a cloud after the glorious party you and His Majesty gave me two days ago." Mr. Brennan celebrated his 100th birthday at the Palais Royale de Valdavia, with a massive party orchestrated by Eric and Angilia. He had the distinct honor of watching Bonnie take Angilia's and Matthew's engagement portraits that morning before his own party began. Angilia wanted to share her joy with Mr. Brennan, knowing his earthly life was nearing its end.

"Thank you for your loyalty and friendship, Mr. Brennan," Eric said as he bent to shake the gentleman's hand, only to be pulled into a hug. Angilia felt tears stinging her eyes as she watched her father and their friend, and Matthew put his arm around her. She smiled at him and quickly dabbed her eyes as more guests arrived, including Billy and his parents.

Billy was now 14 and nearly as tall as Matthew. He shook Eric's hand and bent to kiss Angilia's hand. "Happy birthday, Princess darling. And happy engagement to both of you," he smiled as he shook Matthew's hand. "I am so very happy for both of you."

"Thank you, Billy," Angilia and Matthew replied in unison. Simon and Kimberly Panning, Billy's parents, followed their son in congratulating Angilia and Matthew.  As more guests arrived, they mingled and talked excitedly with one another on the patio, where tables and chairs were decorated.  Angilia's manager and producer Sam Burton arrived with Angilia's four band members: John Herbert, Tim Hanley, Greg Smithson, and Joe Arnold.  They had each met her when she was a six-year-old musical prodigy who had swept former teen idol Tom Greenfield off of his feet at a chance encounter.  The five men adored and loved Angilia, and overflowed with happiness for her as they hugged her and Matthew.

Following them was Dr. Christopher Dalton, her former professor and boss and the President of Wolfson College at the University of Oxford.  Like Sam and the band, he had met her when she was a child, a genius who had earned her doctorate from Oxford and become a professor at the age of 11.  He, too, had watched her grow to adulthood with awe and respect.  As he hugged her, he knew they were forever connected.  She and Eric returned to the University annually to bestow the music scholarship that had been established in Eric's name in 2012.  "I am so very happy for you, Angilia, and so honored to share today with you."

"Thank you, Christopher.  We are so happy you are here to share today with us," Angilia said as she leaned up to kiss his cheek. Matthew shook his hand, his own smile as broad as possible. Accompanying Christopher was perhaps the most surprised guest of all, Anthony Severson, who was soon to graduate from the University; he earned the first Eric DeBruce Martineau Scholarship for Musical Excellence nearly four years earlier.  Anthony was honored to be invited, although he did not know yet why he had been.

Excited voices and squeals announced the six friends Angilia had met through her initial involvement with Christ on Campus in the fall of 2012.  Shannon, Darlene, Amy, Nicole, Amanda, and Scott greeted Eric, and Mitchell smiled when he recalled how Darlene used to faint every time she saw Eric.  Darlene was now 22, and although she still looked at Eric with huge eyes, she no longer needed Mitchell's services when she visited.

The five girls gathered around Angilia for a group hug, their collective chatter and screeches of delight filling the air. They sobbed when they looked at her engagement ring, commenting on its beauty and romance. Their excited comments and hugs overwhelmed Matthew, while Scott hugged and congratulated Angilia and then Matthew.

Angilia had requested no birthday gifts, wanting only the company of her family and friends. They had protested, but she insisted that if they really wanted to give a gift that they consider a donation to one of her charities or foundations. She was so blessed and blissfully happy that she could think of nothing she needed or wanted except to be surrounded by the people she loved most on this most magical day.

Angilia took a deep breath, smiled at Matthew, and they welcomed everyone to the double celebration. While they spoke, Chef Antoine and his staff added the final touches to the buffet. Guests helped themselves to tea, lemonade, mineral water, or coffee as they chatted and mingled, continuing to congratulate Eric, Angilia, Matthew, and their families. Roger, Daniel, Susan, and Bonnie joined the festivities as well, told they were in attendance as friends, not employees.

At 3:00, everyone lined up to serve themselves from the buffet, enjoying a late lunch on the patio, the cool breeze refreshing and soothing. Angilia sat between her father and Matthew, the two most important men in her life, her joyous smile never fading. After everyone finished lunch, Antoine and his staff collected the plates. Angilia and Matthew stood, smiling, and again thanked everyone for coming.

"We know that some of you were surprised by your invitations, but Matthew and I wanted you each here today for a very special reason. We want to ask many of you to be part of our wedding. Susan," Angilia said as she looked at her most-trusted friend, "there is no one else I would rather have as my maid of honor if you would do me the pleasure of accepting."

Susan could not stop her tears, although she dabbed at them as she stood and smiled. "It will be my honor, darling," she replied and she went to hug Angilia with love and gratitude.

Matthew next spoke, looking at Angilia's uncle. "Eduardo, will you do me the honor of being my best man?" he asked.

Eduardo stood, tears filling his eyes, and said, "Nothing would fill my heart more than to be part of your wedding day. I love you both," he declared as he walked to hug Matthew and Angilia.

"Shannon, Darlene, Amy, Nicole, and Amanda, I want to ask you to be my bridesmaids," Angilia stated with a smile as she looked at her friends, who instantly squealed with delight. The five young ladies stood and ran to Angilia for another group hug. As they returned to their seats, Angilia giggled and said, "I take it that means you will," to which the young ladies said they would love to support her on her wedding day.

"As for the groomsmen, I would like to ask Roger, Daniel, Christopher, Scott, and Billy to fill those roles," Matthew smiled and looked at each of them in turn. They all stood and said they would be delighted, and each walked to thank Matthew and Angilia personally. Billy in particular was touched by the honor, and he felt his whole being soar as he shook Matthew's hand and kissed Angilia's.

Matthew continued as he looked at Bonnie. "Bonnie, there is no one else we want to be our wedding photographer than you." Four years ago, she had been a prisoner of war, with Eduardo and eight other journalists, fearing she would spend the remainder of her life in the small room where she had spent 22 years. She owed her freedom and her life to Angilia, and now she would be the Royal Wedding photographer. With tears sliding down her face, she hugged Angilia and Matthew and told them she would be deeply honored to capture their love on their glorious wedding day.

"Anthony, Matthew and I would like to ask you to be our pianist during the church service," Angilia smiled at him. More than anyone else, Anthony was truly stunned, never dreaming of such a distinction. His face registered his surprise, so much so that

Christopher had to gently nudge him to stand.  He did so, and accepted with a bow, and then went to shake Matthew's hand and to kiss Angilia's, as he had done four years earlier at the scholarship ceremony.

Matthew turned and looked at Antoine, who stood unobtrusively behind the buffet table.  "Antoine, Angilia and I would like you to design and to make our wedding cake."  Antoine bowed, thanked them, and said he was deeply privileged to do so.

Angilia beamed at her talented band.  "John, Tim, Greg, and Joe, of course we want you all with us that day, but we also want to ask if you will provide the music for the reception that afternoon, at least for part of the time.  There are no better musicians anywhere, and none who mean so much to us."  The four men stood, tears of happiness shining in their eyes, and said they could think of nothing they would rather do.  Like the other wedding party members, they hugged the happy couple.

"Thank you all for making our wedding day plans so very easy and so perfect.  More than anything, our wedding day is the day our love and union are sanctified by God, and we both want to share it with the people we love most," Angilia said as tears glistened in her eyes yet again that day.  As she looked at Matthew and smiled, the party guests stood and applauded.

At that moment, Antoine carried a gorgeous cake to the buffet table.  The four-tier cake was adorned with white and pink sugar roses and ribbons, and Angilia smiled as she nudged Matthew's arm.  Their wedding colors were white and pink. Antoine's birthday cake could easily be their wedding cake; it was so elegant and beautiful.  Eric stood beside his daughter, his happiness immeasurable.  She smiled at him, pulled him into a hug, and said, "I love you, Daddy."  He kissed the top of her head, choked by his tears, and said another silent prayer of thanksgiving.

Angilia walked to the buffet table, blew out the one heart-shaped candle, and cut the first piece of cake, which—as always— she handed to her father.  She cut a second piece, which she handed to Matthew.  Antoine and his staff served the remaining guests, while everyone continued to enjoy their friendship, love, laughter, tears, and talk. The camaraderie continued into the early evening, excitement unabated, and as the air became a bit chilly, they went to the second floor sitting room until dinner. As usual, Angilia, Alejandro, Juanita, and Mr. Brennan—who was assisted by Ginny—all took the elevator.

At 8:00, they all went to the first floor dining room for a delicious dinner made and served by Antoine, and the room resonated with their talk and laughter as they lingered over desert and coffee. Finally, at 10:00 that night the guests began departing, once more congratulating Angilia and Matthew and wishing her a happy birthday. Mr. Brennan was the last to leave, hugging his friends again before Ginny and Matthew lifted him into the car. Angilia leaned in to kiss him one last time before he left, knowing the day had been exciting but tiring for him, as well as for her grandparents.

Inside, she, Matthew, and Eric shared emotional hugs with their closest friends, Roger, Susan, and Daniel, and then Angilia linked her arms with her grandparents' arms, and they took the elevator to the third floor. Susan quickly arrived, and Angilia asked her to assist Abuela. Eric and Matthew came up the staircase together, their arms around one another. The sight warmed Angilia's heart. She smiled at Matthew, he smiled at her, and they both felt such wondrous peace and happiness. Matthew kissed her hand and wished her a good night as he entered his suite.

Once they were alone in the hallway, Angilia smiled up at her treasured father and pulled him into her sitting room. "Sit with me for a while?" she asked, and Eric nodded. They sat on her oversized sofa, relishing their love and happiness, when they felt a very familiar warmth encircle them. They smiled in unison, both of them knowing who was there. "Uncle Patrick," Angilia enthused when he manifested and plopped himself between them on the sofa.

"Now we can celebrate together," Patrick announced with his handsome slanted smile as he put his arms around his brother and his niece. Without any warning, the radio on Angilia's desk began blaring rock music, and she jumped up to close her suite door and to turn down the volume. Patrick giggled, said they should party all night, and Eric swatted his arm.

"Today has been exhilarating but exhausting for most everyone, especially Alejandro and Juanita, who are trying to sleep next door. Nothing has changed at all, Patrick, nothing at all," Eric said with a twinkle in his eyes and a smile.

"It never will, not now. Why should it? There is far too much seriousness in those Choirs as it is. Besides, God wants me in Heaven, so he is okay with me as I am. He hasn't ever told me to change," Patrick said with a grin.

"Actually, he has, Uncle Patrick. Remember when you hid Great-grandfather's robe on God's throne? When I went to God to get you out of trouble, he told me that you needed to learn restraint. I can only imagine what you've done since I left the Angels Choir."

"They need some excitement there, Little One. I mean, really, can you see me walking around in a tunic constantly, quietly doing my duties while eternity slowly ticks by," Patrick grimaced. Eric leaned his head on his brother's shoulder and laughed uncontrollably as he imagined the sight of Patrick in a tunic peacefully strolling through Heaven.

Angilia half-playfully swatted her father's arm. "Don't encourage him, Daddy. He gets in enough trouble as it is."

"I know," Eric said through his laughter, while Patrick feigned insult.

"I do not get in that much trouble," he insisted, which made Eric laugh more. "I don't. I never have."

"No, of course not. How come you were grounded at least once a week, then?" Eric reminded him.

"Yeah, but Mother and Father always rescinded my punishment. That doesn't count. Look, God wants me in the Angels Choir for some important mission in the future, so he is fine with me, really. Life there would be boring without me," Patrick said with a wink.

"That's one word for it," Angilia agreed, smiling at her impishly boyish uncle. "I am happy you are here, Uncle Patrick. Will you come to the wedding?"

"Of course! Nothing can keep me away." Patrick hugged his precious niece, the girl who had made his transition to death and Heaven painless and who had filled his heart with so much love. He could never truly fathom how much love Eric felt for Angilia, but he knew how very grateful his brother was to have her in his life. He felt his brother's gratitude emanate from Eric's heart constantly. "I love you so very much, Little One."

Eric heard tears in his brother's voice, and marveled at how much love and emotion the three of them shared across the invisible barrier between Heaven and earth. As if sensing Eric's thoughts, Patrick turned and hugged his brother. "I love you so much, Eric. I always have. I always will."

"I know, Patrick, and I have always and will always love you more than you know," Eric said softly as tears choked him again that day.

"I do know, Eric. I know." Patrick held Eric and Angilia close to him. "Death can never separate us. Our love is too strong, too powerful to ever let anything or anyone separate us."

"Yes, it is, Uncle Patrick, always and forever. Our love, like our souls, is eternal," Angilia whispered. She kissed her uncle's cheek, he kissed hers, and they felt their love surge through their bodies.

"Always, Patrick," Eric too whispered as he hugged his much-loved little brother. "Always."

"I love you both, and I am so very happy for you today," Patrick said. "I'll be back," he smiled as he kissed them each again before he vanished into spirit form and whisked away, back to Heaven. Eric and Angilia smiled as Patrick's warmth slowly trickled away, and held each other close as love filled and surrounded them.

§§§§§

*3 January 2016*

*Today was gloriously happy and love-filled, the entire day.  Both Daddy and Matthew gave me letters early this morning, and I treasure them so.  Daddy also gave me the most beautiful and special tiara in the world—the one he had made for Mommy, the one she wore with her veil on their wedding day.  Now, 25 years to the day since their gorgeous and love-filled wedding, I will wear that tiara with my wedding veil!  That day will also be the last day that I wear the same purity ring that Mommy wore until her wedding day.  She is so alive; I know that, for I feel her spirit, her soul, in my heart always.  I love her so, and I know she loves me.  She is the one who brought me back to life twice the day of the shooting.  Just as I did everything I could to make sure Jamieson never altered Daddy's destiny, Mommy made sure my destiny was not altered.*

*I am grateful for that, not only because I treasure my life here with Daddy and now with Matthew, but because had I died, another would never have the chance to live—my future child.  My most important role in this life is to give life to my future son.  Had Jamieson's plot succeeded, several lives would have been destroyed, including my son's.*

*God made sure that never happened.  He brought me and Matthew together on earth, and now we are engaged to marry!  In a few years, our son will join us, and we will share our lives and our love with him.  My life is so blessed, so happy, and I am so thankful.*

# CHAPTER 2

"Hey, Little One!  Can I hear your new song?"

Angilia smiled at her uncle as she sat on the floor in his sitting room, the room she had long called her Thoughtful Place. "Actually, I didn't write this one—you did, Uncle Patrick."

"I did?  I've never written a song in any life," he giggled as he sat on the floor across from her.

"You wrote the lyrics to this one, at least.  All I did was put them to music," Angilia told him.  Patrick's face betrayed his confusion.  "You remember telling me I could read your journals and notebooks?" she asked, and he nodded in reply.  "I'm sure you know I have, a lot, and that I truly love them.  They capture part of you, who and what you were at those moments, what you thought and felt.  Your poems are especially insightful and thought-provoking, Uncle Patrick.  I found one today that I had never seen before, folded in the bottom desk drawer, stuck in the back corner. I sat in here all morning reading and rereading this poem, my heart and my mind so full of pain at what you endured internally at that time.  You were so young and so wise, and finally I just heard this as a song and grabbed my guitar."

Patrick's steel blue eyes flashed recognition and truth as he recalled which poem he had written and hidden, hoping no one would ever find it. "You found that? I should have burned it right away. I never meant for anyone to read that," he said, picking at the shag carpet and no longer looking at her.

Angilia's heart ached. "I'm so sorry, Uncle Patrick. I never want to hurt you, never. No one else will ever see this," she promised him as she crumpled her sheet music into a ball and told him she would take it to the incinerator immediately. As she struggled to stand, she felt his hand on her arm, restraining her.

"Why that one?"

"Your questions, your thoughts, your concerns are all universal. So many people throughout the centuries have asked these questions, although not everyone wrote them down as you did. The purpose of one's life is the most-asked question people have. How many young soldiers thought as you did as they faced their looming deaths, knowing that they, too, would die without children who would carry forward their names and their legacies? How many people think about whether they will be remembered and loved after they die? How many people wonder what dying will feel like and what happens after they die? Uncle Patrick, these are everyman's questions and thoughts, written by a teenager with such angst and yet such hope. That hope is what people need, and you can provide it to them. You and your words can give people first of all the knowledge that they are not alone in asking these questions, and second and most important, the truth that God is in control of our lives and our destinies," Angilia stated as she held his hand and looked into his eyes.

Patrick sat quietly, unmoving, for several moments, while Angilia bowed her head. She had hurt her sweet Uncle Patrick, the last thing she ever intended to do. *Will he, can he, forgive me?* she asked herself as a tear slid from her eye and down her cheek. She felt his soft finger gently brush it away. "If you think so, I trust you. May I hear it?"

Angilia looked at him, nodded as she wiped away her tears, and picked up her guitar. As she began playing the opening chords,

Patrick pulled his knees to his chest, leaned his head on his knees, and listened intently to his niece singing the words he had written so long ago:

*Every day and every night, so many questions fill me;*

*They consume my time and my thoughts to my distraction,*

*As I seek the answers which I pray bring peace to my soul*

*And ease this tumult within which lead all to disruption.*

*Why am I here? Why was I born? My brain keeps asking*

> *God.*

*What is my ultimate purpose? Why was I created?*

*What does my life mean to the rest of this vast universe?*

*Everything about me is a mystery, yet fated.*

*I feel such anguish as I ponder about my future,*

*Sensing that I shall never grow old and will stay alone—*

*Never truly a man, unwed, childless, with no legacy,*

*No mark, no inheritance, to leave behind of my own.*

*I live each day fearlessly, for I hide the fear and angst*

*The whole while I'm wondering if that is my destiny.*

*If I am meant to live fast and die young without children,*

*Then what is the reason, God's reason, for my brevity?*

*What will death feel like at the true moment it strikes me*

> *down?*

*What will happen after death requests me at my gloaming?*

*What influence will I make on those I must leave behind?*

*Will my shadow on this world grow dark or endure glowing?*

*Will I still matter to those whom I continue to love?*

*What purpose will I serve in my eternal life after death?*

*I wish I knew that, but I cannot know until I die.*

*'Til then, I must trust God and live life until my last breath.*

Angilia sat quietly when she finished, watching her uncle's face, seeing the hint of a smile and the glisten of tears. He approved, she felt, and that relieved her soul.

"All of my questions were answered, all of my doubts assuaged, all of my fears allayed, at the moment I died. When you came to us, to me and Eric, to escort me to Heaven, and I saw the love between you and Eric, I knew my purpose. I was the one who allowed you and Eric to see one another long before your physical birth. My death brought the two of you together and propelled your love. You are Eric's reason for living, and you are also my reason for living, Angilia. You are his legacy, but you are also my legacy. I know that. I've known that from the moment of my death. I couldn't fear death or what would happen after my death, because all I saw ebb and flow between you and my brother was the most intense, true love. I—my physical death—allowed that love to come into existence 19 years before your life on earth began."

Angilia nodded as she smiled at him through her tears, and Patrick smiled at her and pulled her into a loving embrace. He felt her heart beating against him, the life coursing through her body, as he softly spoke. "You, my darling niece, took away any fears and doubts I had about death and the afterlife. I mean, I knew what the Bible teaches, but like a lot of people, that never became real and true for me. I always wondered what eternity was like, what I would feel, how I would continue to exist. When I took your hand, climbed that staircase, and entered Heaven, any fears and doubts I had dissipated immediately. I was instantly filled with light, love, and peace. Do you remember how I kept smiling that day?" Angilia nodded. "I was happier than I had ever been. I was in the most beautiful place imaginable. I had just witnessed the most blessed love possible as my brother and my niece looked at each other, sharing unspoken emotions.  You are my reason for living and for dying."

Angilia held him tightly, while she cried against his chest as he gently rocked her.  "I love you so much, Uncle Patrick.  I knew that truth from the moment I came for you, that you are the one who brought Daddy and me together long before my birth.  You.  Reading your poem this morning, knowing God's purpose for you, I felt such guilt and heartbreak for the doubts and fears you held inside.  But those last lines about trusting God took my pain away.  Your words and wisdom will do that for so many other people, too, Uncle Patrick.  You will bring peace to others who doubt their purpose and worry about their lives and deaths."

Patrick kissed her temple and pulled her closer, believing, knowing, more than ever that everything has a reason, a purpose.  He had written that poem on his 16$^{th}$ birthday, January 6, 1974.  He had contemplated tearing it up and burning the scraps.  Instead, he had folded it and stuck it in the back of his bottom desk drawer, where Angilia had found it earlier that morning, on January 6, 2016—on what would have been Patrick's 58th birthday.

§§§§

Eric heard Angilia's song reverberating from the music room as he came upstairs one late afternoon in early February, and turned to Roger with a huge smile.  Roger smiled in return, and he reached for Eric's briefcase and headed upstairs to the office.  Eric stood leaning against the music room door frame as he listened to his daughter play and sing a song she had just written.  She turned and motioned for him when she finished, and he sat on the piano bench alongside her.

"Sounds like you're just about ready to record your next album, Angel."

"I hope it will be our album, Daddy.  I thought it could have 18 songs, six that I sing, six that you sing, and six duets we do together.  You haven't recorded any songs in almost four years, and "Sunshine on My Shoulders" still sells millions of copies and still makes lots of money for Open Heart.  It's time for another album.

The Athletic Association of Valdavia gets the proceeds from this one," Angilia revealed, much to Eric's pleasant surprise.

"Patrick's charity," Eric replied with a teary-eyed smile. "He became their Patron when he was 15. He did so much for them. Thank you, darling."

"He's still doing a lot. Come with me. I want to share something with you, Daddy," she said as she stood and reached for his hand. He took the elevator to the third floor with her, and was a bit surprised when she bypassed both of their suites and turned toward the east wing. She led him to Patrick's suite, closed the door, and motioned for him to sit on the sofa across the sitting room. She pulled sheets of paper from one of the desk drawers and sat beside him.

"On Uncle Patrick's birthday, I found a poem he wrote, a traditional ballad, and set it to music. He came for a visit that day, and I sang it for him. It's such a beautiful, deep, thought-provoking poem, and I told him that it will connect with so many people who have similar questions and feelings. Read it," she said, and handed him the yellowing piece of notebook paper, filled with Patrick's small, loopy handwriting.

Eric read it three times as tears filled his eyes. "I never knew he felt these things. How could I not know? He's right—he hid his fears well. He did seem so fearless and carefree."

Angilia shared with her father everything that Patrick had told her on January 6. Just as Patrick's words had soothed her guilt, they eased Eric's. The three of them knew that the day Patrick died was not the horror Eric had once believed it to be, but rather the most resplendent blessing from God. Patrick was not dead. He still lived, he was still the same, but he now resided in Heaven. Eric, Patrick, and Angilia were indeed bound by God's plan, their souls woven for all eternity. "I love what he said. You are my reason for living, and you are his reason for living. The peace and beauty in that fills my heart, Angilia. And you are right that Patrick's words, his poem, will touch people. This was truly meant to happen as it did. Will you sing it for me, as you did for Patrick?"

Angilia nodded and stood to get the guitar she kept in his suite. She often wrote songs there. Eric listened to his daughter play and sing the song. "You have to record that song," he told her. "You have to."

"I thought we could, Daddy, together. How perfect that we sing the words that Uncle Patrick wrote, the three of us yet again connected across space and time."

Eric sat thinking quietly for a minute, and then nodded. "You're right, Angilia. This song is meant for the two of us. We can bring Patrick's words to the world in his stead. We can carry his message and continue his charity work. This is brilliant. Thank you for this beautiful gift, Angel," he said as he pulled her into a hug. "Thank you."

§§§§

A few days later, Sam, Greg, Tim, Joe, and John arrived to learn the songs for the album and then to record the tracks. They spent two days in the basement recording studio with Angilia, learning the songs she had written, perfecting the six songs. Eric joined them on the third day, handing them a list of the six songs he had selected, as well as the sheet music that Angilia had obtained for them. The band was more familiar with his songs already, having heard them many times over the years. On the fourth day, Eric, Angilia, and the band ran through the six duets father and daughter had chosen, some of them nearly three-quarters of a century old. Finally, Angilia presented them the sheet music to what she called Patrick's song, and the band mastered the ballad within two hours.

While it was fresh, Sam asked them if they wanted to record that song first, right then, and bless the remainder of the recording sessions with Patrick's song. Eric smiled, took a deep breath, and told Sam, "Absolutely. This song is already blessed, and I know it will bless thousands of people." Angilia leaned over and kissed her father's cheek, adjusted the microphone between them, and picked up her guitar. Eric and Angilia sang Patrick's words in harmonization, their voices blending perfectly. When they finished, Eric smiled at Angilia and tears filled his eyes.

Angilia smiled in return and grabbed his hands. "You were impeccable, Daddy, as always." To prove her correct, Sam played the track for everyone, and they listened reverently, knowing it was flawless. Even Eric approved the first take, not because he thought his singing superb, but because his singing was inspired by his love for Patrick. The emotions he felt were evident in his voice. Angilia had heard those emotions while he sang with her, and she knew everyone who listened to the song would sense Eric's emotions, too. The cornerstone song of the album, the one Sam already knew would be the first single and the runaway hit, was complete. Sam, the four band mates, Eric, and Angilia shared a group hug and a prayer as they wrapped up the day's work. They would complete the album over the next two days.

As he often did, Eric sat in the control booth with Sam to watch and listen to his daughter perform her songs the following day. Angilia recently wrote several songs, and she selected six to record for the album, all of them reflective, thoughtful, power ballads that showcased her breathtaking five-octave range. Eric never failed to be stunned, amazed, and impressed when he heard Angilia sing. After each of the first five songs, as he listened to the tracks, Eric felt his pulse race, his heart pound, and his love nearly explode through his flesh and bones. Like every time before, she recorded each song in just one take, hitting each note, each emotion, each dramatic moment with her perfect pitch and phrasing. Her lyrics alone stunned Eric with their depth, truth, beauty, and faith. His little girl truly was ordained and blessed.

Her sixth solo struck Eric's heart with the force of a rocket, much like "The Gift of You"—her song about and for him—had done four years earlier when they recorded in Oxford, England. Eric heard the song for the first time, yet he instantly knew that Angilia wrote it about and for her mother, Eric's one true love, Marisol. Adoration and warmth filled his entire body as he listened to her profound lyrics:

*The soul of a loved mother never dies.*

*Even after the body dies, the soul lives.*

*You can feel her warmth and the love she gives*

*Across space and time, where nothing denies*

*The perpetual bond that always underlies*

*The pain you feel at her loss, a bond that forgives*

*Your guilt, that soothes and calms while it outlives*

*The angst of earth and erases your tears and sighs.*

*The truth remains, your mother's love is eternal*

*And undeniably she makes your soul complete,*

*Culminating on the day you and she shall meet*

*In Heaven, never again torn apart.*

*From first spark of life, she remains your sentinel.*

*Forevermore, the two of you stand heart to heart.*

Angilia looked at her father when she finished, and noticed the tears shining in his turquoise eyes. She placed her guitar on its stand, and joined him in the control booth. She bent and kissed his cheek, and Eric pulled her onto his lap in a hug. Sam brushed a tear from his eye and played the track, to everyone's approval.

After a late lunch, they returned to the studio, where Eric recorded three of his solo songs. He insisted on three or five takes of each, still uncomfortable hearing his own voice. Angilia smiled each time, knowing his takes were faultless, but sticking to her promise made four years earlier that he could do as many takes as he felt necessary until he was satisfied. After a long afternoon, half of his solos were completed, and they went upstairs to relax before dinner.

After breakfast the next morning, they all reconvened in the recording studio and Eric completed two more of his solos by midmorning. The sixth song he wanted to record dated to 1957, the year Eric turned three years old. When Angilia saw "The Twelfth of Never" on the list of songs he chose, she understood that he would sing this to and for the one love of his life, her mother Marisol. Her love for her parents grew stronger and more intense each day, and she remained so very grateful for them and their abiding love.

As Eric sat on the stool across from her and sang into the microphone, Angilia felt tears threaten her when she saw him tenderly caress his gold wedding band.  His love for Marisol was as eternal as the human soul.  Everyone in the studio heard and felt Eric's heart, soul, and feelings in his voice as he sang to his wife.  They all had to fight their tears.  When the song ended, they stood or sat reverently quiet for several minutes, knowing that his performance was not just perfect but touched by God.

After the emotional session, they joined the Taylors, Martínezes, Roger, Daniel, and Susan in the dining room for lunch.  The conversation was light-hearted and joyous, which alleviated the deep-seated sentiments of the recording sessions.  Between their duet of Patrick's song, Angilia's song about her mother, and now Eric's love song to his wife, the sessions had been steeped in emotions.  Knowing some of the remaining duet selections, they anticipated that the afternoon would have its moments, too.

It did.  With Patrick's song already recorded, Eric and Angilia had five duets left to record, all of them songs they had jointly selected.  Four of them were from the 1970s and 1980s, all in the easy-listening vein of The Carpenters.  The fifth, and the last song they recorded for the album, was the oldest, written and first recorded in 1947.  Eric sang the first half of the touching ballad "I Love You Because," and Angilia's voice melded with her father's for the remainder of the song.  This song they sang for and to one another, signifying to the world that their love was true, powerful, and pure.  They nailed it in one take, accompanied only by Angilia's mellow acoustic guitar.  The album was complete, and the seven of them came together in a joyous embrace.

§§§§

The next morning after breakfast, Sam invited everyone to join him in the recording studio to hear Angilia's new album.  They were the first people so privileged other than the band—and of course Eric. Sam purposely did not mention Eric's involvement, for he wanted to surprise Eric's family and friends when they heard the entire album for the first time. Angilia smiled, linked her arms with her grandparents, and took the elevator to the basement with them. She led them to a small sofa along the wall, kissed their cheeks, and sat on one of the stools alongside her father. Everyone else sat on stools, leaned against the wall, or sat on the floor. Matthew stood next to Angilia, excited to listen to her new songs.

Sam introduced the album, telling everyone it contained 18—yes, 18—songs and was called <u>Love's Legacy</u>, a title selected by Angilia because it summed up the songs' overriding theme and connective thread. Although he did not tell those gathered for the private listening party, Sam had arranged the songs thusly: Angilia's solo songs, placing the song about Marisol, "Love is Eternal," last; following were Eric's six solos, with "The Twelfth of Never" his final song; the six duets completed the album, and by unanimous decision, "My Purpose"—what Angilia called Patrick's song—closed the album.

Sam paused after each song, allowing people time to process the impact of each song and to ask a question or to comment. One of Angilia's songs voiced her thoughts about literally facing death, the lack of fear involved, and her faith that God remains in control. That song had wrapped itself around Eric's heart when he watched his daughter record it, and it likewise touched those who listened to it. Juanita sobbed, as did Susan, and Matthew recalled his first sight of Angilia, bleeding to death. She had been unafraid for herself, he knew that. She had impressed him then, and she continued to impress him every moment.

Finally, "Love is Eternal" played, and after the first line, Alejandro, Juanita, and Eduardo knew the lyrics spoke of their beloved Marisol. Angilia's unwavering faith that they and she would reunite with Marisol when they died, as well as Eric's Christmas 2012 revelation that Marisol had brought Angilia back to life on the day of the shooting, soothed their hearts and souls. Their tears contained not pain and grief but rather peace and joy. Marisol, like Patrick, was not dead; she merely lived in Heaven now.

Sam paused the album for several minutes, allowing everyone to express themselves and their heightened emotions. Eric had heard the song several times, yet each time he found his being filled with immense love for his wife and his daughter. Angilia's faith and truth touched people around the world, none more deeply than her father. Matthew placed his hand on her shoulder, feeling his own emotions raging through him. Angilia smiled up at him and reached up to squeeze his hand. The guardian angel Matthew had spoken of the day of her emergency surgery was her mother, the woman who fought for Angilia's life from the beginning. Daniel and Roger wiped tears from their eyes as they recalled Eric's wedding, Marisol's pregnancy and death, and Angilia's birth. The love shared between Eric, Marisol, and Angilia had always been palpable and powerful.

When Sam finally pushed the play button and the familiar melody of a vintage Hollies song began, people were admittedly confused. Angilia rarely recorded covers of others' songs. When they heard Eric's voice instead of Angilia's they were all pleasantly surprised. None of them had known that he had any plans to record again. Roger and Daniel, his best and longest friends, smiled and enjoyed the first five songs immensely. Angilia beamed, her smile seeming a mile wide, as she listened to her father and watched everyone's reactions. When the fifth song ended, though, she knew that Abuelo, Abuela, and Uncle Eduardo would feel tremendous joy and perhaps pangs when they heard his loving rendition of "The Twelfth of Never."

Angilia saw the instant recognition in their eyes as the song began. They knew, as did Susan, Roger, Daniel, Katherine, Mitchell, and Matthew, that Eric sang to his wife. Susan, Katherine, and Mitchell bowed their heads, overcome with emotions, Eduardo smiled through his tears at his brother-in-law's love and devotion, Alejandro and Juanita stared into one another's eyes as the beauty of Eric's song filled their hearts, and Matthew's hand tightened on Angilia's shoulder. Daniel and Roger once more relived the key moments from their best friend's all too brief life with Marisol. As Angilia had known it would, her father's song to and for his wife touched each person in the room.

With tears in his eyes, Sam stopped the album for a while, giving everyone time and space. Juanita stood and walked to Eric, grabbed him in a hug, and whispered in his ear. "Mi hijo, yo amor tú. Yo amor tú. You and our precious Angel keep Marisol alive. I feel your undying love for her always.  When I first met you, I knew, I saw, your true love for my daughter.  I knew your union was blessed by God.  I am so grateful for you, mi hijo."

"I love you so much, Mamá, so very much.  I love Marisol for all eternity.  She is my love, my wife, for all eternity."  Eric pulled Angilia closer to him.  "Our daughter knows that, and she knows that our family will be together for all eternity.  Nothing is more miraculous than our love and our eternity," he softly said as he kissed Juanita's cheek.  Juanita kissed his cheek and then Angilia's forehead, told them how much she loved them, and wiped her tears as she returned to her husband's embrace.

After several moments, Sam asked if they were ready to hear the remaining six songs on the album.  They all answered in the affirmative, so Sam smiled and began the tape, knowing the duets would thrill them.  Sure enough, the first song, which Eric and Angilia sang together in its entirety, stunned everyone.  Few of them had ever heard father and daughter sing together.  Katherine, Mitchell, Matthew, and Eduardo never had; Alejandro and Juanita had heard them duet once or twice; Susan, Daniel, and Roger had heard them a few times.  Until the album rehearsals, Sam and the band had never heard them duet.  All of them were touched and amazed at how seamlessly the voices blended, although Eric laughingly attributed that to Angilia's vocal range and skill.  "With that breathtaking voice, Angel can harmonize with a garbage disposal," Eric giggled.

"Don't be silly, Daddy.  You brought that out in me when I was very young," Angilia replied, remembering the first time she sang with him when she was two years old.  Eric simultaneously recalled that earth-shaking moment, and smiled as he kissed her nose.  The next three songs equally delighted everyone, as they harmonized on a David Cassidy song, a Spandau Ballet song, and a Bryan Adams song, all soft rock or easy-listening ballads.  The covers were not mere cookie cutter copies of the originals, but bore Eric's and Angilia's joint thumbprint.  They sang songs Eric had played frequently when she was a child, some of which he often sang along to as she gleefully listened.  They made the songs fresh, unique, and new.

So they did, too, with the sixth duet of the old standard, "I Love You Because," a song they chose for its message and theme: their love was pure, ordained, and lasting.  As stated in the lyrics, Eric and Angilia supported one another, stood by each other, and shared abiding love.  The love between father and daughter filled the room, not just as the song resounded, but from their hearts.  Their love was all but tangible to all who met them, as Patrick had said in his own words to her on January 6.

Patrick's song ended the album, and everyone felt peace and hope from within, not pain and despair, as they listened to the lyrics. Roger and Daniel, who had known Patrick, smiled throughout the song, knowing in their hearts that Patrick's spirit lived.  Patrick's legacy was evident in Eric and Angilia, who loved him so dearly.

That love affected each person in the recording studio, all of whom felt their sensations spring from deep within them in the form of tears.  No one was sad, but instead they all were filled with happiness and joy at sharing the love at that moment.  Angilia always called them happy tears, and indeed they were.  As the album concluded, everyone gathered around Eric and Angilia to not just congratulate them but to thank them for sharing such a beautiful gift with them and with the world.

§§§§§

*7 March 2016*

*This evening, Daddy and I perform a concert to debut our new album. Daddy has rarely sung in public, and I am extremely excited and happy.  What makes us both happy is that Uncle Patrick's song becomes the first single from the album when it is released tomorrow!!  I played the tape to Uncle Patrick last week when he came for a visit, and he is thrilled to hear his brother sing his words and also that his favorite charity, The Athletic Association of Valdavia, receives 100% of the album's proceeds.  Even if Uncle Patrick had not wanted us to use his poem, I had already decided to make AAV the beneficiary of this album.*

*Daddy became the honorary Patron of AAV in 1978, but no one has filled Uncle Patrick's role since mid-1977.  That will likely change soon. Matthew asked me about AAV and told me he would like to become their Patron—if Daddy and the board members agree.  I talked this over with*

*Daddy, and he is thrilled that Matthew wants AAV to be his first charity. Daddy has a meeting with the Board of Directors next week to discuss Matthew's patronage, and he is certain they will accept and also be excited and ecstatic. I love Matthew more for wanting to do this, and for telling me that he is never replacing Uncle Patrick as Patron, but rather doing the work on Patrick's behalf.*

*It's been four years since we recorded <u>Heart-Glow</u> and Daddy's "Sunshine on My Shoulders" stormed the world. His song still sells millions of copies each year! Other than "A Time for Us" and "Love Was Born on Christmas Day," I have only recorded an album of piano solos. It was time for us to sing again, and this time the album truly is OUR album! I keep playing my copy as often as I can, listening to Daddy's songs time and again. He is so spectacular, and he really has no idea how great he is. Wait until everyone sees him on stage this evening—and hears him sing again! No one else knows that he is part of the album, so his appearance and performance tonight will utterly shock and surprise everyone in the theatre. I can hardly wait.* ♥

§§§§§

Angilia and Eric dressed for the concert and left for the downtown theatre that afternoon in Eric's Aston Martin. During the two hours before the concert began, they would join the band for the sound and light checks and ensure that everything was set and ready for the 5:00 start time. The tickets had sold out in minutes, with several attendees flying from France, England, Spain, and even the United States and Japan for Angilia's concert, which astonished everyone, particularly since the concert was announced less than two weeks earlier.

Angilia smiled at her father when they arrived at the theatre. He got her guitar case from the car trunk, and when she took it from him, she felt his hand shaking. He was nervous, she knew that, and she put her arm around him as they entered. The band and Sam had arrived moments earlier, and their instruments were being set up on the stage. They all chatted casually until the drum kit was assembled and the piano, bass, and electric guitar were wired to the speakers.

Finally, Tim, Greg, Joe, and John jumped on the stage and took their places at their respective instruments. "Ready, Daddy? You've been on this stage many times."

Eric giggled. "Not singing to everyone, I haven't." He took a deep breath and winked at her. "I'll just take your advice of four years ago and look only at you. Just don't go too far away and leave me front and center all by myself. Please?"

Angilia hugged and reassured him. "I promise, Daddy. I will never leave you." He kissed the top of her head and took her hand as they walked up the steps onto the stage.

Angilia plugged in her acoustic guitar, adjusted the microphones, and she and the band played one of her older songs to test the sound and feed in the building. The sound engineer needed to adjust some settings, so they performed a few more songs before he asked them to run through a short set of four songs so he could make sure everything sounded as it should throughout the theatre. Eric sang one of his solos to test his microphone, and the fourth song of the test was one of their duets. While they performed, the lighting designer checked his equipment and cueing, making any last second adjustments as necessary. With 45 minutes remaining until they were introduced, Angilia, Eric, and the four musicians headed backstage to freshen up before the audience was admitted in 15 minutes. Finally it was time for them to take their places on the stage before the curtain rose. Angilia kissed her father and Sam as she went on stage and slipped her guitar strap over her shoulder.

The President of The Athletic Association of Valdavia briefly greeted Sam, Eric, Angilia, and the band before stepping in front of the red velvet curtain at precisely 5:00. "Good afternoon, everyone! I am Wayne Chambliss, the president of the honored and proud recipient of 100 percent of the proceeds from Her Royal Highness' album and of this evening's concert. The album, <u>Love's Legacy</u>, is released tomorrow, and the board, staff, and members of The Athletic Association of Valdavia are blessed by Her Royal Highness' kindness.

"I was a young, new staff member of the AAV 43 years ago, fresh out of college and a sports fanatic, when our new Patron breezed into the office building, full of energy and enthusiasm. His Royal Highness Prince Patrick was 15 years old and still in high school, but the AAV became one of his most passionate causes. He loved sports, as I did, and he later took up speedboat racing. His Royal Highness wanted to support his fellow athletes, and that is what he enabled the AAV to do through his tireless programs and fundraising.

"Now his niece carries on His Royal Highness' charitable work with the AAV, and I know I speak for everyone involved with the AAV that we are so grateful and touched. You—each of you in attendance—carry that legacy, too, by purchasing your concert tickets and, we are certain, copies of <u>Love's Legacy</u>. I am deeply honored to introduce to you Her Royal Highness Princess Consort Angilia, who debuts her new album for all of us tonight." The audience stood as the curtain rose and revealed Angilia front and center, attired in a vintage ivory Gunne Sax dress paired with pale pink granny boots. Everyone applauded for more than 10 minutes, until she finally convinced them to stop.

"Thank you each so very much for coming and for supporting the Athletic Association of Valdavia. Your generosity means so much to me and to my family. AAV was the first and only choice as beneficiary for this album, and I am truly privileged and honored to be part of this beautiful synergy. I know my uncle is pleased, as well, that AAV receives your donations from your ticket purchases. Thank you.

"Before we share the songs with you, I want to introduce this wonderful band, these fabulous musicians, to you. On electric guitar is Tim Hanley. At the drums is Joe Arnold. On bass is John Herbert. At the piano is Greg Smithson." Angilia turned and applauded her friends as the audience cheered them. After a few minutes, Angilia turned to face the audience, and asked them, "Are you ready to hear our songs?" They screamed excitedly, and Angilia smiled as the band launched into her first solo song. The standing-room-only crowd listened admiringly, taking in her words and voice, but stood in rapturous applause when the song ended.

Eric watched from stage left, tears of joy threatening him. Sam put his arm around Eric's shoulders, knowing how emotional the experience was for everyone, particularly Eric. No one spoke of it, but they all knew the significance of the day—four years earlier to the day, on March 7, 2012, Matthew fought to save Angilia's life during a several-hours-long emergency surgery. She had literally taken bullets and willingly risked her life to save her father's life that day. Watching her, listening to her, seeing peoples' reaction to her performance, was truly a miracle for Eric. As she sang, he prayed silently to God, thanking him once more for Angilia and her life.

After her fifth song, Eric also silently spoke to his wife: *Dearest Marisol, our beautiful Angilia's next song is for you and about you. I know you, like I do, feel her love and respect. I know you are with us every moment. I love you so very much.* As he heard and felt Angilia's tribute to Marisol, he sensed his wife's soul and knew such serenity and love. When Angilia turned and looked at him, his buoyant smile and shining eyes filled her being with tremendous joy. She, too, felt her mother's soul hovering over them, and she sang about her mother with such intense emotions in her voice. The audience was dazed by the experience. When the song ended, they stood and applauded, many of them crying simultaneously.

Angilia thanked them, her smile now huge as she prepared for her father's surprise entrance. "Thank you so very much," she said when the audience sat. She knew they would jump to their feet in euphoric cheers when she introduced her father. "We have someone very special joining us for the remaining 12 songs, someone very dear to me and tremendously loved by me. I know how much you love him, too. Please join me in welcoming to the stage my father, Eric DeBruce Martineau," Angilia beamed as the audience erupted into the elated cheers and screams she had anticipated.

Eric walked across the stage to his daughter, his own smile radiant as he turned to wave at the audience. He pulled Angilia into a hug, while the reaction to his unannounced appearance generated a very lengthy standing ovation. Angilia and Eric could do nothing but stand there, feeling the building vibrate from the massive sound of five thousand screaming voices blending and reverberating from the ceiling. Eric motioned them to sit, which they finally did. He looked at Angilia, shrugged his shoulder, and stepped to his microphone. "Thank you for your amazing greeting. Now I just have to live up to that," he said to more cheers and some laughter.

Angilia stood next to him, at her microphone, and promised him, "You will," which elicited more cheers. She asked the audience, "Are you ready to hear my father?" In response, thousands of people yelled "Yes" in very loud unison. Angilia giggled and quietly asked Eric if he was ready, to which he said, "As ready as I can be." She and the band began playing his first solo song, and everyone sat in awed reverence as they listened to Eric's velvety baritone. After each of his first five songs, the audience members stood and cheered their appreciation. Each time, Eric looked totally flabbergasted by the reaction, certain that the frenzy around his recording of "Sunshine on My Shoulders" four years earlier was merely a novelty, a one-off response to his unexpected recording. Angilia's huge smile throughout her father's performance told him how happy she was, but she had always encouraged and supported him. He had never predicted and expected this level of response.

Finally, the noise lulled, and Eric stepped to his microphone to tell everyone, "Thank you. I have one more song before Angilia and I share our next surprise with you. I dedicate this song to my one true, eternal love, my wife Marisol." Everyone in the audience gasped, many sobbed, and all sat quietly reverential, respectful, and already emotional. Eric bowed his head as the band and Angilia played the opening chords of the song, and when he raised his head to sing, he felt everyone and everything else fade as he recognized the warmth of his beloved wife's soul surround him. His performance was heartfelt, passionate, and spiritual. In the Royal box, Juanita, Alejandro, and Eduardo cried and embraced while they watched and listened to Eric, knowing how deep and lasting his love for their Marisol truly remained.

When Eric finished, he bowed his head again for a moment, while the audience sat quiet and still for several seconds, feeling as if they had experienced the most sanctified moment. Finally, they stood in solidarity and applauded for several minutes. Eric looked at his daughter and smiled at her through his tears, holding her hand. She stood on the toes of her left leg and kissed his cheek, which touched everyone even more deeply. She asked him quietly if he wanted to take a short break before the duets, and he shook his head.

"Thank you all so very much," Eric finally said. "Thank you. Angilia and I have six more songs to share with you from the album. If you are ready to hear them, we're ready to sing them," he told them with a smile, which elicited shouts of approval. Without another pause, Angilia, Greg, Tim, Joe, and John started the first duet, and everyone once again exploded in cheers when they heard Eric and Angilia singing together for the first time publicly. The audience cheered relentlessly throughout their first five songs, obviously elated at what they heard. Sam and Wayne, who watched from stage left, enjoyed the concert, and both men knew that <u>Love's Legacy</u> would sell several million copies and make billions of euros for AAV.

Eric, Angilia, and the band paused before the final song. "Thank you each. We are so appreciative of you all, truly we are. My father and I have one song remaining to debut, and I want to tell you about this very extraordinary song. This is not a cover of a favorite song, as the other duets are, but a new song for which I am listed as the composer. I did not write the lyrics. Someone extremely dear to me did, on his 16th birthday, January 6, 1974. Forty-two years later, to the day, I found a poem, a traditional ballad, that my Uncle Patrick wrote, and that poem became this song. I was blown away by my uncle's words, and I am certain you will be, too," she concluded as she gave the four musicians the signal to start.

Angilia and Eric looked into one another's turquoise eyes as they sang Patrick's words, knowing they had his blessing and that his song would touch millions of people deeply. As they sang, they smiled at one another, feeling very familiar warmth envelop them: Patrick was there. He had come to experience and to share the debut performance with them. When they sang the last note, Eric and Angilia embraced while the audience jumped to their feet in jubilation. Prince Patrick had never been forgotten, and he was still touted as the poster boy for handsome, fun-loving, charity-driven young princes. He was the first superstar prince of the modern era, with his dashing looks, charm, and outgoing, playful personality.

Angilia saw the tears in her father's eyes and knew that he was too emotional to speak.  She leaned toward the microphone.  "Thank you more than we can say.  On behalf of my remarkable Uncle Patrick, we thank you so very much.  I can honestly tell you that his soul is elated today, knowing that his song is helping his favorite charity, The Athletic Association of Valdavia.  I can also tell you that Patrick's song is the first single from the album, both released tomorrow, and as you know, 100 percent of the purchase price for any of the songs or for the entire album goes to AAV."

"Angilia is correct.  We do thank you more than our words can tell you.  My brother is remarkable, as Angilia said, and I am so extremely proud that his charitable work continues through his song and this album."  As Eric spoke, Angilia quickly stepped to John and asked him to hand her something from his jacket pocket.  "I am also proud of my equally-amazing daughter, who brought Patrick's words to the light and for wanting to dedicate this album to him.  Angilia planned to donate the proceeds of this album to AAV before she found Patrick's poem, and I am grateful for that," Eric smiled at her.

Angilia returned his smile and said, "Mr. Chambliss, will you please join us for a moment?  My father and I have something we want to give you."  Both Eric and Wayne were caught by surprise, neither of them knowing what she meant.  Sam motioned for Wayne to walk on stage, and he gathered his poise and did so, thanking them for an amazing concert.  He stood between Eric and Angilia as she handed him a check in the amount of €50,000 and stated, without boasting of the amount, "This is our gift to AAV on behalf of Patrick."

Wayne stared at the check, overwhelmed.  "This is not only a generous surprise, but a much appreciated gift.  The AAV Board of Directors has created an athletic scholarship in Prince Patrick's name, actually, which I planned to announce tonight anyway.  With this, we can initiate the scholarship immediately.  That means any high school or collegiate athletes can apply soon for the Patrick DeBruce Martineau Athletic Excellence Scholarship.  Thank you from the depth of my heart, Your Royal Highness, Your Majesty."  Wayne shook their hands and spoke with them briefly as the audience rose for another standing ovation.

Angilia turned her attention to the audience. "Thank you all for coming and sharing the evening with us. Thank you each most of all for continuing Patrick's charitable work. That means more to me than you shall ever know."

Eric, too, offered closing remarks to the audience, as did Wayne, and finally the three of them exited the stage. After talking with theatre officials and a few trusted press reporters and photographers, Eric and Angilia agreed to sign autographs for concert attendees. Roger had come to assist them, but Eric asked him to make sure everyone else got home safely and to please have dinner without him and Angilia. "We'll be fine, Roger. Mike is staying, and we'll eat when we get home. It doesn't make sense to keep all of you waiting," Eric assured Roger.

A table and two chairs were placed on the stage for Eric and Angilia, and theatre ushers organized the autograph line at the stage right steps. One person at a time approached the table, spoke to the King and Princess Consort briefly, and got the requested autographs, whether on a copy of <u>Heart-Glow</u>, a photograph, magazine, newspaper, or one of Angilia's books. Three hours after they began, they finished. Unlike walkabouts, the post-performance autograph lines were well orchestrated. Angilia and Eric thanked the theatre staff. Sam bid them farewell and headed to the hotel where he and the band were staying for a few days.

Eric and Angilia placed her guitar case in his car's trunk and went home to eat a late dinner together at the kitchen island. They remained relatively quiet as they ate, still taking in and feeling the intense emotions of the evening. Finally, as they finished eating, Angilia said, "I am so blessed, Daddy. Thank you for today. You are magnificent. I love you more than you know."

Eric smiled at her, pulled her to him, and replied, "I do know, Angel. I have always known. I felt your love from that first moment so long ago."

She smiled and softly said, "Uncle Patrick gave us his blessing today, Daddy. I am so grateful that he is part of this. I really am."

"So am I, baby. So am I."

§§§§§

"Welcome to the news for Tuesday, March 8, 2016. I am Franklin Sydney, and I am live at the Clover Music Store, where the excitement over His Majesty's and Her Royal Highness' album <u>Love's Legacy</u> has been at a fever pitch since midnight, when the store opened early to meet the public demand for this highly-anticipated CD. As we reported six hours ago, during the noon news, sales have been nonstop throughout the day, with long lines of people waiting patiently to purchase copies of the CD.

"Moments before we went live, I spoke via telephone with Sam Burton, the Princess Consort's producer and manager, who told me that initial reports he received today indicate that <u>Love's Legacy</u> hit gold record status earlier today. Ladies and gentlemen, we are witnessing recording history yet again, it seems, as this album appears close on the heels of <u>Heart-Glow</u> as another diamond-certified album. The most remarkable piece of this historical event is Prince Patrick's posthumous participation. He wrote the lyrics to "My Purpose," the first single from the album and the most-downloaded track from the album according to first-day reports. If you have not yet heard the album, I highly recommend you listen to it. Buy it if you can, since all of the proceeds go to The Athletic Association of Valdavia."

# CHAPTER 3

"Welcome to the most anticipated and special day in recent memory. I am Franklin Sydney, and today is Sunday, June 26, 2016—Royal Wedding Day. We are bringing you exclusive live coverage of the day as events unfold."

"Yes, we are indeed. I am Laurie Dougray, and today we will all witness a real-life fairy-tale when our beloved Princess Consort Angilia and Dr. Matthew Taylor wed on the 25th anniversary of King Eric's marriage to Queen Consort Marisol. Today promises to be filled with love, romance, beauty, joy, and emotions."

"It most certainly does, Laurie. The wedding ceremony begins at 1:00 this afternoon in Christ Church Valmondois. Before that, though, we have the morning Mother's Day church service, which the Royal Family, the Taylors, and their friends will attend as usual. Our coverage will go live to the church the moment the Royal party arrives, which should be shortly before 8:00."

"That's right, Franklin. We expect notice momentarily that their car has left the palace. The drive to the church is brief, which is one reason why the bride's procession to the church this afternoon has been altered. Thousands of people have already staked out prime locations along the route His Majesty and Her Royal Highness will take to the wedding ceremony. Everyone, it seems, wants to see the beautiful Princess Consort and the first glimpse of her top-secret wedding gown."

"Who can blame them, Laurie?  Last evening, as you may know, I interviewed several spectators who have in fact been staking their places outside the church all week.  They want to see Her Royal Highness up close and share this most joyous day with her.  Some of the people we see already crowding the route came from across Europe, the United States, Canada, Japan, and Africa.  Royal Wedding fever is at its highest pitch this morning as we will see Her Royal Highness and Dr. Taylor, together, prior to their marriage.  I dare say, this is unprecedented for a Royal wedding as far as my research revealed."

"Yes, Franklin, many people were startled when the Princess Consort addressed concerns about her wedding date falling on a Sunday.  She was often asked how that would complicate her wedding ceremony plans.  Her Royal Highness issued a statement reassuring everyone that she and her family and friends would attend the morning church service as always, return to the palace for a light lunch, and then they would prepare for the ceremony, which as we noted begins at 1:00 this afternoon.  Princess Consort Angilia stated there was no reason for a Sunday and the annual Mother's Day church service to interfere with the wedding ceremony, and in fact, Mother's Day Sunday only seems to make her special day all the more reverent and joyous," Laurie added with a smile.

"Today is glorious, and the perfect day for Her Royal Highness' wedding," Franklin enthused.  "The most often-asked question I received when I was among the crowds here in Valmondois last evening was what the Princess Consort's wedding gown looks like.  We will not know that until her procession leaves the palace at 12:30 this afternoon.  More than likely, we shall not get a clear view of her gown until she emerges from the carriage at the steps of the church.  We do know that a press embargo containing details regarding the wedding gown and the bridesmaids' dresses shall be released to us at the exact moment His Majesty and Her Royal Highness leave the palace.  The embargo will provide us with details regarding the design, the fabrics, and a statement from Her Royal Highness as to the gown's significance to her."

"We eagerly wait with everyone else for the first sight of our beautiful Princess Consort in her wedding gown.  Regardless of what her gown looks like, we know she will be stunning.  Franklin, we have just received word that the Royal party has departed the palace in one of His Majesty's cars. They shall arrive at the church shortly, and we shall get our first glimpse of His Majesty, Her Royal Highness, and Dr. Taylor on this most magical of days," Laurie informed everyone.

"Laurie, they have just arrived and parked at the church. His Majesty drove them, which is quite common, and he has exited the Rolls Royce to cheers. King Eric is assisting his parents-in-law from the car, as the others get out. In a very gallant gesture, Dr. Taylor is opening Her Royal Highness' car door and taking her hand to assist her. Could there be a more romantic gesture on the morning of their wedding?"

"Absolutely not, Franklin. Excuse me for suddenly seeming to shout, but as the Princess Consort and Dr. Taylor came into view, the screams and cheers from those already standing outside the church became extremely thunderous. Angilia and Matthew are waving to everyone, their smiles showing how happy they are today. Oh, is that not sweet? A little girl ran from the crowd to give a posy of violets to Her Royal Highness."

"The Princess Consort and Dr. Taylor have actually crossed the street to talk with those who are there, which is a most delightful and unexpected surprise. The Princess Consort is stunning this morning in an emerald green dress, which as many people know is her mother Queen Consort Marisol's birthstone color. Her dress honors the woman who cannot be here physically, but as Her Royal Highness has stated on many occasions, Queen Consort Marisol is here in spirit. Her choice of dress is so appropriate on a day that is not only the Princess Consort's wedding day and her parents' wedding anniversary but is Valdavia's fifth Mother's Day. How emotionally charged the day begins, Laurie."

"The entire day will no doubt be steeped not just in tradition and reverence, but in emotions, as well," Laurie added. "The Royal party is entering the church, and His Majesty, Her Royal Highness, and Dr. Taylor are waving to the crowds as they stand in the doorway. What a beautiful start to this day, Franklin, to see the young couple together and so obviously in love and at ease."

"Yes, it is, Laurie.  Both of them have said that they are not nervous or scared about the wedding, as they are confident and secure in their love as they begin their lives together.  The doors to the church have closed, and our coverage of the Royal Wedding Day will continue until the service concludes and the Royal Family emerges to return to the palace for wedding preparations."

During the church service, Laurie and Franklin maintained their live coverage not by calling in so-called royal experts or fashion designers to speculate on the ceremony or gown, but by talking with many of the people who had come from all across Valdavia and in many cases from around the world just to see Angilia on her wedding day.  The church service, as most people knew, was typically one hour in length.

At 8:50, therefore, Laurie and Franklin resumed their seats in the temporary reporting booth near the church, waiting like everyone there for the congregation to step outside.  "Franklin, the church doors have opened, which means the Royal party shall emerge momentarily."

"Yes, and we expect them to greet the people, albeit briefly, and to return to the palace almost immediately.  All of them must prepare for the wedding ceremony in the few short hours between now and 12:15," Franklin added.

"That is when the family members begin leaving the palace for the church.  The wedding party next leaves, and then the groom's procession makes its way to the church.  Finally, His Majesty and Her Royal Highness emerge from the palace gates in a horse-drawn carriage at 12:30 sharp.  Their carriage will circle the heart of Valmondois, expected to arrive at Christ Church Valmondois at 12:55 this afternoon," Laurie informed everyone.

"Yes, and all expectations are that they will stick to that time-table.  His Majesty and Her Royal Highness shall enter the nave and shortly thereafter begin their slow walk down the aisle.  Here come members of the congregation, including Billy Panning, who is one of the groomsmen today, with his parents.  How often we have seen Billy with Her Royal Highness over the years.  He must be thrilled to be part of this momentous occasion, Laurie."

"I can only imagine how the members of the wedding party do feel today.  I think we all sense the love and happiness of His Majesty, Franklin, and I am certain that Dr. and Mrs. Taylor share his emotions.  Their son becomes a member of the Valdavian Royal Family today upon his marriage to the Princess Consort.  Dr. Matthew Taylor makes history today as the husband of the heir to the throne, the future Queen de Valdavia," Laurie enthused.

"And here they are, Her Royal Highness, on her father's arm, with Dr. Taylor alongside her.  The crowds have yet again launched into uproarious cheers at the mere sight of them," Franklin announced.  Angilia, Matthew, Eric, the Taylors, the Martínezes, and their friends, waved to those gathered, as the crowd continued to grow moment by moment.  Angilia blew them a kiss, as Eric and Matthew escorted her to the car.  Soon, Eric drove them home, where they relaxed for a while before an early light lunch.

§§§§

The mood during the 10:30 lunch was joyous and lighthearted.  No one seemed stressed, as everything was ready: clothes, shoes, jewelry, cars, drivers, the carriage, the horses, and Joseph, who would drive the carriage.  Security would leave at 11:00 to take their appointed places along the route and at the church.  Mike and Tony would change prior to the ceremony and act as footmen on the carriage that would transport Eric and Angilia to the church and afterwards carry Angilia and Matthew to the palace, their guns concealed in their uniforms as a precaution.  Everything was minutely planned, to the last detail, and getting dressed was the main task ahead for everyone.

While Susan and Daniel went to assist Juanita and Alejandro in changing clothes, Eric noticed that Angilia and Matthew walked toward the east wing together.  They went to the palace chapel.  Eric smiled at Mitchell and Katherine, and the three walked toward the patio.

"We best get ready, Eric.  That way we can help with any last minute needs if necessary," Katherine said.  "Are you two men as happy as I am today?"

Mitchell said he was, but Eric smiled with a hint of tears in his eyes and said, "Happier, I dare say.  Remember when I told you after Matthew's 26th birthday in 2012 that I knew our children were destined to marry?  They are.  They always have been.  Today truly is blessed by God."  Katherine hugged him, knowing he spoke the truth, and Mitchell, too, grabbed Eric into a hug.

They parted ways, and Eric walked upstairs to his suite, ready to shower, freshen, and change into his military uniform.  In two hours, his daughter's wedding would begin.  Eric caught sight of his own face in the mirror as he pulled off his suit jacket in his changing room.  His smile seemed a mile wide.  He felt as if he could not stop smiling, his heart and soul were so full of love and happiness.  He sighed while he removed his suit, put on his robe, and entered his shower.

Daniel came in just as Eric finished, made sure the uniform was ready, and gave it a final brushing when the last medal was pinned in place.  Eric smiled at one of his best friends.  "You need to get yourself ready, Daniel.  You, Roger, and Eduardo actually need to get into your tuxedos.  We all have important jobs today, Daniel.  It's my little girl's wedding day."

"I know, Eric.  Roger and I were beside you from the first moment, and we will remain beside you."  He cleared his throat.  "I'll make sure Eduardo and Roger are getting ready, and then I will hop to it," he promised.  "Today will be amazing."

It certainly would, Eric thought, his smile still lighting his face.  Twenty-five years ago, he and Marisol married, and he looked at the gold wedding band he had faithfully worn every second since she had slipped it on his finger.  *My darling Marisol, happy anniversary my beloved.  You know, I know you do, that our beautiful, remarkable daughter marries her true love today.  They will share our anniversary.  How incredible is that?  I know that you will watch with me as Angilia and Matthew marry.  Is your soul as filled with peace and love as mine is today?  I love you so very much, Marisol.  We both love Angilia more than our words could ever say.*

§§§§§

Meanwhile, Angilia and Matthew had spent several minutes alone in the chapel before their marriage.  They stood before the altar holding hands as they prayed.  Still holding hands, they turned to look at one another, their eyes filled with love and their souls embracing.  Matthew smiled at her, and softly said, "I love you so very much, Angilia.  Now that I know love, I also know how impossible it is to describe my love for you with words.  That must be why all of the poets use such grandiose terms to even attempt to describe what I feel for you."

Angilia smiled in return.  "True.  I know love now, too, and I understand how impossible it truly is to tell someone what is really felt within.  Love is more than a sensation, more than a feeling.  Love fills the soul to its capacity.  We are meant to be together, Matthew.  We were always meant to marry, just as I was always meant to be born to my father.  We are so very blessed, more than we likely know."

"We are.  Today we become husband and wife, and we fulfill our destiny."  They smiled as they held hands and walked to the elevator, riding it to the third floor.  Eric watched them part in the hall, going into separate suites for the last time.  He smiled when Matthew kissed her hand before she joined Susan and her bridesmaids in her suite.  Soon, Eric would ride with his daughter to her ordained marriage to her best friend and soul mate.

§§§§§

Susan, Shannon, Darlene, Amanda, Nicole, and Amy were dressed in their pale pink bridesmaids' dresses, their hair adorned with coronets of pink and white roses.  Angilia quickly showered, put on her lingerie, and then Susan dried and styled her hair as she had done so often.  Angilia wanted to look like herself on her wedding day; she did not want to look any differently than she typically did.  Susan styled her long hair into a herringbone braid, as usual, with most of Angilia's long ash-blonde hair long and loose.  Her tiara would sit atop her long hair as her tiaras always did.  This princess bride did not want or need an elaborate up-do for her wedding day.  When Susan finished, Angilia applied her make-up, which was minimal and understated as always.

Finally, Angilia stood, took a deep breath, and allowed Susan to help her into the hoops which would support her extravagant skirts. Once the hoops and slip were in place, Susan and the girls assisted Angilia into the silk taffeta underskirt, and then the overskirt which fell into a wide, long train. Angilia slipped on the bodice, which Susan fastened in back. Angilia slipped her feet into clear acrylic pumps, real-life Cinderella-like "glass" slippers. At the front of each shoe was a clear crystal heart.

Finally, Angilia picked up the tiara which her father had given her on her birthday, the lace veil attached. Susan fastened it to Angilia's hair, smoothed the veil and train, and found herself crying. Soon, the five girls were crying, too, moments before they had to leave in one of the cars for the church. Angilia calmed them as they frantically wiped tears and reapplied make-up.

"Thank you all for sharing today with me," Angilia told them. "As a token of my thanks, I want you to have these," she said as she handed the six of them jewel boxes. The girls gasped when they saw the lustrous pearl necklaces, with garnet and sapphire clasps—Angilia's and Matthew's birthstones. They scurried to fasten one another's pearl necklaces, the perfect final touch to their fairy-tale dresses.

Finally, a knock on the door alerted the bridesmaids and Susan that they would leave soon. The maid explained that Juanita, Alejandro, Mitchell, and Katherine had left in their Rolls Royce seconds earlier. Susan, the bridesmaids, and the groomsmen would leave in a moment. The girls hugged Angilia and rushed to the garage, with Roger, Daniel, Christopher, Scott, and Billy right behind. Their car pulled out, the convertible top down so that the well-wishers could see them, and they received ecstatic cheers as everyone realized that the bride and her father would appear soon.

"Laurie, here is the bridal party. There is Susan Pierce, Her Royal Highness' Lady-in-Waiting, acting as maid of honor today. She and the bridesmaids are wearing pale pink dresses designed by the same couturier who made the Princess Consort's gown."

"Yes, Franklin, and I notice a Victorian style to their lovely dresses. Of course, we all know that pink is Her Royal Highness' favorite color, so its use today is not surprising. Are they not lovely? And the groomsmen are quite handsome in their classic black tuxedos. There is Billy Panning, a lifelong friend of the Princess Consort. His smile says it all, does it not, Franklin? Happiness is the prevalent feeling today."

§§§§

Before the bride and her father appeared, however, Eduardo made sure that Matthew was ready, and he smoothed and brushed the groom's black tuxedo one last time. Eduardo then assured Matthew that he did indeed have Angilia's gold wedding band in his jacket pocket. Matthew took a deep breath, smiled, and clapped Eduardo on the shoulder. "Are you ready?"

"To see my precious niece marry? Of course, I am ready. I am so happy for you, Matthew," Eduardo said, and he hugged Matthew before they went downstairs and to the garage. The two men settled into the third Rolls Royce of the procession, and as soon as their car turned out of the garage and approached the palace gates, the cheers escalated. Their adored Princess Consort loved Matthew, so the people loved him, too. Thousands of people pelted his car with rose petals, much to his delight. Matthew smiled and waved at everyone for the short drive to the church. When his car arrived and he opened his door, followed by Eduardo, people screamed his name. Matthew stood at the foot of the church steps for a few moments, waving and smiling still, as cameras flashed and people screamed.

"Franklin, this is truly an amazing day. Dr. Taylor was thrust into the Princess Consort's life four years ago, and now their love story culminates in this historic wedding."

"Yes, it does, Laurie. As we mentioned earlier, Matthew Taylor is soon to marry the future first hereditary Queen de Valdavia. When Angilia assumes the throne, she will indeed be the first hereditary Queen. There has never been a King Consort before, so what Dr. Taylor's titles will be is a mystery at this point. As he told us, though, he cares little for titles. His love for Her Royal Highness is clearly evident, Laurie," Franklin commented as Matthew climbed the stairs, walking the red Royal carpet for the first time, and turned to wave once more before he entered the church.

§§§§

Eric stood in the hall watching with his perpetual smile as Susan guided the five bridesmaids downstairs, where the groomsmen were waiting for them. As soon as the ladies left Angilia's suite, he tapped on the door to see her standing in her sitting room smiling at him. They met in a loving hug, and he softly said against her veil the familiar line that always sent a surge of loving warmth through her. "I love you, my beautiful daughter Angilia."

"I love you, my magnificent father," she replied against his chest. "I love you so very much, Daddy. I literally always have. My love for you is eternal."

"As is mine for you, Angel. Today is gloriously happy as you marry your best and longest friend," Eric winked, alluding to her revelation that she and Matthew had first met in a part of Heaven known as the Unborn Children Sphere. "From the moment you shared that with me, I knew that God had meant for you and Matthew to reunite and to marry. Today we stand before God, our family, and our friends as you and Matthew become man and wife."

"I am so thankful and so blessed, more than I realize. I know that. I would not want anyone else beside me on this day, Daddy." Angilia stood on the toes of her left foot—as she had to do since the shooting damaged her right knee—and reached up to kiss his cheek. "Everything feels so right and so calm, because I know that we are fulfilling God's plan for us. Matthew and I went to the chapel after lunch and prayed together. We both said the same thing—our union was pre-destined and is ordained by God. People kept asking me if I felt nervous in the days leading up to now, and I honestly kept saying no. Why should I be nervous when everything is so true and right?"

"I know. People asked if I were sad at giving away my daughter. I am not giving you away. You will always be my little girl, my beautiful daughter. No one and nothing can change that. I am sharing this beautiful moment with you as I, too, fulfill God's plan. Oh, Angilia, my words can never express how I truly feel today," Eric smiled as tears yet again filled his eyes. He held her at arms' length and looked at his most beloved daughter. "You are so beautiful, Angilia. Your gown is gorgeous, too," he smiled. "You will take everyone's breath today. Are you ready?"

"Yes, Daddy, I am ready." She paused. "But not before Uncle Patrick shows himself," she smiled as his familiar warmth greeted them.

"Little One! Look at you! You have got to be the most beautiful bride ever," Patrick said to his niece as he gently kissed her cheek. "Eric! You are the father of the bride today! I am so happy for you both." Patrick and Eric hugged. "I won't keep you. I'll be at the church, you know. Don't be surprised if you feel me hanging around."

Angilia quickly kissed her uncle's cheek. "I love you so much, Uncle Patrick, and I am elated that you are here today. You have to come to the reception, too, you know."

"I love you, Patrick," Eric said as he hugged his brother, waved, and helped Angilia carry her train for the elevator ride to the first floor. She picked up her bouquet and blew a kiss to her uncle before she and Eric left to board the horse-drawn carriage.

Joseph had the carriage waiting at the garage for them, and Angilia kissed her golden palomino Starlight, who led the team of three horses. Mike and Eric assisted her into the carriage and helped her arrange her large skirts and train. Eric sat on her left side and noticed that she moved her mother's purity ring and her engagement ring to the ring finger of her right hand. Matthew would place her gold wedding band on her left ring finger, and during the signing of the register, she would slip her engagement ring alongside her wedding band. She smiled at her father and held his right hand as the carriage began its slow trek through town and to the church.

§§§§

"Laurie, the King and Princess Consort are leaving the palace at this moment, at 12:30 sharp as scheduled. Let's watch and listen live as we get our first glimpse of the bride and her father," Franklin told his global audience with tremendous enthusiasm.

As the horse-drawn carriage turned the corner from the garage and came into view as it approached the palace gates, the sound of several thousand well-wishers screaming in unison filled Valmondois.  Large screens lined the route so all could see every moment of the wedding as it occurred.  When they saw Angilia, people shouted, jumped, screamed, and cheered.  When the carriage exited the palace courtyard and turned onto the street, it and its occupants were showered in red and white rose petals.  Angilia smiled in utter happiness and joy, squeezed her father's hand, and then waved at those gathered to celebrate her marriage.

The carriage traveled slowly, giving all who crowded the route a chance to see Eric and especially Angilia on this most astoundingly beautiful day.  Cameras and cell phones were held aloft as people took hundreds of pictures, all the while thousands more people tossed handfuls of rose petals and shouted their blessings to Angilia.  She and Eric radiated pure happiness as their carriage traveled through the heart of Valmondois and they waved at people who cared enough to share the day with them.

As the carriage wound its way slowly along the route, everyone was focused on Angilia's wedding gown, trying to see as much of it as possible.  At the exact second the carriage left the palace, Eric's Press Secretary, Carol Schuman, released the press embargo containing details of the wedding gown.  "Franklin, I dare say that Princess Consort Angilia's wedding gown is unlike any other we have ever seen.  We are watching her and His Majesty, but also looking through the embargo that we received when the bride's procession began.  The Princess Consort's custom, one-of-a-kind wedding gown was designed by Sherry Greenleaf, who has designed and made several beautiful gowns for Her Royal Highness over the past four years.

"The wedding gown, according to Ms. Greenleaf's statement, was a collaboration between her and Her Royal Highness, with the ultimate choice of style, fabrics, and trims made by Her Royal Highness.  Ms. Greenleaf began by asking the Princess Consort her favorite era of fashion, and thus the wedding gown and bridesmaids' gowns are indeed Victorian in style.  Princess Consort Angilia's gown is made of cream pure silk taffeta, with antique rose colored lace, white lace, and rose-printed silk jacquard trim.  The overskirt falls into the long train, and the skirts are typically full over supporting hoops.  The lace veil is attached to a family heirloom white gold and diamond tiara.  The bouquet of pink and white roses is held by a white lace bouquet collar which is made from the same white lace used on the gown.  Franklin, this is the one most stunning wedding gown I have ever seen," Laurie stated.

"The Princess Consort's gown is absolutely gorgeous, Laurie, and a very personal choice.  The Princess Consort wears acrylic Cinderella shoes, and wears the same tiara which her mother Marisol wore with her wedding veil 25 years ago to the day.  In her statement, Her Royal Highness said she wanted her wedding gown to visually represent her love, joy, and blessings on her wedding day.  What a glorious sentiment, an emotional sentiment, from this young lady who has amazed and besotted us all her entire life," Franklin continued.

"It truly is, Franklin.  While the carriage turns for its final stretch before reaching the Christ Church Valmondois, we can see some of the details on the gown's bodice as the camera zooms in for a closer view of Her Royal Highness.  We will not get a true look at this gown until she steps from the carriage to take her father's arm and walk the red carpet up the steps of the church.  What a dream come true that will be for them, as well as for all of us who are watching," Laurie sighed.

"Indeed.  The carriage is circling the mall again before stopping in front of the church steps.  Our cameras remain on the bride's carriage, but Reverend Hutchins is awaiting His Majesty and Her Royal Highness at the church entrance.  He will lead the bride's procession down the aisle, Laurie."

"That's correct.  The bride's procession begins with Reverend Hutchins, who is directly followed by His Majesty and Her Royal Highness.  Behind them is Susan Pierce, the maid of honor, who in turn is followed by pairs of bridesmaids and groomsmen thusly: Shannon Mazier and Roger Rocard; Nicole Taulbert and Daniel Sein; Amanda Darcy and Christopher Dalton; Amy Wilson and Billy Panning; and Darlene Somers and Scott Ransdale.  They will join Dr. Matthew Taylor and best man Eduardo Martínez at the altar.  At that point, the traditional ceremony will commence."

"Everyone's excitement grows as the bride's carriage pulls in front of the church, Laurie, and the footmen, Mike Connery and Tony Reynolds, alight from their posts on the rear of the carriage to open His Majesty's and Her Royal Highness' carriage doors.  King Eric steps down to loving cheers, and his smile says it all as he waves to those whose elation is nothing compared to his, Laurie."

"His Majesty is so handsome and dashing in his white military uniform, and his eyes shine with happiness today," Laurie commented.  "His Majesty has stepped around the carriage to assist his daughter, who waves to everyone just before she takes her father's hand and steps down from the carriage.  Susan is there to straighten the train and to hand the bride her bouquet before the Princess Consort makes the most joyful walk of her young life.  People are glimpsing the gown for the first time, and the screams of delight are truly deafening, Franklin," Laurie had to practically scream.  "Let's watch the King and Princess Consort."

As the carriage pulled away to the side of the church and everyone saw Angilia in full view for the first time, the whole city of Valmondois seemed buried in an avalanche of screams that blocked out every other sound.  Angilia and Eric waved to everyone, and then walked to the top of the stairs, where they turned to allow everyone who had waited so patiently several moments to savor this one gorgeous moment.  Angilia waved, Eric waved, they both beamed with smiles, and both enjoyed seeing so many of their friends and neighbors there to wish them well.  With seconds to spare, Angilia blew them a kiss, slipped her arm through her father's arm, and walked into the church.

Inside, Susan once more straightened the train and fluffed the skirts, before making sure the bridesmaids and groomsmen were paired and in place.  Everything was perfect and on schedule.  Reverend Hutchins said a prayer with Eric and Angilia before they began the procession, kissed her cheek, and asked if they were ready.  Angilia and Eric looked at one another, still smiling, and said simultaneously, "Absolutely."

§§§§§

Just before the processional began down the nave, Angilia leaned close to her father and whispered, "You are my greatest love, always, Daddy." Eric squeezed her hand and gently kissed her cheek as he felt tears threaten his eyes yet again that day. Reverend Hutchins began his reverently slow walk down the aisle, and just as their cue sounded, Eric and Angilia took their first step and smiled at one another again. Susan followed several paces behind them, and then the pairs of bridesmaids and groomsmen walked in steady progression behind the maid of honor.

When Eric and Angilia came into the view of the guests seated near the back of the church, gasps and sobs were heard. The lights made the silk of her gown sparkle and the diamonds in her tiara shine like the brightest stars. The diamond earrings she wore, which also caught and reflected the light, had belonged to her maternal grandmother. Eric had given them to her on her 16th birthday, and they perfectly suited both the tiara and her Victorian gown. Occasionally, the tip of a "glass" slipper peeped from beneath her voluminous skirts. To the world, Angilia was a real-life princess bride, living her real-life fairy-tale come true. Her gloriously happy smile proved that to everyone who watched her with love and awe that day.

In front of the altar, Eduardo touched Matthew's elbow and whispered for him to look down the aisle. Matthew breathed deeply and turned to see his breathtaking Angilia seemingly gliding across the red carpet toward him. Very soon, she would stand beside him as they exchanged wedding vows and were pronounced husband and wife before God and their families and friends. Angilia caught his eye and smiled at him, and she saw, even from a distance, the glimmer of tears in Matthew's amber eyes.

Angilia smiled and nodded at their friends as she and her father walked down the aisle, so thankful that those who mattered to her shared her wedding with her. When they neared the altar, she saw dear Mr. Brennan next to Mitchell in the Royal pew. She was especially grateful that he was with them today, as she knew how frail and weak he had been for a while. He smiled at her and Eric as they came into his view. Angilia and Eric knew well what today meant to Mr. Brennan, their friend and supporter who had watched every Royal wedding since his 1916 birth from a vantage point along the route. Today, this ardent royalist witnessed Valdavia's future Queen wed her true love, in a place of honor beside his King.

Eric and Angilia finally stood in front of the altar alongside Matthew, and both felt the truth that God's destiny was now moments from fulfillment. Eric lifted a silent prayer to God, while Angilia and Matthew smiled at one another, knowing their union was blessed and meant to happen. As the last piano note struck, Anthony smiled, and the traditional wedding service began.

§§§§

The screaming, cheering crowds watching outdoors on the large screens throughout Valmondois grew respectfully, reverently quiet as the ceremony began. Everyone longed to see and to hear their darling Angilia's wedding in its entirety. King Eric smiled at his daughter and soon-to-be son-in-law Matthew as Reverend Hutchins took his position at the altar.

"Dearly beloved, we are gathered here in the sight of God and in the face of this congregation, to join together this man and this woman in Holy Matrimony; which is an honorable estate instituted by God himself, signifying unto us the mystical union that is betwixt Christ and his Church; which holy estate Christ adorned and beautified with his presence, and first miracle he wrought, in Cana of Galilee, and is commended in Holy Writ to be honorable among all men; and therefore is not by any to be enterprised, nor taken in hand, unadvisedly, lightly, or wantonly; but reverently, discreetly, soberly, and in the fear of God, duly considering the causes for which Matrimony was ordained.

"First, It was ordained for the increase of mankind according to the will of God, and that children might be brought up in the fear and nurture of the Lord, and to the praise of his Holy name.

"Secondly, It was ordained in order that the natural instincts and affections, implanted by God, should be hallowed and directed aright; that those who are called of God to this holy estate, should continue therein in pureness of living.

"Thirdly, It was ordained for the mutual society, help and comfort, that the one ought to have of the other, both in prosperity and in adversity.

"Into which holy estate these two persons present come now to be joined.

"Therefore if any man can shew any just cause, why they may not lawfully be joined together, let him now speak, or else hereafter for ever hold his peace." Reverend Hutchins paused for 30 seconds, allowing the traditional time for this matter to be addressed if needed, and also allowing time for Angilia and Matthew to look at one another with love and smiles. Everyone watching around the world clearly noticed the devotion and love shared between the young couple.

Reverend Hutchins looked directly at Angilia and Matthew. "I require and charge you both, as ye will answer at the dreadful day of judgment when the secrets of all hearts shall be disclosed, that if either of you know any impediment, why ye may not be lawfully joined together in Matrimony, ye do now confess it. For be ye well assured, that so many as are coupled together otherwise than God's word doth allow are not joined together by God; neither is their Matrimony lawful."

Angilia and Matthew looked into Reverend Hutchins' eyes, neither speaking words, yet saying everything with their eyes. Reverend Hutchins nodded once in understanding, and then he looked at Matthew, who felt his heart raging as he knew the vows were next. That was the moment for which Matthew had waited for four years. "Matthew Aaron, wilt thou have this woman to thy wedded wife, to live together after God's ordinance in the holy estate of Matrimony? Wilt thou love her, comfort her, honor, and keep her, in sickness and in health; and, forsaking all other, keep thee only unto her, so long as ye both shall live?"

"I will," Matthew replied, his voice clear yet filled with what Angilia perpetually called happy tears.

Reverend Hutchins looked at Angilia, whom he had known since her birth, and flashed a small smile. "Angilia Erica Charity, wilt thou have this man to thy wedded husband, to live together according to God's law in the holy estate of Matrimony?  Wilt thou love him, comfort him, honor and keep him, in sickness and in health; and forsaking all other, keep thee only unto him, so long as ye both shall live?"

Angilia silently thanked God for their blessed union, and answered in a clear, confident voice.  "I will."  She knew, though, that the most emotional moment of the service was seconds away.  Just before Reverend Hutchins continued, Angilia felt the familiar warmth of her Uncle Patrick's presence as he surrounded them with his love at this key moment.

"Who giveth this Woman to be married to this Man?"  Reverend Hutchins asked as he looked at Eric, who stood at his daughter's left.

"I, her father, do," Eric said with tears shining in his eyes and a smile radiating on his face.  Eric slipped his left hand under Angilia's right hand and lifted their hands before Reverend Hutchins.  Reverend Hutchins placed his right hand over both of their hands and then placed his left hand over Matthew's right hand.  After blessing the three of them, Reverend Hutchins brought their hands closer and transferred Angilia's right hand from her father's left hand onto Matthew's right hand.

"Matthew Aaron, say after I do," Reverend Hutchins ordered, as he recited the vows line by line for Matthew to repeat.

"I, Matthew Aaron take thee Angilia Erica Charity to my wedded wife, to have and to hold from this day forward, for better for worse, for richer for poorer, in sickness and in health, to love and to cherish, till death us do part, according to God's holy ordinance; and thereto I plight thee my troth."

Angilia and Matthew smiled at one another as they separated their hands for her wedding vows.  Angilia then placed her right hand below Matthew's right hand and likewise repeated her vows after Reverend Hutchins.

"I, Angilia Erica Charity take thee Matthew Aaron to my wedded husband, to have and to hold from this day forward, for better for worse, for richer for poorer, in sickness and in health, to love and to cherish, till death us do part, according to God's holy ordinance; and thereto I plight thee my troth."

Angilia and Matthew separated hands and each took the wedding bands from Susan—who had safeguarded Matthew's ring—and Eduardo—who had protected Angilia's ring—and placed the gold bands upon the book which Reverend Hutchins held. The congregation bowed their heads as Reverend Hutchins said a prayer for the blessing of Angilia's ring.

"Bless, O Lord, this ring, and grant that he who gives it and she who shall wear it may remain faithful to each other, and abide in thy peace and favor, and live together in love until their lives' end. Through Jesus Christ our Lord. Amen." Reverend Hutchins lifted Angilia's ring and placed it in Matthew's left hand.

Matthew smiled at his Angilia as he tenderly slid the ring onto the fourth finger of her left hand and said, "With this ring I thee wed; with my body I thee honor; and all my worldly goods with thee I share: In the name of the Father, and of the Son, and of the Holy Ghost. Amen."

Reverend Hutchins offered his prayer for the blessing of Matthew's wedding ring. "Bless, O Lord, this ring, and grant that she who gives it and he who shall wear it may remain faithful to each other, and abide in thy peace and favor, and live together in love until their lives' end. Through Jesus Christ our Lord. Amen." Reverend Hutchins placed Matthew's gold band in Angilia's left hand.

Angilia slipped the ring onto the fourth finger of Matthew's left hand as she smiled joyously at him. "With this ring I thee wed; with my body I thee honor; and all my worldly goods with thee I share: In the name of the Father, and of the Son, and of the Holy Ghost. Amen."

At that moment, Angilia and Matthew knelt onto the same kneelers that had been made for her parents' wedding 25 years earlier. Eric discreetly stepped to his seat in the Royal pew, next to Mr. Brennan, who motioned for Mitchell and Eric to assist him to stand for the consecration of the vows. Eric and Mitchell supported him during the prayer.

"Let us pray," Reverend Hutchins said.  The congregation all stood and bowed their heads.  "O eternal God, Creator and Preserver of all mankind, giver of all spiritual grace, the author of everlasting life; Send thy blessing upon these thy servants, this man and this woman, whom we bless in thy name; that living faithfully together, they may surely perform and keep the vow and covenant betwixt them made, whereof these rings given and received are a token and pledge; and may ever remain in perfect love and peace together, and live according to thy laws; through Jesus Christ our Lord.  Amen."

Reverend Hutchins took Angilia's and Matthew's right hands in each of his hands and joined their hands to signify their marriage and said, "Those whom God hath joined together let no man put asunder."  Angilia and Matthew smiled at one another and she gently squeezed his hand.  She could feel Matthew trembling, and she understood how emotional this was for him.

"Forasmuch as Matthew Aaron and Angilia Erica Charity have consented together in holy wedlock, and have witnessed the same before God and this company, and thereto have given and pledged their troth to each other, and have declared the same by giving and receiving of rings, and by joining of hands; I pronounce that they be man and wife together, In the name of the Father, and of the Son, and of the Holy Ghost.  Amen."  Reverend Hutchins had placed his hands atop their heads to bless them as he spoke.

At the moment Reverend Hutchins pronounced Matthew and Angilia husband and wife, the crowds outside erupted in rapturous cheers.  Even with the heavy church doors closed, those inside could hear the screams and cheers of happiness and delight.  Angilia and Matthew yet again smiled at one another.

The blessing continued.  "God the Father, God the Son, God the Holy Ghost, bless, preserve, and keep you; the Lord mercifully with his favor look upon you; and so fill you with all spiritual benediction and grace, that ye may so live together in this life, that in the world to come ye may have life everlasting.  Amen."

At that point, Matthew took Angilia's hand and helped her to stand, knowing that kneeling on her knees—even for her joyous wedding—was painful for her right knee. He helped her into one of two seats that had been placed for them to the right of the altar, and as soon as the bride and groom were seated, the rest of the congregation sat. The choir sang the hymn that Angilia and Matthew had selected, "Christ is Made the Sure Foundation," her father's favorite hymn that had been sung at his wedding to Marisol.

Afterward, the Reverend Paul Minor, who had led the services at the church Angilia had attended in Oxford, England, approached the altar to read the Lesson, I Corinthians Chapter 13.

Reverend Hutchins returned for the Address, which no one had heard or read prior to the ceremony, although Eric had provided a bit of information for the Address. Reverend Hutchins spoke from his heart, having known Angilia her entire life and being quite fond of her. "Today, we have witnessed a real-life fairy-tale, in which the beautiful and kind princess falls in love with and marries her one true love. While that analogy appears romantic and sweet, we should take our true analogy from the Princess Consort Angilia herself.

"She has stated many times in the past that her life is a fairy-tale, but never because she was born a princess and heir to the throne of Valdavia. Her life is magical, because God has seen fit to bless her abundantly. As Angilia moves from this day forward, she does so knowing that she is the daughter of His Majesty King Eric de Valdavia and the wife of His Royal Highness Matthew Aaron, Duc de Valmondois, but more importantly that she is a child of God.

"Both her father and her husband are children of God, as well, and together they shall continue to love and to support Angilia in her work. Likewise, she will continue to love and to support her father and her husband. All of us who love them will continue to provide them our love and support, and in return the King, the Princess Consort, and the Duc shall love and support us as they have always done.

"Love for God, for ourselves, and for one another is crucial in this world of the 21$^{st}$ century. God has blessed Valdavia, and the world, with a King, a future Queen, and a Duc who understand and practice God's commandments daily for the salvation of their own souls and also for the benefit of our well-being.

"God tells us that love is the greatest gift we can give to another human being, and we see this evidenced daily in the lives of His Majesty and Their Royal Highnesses. Today is all about love, as we rejoice in the marriage of Angilia and Matthew."

Reverend Hutchins bowed his head and moved to stand to the left of the altar. The choir sang The Lord's Prayer, Psalm 23, newly set to music by Angilia specifically for the wedding ceremony. Immediately at the hymn's conclusion, Reverend Hutchins continued the blessing of the Royal couple. "Almighty God, gracious Father, heap upon you both his grace and his sanctity, that you may honor and please him in body, in heart, and in soul throughout your earthly lives, so that you may live together in holy love not just in this life on earth but in your eternal life in Heaven."

The congregation rose to sing the National Anthem of Valdavia, and Eric looked at his daughter, his love and joy evident on his face. She looked at him, too, and he saw that oh so familiar look of tremendous love for him sparkling in her eyes. She smiled at him, he smiled at her, and they knew that they had truly fulfilled God's plan. Matthew smiled at his father-in-law, as well, his whole being so full of love and happiness.

When the National Anthem concluded, everyone remained standing while Angilia and Matthew linked arms and followed Reverend Hutchins to the Register Room. Susan and Eduardo walked behind the newlyweds, Eric entered the line after them, and finally Mitchell and Katherine joined them. While they were all in the Register Room, signing the Church Register and the Marriage License, Anthony Severson resumed his seat at the piano. He played the piece that Angilia wrote for her husband, a piano solo she titled "Love's True Blessing." The piece lasted seven minutes, just long enough for the signing—they all signed the Church Register— and a moment of hugs and kisses.

For the first time since they began their walk down the aisle, Angilia kissed her father's cheek and hugged him close to her. Katherine pulled her handkerchief from her purse, ecstatic for her son and new daughter-in-law.  Matthew looked at his Angilia and leaned close to her, whispering in her ear.  She smiled, nodded, and whispered her reply in his ear.  Eric was close enough to hear them tell one another "I love you," which made his smile even more resplendent.  Angilia took a moment to pull the 1991 Church Register from the shelf and flip to 26 June 1991—to her parents' wedding register.  Tears filled her eyes as she looked at her father's signature and then at her mother's.  Eric put his arms around her, knowing what she felt.  She smiled up at him, tears threatening to spill down her cheeks, and softly said, "I love you both, Daddy and Mommy.  Happy Anniversary."  Eric kissed the top of her head, unable to speak for the moment, and thanked God for his abundant blessings.

Angilia returned the Church Register to the shelf, cleared her throat, and smiled at everyone.  What a wonderfully glorious day!  Reverend Hutchins congratulated Angilia and Matthew and then led them all back to the altar, where Eric, Mitchell, and Katherine returned to the pew.  Susan and Eduardo resumed their places near the bride and groom as the wedding ceremony reached its conclusion.  Before they turned to face Reverend Hutchins, Angilia curtseyed and Matthew bowed to Eric.

Reverend Hutchins offered his final blessings to Angilia and Matthew with a recitation of an Orlando Gibbons prayer.  "God the Holy Trinity make you strong in faith and love, defend you on every side, and guide you in truth and peace; and the blessing of God Almighty, the Father, the Son, and the Holy Spirit, be among you and remain with you always.  Amen."

Susan handed Angilia her bridal bouquet and Reverend Hutchins made one last statement before the Princess Consort and Duc led the processional.  "Honored guests, I am pleased to present to you Her Royal Highness The Princess Consort, Angilia Erica Charity, Duchesse de Valmondois and His Royal Highness Matthew Aaron, Duc de Valmondois."

Matthew was unaccustomed to the sound of his new and surprise title, although he followed his wife's lead and turned for their walk down the aisle.  The congregation stood, Mr. Brennan supported by Mitchell, as the Royal couple heard the fanfare and smiled at one another. Angilia gently nudged Matthew, and they slowly walked down the red carpet, where the doors opened to the most ear-shattering screams Matthew had ever heard. Susan and Eduardo followed, and then the pairs of bridesmaids and groomsmen. Eric joined the procession next, and then Mitchell and Katherine, Alejandro and Juanita, and at the end of the procession walked Reverend Hutchins.

Angilia and Matthew approached the door, and she felt him trembling, unused to the screams and attention. She tightened her hand on his arm and smiled reassuringly at her husband. Her husband! He smiled at her as the same reality hit his brain—that his Angilia was now and forever his wife. When they stepped outside the church, they stood to allow everyone who had shared their wedding a few moments to view and to greet them. Angilia waved at them, her wide smile and bright eyes relaying her happiness. Matthew waved, as well, feeling the love and respect everyone held for his wife. How could they not love Angilia? he thought.

The carriage pulled in front of the church, and they slowly walked down the stairs as they waved occasionally to the well-wishers. Just as she prepared to enter the carriage, Angilia turned and blew a kiss to her father, which caused everyone to once more erupt into shattering cheers. Matthew and Mike assisted her, and Matthew arranged her skirts and train as she settled on the seat. He walked around the carriage, while Tony held his door, and sat beside his wife. Matthew and Angilia waved at everyone while the carriage slowly retraced its earlier route through Valmondois.

As they approached Main Street, they both leaned closer to one another and spoke privately under cover of the tumultuous screams for a few minutes. "I love you so much, Angilia. I am so happy. I never thought I would ever be this happy," Matthew said as tears trickled from the corners of his eyes.

Angilia smiled at him, intuiting his feelings. "I love you so very much, Matthew. I always wondered if I would feel this way, this deep, true love my parents share. Thank you for waiting for me. I know that wasn't very fair to you, Matthew."

He smiled, yet shook his head. "I meant it. I would wait forever for you. You are my one and only love, Angilia. I know that." The people lining the route were screaming frantically, expecting an impromptu kiss at any moment. As rose petals besieged them, Matthew cleared his throat and waved at everyone. He suddenly realized that he had never kissed Angilia, except on the cheek or the hand. That would change once they were in the privacy of the palace. When the moment was right, he would kiss his bride for the first time!

After nearly 30 minutes, the carriage approached the palace, and the throngs gathered on the mall beseeched them to prolong their stay there. Angilia shouted that they would make the balcony appearance very soon, which garnered shouts of approval. One extremely excited admirer ran to the carriage as the palace gates opened, and the woman handed Angilia a white teddy bear with a pink ribbon around its neck. Angilia's wedding colors. Angilia showed the stuffed animal to Matthew and thanked the tearful woman for the gift.

Soon, the carriage pulled up to the garage, and Bonnie Glaser was there to capture the moment when Angilia and Matthew alighted and entered the palace for the first time as wife and husband. Matthew and Mike once more assisted Angilia from the carriage, with her train, and onto the walkway to the patio. As Bonnie walked ahead of them taking photographs, Angilia and Matthew were greeted by their family and friends on the patio. Katherine hugged Angilia while Eric hugged Matthew, and then Mitchell hugged the young lady who was now his daughter-in-law. Katherine and Mitchell hugged their son, although Katherine was so emotional that she barely let go of Matthew for two seconds. Alejandro and Juanita cried tears of joy as they embraced their beloved granddaughter and grandson-in-law. Their hearts were so filled with love and joy. The wedding party hugged the happy couple, tears in plentiful supply that afternoon.

Mr. Brennan reached for Matthew, Valdavia's new Duc, and hugged him. "You will make a wonderful Duc, dear boy. Just wonderful." Angilia beamed as the two men hugged.

Mr. Brennan smiled at Angilia with tears sliding from his eyes down his cheeks, and he reached his arms to her. She bent to hug him, and he could barely talk. "My dear Princess Consort, you must know how much I have looked forward to today. You know how I prayed to live long enough to see today, and I thank God that I have. You make me so very happy, my dear. So happy."

"You are very special to me, Mr. Brennan. I am grateful you are here with us today, to share our wedding with us. I am thankful that God created our friendship. I love you, Mr. Brennan." Eric and Nurse Ginny felt their throats ache as tears gathered in their eyes. They all recognized the reality that Mr. Brennan, at an amazing yet frail 100 years of age, was nearing the end of his earthly life. They knew how much Angilia's wedding day meant to him, and his joyfulness made them instantaneously happy and appreciative of their blessings. Bonnie wiped tears as she took photographs of Angilia and Mr. Brennan.

§§§§§

Most of the wedding party and family members spent the following 15 minutes freshening up, although Matthew, Angilia, and Eric remained together in the foyer. Eric finally stepped to his daughter and pulled her into a hug. Neither spoke, not needing to say with words what they shared in their hearts. Matthew smiled as he watched them, blessed beyond measure to witness and to share their love. What he had once envied he now treasured.

Simultaneously, Angilia and Eric reached for Matthew and pulled him into the embrace. Matthew was now connected to them for all eternity. Angilia smiled as they felt warmth encircle them. Matthew glanced around the foyer and asked, "What is that?" He had never felt a warm breeze like that before in the palace.

Angilia giggled. "You mean who. That is my Uncle Patrick."

Matthew looked as confused as he felt. He knew her paternal uncle had died in 1977. He remembered her Christmas 2012 drawing of Patrick and her explanations that she had known him when she was in Heaven. Still, Matthew wondered what Angilia meant that Patrick was there. She saw the questions on her husband's face and answered them.  "Uncle Patrick visits a lot, Matthew.  He was at the church earlier, near the altar with us.  Didn't you feel him?"

"I felt warm air blow around us, yes, but I thought it was the church heating and cooling system."  Matthew looked at Eric and Angilia for a moment.  "Are you telling me that your uncle is here right now?  He was in the church?"  Angilia understood that Matthew tried to comprehend what she told him, and that it was difficult for him to do so.

"Yes.  Uncle Patrick is around quite often, Matthew.  I've felt and seen him all of my life.  You will love him, I know you will.  I know he is thrilled that you want to become the Patron of the AAV.  He can answer any of your questions about that, you know, and give you lots of tips and ideas.  Just ask him the next time he manifests."

"Manifests?  What does that mean?"  Matthew appeared almost afraid of the answer.

"Souls manifest when they take on their earthly physical appearance," Angilia explained.

"I first saw Patrick's manifestation on Christmas Day 2012," Eric smiled.  "Other than Angilia, my brother's manifestation is the most wonderful Christmas gift I have ever received."

"You can actually see him?" Matthew asked, still befuddled.

"Sure they can," Patrick said as he appeared between Angilia and Matthew, his arms around their shoulders.  "So can you, nephew."

"Uncle Patrick!  Meet my husband Matthew.  Matthew, this is my Uncle Patrick," Angilia said, as if she introduced her dead uncle to people every day.

"I am so very happy for you, Little One.  Matthew, I know how much you love my niece and how much Angilia loves you.  I've seen it clearly since you first met her four years ago, at least from your end," Patrick giggled as he hugged Matthew.

Patrick looked real, he sounded real, and he felt real, as human as any of them, yet he was dead, Matthew thought. Matthew looked at Angilia's radiant face, and at the ease and naturalness of Angilia's and Eric's interactions with Patrick. Patrick died long ago, but he was still alive. Matthew finally truly understood Angilia's talk of eternal souls. She had said more than once that people do not cease living when their earthly bodies die. Matthew returned Patrick's hug, forgetting the unusualness of the exchange and feeling only the genuineness of the exchange. "Thank you. I know how much Angilia loves you, too, Patrick. She talks of you very often," Matthew told Prince Patrick.

"Aw, thank you. Well, I best disappear for a while. I hear the others. I'll be at the reception, though," Patrick said when Roger came rushing down the stairs to organize the balcony appearances. Without another sound, Patrick was gone as quickly as he had come. Matthew almost—almost—doubted the reality of what had just happened.

§§§§

Roger and Daniel opened the red velvet drapes and the double French doors leading to the fifth floor balcony, which elicited excited screams and cheers. As the balcony appearances drew nearer, thousands of people ran to the mall, hoping to see Angilia and Matthew again. Many people brought telescopes or binoculars, as well as zoom lenses for their cameras, to better glimpse the newlyweds. Angilia took her bouquet from Susan, and then took hold of Matthew's hand. "Are you ready?" Matthew smiled and nodded, far too happy to let his nervousness bother him.

The Royal couple walked onto the balcony to several thousand people crowding the mall, more running to the mall, and joyful cheers, banners, and balloons. The afternoon sunlight glistened and gleamed on the statue of Valdavia's first ruler, King Christophe, as well as Angilia's diamond tiara and earrings. Magical stars appeared to brighten the fairy-tale afternoon.

Angilia's and Matthew's smiles shone just as brightly, as they radiated such happiness and love. Their waves were answered with screams of delight, as well as shouts for King Eric, whom everyone adored.  Angilia turned and called for her father.  "They want you, Daddy.  They're calling for you," she said with a smile.

"This is your moment, Angel.  We'll join you soon."

Several minutes later, Matthew turned and told Eric, "They want to see you.  You might as well come out here now before they storm the palace."  Roger gently pushed Eric toward the balcony, so he finally relented and stepped out to join Angilia and Matthew.  As soon as he did, those on the mall saluted and cheered the man long ago dubbed the King of the People.  Eric earned peoples' love and respect, which was clearly evident to everyone around the world who watched the Royal Wedding coverage live on televisions, computers, or tablets.  As Eric waved, Angilia smiled up at her father, overjoyed as she always was when people showed their love for him.

Roger soon sent Mitchell and Katherine out, as well, and they were pleasantly surprised to receive generous cheers.  The reality that their son was now a member of the Royal Family, a Duc, finally registered in their brains as they saw people holding signs and waving flags with Angilia's and Matthew's engagement portraits on them.  Neither of them had known that Eric would bestow the title Duc de Valmondois upon Matthew.  Only Roger and Reverend Hutchins had known.  Royal titles had never entered their thoughts, as Eric well knew.  He had created the title Duchesse de Valmondois for Angilia as her 16th birthday surprise.  He felt it quite fitting to create the title Duc de Valmondois as a surprise wedding gift for Matthew.

As they watched in delight from inside, Alejandro and Juanita were encouraged to join those on the balcony, and they, too, were greeted with tremendous love and respect.  Many of those watching remembered seeing Alejandro and Juanita as the parents of the bride 25 years earlier.  Now they were the grandparents of the bride.  The thought made many in the crowd emotional and even cry, knowing the love they felt for Angilia and she for them.

Finally, Roger shepherded the wedding party onto the balcony, which was admittedly nerve-inducing for most of them.  Angilia noticed and smiled at them as she told them to have fun and just enjoy the experience.  Billy stared wide-eyed, having been in the crowd below many times over the years.  She pulled him close and held his hand as she encouraged him to wave.  "You know you are one of the most popular people out here today, Billy.  Everyone in Valmondois already knows you and adores you.  Just wave to let them know you appreciate their kindness and love."

Billy doubted his adored Princess darling, but he smiled and timidly waved.  So did the girls and Scott.  They, like Billy, had never experienced anything remotely similar before.  Sure, Scott had portrayed Romeo to Angilia's Juliet, which received lots of attention, but not with several thousand people screaming at him at once.  This was dreamlike for most of them.  Even Susan, Daniel, and Roger had never appeared on the balcony with the Royal Family before.  They had always been behind the scenes.  Still, the love, joy, and peace they all felt buoyed their spirits and made the experience itself euphoric and memorable for everyone.

Suddenly, the crowd's cheers turned into a chant, and Eric leaned closer to his daughter and son-in-law to repeat the request with a smile.  "They want you two to kiss."

Matthew looked at Angilia, and she smiled at him.  He lifted her left hand and kissed it, in a gallant and romantic gesture, which may not have been what people wanted and expected, but which charmed and delighted them nonetheless.  The screams and cheers escalated in appreciation, and that moment was captured in dozens of photographs that headlined newspapers, magazines, and commemorative books around the world.

§§§§

The wedding party gathered in a room few of them had seen.  Susan, Daniel, and Roger had been in the throne room for official occasions, photographs, and portrait sessions, although the throne room was the least used room in the palace.  Alejandro and Juanita had been there twice before, once when Eric was coronated King de Valdavia and Marisol Queen Consort de Valdavia.  They led Mitchell and Katherine to the room, also on the fifth floor, seemingly tucked away opposite the grandeur of the huge ballroom.

Bonnie trailed behind them, several cameras in her bags. Her hired crew had sat up the lights in the throne room during the wedding ceremony, and they stayed to assist in moving and adjusting the large lights for the official wedding photographs. Several of Eric's security staff stood guard in the throne room, primarily because the vault which contained the Royal jewels was built into one of the walls and covered—as were all the walls—in rich red velvet. No one would know the vault were there unless they had been shown the hidden panel which disguised it from view. Of those present, none had ever entered the vault. Most did not know it existed.

While most people were admiring the room, with its red and gold décor, Eric, Angilia, and Matthew entered. Angilia had requested that Bonnie take the family and group photographs first so that her grandparents and the others could relax and rest a bit prior to the reception. Bonnie organized Angilia, Matthew, the wedding party, the families, the foreign Royal guests, the politicians and dignitaries who had attended, Mr. Brennan, and a very special guest who appeared seemingly out of nowhere to Angilia's immense surprise and pleasure. He was placed slightly behind Eric and Angilia, and she turned to thank him while Bonnie finished arranging everyone for the group photographs.

"Your Excellency, I am so honored and happy that you are here today. You are such an inspiration to me," she told him, feeling as if she were speaking with a dear friend rather than a revered international figure.

"As you are to me, dear Princess. I am quite pleased to be here to share your happiness today. And please, call me Bibi," the Israeli Prime Minister winked at her just as Bonnie called everyone to order and took several group pictures to make sure she had just the right ones.

Next, most of the Royal and political guests were excused and told they could go to their overnight suites to freshen up before the reception began. Maids escorted the guests to suites on the third floor, while Angilia, Matthew, the wedding party, and their family members stood for their photographs. So that Alejandro and Juanita could relax soon, Bonnie next photographed the bride, groom, and their family members. Before they went to their suite to rest for a short while, Juanita hugged and kissed Angilia and Matthew, and Alejandro struggled to contain his happy tears as he hugged them.

The wedding party rejoined the Royal couple for their pictures, and then Mr. Brennan was asked to join Angilia and Matthew for a very special Royal souvenir—his photograph with the newlyweds. Eric joined them for another picture to grace Mr. Brennan's photograph album, much to his delight. Angilia kissed him before Nurse Ginny took him to a suite to freshen and to take his medications.

Another very important guest posed with the newlyweds. No one except the family and wedding party ever saw these photographs, but they remained cherished by the Valdavian Royal Family thereafter. Angilia, Matthew, and the Prime Minister of Israel smiled happily from the family photograph album for many centuries. Angilia called her uncle Eduardo to them and introduced him to the Prime Minister, and Bonnie fought her tears as she took photographs of the four of them together. Angilia then introduced Bonnie to His Excellency, and she kissed his hand. The Prime Minister asked someone else to take a picture of the five of them: Angilia, Eduardo, His Excellency, Bonnie, and Matthew. Copies of that historic picture hung on Bonnie's wall and stood on Eduardo's desk for the rest of their lives.

Finally, after drying her tears, Bonnie took the photographs of the couple, including portraits of each of them alone. At one point, Angilia leaned her head on Matthew's shoulder and Bonnie quickly captured the tender moment. Matthew's amber eyes once more seemed lit from within as he looked at his wife, his Angilia, and lifted her left hand to gently caress her engagement and wedding rings. Angilia beamed at him and leaned up to kiss his cheek.

When Carol released the official wedding photographs the following day, people gasped once again at the immense beauty and love so very evident in the photographs and throughout the historic day. Matthew and Angilia were gifted a white and pink album by Bonnie, with each of the day's pictures inside. Years later, that album would be looked at with love by their son, just as Angilia often looked at her parents' wedding album with love.

§§§§§

Maids and butlers escorted the wedding guests to the fifth floor ballroom as they arrived at the main entrance of the palace. Everyone was there by 5:50, happily waiting for Angilia and Matthew to make their entrance at 6:00 sharp. As they stood in their sitting room in the minutes before the reception began, they stood close, holding hands, while they shared their first private moment since becoming wife and husband.

"I feel so incredibly happy, loved, and blessed today, Matthew. I do love you, you know that, I hope," Angilia told him, those remarkable turquoise eyes of hers shooting Cupid arrows into his heart again.

"I do know, Angilia. I love you so very much, but yet that sounds so feeble compared to what I truly feel for you. If anyone is blessed, I am, for every dream that I ever dreamed has come true in one day," Matthew replied with tears choking his voice. "I love you, my precious Angilia. I love you."

"I know, and I thank God for bringing us together again."

"So do I. Even if I don't remember anything from the Unborn Children Sphere, I know it is true. I knew there was something about you even that first moment when I was so scared. I've never told anyone how very scared I was that day, scared that I would lose you when I had just found you. I loved you from the very first second I saw you. None of it made sense to me then, but when you showed me your diary and I read it, everything made sense. God did reunite us, Angilia. He intended all along for us to marry. That's why I never even looked at another woman. I was waiting for you, my love. Only you."

A tear slid from Angilia's eye, Matthew gently wiped it away, and they bowed their heads in a prayer of thanksgiving before joining their family and friends for the celebration of their union. After they said "Amen" in unison, Angilia picked up her train, draped it over one arm, and walked with Matthew to the elevator.

Outside the ballroom, he smoothed her train and veil for her, kissed her cheek, and linked arms with his beautiful wife.

Eduardo stood near the entrance, where he could see them arrive, and just before they entered, he introduced them. "Ladies and gentlemen, Their Royal Highnesses The Duc and Duchesse de Valmondois!" Everyone except Mr. Brennan stood and applauded Matthew and Angilia as they walked into the center of the ballroom. She curtseyed and Matthew bowed to Eric, and Matthew kissed her hand as Eric approached. Matthew slid Angilia's hand into Eric's for the father-daughter dance.

Angilia selected the song, which Dave Rodan, the most popular disc jockey in Valdavia, played for them. Angilia and Matthew had asked him to DJ the reception, when the band wasn't playing live, and he had been ecstatic to accept. He understood well the significance of the song Angilia had selected for the first dance with her beloved father. So did the guests when they heard John Denver's "Sunshine on My Shoulders" begin playing and saw Eric and Angilia dancing.

The guests stood watching them, tears yet again freely flowing, their awe and enchantment greater than ever. When the song ended, Angilia reached up and kissed her father's cheek. With happy tears shining in his turquoise eyes, Eric kissed his daughter's cheek and told her, "I love you, my beautiful daughter Angilia."

The guests applauded as Eric hugged Matthew and slipped Angilia's right hand into Matthew's hand for their first dance as husband and wife. Matthew chose the only song that even came close to capturing what he felt for his Angilia, and everyone sighed when the romantic and familiar notes of Elvis Presley's "Can't Help Falling in Love" sounded and the newlyweds began waltzing. Matthew and Angilia stared into one another's eyes and souls as they glided across the floor. Katherine and Juanita cried proverbial oceans of emotional tears as they watched the young couple, who were so obviously in love and happy.

Eric watched them as he felt his beautiful wife's spirit encircle him. Marisol, too, witnessed their daughter's love and joy while Angilia danced with her husband. Eric touched his wedding band, remembering that moment 25 years earlier when Marisol had slid the ring on his finger and they were pronounced man and wife. Now their daughter knew that love, happiness, and blessing as she shared their wedding date. What a beautiful experience.

The next dance was shared by Eric and Katherine, as well as Mitchell and Juanita. The two families were truly one now and forevermore. Angilia had signed her new name for the first time in the Church Register and then on the Marriage License: Angilia Erica Charity DeBruce Martineau Taylor. The surname had changed in 1578 after the marriage of the future King Leon II to Muriel Darrell, a direct descendant of King Robert the Bruce. The Martineau dynasty became the DeBruce Martineau dynasty via that marriage. Now the dynasty bore a new name for the third time in its 685 year history.

After several dances, including Angilia's emotional waltz with her adored Abuelo, Angilia sensed a very special guest indeed. She looked knowingly at her father and her husband as warmth encompassed them for the third time that day. Patrick kept his promise to her. He did attend her reception. Angilia unexpectedly felt a tap on her shoulder and turned to greet her next dance partner.

Her eyes sparkled like the diamonds in her tiara when she saw her handsome uncle standing there in a black tuxedo and smiling at her. "May I have the next dance with the bride?" he asked with the hint of mischief in his eyes.

"Absolutely, Uncle Patrick! I am so very happy you are here," she said, her smile proving her words. Patrick nodded to Dave Rodan and the next song caught everyone by surprise, particularly Eric. His recording of "The Twelfth of Never" resounded, Patrick's tribute to his brother's anniversary and his niece's marriage. The dance floor cleared as Angilia danced with her uncle, although most people did not know who the handsome, mysterious guest was. Matthew stared at Patrick in disbelief, never expecting Angilia's uncle to actually materialize—or was it manifest?—at the reception in such a very public way.

Roger and Daniel recognized him instantly and quickly made their way to Eric's side. As softly as he could, Roger asked, "Is this for real? Is that really him?" Eric smiled and nodded, never looking at Roger or Daniel, just at his brother and daughter.

"How? He looks so real. I don't understand," Daniel mumbled. Matthew shushed Roger and Daniel, knowing how unreal this seemed to them, especially since they had known Patrick. Heck, Roger saw Patrick die in 1977.

Unexpectedly, Mr. Brennan recognized Prince Patrick immediately. Mr. Brennan smiled delightfully, knowing the truth of the Princess' background as an angel and never questioning that her uncle had returned from Heaven for Angilia's wedding. When the dance ended, Mr. Brennan called for them excitedly. He pulled them close and said, "What a most beautiful sight, I do say. I know I am not meant to live all that much longer here," he said, "but I am no longer scared or doubtful about that, you know, my dear. Once I got to know you, I sensed the truth about you, you knew that I did. And you," Mr. Brennan looked at Patrick, "I watched you all of your life, just like I have watched your family since 1916. I remember very well how full of spunk and energy you were, and you still are. You have not changed at all, you little scamp. Both of you have actually made me look toward my own death with a bit of delight. How often have you heard someone say that?"

Patrick burst into his familiar laugh, which made Roger question his sanity. Matthew quickly explained what Angilia had told him earlier about manifestations, but Roger just stared at Patrick in stupefaction. Mr. Brennan noticed. "I think you have some explaining to do to Roger, though. The poor man looks completely befuddled," he said and scooted them off toward Roger.

Eric, who still stood next to Roger, smiled broadly at his brother, although Roger looked like he might run away or faint to the floor. Patrick smiled at Roger and grabbed him in a hug, which literally made Roger jump in utter shock. He had watched Patrick die almost 39 years earlier. How could Patrick be at Angilia's wedding reception?

"Hey, Roger, there's no reason to be afraid. It's just me, Patrick. Hi, Daniel! Gosh, it's great to see you two again."

"Eric? What is going on?"

"Patrick's just visiting, that's all, Roger.  I know it's a bit of a shock at first, but he's still Patrick," Eric assured him.

"That's right, Roger.  Mr. Brennan just told Patrick that, in fact.  He said Patrick seemed the same as he did as a teenager.  Didn't you see how overjoyed Mr. Brennan is to see Patrick?" Angilia's smile, the way she hugged her uncle, the ease with which she talked to him struck Roger and Daniel as odd at first, but the more they watched her—and Eric—the more they began to accept the idea.  Just as Matthew had earlier that afternoon, Patrick's friends saw him, heard him, and felt him, and therefore they knew he was real.

"Patrick?"  Roger tested the waters, a bold step for him.  Angilia had long known how timid he was about anything "spiritual," as he called it.  Talking face to face with his dead friend had to be at the top of Roger's list of spiritual oddities.

"Yep.  Isn't my niece the most beautiful bride you have ever seen?  Everyone thinks so.  Oh, I have something for you, Little One, before I forget."  Patrick fumbled in his jacket pocket for a moment and finally pulled out a cloth that wrapped something odd shaped.  "This is from Michael."  Angilia's eyes glistened and her smile trembled at the sound of the Archangel's name.  "Open it later, in your room, not here.  People will ask too many questions if they see it."

Roger nearly choked on his mineral water.  "If they see that?  What about you?  Do you know how many people here recognize you?"

"Relax.  They don't recognize me unless they're supposed to, like you and Daniel and Mr. Brennan.  I knew he'd get a kick out of this," Patrick giggled.  "I had to be here.  I would never miss Little One's wedding for anything or anyone.  I even got permission to come, Eric, so don't worry.  This is fine with, well, you know who," Patrick winked, and Eric knew that his brother referenced God.

Patrick talked with Roger and Daniel for a long time, while Angilia and Matthew circulated among the guests, making it a point to talk to each person.  Finally Eduardo called everyone to order for the toast.  "Angilia and Matthew, what an enormously blessed and beautiful wedding day you shared with all of us.  I am so unbelievably happy for both of you.  We all are, I know that. Angilia, my incredible niece, I met you just over four years ago, and in that short time my love for you has steadily increased.  You are amazing.  Matthew, even I saw how you felt for my niece then.  You really never hid it well at all, except from her.  Those of us who saw your love for Angilia pretty much knew that this day was fated. Today truly was your destiny, Angilia and Matthew.  I know—we all know—that you are meant to be husband and wife.  We know your marriage will remain steeped in love and blessings.  We love you both."  Everyone raised their crystal glasses of mineral water and sipped to seal the toast.

Dinner was served after the toasts, and Mr. Brennan had a seat of honor between King Eric and Prince Patrick.  Angilia and Matthew sat at the Prime Minister's table, and members of the wedding party and family were seated at various tables, as well, so that each table had a member of the family or wedding party. Antoine and his team had prepared several of Angilia's and Matthew's favorite foods, as well as a variety of dishes to satisfy any palate.  Angilia enjoyed the chance to talk with His Excellency, a man she had long admired for his empathy, compassion, and Biblical adherence.

Matthew quickly glanced around the room, and he knew that everyone felt relaxed, content, and congenial.  He was pleased.  He and Angilia wanted everyone to enjoy the day rather than to in any way feel it was a burden or an obligation.  After Antoine's staff cleared the dinner plates, Eric stood and announced it was time for the bride and groom to cut the cake.

Angilia and Matthew stood, still smiling—as they had done all day—and walked to the round table which held Antoine's divine white cake which was adorned with pink sugar roses and ribbons. He had not seen her gown before the ceremony, yet the cake looked inspired by the gown.  Angilia thanked Antoine with a kiss to his cheek, and he bowed and blushed.  Angilia and Matthew picked up the same gold cake knife that Eric and Marisol had used to cut their wedding cake.  Their hands clasped over the handle, they cut one perfect piece of cake.

They did not follow the example of many couples and messily feed one another.  Instead, they cut two more pieces which they placed on separate plates.  Angilia picked up two of the plates and Matthew picked up one plate.  Angilia walked to Mitchell and Katherine and handed each of them a piece of wedding cake as she bent to kiss their cheeks.  Matthew handed his plate to Eric and hugged him.  The guests were truly charmed and delighted, and all of them respectfully applauded.

Matthew and Angilia returned to their seats while Antoine and his team sliced the cake and served pieces to the guests.  After the delicious cake, the tables were cleared and dancing resumed until well after midnight.  "Matthew, Mr. Brennan looks exhausted.  So do Abuela and Abuelo.  This has been a very emotional and long day for all of them."  Matthew nodded, and realized that Mr. Brennan had pushed himself too hard throughout the day.

Angilia motioned for her father, and he agreed that Mr. Brennan and Ginny should stay in the palace for the rest of the night.  Soon, guests began feeling the effects of the day, and the first few offered their congratulations and blessings to Angilia and Matthew and went to their suites, hotel rooms, or homes for the night.  Finally, the wedding party and family were left in the ballroom.  Angilia thanked and hugged her bridesmaids, Scott, and Billy, all of whom lived relatively nearby.  Security would drive them home.

Angilia hugged Susan, who said she would check on Juanita and then come to assist Angilia with her gown.  Christopher and Anthony likewise hugged and congratulated the newlyweds, and then headed to their third floor suite.  Eduardo hugged his niece and new nephew to him for several minutes, as tears won their battle and spilled from his eyes.  He kissed them both and croaked out a tear-choked, "I love you" before he checked on his parents and retired to his suite to try to sleep.

Mitchell and Katherine joined Eric, Angilia, and Matthew for a family hug.  They had long felt like family.  Now they were family.  After several hugs, kisses, and a prayer, Mitchell led a sobbing Katherine from the ballroom, down the stairs, and to their house on the palace grounds. Eric, Angilia, Matthew, and Patrick were now alone again, with more time together.

"Patrick, you never fail to amaze me," Eric said as he hugged his younger brother. "You even changed into your old tuxedo! I was going to say how incredible that it still fits you, but then I remembered that you haven't changed or aged at all in 39 years, little brother."

Angilia and Patrick giggled, and Patrick looked at Matthew, Angilia, and Eric. "I couldn't very well come to my niece's wedding reception in blue jeans and a red hoodie. Yeah, when I left you guys in the foyer, I went up to my rooms and hung around for a while. I played some old eight tracks, danced a bit, and then dug the old tux out of the dressing room and changed. I almost forgot how to do the bow tie. But I think I look pretty good for a guy who's worn the same clothes for 39 years," Patrick said as he made a 360 degree turn for them.

"You really haven't changed at all, Patrick. I'm so happy you visit us. I missed you all those years, you know. I missed your smile, your voice, your jokes, and your kookiness," Eric said to his brother.

"What kookiness? I am a serious poet, you know," Patrick said and tugged on his jacket lapels in mimicry of the stuffy men who used to visit their father.

After the giggles subsided, Angilia hugged her Uncle Patrick. "I love you so much just the way you are. You know that. You might be a little kooky, but you are very loving and compassionate, too. I know you get teased about it sometimes, but you really are perfect as you are. God is fine with you, you're right about that. You wouldn't be an angel if he weren't. I'm glad you never changed." Angilia pulled him down and kissed his cheek, which brought tears to Eric's eyes yet again.

"I'm glad you came, too," Matthew softly said, to the others' massive joy. "Thank you for making our day even more special and for making my wife so very happy." Tears shone in Matthew's eyes at the sound of his own voice calling Angilia his wife.

The four of them shared a group hug as Patrick whispered a prayer of thanksgiving and blessing. He hugged his brother and told Eric he loved him. Then he hugged Matthew and said how much he loved him and welcomed him to the family. Finally, Patrick pulled Angilia close to him and held her as if he did not want to let her go. "I love you so much, Little One, so very much. You really are my angel. You gave me my purpose and taught me what is most important in mortal life and in eternal life. I know we won't be together up there for a long time, you guys, but we will, and then we can really have tons of fun! I've already told Michael that I am the one who gets to show all of you around, so just know that. Heaven won't ever be boring if you stick with me. Right, Little One?"

Angilia tilted her head and smiled up at her uncle. "That's guaranteed, Uncle Patrick. Just promise not to lead anyone into trouble. Please?"

"Whatever. What's life here or there if you can't have a bit of fun? You agree with me, right, Matty?"

Matthew was flabbergasted by the conversation, as if they were talking with a reform school student and not an angel. And did Patrick just call him Matty? No one had ever called him that. "I suppose, sure," Matthew mumbled, unsure what to say.

"I do love you all, more than you know," Patrick said, and hugged them once more. "I know it's been a long day for you, and besides, I have to leave now. I got permission, but it came with a curfew, if you can believe that!" He giggled as Angilia leaned up to kiss him again. Then he was gone, vanished into the air.

While Eric, Angilia, and Matthew slowly walked from the ballroom to the elevator, they heard Patrick giggle. "Now it's goodbye for real. I forgot to change back into my jeans and hoodie! See ya!"

"Bye, Uncle Patrick," Angilia said as he swooshed by them on his way back to Heaven. Eric giggled, Matthew looked above his head, and they entered the elevator with the happiest smiles of the day.

§§§§

In the hallway between Eric's and Angilia's suites, the three of them stood for a few moments for happy goodnight wishes. For the first night of their married life, Matthew entered what was now the suite he and Angilia shared. They left the hallway door open, and soon Susan came in to assist Angilia in removing her beautiful wedding gown. When the gown was hung, Susan tearfully hugged and kissed Angilia, realizing that the girl she had known from birth was now a married woman. Susan wiped her tears and left Angilia to shower and change into her nightgown alone.

Most of Matthew's belongings were moved to their suite during the day, which kept maids and butlers busy long before the reception guests arrived. One week prior to the wedding, two maintenance staff members had converted an unused large walk-in linen closet next to Angilia's wardrobe/changing room into Matthew's wardrobe/changing room, and all of his clothes, shoes, and accessories were now there. He had entered it to change from his tuxedo while Angilia showered. When he walked out, in pajamas and robe, he saw Angilia sitting at her vanity.

Matthew stood near her open wardrobe door and smiled as he watched her brush her long blonde hair. Yes, she was stunningly beautiful, but he did not love her for her beauty. He loved her essence, her soul. Her physical beauty was a very nice added bonus. She turned her head and smiled at him, and she held the brush in mid-air. "What are you smiling about?" she asked him.

"You. I am so very happy, Angilia, I truly am. I am the luckiest—I mean most blessed—man alive. I do love you."

"I love you, Matthew," she said, placed the brush on her vanity, and stood. She stepped out of her wardrobe/changing room and noticed that the bed sheets were already turned back. She reached for Matthew's hand, and motioned him to follow her into the sitting room. She picked up a box from her desk and handed it to him. When he opened it, Matthew saw a 2016 diary that resembled hers and Eric's. His first Royal diary.

Matthew smiled and kissed her cheek. "Thank you. I know what I will write first, most definitely. Today—I mean yesterday— has been a dream come true, hasn't it?"

Angilia nodded. "Absolutely, Matthew. Do you mind if I open the gift that Uncle Patrick gave me?" Matthew shook his head, and Angilia pulled the gossamer cloth from her robe pocket. She placed it in one palm and carefully unfolded the corners. On a long gold chain hung what looked like a miniature planet. Angilia lifted it, looked into its depths, and gasped when she saw what it represented. Matthew appeared concerned when tears fell from her eyes and she seemed to collapse onto the sofa.

"Angilia, what's wrong? What happened?"

She shook her head, a smile now combining with her tears. "Happy tears," she said as she wiped her tears with the back of a hand. "This is the most wondrous gift, Matthew. Look." She held it aloft and Matthew peered into the miniature globe. He saw a brunette woman strolling amongst flowers, and she turned and smiled as someone approached her. Matthew gasped. The woman looked just like Angilia's mother. A man's hand took the woman's hand, and he spun her into an embrace. Eric! Eric and Marisol! After sharing a kiss, the two held open their arms and Angilia ran to them with that jubilant smile of hers. Eric, Marisol, and Angilia hugged, and then walked along a golden road that was bordered by the most beautiful flowers. Suddenly, Angilia held open her arms, and Matthew came to her in a hug. The four of them laughed, talked, and sat on lush green grass together.

Angilia smiled at Matthew. She recognized the confusion on his face and took hold of his hand. "Matthew, this is the most beautiful gift ever. Don't you see what this is? Michael gave us a glimpse of our future! Daddy, Mommy, me, and you, together in Heaven! I could only try to imagine this future, even with my prior knowledge. Michael knew what our wedding day really means to all of us, and he showed us our happy, glorious future, our eternal future. Oh, Matthew, I am so incredibly happy, peaceful, and blessed," she wept as she leaned her head on his shoulder.

As he held her, they looked at the four of them, together, in a remarkably beautiful place. Matthew could almost hear the birds, the crickets, and Gabriel's symphonic music. Angilia had described Heaven to him when she had revealed her past to him on his 29th birthday the previous September 30. He believed her, just as

Marisol had believed Eric's certainties about their daughter in 1995, for Angilia's earnest, honest eyes demanded his belief.

"This is incredible.  If I hadn't seen your uncle give this to you, I question whether I would believe this.  So we can see ourselves as we will be after our deaths.  That's quite mind-blowing, don't you think?" he smiled and giggled.

"Oh, I suppose it is at first, but how like Michael to do this.  He never thought I would remember anything from my time in Heaven, you know, but since I do, he understands what this means to me.  Seeing Mommy so alive and vibrant is the most extraordinary gift I could receive on our wedding day, which is her anniversary.  I thought of her and felt her essence all day, Matthew.  Now we all know that our physical deaths open the door to that next life.  Like Patrick shows us, nothing about us changes when we die and enter Heaven.  Nothing changes.  We will all be together there, just as we are here.  Is that not the most magnificent reality?"

Matthew looked at Angilia, her turquoise eyes so full of love, joy, and peace.  How could he not rejoice with her?  He had been shown their future.  They were as alive and animated as they were every day on earth.  "Yes, it truly is, Angilia, my love.  It truly is."

They held hands and bowed their heads as Angilia prayed.  "Dear God, Thank you so very much for your love and protection of us, our parents, our families, and our dear friends.  Thank you for reuniting us and for leading us on the path you destined for Matthew and me to walk as husband and wife.  Thank you for the gift of Uncle Patrick's presence today, as someone I love so dearly and Matthew now knows.  Thank you for the gift from Michael that soothes our hearts and souls.  The beauty, exultation, peace, and blessings revealed in his gift show us the reward we shall receive when our earthly lives end.  That is your promise to us, and we vow to you that we shall do all we can to earn that reward.  We long to do your will, God.  Please walk with us during this life so that we do fulfill your destiny for us.  With our loving gratitude, Amen."

"Amen," Matthew whispered.  Angilia smiled at him, slipped the necklace from Michael over her head, and hugged her husband.  Matthew stood and lifted her into his arms.  His joyful smile lit his face as he carried his bride to what was now their bed.  Matthew gently placed her atop the bed, covered her, and then walked to the other side, where he slid onto the bed beside her.

Angilia turned onto her right side and rested her head on Matthew's shoulder.  She slipped her arms around him just as he put his arms around her.  He kissed the top of her head, and she smiled up at him and softly said, "I love you, Matthew."

Matthew smiled at her, tears again in his beaming eyes, and for the first time, their lips met in a tender kiss.  "I love you, my darling Angilia," he whispered as moonbeams danced across the floor, ceiling, and bed canopy.  Matthew and Angilia drifted asleep, smiles still illuminating their faces, in a loving embrace.

# CHAPTER 4

After lots of hugs, tears, kisses, and promises to call, Eric drove Matthew and Angilia to the airport, accompanied by Tony. The newlyweds were flying to Ayrshire, Scotland for their one-month honeymoon. Thousands of well-wishers lined the route from the palace to the airport, there to see the Duc and Duchesse again. Many took pictures and videos of the Royal Family as they slowly drove by, often waving, always smiling, happiness radiating from all three. Speculation had run rampant about Angilia's going-away outfit, and those who saw her were not disappointed.

Angilia wore a new dress designed for the occasion in sapphire blue silk trimmed with garnet lace at the sleeves and hem. Most people understood the significance of the colors: Matthew's September birthstone and Angilia's January birthstone. Angilia's clothes often reflected her emotions and honored important people or dates. Like her Victorian wedding gown, her going-away dress was in a vintage style, this time of the 1970s, which was her nod to her Uncle Patrick.

Eric parked his car near the private airplane, and smiled as Matthew assisted Angilia from the back seat. The three of them greeted people for several minutes, accepting flowers, gifts, and cards as long as they could. Finally, Tony mentioned that their take-off time was nearing and they had to board the plane. Eric followed Matthew and Angilia onto the plane for private good-byes. Mike was already aboard to make sure all was in order. The couple's luggage had been brought earlier, and everything was ready.

Eric smiled and took a deep breath as he held his daughter close. "I love you, my beautiful daughter Angilia. I am so very happy for you, for both of you," he added, pulling Matthew to him. "Have fun, enjoy yourselves, and just relax and forget work. This is your time together."

Angilia hugged her beloved father tightly. "I love you so much, Daddy. We will truly enjoy Scotland and our time alone together, but we will miss all of you, too. We'll call all of you, of course we will." She stood on her left toes and kissed his cheek. "Thank you for everything. Everything."

"We do love all of you," Matthew added. "We love each other, and we will have a wonderful time. I will protect her, pamper her, and love her always," he said as he smiled at his Angilia. Eric patted Matthew's back, his own smile huge, and knew that Matthew spoke the truth.

Eric hugged Matthew and kissed Angilia again before he waved farewell and left the airplane. He and Tony leaned against the Rolls Royce, watching until the plane was no longer visible. Tony found himself smiling at the happiness that permeated the Royal Family, especially when he recalled the near-fatal events of four years earlier. Tony had fired the fatal bullet into the hired assassin's head when he saw that man shoot the Princess in the heart. He was haunted by the sight of blood pouring from her, but not by the killing. Tony never regretted killing the gunman. Never.

Eric turned and smiled at Tony, and they entered the car for the return drive to the palace. Life was indeed gloriously wonderful, Eric thought, knowing his daughter and son-in-law remained happy, loved, and blessed. Eric smiled and waved at the people who still lined the route, and beeped his car horn in thanks as they applauded him. As he pulled into the palace gates, Eric silently thanked God for his family's generations of blessings. Despite the personal tragedies and pain over the centuries, their faith never wavered. God's loving grace had embraced them and would do so for all time. Eric knew this.

So, too, did Angilia and Matthew as they looked out at the clouds. They held hands, and Mike smiled when he walked down the aisle and saw them. Like Tony, he could not help but remember that Angilia nearly died for her father, and seeing her so happy and in love did touch his heart. Yes, he was a hired security officer, but during the past four years, he had grown to know and to love Eric and Angilia. He would guard and protect Angilia and Matthew as discreetly and intensely as possible on their honeymoon.

"We'll be in Scotland in a couple of hours, Angilia. On our honeymoon. I cannot begin to tell you how happy I am," Matthew said as he smiled at her.

Angilia squeezed his hand and smiled at him. "You don't have to, Matthew. I feel your love. We are living a fairy tale, my dear. Our love is literally eternal and meant to exist. I don't believe in Cupid, but I do know that God planned our marriage a very long time ago. We are living the life God wants us to live."

Matthew felt tears—happy tears—sting his eyes as he looked at his beautiful Angilia. While their plane soared amongst the clouds, Matthew slipped his arms around his wife and pulled her gently into a kiss. She looked up at him with those remarkable turquoise eyes, and she felt his heart flutter against her.

§§§§

*28 June 2016*

*Matthew and I arrived at our lovely room at the Turnberry Resort. As I sit at the desk and write this, I also look out of the window and see the Turnberry Lighthouse and the ruins of Robert the Bruce's Turnberry Castle! My heart pounds dizzily at the sight of the ruins! We chose the Resort so that we can be close to the castle. I love my family—past, present, and future—so very much. To be where Robert lived, loved, and fought fills me with awe. I admire him immensely, and Matthew suggested Ayrshire for our honeymoon so that we can visit the castle together! I cannot believe I ever questioned or doubted that he is the same Matthew I knew long ago in the Unborn Children Sphere. How could I? He is the same, yet more loving and kind. I do love him so.*

§§§§

After Angilia and Matthew unpacked, they left the Resort and took their rented car into town, with Mike insisting on driving.

99

They walked along the sidewalk, gazing in shop windows and drawing a huge crowd of followers. Angilia was stopped several times and asked to sign autographs, and she and Matthew were asked to pose for pictures with admirers. As they strolled, people took pictures and videos of them, which seemed to make Matthew uncomfortable. "Just ignore it, Matthew. It happens, and people don't mean any harm in it. I've watched Daddy go through intense public attention from the second day, and I feel how much everyone loves him. When he took me home the day after my birth, several hundred people were waiting for him. I remember all of the bright lights from the camera flashes. It's always been that way for him."

Matthew unintentionally interrupted her with his laughter, and she asked what was so funny. "I'm sorry, darling. I'm sure people wanted to see Eric that day, but you do realize they were really there to see you. They wanted to see the newborn Princess. Heck, even I remember seeing all of that on the news that day. I was nine, and Mom was watching the midday news, and the lead story was your leaving the hospital. That day was all about you, Angilia. People have followed your life since its beginning, you know. I never once thought that the baby I watched on the news that day would become my wife," he smiled at her.

Angilia giggled happily and leaned close to her husband. Matthew put his arm around her just as they came to a small souvenir shop. Outside, on the sidewalk, was a revolving rack of postcards, and she gleefully selected one with a picture of Turnberry Castle. "I have to send this one to Daddy," she proclaimed, and she grabbed his hand as she went inside the shop to pay for the postcard. Matthew picked up a snow globe of the castle and decided to buy it as a surprise for Angilia. While she wrote her note to her father and mailed the postcard at a nearby postal box, Matthew paid for the snow globe and tucked the package in the backpack he carried on his shoulder.

Moments later, they stopped for lunch at a café and sat at an outdoor table with Mike. As Matthew held her chair for her, the other patrons spontaneously applauded them, which drew a smile and a wave from Angilia and a blush from Matthew. So much for a private honeymoon, he thought, although he was so proud and elated by the love everyone showed to Angilia. When the waiter brought their tea, he handed Angilia a red rose.

After a couple more hours of walking, Matthew suggested they return to the Resort to rest a bit before dinner. She had walked quite a lot that day, and he did not want her to overtax herself. In fact, they sat alone together snuggled in a chair in front of the large windows of their room, overlooking the lighthouse and castle. Angilia picked up her diary from the desk and read her earlier entry aloud to Matthew.

"We will go there soon, darling. We can go as often as we like, actually. I thought we could even spend a whole day there and take a picnic lunch with us," Matthew told her, his amber eyes lit from within.

Angilia smiled up at him. "Really? We can do that? We can spend the day at Robert's castle?"

"Of course we can," he giggled. "You are the man's 18th great-granddaughter, after all. It's all arranged, actually. Roger helped me set it up before we left. Our picnic is scheduled for July 11." Matthew watched her face as the significance registered in her brain. He smiled when tears formed in her eyes and she hugged him.

"The anniversary of Robert's birth! His 742nd anniversary. Thank you, dear Matthew. Thank you." She sobbed on his shoulder, murmuring her constant thanks and love to him. Matthew kissed her head and told her he could think of no better gift for her than to celebrate her much-loved ancestor at his castle. At that perfect moment, Matthew handed Angilia the snow globe. "This is lovely, Matthew! Thank you, my dear." She shook it and watched the white flakes swirl around the miniature castle. "I will treasure this forever, Matthew. Thank you." She kissed his cheek and snuggled against him as she kept shaking the snow globe and admiring the recreation of the castle.

After an hour of cuddling and watching the sunset, Matthew reminded her that they needed to get ready to go down for dinner soon. Several moments later, they and Mike entered the Resort's 1906 restaurant, and were escorted to their reserved table. Guests nodded to them as they passed, offering congratulations and best wishes. Angilia and Matthew smiled and thanked them. Their table overlooked the lighthouse and castle ruins, as well, which delighted Angilia. They sat next to one another, and when their meals were served, they bowed their heads in prayer.

Angilia and Matthew enjoyed the pasta meal, but more importantly, they enjoyed their time together. They did not exclude Mike from the dinner conversation, though, and Matthew even mentioned that he and Mike should enjoy a game of golf one afternoon during their month-long stay. Angilia smiled and agreed that they would enjoy their game. "I'll have to take some pictures to send to your father, you know," she winked at Matthew, who was known for his good-natured teasing of Mitchell's passion for golf. "That will be a nice time for me to sit at the castle and do some writing, I think," she added.

$$\text{SSSSS}$$

After dessert, the three returned to their neighboring rooms for the night. Angilia filled the tub with a hot bubble bath and relaxed in its soothing warmth while Matthew took a shower. He finished and brushed his teeth while Angilia still soaked in the hot bath. While Matthew put on his pajamas, Angilia dried, put on her warm robe, and blow-dried her long blonde hair. As she changed into her nightgown in the walk-in closet, Matthew closed the drapes and pulled back the bedclothes.

He turned to see her just as she stepped out of the closet. His breath caught in his throat. Her hair was long, loose, and flowing. Her bright blue eyes revealed her love and wonder. Her pink silk gown and robe skimmed her slender curves. Matthew had never seen a woman as beautiful or wondrous as his Angilia. He walked to her slowly, placed his hands upon her shoulders, and kissed her soft pink lips.

Angilia's arm went around Matthew, and he felt his heart pounding fiercely against his sternum. "I love you, Angilia," he managed to whisper. "I have never loved another, only you."

Matthew stared into her eyes, seeing her love for and trust in him. He gently massaged her shoulders and slid the silk robe down her arms. It puddled in a shimmering heap at her feet. Matthew picked her up, lovingly placed her on the bed, and lay next to her. His left hand caressed her stomach, and her left hand cupped his shoulder. Matthew leaned over, and they kissed again as he pulled her closer.

"I do love you so very much, Angilia. I always have. You are why I never was interested in or tempted by anyone else. I was waiting for you, my love, only you."

"And I you, Matthew. I love you." She kissed him, put her arms around him, and felt his heart pounding.

Matthew lovingly slipped the strap of her gown off of her shoulder and kissed the soft skin there. He saw the small scar where he had inserted the central venus catheter in March 2012, and he kissed the spot. His head moved down, and he likewise kissed the top of her thoracotomy scar. "I thank God you are with me, that we are one, Angilia."

He kissed her as he slid his pajamas off and then slowly pulled her nightgown down her willowy body. His eyes asked if she were ready, and she smiled, nodded, and kissed him. Matthew kissed her as he moved atop her and their bodies joined and truly became one. A while later, a tear fell from Matthew's eye, and Angilia softly brushed it away. "I love you, Matthew," she breathed into his ear and felt his body tremble.

Matthew buried his face against her neck, overcome with powerful sensations, and she held him and kissed his cheek. "I love you. Thank you for being so gentle with me, Matthew. All I feel is love, my dear."

"I do, too, darling," he said as he held her close. "I never knew anyone could feel so much love, Angilia. I keep saying I love you, and I do, but what I feel is so much more than that."

Angilia smiled and leaned into him. "I know. Even with the millions of words we have, there is no one word to explain how I feel. I do love you, but what I truly feel is so much deeper than that, Matthew."

He smiled, kissed her, and pulled the sheet over them. Matthew fell asleep with his head on her shoulder, and Angilia kissed the top of his head and smiled. She whispered a prayer: "Dear God, Thank you for the gift of Matthew. His love, devotion, and tenderness amaze me. I feel such serenity and security with him, and I know that our love will bring earthly life to our son. The joy I feel now is honestly indescribable, but I know I need not describe it for you. I know you see and know how I feel. Thank you for blessing me so much. Amen."

§§§§§

The next morning, Matthew awoke at sunrise to Angilia's loving smile. He kissed her and breathed deeply, savoring his contentment. "I love you, Angilia," he told her as his hand traced the curve of her waist. She repeated the sentiment, kissed him, and went to the shower before breakfast. While she showered, Matthew pulled on his robe, sat at the desk, and wrote in his diary.

*29 June 2016*

*My heart is so happy. Can a man feel too much love? Is that possible? At times, it fills me to such capacity that I fear I will literally burst. I always wondered in my teens and early 20s if something was wrong with me. I was never romantically interested in or attracted to any girl or woman I met. Something felt wrong and missing in my life all those years, and I blamed my schooling, my career, the women, and finally myself. That moment I ran to Angilia and saw her dying, I knew the truth. She was the one, my one and only. My father was right. I did fight for her life as I had never fought for anyone's life. I loved her instantly, heart and soul, and I was not about to let her go when I had just found her. Angilia is the one for whom I had waited. Angilia is the one God meant for me to marry. I know that. We are married. We are so happy. I finally have the one woman who matters, the one to whom I gave the sacred gift only she deserved. Everything about last night felt so true, pure, and right. Just like my Angilia!*

§§§§§

Matthew, Angilia, and Mike left the Resort very early on Friday, July 8 for a very special day trip. Matthew and Angilia settled close to one another on the back seat while Mike drove the 135 miles to Melrose Abbey in Roxburghshire. Angilia's black dress and Matthew's black suit reflected the solemn journey. As they neared the Abbey, Angilia asked Mike to stop at a flower shop, where she bought one dozen white roses. Three hours after they left the Resort, Mike parked near the Abbey, and Matthew assisted Angilia from the car.

Mike followed them discreetly as they were welcomed by the director, who refused to charge them the usual ticket prices for their visit. Matthew and Angilia were given a private tour of the Abbey, during which they stopped to pray at the altar. Their tour continued as they were shown the ruins of the Abbey which had been burned at the order of King Edward II. Matthew felt Angilia breathe deeply, knowing that the conflict between her ancestors affected her.

Angilia felt Matthew tense as the director showed them some of the ruins and discussed Edward II's destruction of the Abbey. She knew he never forgot that the battle for the throne of Scotland—involving Angilia's ancestors Robert the Bruce, Edward I, and William Wallace—led Gregor Jamieson on his heinous plot to assassinate Angilia four years earlier. She put her arm around him, kissed his cheek, and softly said, "It's all right, Matthew. What happened to me is not their fault." He gave her a small smile and kissed her cheek in gratitude for her prevailing positivity.

The director led them to the Abbey cemetery and showed them several historic graves before pointing toward the reason they had come. "Thank you both for coming, Your Royal Highnesses. If you should need anything while you are here, please do let me know. I shall leave you to pay your respects in private."

"Thank you so much for welcoming us and allowing us to visit the Abbey. This means more to me than you know," Angilia said as she shook his hand. The gentleman bowed to her and Matthew before he walked away. Angilia took a deep breath, smiled at Matthew, and slowly walked to the plinth which marked the burial place of Robert the Bruce's heart.

Angilia bowed her head in prayer, as did Matthew and Mike—who stood several feet away to provide them privacy. "A noble heart may have no ease without freedom," Angilia translated the line from John Barbour's 1375 poem which was etched into the plinth. "My dear Robert, I know your heart is at peace. You lived and fought for Scotland's freedom and independence, and you changed the world completely. You are the eternal symbol of courage and freedom. You are my beacon of hope." She knelt to place the white roses atop the plinth, her tears falling unashamedly down her face. "You belong to the world, but you truly belong to me. You are part of me, of who and what I am. I do love you. I look forward to our meeting in Heaven, when I can tell you how very much I love you."

Matthew knelt beside his wife as she cried, not in sadness but in love. He knew this was a very emotional experience for her. He gently helped her up and sat with her on a bench which the director had placed there for them. Matthew had mentioned that they would like to stay for a while when they visited. He removed his handkerchief from his jacket pocket and handed it to her as he continued to hold her. They sat there in silence for more than one hour.

"King David II wanted his father's heart buried here. He knew what that meant and will always mean. Robert knew he was dying, and he asked his friend Sir James Douglas to take his heart on the crusade. Even in death, Robert continued his mission and his message. Sir James was killed before he could return to bury Robert's heart, but David made sure his father's heart was honored and consecrated. Matthew, this has filled my soul with such awe and love. Thank you for this."

Matthew pulled her close. "I could think of nothing more important for us to do. I wanted to bring you to Scotland not just for our alone time, but so that we can pay respect to Robert. I know what this means to you, darling. We have one more destination today, too, on our personal crusade. When you are ready, Mike is driving us to Dunfermline Abbey."

Angilia looked at Matthew with tears and a smile. She kissed him and told him, "Thank you. Thank you, my dear."

Matthew held her, her head resting on his shoulder, for the 90 minute drive to Dunfermline Abbey. Matthew asked Mike to stop in the village, and he got out to buy some white roses and a bouquet of red roses, which he handed to Angilia when he returned to the car. "Red roses, the color of his ruby birthstone. White roses for your other ancestors," he smiled at her.

"Thank you, dear Matthew. Thank you for today."

Several moments later, Mike parked the car at the Abbey, and Matthew helped Angilia from the back seat. Just as he closed the door and took her arm, the Abbey's Reverend Rennie approached and welcomed them. She knew why they had come, and she curtseyed to Angilia and then to Matthew. "Welcome to Dunfermline Abbey, Your Royal Highnesses. I am honored by your visit. I thought I might give you a tour of the Abbey, including the tombs of King Robert I's wife and daughter and Mrs. Wallace's memorial. After that, I will escort you to the pulpit and leave you alone to pay your respects."

"Thank you, Reverend Rennie. Matthew and I truly appreciate your taking the time to accommodate our visit. I am honored to be here," Angilia replied as they began walking across the lawn.

"I understand you spent the morning at Melrose Abbey, which I am sure must have been quite an emotional experience for you," Reverend Rennie added.

"It truly was. I know Dunfermline Abbey will be, too, so please forgive me if I do get a bit weepy."

"Not at all, Your Royal Highness," the Reverend assured Angilia as she showed them around the grounds, stopping at a thorn tree. "Mrs. Wallace is buried at the Abbey, although her exact location remains unknown. Many years ago, this thorn tree was planted here as a memorial to her."

"Margaret. William was only seven years old when she died," Angilia softly said. "She was 14 when she married Malcolm, and despite everything, they were happy together. Her life was not very long, but she knew love with her family. The blessing is that she did not live to see what happened to her husband and sons." Matthew's arms encircled Angilia's waist as she bowed her head in prayer, and he and Reverend Rennie followed suit. "Amen," Angilia whispered when she finished, and then knelt to place a white rose at the base of the tree.

Reverend Rennie took them to the tomb of Elizabeth DeBurgh, who married Robert the Bruce when she was 18 and he was 28. A tear slid from Angilia's eye as she thought of this young woman who became her $18^{th}$ great-grandmother. "She and Robert loved each other so much. I feel so close to her, probably because of the similarities in our lives. Love, family, faith, and honor were vastly important to her, just as they are to me. She married for love in a world where that was not the norm. She was almost my mother's age when she died two years before Robert. He lived without her for two years," Angilia whispered as another tear fell down her cheek. She bowed her head to pray, with Matthew and Reverend Rennie, and bent to place a white rose on the tomb. "Thank you for everything, Elizabeth. Your daughter Matilda became my $17^{th}$ great-grandmother. Without you, I would not exist."

After several moments of silent introspection, Reverend Rennie put her hand on Angilia's back and quietly asked her, "Are you ready to visit Matilda's tomb?" Angilia smiled, nodded, and walked with the Reverend to Matilda's tomb. She unexpectedly leaned against Matthew in tears, and he held her as he patted her back.

"I'm sorry. It's my emotions again. I was just struck by how much Matilda loved her father and asked to be buried here where her parents are buried. She was the same age as her mother, 43 years old. My mother was 44. Like her mother and my mother, Matilda married for love. Her courage to do that united our two families together for eternity. Thank you, Matilda dear." Once more, Angilia said a prayer of thanksgiving and placed the final white rose on Matilda's tomb.

Matthew handed her his handkerchief again, and she dried her tears and took a deep breath. "When you are ready, I will take you to the pulpit," Reverend Rennie told Angilia. Several minutes later, Angilia told them she was ready, and she and Matthew walked with the Reverend to the newer section of the Abbey which was rebuilt in 1818 after the great tower collapsed.  An intricate pulpit of Scottish oak was carved by William Paterson at the request of the Earl of Engin and Kincardine and gifted to the Abbey by him in 1890.  That pulpit was installed over the tomb of Scotland's most revered king.

Reverend Rennie saw the emotions in Angilia's eyes and on her face as they approached the pulpit and the tomb.  "I will leave you alone now," she softly said.

Angilia asked her to stay.  "I'd like to ask you a favor, Reverend Rennie.  Will you lead us in prayer please?"

"I would be honored," Reverend Rennie replied, and as the three of them joined hands and bowed their heads before Robert the Bruce's tomb, she spoke a prayer of thanksgiving and love.  When they said their collective "Amen," Angilia thanked and hugged the Reverend.  "It is truly my privilege to meet you," Revered Rennie smiled.  "Too often we forget the human aspects of our heroes' lives, and you reminded me of that today, Your Royal Highness.  Robert the Bruce is often worshipped as a national hero, but your love for the man behind the legend is quite inspiring.  Thank you for that, Your Royal Highness," Reverend Rennie smiled.  "If you need anything, I shall be in the office."

Angilia looked down at the carved gold tomb for many minutes, her love for this historical figure who was her direct ancestor filling her being.  "Oh, Matthew, I feel his spirit so strongly today.  So very strongly.  He knows we are here.  He knows we love him.  He came to the Abbey during his life, and his body rests here.  He and Elizabeth knew they would be entombed here, and Matilda wanted to be near her parents.  Their bodies are together here, and their souls are together in Heaven."

Matthew kissed the top of her head as he stood behind her, holding her close.  He could feel the emotions surging through her, and he knew that her love, not sadness, drove her emotions.  Angilia smiled up at him, took his hand, and knelt to place the red roses over the effigy's heart.  She kissed her fingertips and pressed them to the tomb. "I love you, great-grandfather. I love you," she whispered through her tears.

§§§§§

After a peaceful breakfast in their room, Angilia and Matthew joined Mike at the front desk. He had picked up the packed picnic basket which contained their lunch, and the three of them boarded a golf cart for their ride to the lighthouse and castle ruins. Mike drove slowly over the uneven terrain, and Angilia smiled as the comfortable morning wind blew her hair. Soon they arrived, and Mike took the basket from Matthew as he helped his wife alight from the golf cart. Matthew picked up the blankets and held Angilia's hand as they walked to a small mound of rubble.

She smiled at Matthew and looked off into the distance at the gentle waves. She took a deep breath and looked down finally to see the remains of Turnberry Castle. Matthew felt her shiver, knowing it was not the air, but rather her emotions, that made her react so. She had already seen the tombs of his heart and his bones, and now she stood at his birthplace. She remained silent in reverence, her hands folded prayer-like before her heart, as she took in the reality of her experience.

"Robert was born here 742 years ago today. What did he know about his future when he was a child? What were his visions of his future as he looked out at the peninsula? Did he know then that he would become so ensconced in history?" Angilia asked as they stood amongst the ruins of Turnberry Castle.

"I don't know, darling," Matthew replied and pulled her to him. "But you can ask him yourself someday, and he will tell you everything about his life that has been shrouded in myth and mystery for centuries."

Angilia giggled and pulled Matthew's head down to her for a kiss. "Yes, I will, my dear. Like Michael showed us, we will all be together in gloriousness for eternity," she said and pulled up the chain that was tucked underneath her blouse. She wore Michael's pendant every moment, except for baths and showers. Matthew laughed in joy, hugged her, and took her hands as he led her to the edge of the promontory.

Matthew pointed at some remains there at the edge of the water. "That must be where the drawbridge was. Let's go down for a bit." Matthew called for Mike, who helped Matthew lift Angilia onto the ground below. She grinned, took off her topsiders and rolled up her jeans. She walked into the water as it ebbed and flowed on the shore, knowing she stood where her amazing ancestor had stood. How many times had he disembarked from a boat and walked that land onto the drawbridge? Matthew pulled out his smart phone and took a picture of her as she stared across the peninsula, the breeze blowing her long blonde hair and the sun shining on her. Before she turned and rejoined him, Matthew quickly sent the picture to Eric with a brief message telling him where they were.

Finally, Angilia slid her feet into her shoes, and Matthew and Mike lifted her onto the grass above. The Resort had restricted access to the lighthouse for the day, which meant the newlyweds had Turnberry Castle to themselves all day. Angilia and Matthew walked every possible inch of the ruins, and she took several pictures with her smart phone. She talked excitedly while Matthew smiled and enjoyed her happiness.

Realizing that they had been standing and walking for several hours at that point, Matthew spread the blankets out next to what was left of a castle wall. He leaned against the wall and he helped Angilia down to sit against him between his legs. Matthew wrapped his arms around her, she wrapped her arms around his arms, and she smiled up at him as they shared a kiss.

"Mike, come on! Join us, and let's have lunch now," Matthew called to Mike, who remained vigilant yet out of the way. Mike grabbed up the basket and joined them on the blankets as they enjoyed the fruit, sandwiches, and juice as much as they enjoyed the sunshine and cool breeze. The three of them chatted as they ate, and Mike could not help but recall that tragic picnic in his memories. Angilia noticed the change in his expression, and she knew what he thought. She smiled at him in silent reassurance, and he smiled in return. She was right. This day was filled with love and peace.

He finally picked up the remaining scraps of the lunch, tossed them in the basket, and told them he wanted to look around a bit on his own.  Matthew and Angilia thanked him, knowing he gave them as much privacy in public as he could.  Angilia leaned her head back against Matthew's shoulder and kissed the hollow of his neck.  He smiled, kissed her cheek, and took a deep breath.

"Angilia, when you told me everything last September, I said I believe you, and I do.  I also said I don't remember anything about that, about the Unborn Children Sphere.  I wish I did, but I don't."

"I know, Matthew.  According to Michael, no one is supposed to remember," she smiled up at him.

"You do, though, and we know there's a reason that you do. Is it all right if I ask you something?  I mean, that's not against any rules, is it?"

Angilia giggled.  "No.  I told Daddy four years ago.  The anniversary of that is eight days away, you know.  July 19 is the anniversary of Uncle Patrick's death, when I first met him and first saw Daddy.  You can ask me anything, Matthew."

"What does it look like there?  I mean, I know how you described it and compared it to Grecian temples and castles, but what does it really look like?  I have tried to remember, I really have, but I don't.  I can't even really imagine it, because all I know is earth-bound, like the temples.  I know it's got to be far grander."

"It is far grander than anything on earth," Angilia smiled. She described it in detail for Matthew, although she knew a description did little to show him.  "You brought your sketch pad. May I use it?  I think if I draw it, you will see it better.  Words just don't do the beauty there any justice," she said as he pulled his sketch pad and colored pencils from his messenger bag and handed them to her.

For many minutes, Angilia drew, shaded, and recreated on paper the place she and Matthew first met.  Finally, she held up the pad.  "I did my best to capture the Unborn Children Sphere, inside and out."  As Matthew looked at the sketch of the exterior, he saw a very large white-gold carved temple.  He asked her if it was marble. "It's actually gold limestone.  We sought the answer to that once, Matthew," she giggled.  "We were standing in what we called our tower, at the ledge, when you asked what the stone was. We left the tower and kept asking people, until we had asked everyone in the Sphere, never getting an answer. We walked back up to the tower, and Michael was there waiting for us. He smiled and told us that our temple is made from gold limestone. I'm not sure that meant anything to us then, since we had no reference to any other stones, though."

"Michael? Your Michael?" Angilia laughed and said he was not her Michael, but rather God's Michael. "Yeah, but you got to know him more than anyone has probably, well, except your Uncle Patrick. Seems like I'm still asking the same questions, too," he giggled.

Matthew turned the page and looked with wide eyes at the interior, with thousands of bookshelves carved into the walls, laboratories, podiums, music rooms, stages, school rooms, museums, pillars, statues, grand staircases, and so much more. Angilia's drawing made the temple seem alive, and Matthew studied the drawing with wonder. "How could I not remember being here?" he softly asked. "This is magnificent and stunning."

Angilia smiled at him, sure she now knew the answer. "Most people never remember the Unborn Children Sphere. I've never read about it or heard anyone mention it. Have you?" He shook his head. "I do think I know why you don't remember, though." Matthew looked at his wife, his eyes asking her to tell him. "You told me that you were never romantically interested in anyone else before we met. You became a cardiac surgeon, not the artist you longed to be. Had you followed your first desire and gone into art, we probably wouldn't have met on earth, and you would have loved and married someone else, Matthew. God planned everything perfectly so that we did meet. You asked me four years ago if our meeting was part of God's plan, and I said yes. But we couldn't have met had you not been the cardiac surgeon on duty that day I was shot. My mother and you kept me from dying so that God's plan would come to fruition in our marriage."

Matthew pulled her closer, held her as tightly as he dared, and unabashedly cried on her shoulder. Angilia held him as they sat against the ruins of the castle wall and the summer wind flitted around them. "Matthew, everything is just as it should be, my dear. Our friendship was forged long ago in that tower, and even if you don't remember the details, you do carry those feelings. I know you do. So does Daddy. We both saw flashes of recognition in your eyes over the past four years. It's all there somewhere deep inside you, and it is actually what you and I both felt that first moment in the ambulance."

"Oh, Angilia. Why did it have to take nearly losing you for us to reunite? Why?"

"Matthew, God had no control over Gregor Jamieson, because he had shut God out of his heart and life. God did not let me die that day, though, because that would have destroyed his plan, his destiny, for us and for future generations. He made sure everything was aligned for our reunion on earth."

"I am so grateful for that, Angilia, so very grateful. I don't remember being in the Unborn Children Sphere, but I do believe that I befriended and loved you there. How could I not?" he asked as he held her and pulled her to him in a passionate kiss.

Moments later, Matthew picked up the sketch book, turned the page, and stared at the tower where he and Angilia spent most of their time in the Sphere. She felt him shiver, and she wondered if another latent memory was triggered. "This is our tower," he softly said. "It is much like the watch tower, you're right. This is where we stayed, just the two of us? Didn't anyone else come up there?"

Angilia shook her head. "No. Michael visited us sometimes, but none of the other children ever came there, no. I have no idea how long we were there. You were already there when I arrived, Matthew. I do know we were there a very long time, though, because I remember other people I met there. I know when they were born, so that gives me a bit of a timeline."

"What do you mean you know when they were born? How do you know?"

"Everyone knows when they were born. Like Robert, their lives are recorded in history, Matthew." She watched him as his brain registered what she said.

"You mean famous people, right?  You met famous people before they were born?"

Angilia nodded her head.  "So did you.  You were with me pretty much all the time."

"Except I don't remember any of this.  You do.  Can you tell me who they were?  What were they like then?  Did you know who they were, what they would do, and how they would be remembered?"

Angilia smiled at his questions, understanding that he was both perplexed and amazed by everything she showed and told him. "I knew who they were, yes, because everyone had the name we would have on earth.  Our identities were already decided and known.  My 2001 drawing of you says Matthew underneath.  When we met, that's how you introduced yourself to me.  I told you my name is Angilia.  Just like we do now, we then called one another Matthew and Angilia.  Everyone used the names there that they used on earth.  God assigned us to our parents centuries before our births.  God named us.  God planned everything perfectly for each person, just as he did for us, Matthew.

"Can I tell you who they were?  Sure.  I'm not breaking any rules by sharing this with you.  One young man in particular stands out, though I doubt most people would believe me.  Once when we walked down from our tower, I saw a young man sitting alone in a chair, bent over reading a book.  I grabbed your hand and went to him, and he looked up at us with a thin-lipped but kind smile.  He greeted us and shook our hands.  I introduced myself, and then you introduced yourself.  He stood and bowed.  He was so tall, probably as tall as Uncle Patrick, and he is six feet three inches tall.  As he stood from his bow, he said, *I am pleased to meet you, Angilia and Matthew.  I am Abraham.'*

"His dark hair was mussed, and when he ran his hand through it a few times, I knew why.  We talked to him for a while, and he read aloud something from the book he held.  I never forgot the stanzas he read, and I looked them up years ago in the library. He read to us the Epitaph of Thomas Gray's poem "Elegy Written in a Country Churchyard":

*Here rests his head upon the lap of earth*
*A youth to fortune and to fame unknown.*
*Fair Science frowned not on his humble birth,*
*And Melancholy marked him for her own.*

*Large was his bounty, and his soul sincere,*
*Heaven did a recompense as largely send:*
*He gave to Misery all he had, a tear,*
*He gained from Heaven ('twas all he wished) a*
*friend.*

*No farther seek his merits to disclose,*
*Or draw his frailties from their dread abode,*
*(There they alike in trembling hope repose)*
*The bosom of his Father and his God.*

"He said something a moment later that I never forgot, Matthew. He sat in the chair again, rested his arm on the back of the chair and looked at the poem for a moment before he closed the book and left it on his lap. He took our hands in his, gave us a sad smile, and said, '*I dare but hope people will think of me and remember me with the tenderness and truth in these stanzas. I can only pray that whatever I am meant to do on earth will meet the trust and responsibility placed upon me, my dears.*' I remember feeling so incredibly despondent, and you put your hand on my back, as you often do now, to soothe me. Abraham pulled me to him and held me while I cried. After a long while, he told me, '*Angilia, please do not cry for me. Whatever my path through life, I will do what I must. So shall you.*' He kissed my cheek, pulled me away from his shoulder, and winked at me. '*When you do think of me, know that no matter how difficult or full of despair my life, I did the best I could. You will go to earth long after I return to Heaven, but we will meet again someday, my dear.*' There are things I remember that I have never written. That is one of them. I started to write it in the diary, but the memory is too much for me. You are the only one I have told about that."

"Abraham? A tall, dark man named Abraham? We met Abraham Lincoln?" Angilia smiled while tears shone in her eyes. "Angilia, your life is a living history book. You met the future President of the United States before he was born and you remember every detail. I know you remember what he wore, even. This is beyond amazing." He saw the sadness in her eyes, though. "But it's been so much for you to carry within you for goodness knows how long, darling. Lincoln was born in the early 1800s. You met him before that. That is a very long time to keep all of this inside of your heart. I mean, he seemed to sense or to know what would happen to him, and he seemed to know you did, too. That's pretty heavy stuff to carry for centuries, Angilia."

"I know, Matthew. Who besides Daddy and now you would believe me, though? Who could I tell any of this?"

"Lots of people, Angilia. How many people do believe in Heaven and angels? Quite a lot of people would believe you. People love to read or hear stories from those who have died and come back to life, those who got a glimpse of Heaven. Those stories give people hope. Your life story is so much deeper than that, darling. You lived in Heaven before you lived on earth, and you can share that truth with people. I do think Mr. Brennan had a perfect idea when you were working on his memoir. You should write your own." She looked at him, her eyebrow raised in a question. "Seriously. You can be God's messenger on earth, Angilia. I do think you need to write your memoir, at least for our family. You adore your family history. Imagine the history your memoir will leave for future generations of our family."

"I suppose. Maybe I should write down everything for the family archives," she replied. "I know how important each person's story is, so it's only right that I record mine, too. I will, Matthew, I promise. I will write my autobiography for you, Daddy, and everyone else in our family."

§§§§

*19 July 2016*

*Hello Uncle Patrick! 39 years ago today, we met and I saw Daddy for the first time! Our three lives changed forevermore at that moment, and I love you so very much. Thank you for just being you, dear Uncle Patrick! You know that I love you for all eternity.*

§§§§§

Angilia called her father while Matthew showered, and she shared with him her surprise trip for Matthew that day. "He planned those two glorious days at the Robert the Bruce places for me, and I will never forget them, Daddy. There is so much to tell you when we return in a few days."

"I look forward to that, Angel. I know you two are having a wonderful time, and I am so very happy for you, but I do miss you. I sound selfish don't I?" Eric giggled.

"No, Daddy. I miss you, too, you know. Our month in Scotland has been so blissful and beautiful, and we shall remember it always. I think we are both ready to come home soon, though."

"You just enjoy your remaining days there, Angilia. We'll all be here to greet you on Friday when you return, never fear. What are your special plans for these last three days?"

"I've planned a special day for Matthew, actually. Mike is driving us to Edinburgh, which is a nice one and a half hour drive. I got Matthew, me, and Mike day passes to the Scottish National Gallery, so Matthew can spend the day there and see all of the special exhibits. We'll even have lunch there, and I know he'll enjoy seeing everything. We have the whole day there, and since we're not on a tight schedule, we can stay as late as we want, and even have dinner nearby afterwards."

"Sounds like you two are enjoying yourselves a lot, baby." Matthew hugged her as he stepped from the wardrobe dressed in slacks and shirt. "Say hi to Matthew for me."

"You can do that yourself. He's right here," she said, and handed Matthew her phone. Matthew talked with Eric a while, then to his mother, before he hung up and pulled Angilia to him for a kiss. Angilia had showered and dressed earlier, before their breakfast was delivered, so they were ready to set out. She picked up her tote bag, Matthew slung his messenger bag over his shoulder, and they joined Mike at the elevator. Soon they were on their way, and try as he might, Matthew could not convince Angilia—or Mike—to tell him where they were going.

After a while, Mike stopped to top the gas tank, and Matthew went into the quick mart to get himself a cup of coffee and Angilia a cup of herbal tea. They snuggled close as they sipped their drinks, and soon they entered Edinburgh. Matthew looked at Angilia in surprise. "Are we having lunch with Her Majesty?" he teased her.

"No, silly. I think you'll like this much better than a formal tea, though. We'll be there in a few minutes," she promised him. Sure enough, Mike pulled the car into the museum parking, and Matthew looked at the building with wide eyes and slightly agape mouth. "Was I right?" Angilia asked him.

"Absolutely, darling. This is fabulous," Matthew said and kissed her again. She giggled as he helped her from the car. They placed their empty cups in trash bins as they walked to the entrance, although they were instantly recognized and besieged with picture and autograph requests on their way. Matthew found it dreamlike to sign magazines and books commemorating their wedding. He reminded himself of her words about Robert the Bruce. Angilia belonged to the world in many ways, but she was his wife and she belonged only to him in other ways. He was just getting used to differentiating between the globally-famous Angilia and the private Angilia. She was the same person regardless of the circumstance or situation, yet he knew her as no one else ever had or ever would. He could never resent the love others had for Angilia, but he understood that their love came from a distance. He was blessed to share an intimate, personal love with Angilia.

As they slowly walked through the museum, they were occasionally asked for autographs or pictures, but not to the extent that it prevented them from enjoying the experience. After several hours, Matthew glanced at his watch and realized it was 1:00 and that they should eat lunch soon. He asked Angilia where they might go for lunch, and she smiled and said they could enjoy lunch in the museum's Scottish Café and Restaurant. "It overlooks the Princes Street gardens, so we'll have a lovely view, Matthew."

They enjoyed their relaxing lunch for one hour, and then resumed their walk through the museum and exhibits. Matthew stopped at one point to sketch a sculpture that caught his fancy, and he giggled when Angilia took a picture of her husband the artist at work and sent it to Katherine, Mitchell, and Eric. Angilia and Matthew adored the day together, and they were among the last to leave when the museum closed at 5:00.

Outside, they agreed to walk and window shop for a while before dinner. Neither could resist a bookstore, though, and they entered to browse the shelves. Angilia purchased a Scottish art book for Matthew, while he bought an antique book about Robert the Bruce from their collection as a gift for Angilia. They strolled for another block before Matthew felt the chilly air and insisted they return to the car.

Mike drove them to Gusto Italian restaurant on George Street, where they relaxed at their candlelit table and enjoyed their meals. They excitedly shared their thoughts and memories of the museum as they ate, and finally left satiated, warm, and happy for the drive back to the resort.

That night, after her bath and his shower, Angilia handed Matthew the bag with the art book at the same moment he handed her the bag with the antique book. They giggled, kissed, and opened their gifts as they sat on the bed. After the long, fun, yet tiring day, Matthew pulled Angilia to him and covered her with the sheet. He knew how grueling walking and standing all day had been for her, despite her never even hinting at pain or fatigue. She never did. He kissed her tenderly and held her protectively against him as she slipped into sleep.

§§§§§

Eric, Mitchell, and Katherine stood beside the Rolls Royce as they waited for the airplane carrying Angilia and Matthew. Tony stood near them, as always, and he watched the sky for any sight of the plane. Eric's phone signaled a text message, and he quickly checked to find a message from Angilia, telling him their plane was nearing the Valmondois airport. "They'll be here in a moment," Eric told the Taylors with a smile.

Sure enough, they all saw Eric's plane come into sight and approach the runway. So did thousands of people who were also there to greet the newlyweds on their return to Valmondois. The plane landed, and after what seemed like hours, the door opened and the stairs lowered. Mike exited first, just as a precaution, and then Matthew and Angilia stepped out arm-in-arm. They were genuinely surprised by the cheers that greeted them, for they were unaware that anyone outside the family even knew or cared about their arrival date. They waved, though, as they stood for a few moments to allow people to see them clearly.

Angilia, however, longed to see only one person, and she turned her head to see her father standing nearby waiting for her. Matthew helped her down the stairs, and knew it was all she could do not to run to her father. Finally, she stood before him and grabbed him in a hug. "Oh, Daddy, I love you. Matthew and I had an amazing month in Scotland, but it is wonderful to come home. I am so incredibly happy."

"I love you, too, Angel, so very much. You look happy, both of you do, and that makes me happy," Eric said as he held her. Mitchell and especially Katherine hugged and greeted their son, and Mitchell handed Katherine his handkerchief when she began crying. At that point, the seven of them settled into the car and Tony drove them home to the palace. The convertible top was lowered to allow well-wishers to greet Angilia, Matthew, Eric, and the Taylors.

Soon, they were inside the palace foyer, where Eduardo waited with his excited parents, as well as Roger, Susan, and Daniel. One month had seemed far too long for Juanita and Alejandro to be without their granddaughter, even though they had phoned, texted, and video-called several times over the month. After tearful reunions, Matthew and Angilia took the elevator to their suite so they could change clothes and relax.

The family spent the day catching up, even walking the grounds after lunch for some fresh air and sunshine. Angilia took some time to print her pictures that afternoon so that she could share them with everyone. Eric smiled at her happiness and peace. He knew, as did she and Matthew, that their lives were just as they were destined to be. He did not even once think of Gregor Jamieson when Angilia emotionally shared the time they spent at the three sights connected to Robert the Bruce. All of their past pain was just that—a thing of the past. It did not control their present. Angilia leaned over and kissed her father's cheek, sensing his thoughts. Her smile confirmed their blessed, peaceful present.

After dinner, Angilia sat with Eric in the sitting room window seat and her smile vanished suddenly. "Daddy, how is Mr. Brennan? He's been in my thoughts and heart for the past several days. Have you seen him or heard anything?"

"I visited him earlier in the week, and he was in bed resting and watching television. Ginny stays with him constantly. He's weak, darling, but I suppose that's to be expected. He did receive your postcard, and he was very happy and excited about that," Eric tenderly smiled at her.

"I'll go visit him after breakfast tomorrow. I'll call Ginny tonight and let her know to expect me. I have to go tomorrow. Something in my heart tells me I have to. I just wish I could locate his daughter. No one I've contacted in Australia has any information about Amelia. He needs to see her again before he leaves earth," she said as she looked out at the sunset.

§§§§

After breakfast, Angilia told her father and her husband that she was going to Mr. Brennan's house to visit him and that she would likely stay most of the day. "I promise I will call both of you with an update sometime today," she told them as she kissed them and left with Mike, who drove her to Mr. Brennan's home.

Ginny greeted her inside, and quietly explained that Mr. Brennan was very weak and receiving hydration and nourishment via intravenous tubes. "I know your visit will do him well, though. He was so very happy when he received your postcard. Don't be afraid to talk to him, even if he appears asleep. He will hear you."

Angilia sat in a chair next to Mr. Brennan's bed and bowed her head in silent prayer. She held his hand and softly talked to him, reassuring him that she was there. "Mr. Brennan, Matthew and I had a marvelous time in Scotland. Matthew surprised me with visits to Melrose Abbey and Dunfermline Abbey, where Robert the Bruce's heart and bones are buried. I'm sure you know how emotional those visits were for me. We also spent an entire day at the ruins of Turnberry Castle. How splendid that was, Mr. Brennan. You were right that we would enjoy Scotland."

Angilia felt his fingers barely move, and Ginny smiled at her. "He hears you, Angilia. Keep talking to him."

"Mr. Brennan, when Matthew and I were sitting against the remains of a Turnberry Castle wall, Matthew brought up something you had mentioned in 2012. He agrees with you that I should write my memoir, going all the way back to my earliest memories. He said my story can help people, and I suppose I can understand his point, but I'm not completely sure about making it public. It's one thing to write it for my family, so they will know my story in its entirety, but sharing it with the world is perhaps a bit much. I'm not sure yet what I will do."

"You must share it with the world, Princess," Mr. Brennan very softly said. His breathing was labored, and Angilia did not want to overburden him. Ginny kept a close watch of his vital signs, though, and nodded to Angilia.

"So you and Matthew agree on that. I suppose I need to pray about that, then. Of course I want to help people if I can, but I do not want to displease God, either," Angilia replied.

Mr. Brennan weakly squeezed her hand as he opened his eyes and offered her a tired smile. "You can never displease God, my dear. But you are right. You need to pray about this before you take this to the public. That's only right." He took several shallow breaths, trying to marshal his strength. "So your honeymoon was quite the experience.  I am happy for you, Princess.  Tell me more about the Bruce please," he requested as his eyes closed.

Angilia continued to hold his hand as he rested, and she spent a few hours telling him in detail about Matthew's surprise day trip to the Abbeys and then their day at the castle ruins.  She knew he was weak, and she preferred to talk to him so that he could rest during what Angilia knew was his last day on earth.

After a few more hours, she kissed his cheek, told him she would be back, and stepped outside to call her father.  When he answered, she told him, "Daddy, you and Matthew need to come to Mr. Brennan's house.  He will die soon, sometime this afternoon."

"We will be there soon, Angel," Eric assured her.  They were.  They arrived within minutes, and Matthew brought his medical bag, as well, so that he could monitor Mr. Brennan.  Matthew had talked with Angilia the night before, as he held her close.  He explained that Mr. Brennan was dying of senescence and that they needed to keep him comfortable until his death.

Ginny led them to the bedroom, where Angilia still sat holding Mr. Brennan's hand and telling him stories.  "Mr. Brennan, Daddy and Matthew are here to visit you, too."  She felt his fingers twitch at the mention of Eric, who sat in a chair next to Angilia.

"Mr. Brennan, I said I would visit again, and I kept my promise.  I would have come yesterday, but these two newlyweds flew home from Scotland yesterday.  Angilia just had to come see you as soon as she could, you know," Eric told him and he placed his hand over Mr. Brennan's and Angilia's.

"I am honored you are here, Your Majesty.  This is actually better than a state funeral," Mr. Brennan managed to say as he gasped for air.  "My King is here for my farewell," he added with a hint of a smile.  Eric fought his tears, and Angilia kissed his cheek.

"Princess, you write that book.  I told you and your uncle on your wedding day that you took away any fear of death I had.  You.  I saw you for the angel you are, and that is why.  I am not afraid of dying or of where I am going.  My only regret is that I never saw my daughter again, but I will see her someday, as we know."

Angilia looked at her father with tears in her eyes, knowing that she could not fulfill Mr. Brennan's one desire before he died. "Mr. Brennan, if I do publish that book, I have to dedicate it to you. Other than my family, you are the only person who knows, and you knew without my having to tell you anything.  You are very special yourself, Mr. Brennan.  No one else has ever seen me for what I really am."

Mr. Brennan smiled weakly and closed his eyes.  His breathing grew more labored, and Matthew listened to his heart and lungs.  He shook his head, letting Angilia, Eric, and Ginny know that Mr. Brennan would die very soon.  Angilia bowed her head and said a prayer for Mr. Brennan, and he gasped for air as they all four said "Amen."

At that moment, Angilia looked up and saw a woman standing at the foot of Mr. Brennan's bed.  Angilia smiled, nodded to the woman, and leaned down to speak to Mr. Brennan.  "Mr. Brennan, open your eyes and look ahead.  Your daughter is here for you, Mr. Brennan."  Eric, Matthew, and Ginny never saw anyone there, but when Mr. Brennan opened his eyes, his face filled with indescribable joy.

"Amelia, you came."  He turned his head and smiled at Angilia.  "She came to take me home, didn't she, Princess?"

"Yes, she did, Mr. Brennan.  Amelia will take you to your wife and son soon.  I love you, Mr. Brennan," Angilia said, and she kissed his cheek.

"I love you, Princess.  Thank you."  Mr. Brennan looked at his daughter, his smile still radiant, as he took his last breath. Matthew confirmed Mr. Brennan's death at 4:31 on the afternoon of Saturday, July 30, 2016.  Mr. Brennan's life spanned 100 years, six months, and 29 days.

§§§§

Late that afternoon, Eric wrote a Royal Proclamation and asked Carol to release it immediately. Most people outside of Valmondois knew Mr. Brennan from the memoir that Angilia had written with him, a book that had pleasantly surprised him by becoming a best-seller. Eric's proclamation brought tears to many as people sensed the love, respect, and admiration embedded within the words.

*Royal Proclamation*

*by*

*King Eric de Valdavia*

*Valdavia lost one of its most respected and valued citizens today with the death of Mr. Arthur Brennan. Mr. Brennan was a lifelong loyal servant of God and of Valdavia. We are all richer for his life.*

*Mr. Brennan left this world at 4:31 this afternoon at 100 years of age. His life was not notable for its length, but more so for his dedication to God, his family, his work, and his country. His joy, love, and serenity touched all who knew him, either personally or through his memoir. He certainly touched the lives of my family, and for that we are grateful.*

*In honor of this noble man, I hereby declare Monday, 1 August 2016 a day of national reverence for Mr. Brennan's life. I hereby order that all Valdavian flags be flown at half-staff in Mr. Brennan's honor. A state funeral for Mr. Arthur Brennan shall be held on that day as a celebration of his life and service.*

*Signed:  King Eric R*

*Date:    30 July 2016*

§§§§§

Angilia awoke early and prepared for the funeral. She left a note for Matthew on her pillow, letting him know where she was. She entered the chapel on the main level, where Mr. Brennan's coffin rested prior to the funeral. She stood before the coffin, bowed her head, and prayed. She felt her father's arm around her shoulders when he joined her. They stood quietly together for a few moments, both reflecting upon similar thoughts of this man they had known for just four and one half years.

"It's actually difficult to realize that Mr. Brennan was part of our lives for just four years. He was always so full of joy and happiness that it became contagious. He banished any sadness or gloom that crept into my personal space. His love of life was immense and childlike. I admit, I will miss that here every day," Angilia confided to her father.

"I will, too, Angilia. Saturday was quite emotional, wasn't it? Matthew, Ginny, and I never saw his daughter, but we know she was there. I will never forget the look on his face when he saw her. His final wish came true, and he saw his daughter. What a beautiful experience to share with him."

"I know, Daddy. He is with his family again, all of them, and I know what that means to Mr. Brennan. His death itself is not sad, but not having him here with us is sad. He's right, though, that we will resume our friendship in Heaven someday."

Eric breathed deeply and kissed his daughter's temple. "Yes, we will. We have a very important day, Angel. Let's join everyone for breakfast before we have to face the emotional moments ahead." Eric and Angilia walked from the chapel to the dining room as everyone else made their way to breakfast. Matthew joined Eric and Angilia as they greeted Alejandro, Juanita, and Eduardo.

Two hours later, everyone gathered in the foyer before the funeral procession and cortege left the palace for Christ Church Valmondois. The gun carriage was brought near the front entrance of the palace. Angilia, Katherine, Juanita, Susan, and Bonnie lined up to face the back of the carriage while Mr. Brennan's coffin was placed atop. Matthew, Roger, Daniel, Eduardo, and Alejandro served as pallbearers, carrying the flag-draped coffin. Eric walked at the foot of the coffin. He, the women, and hundreds of mourners on the mall bowed their heads in respect as the coffin was placed on the gun carriage.

Two soldiers standing at the front of the carriage gave Mr. Brennan a 21-round salute and then a trumpeter played the Valdavian National Anthem. Several people on the mall began crying, especially since nearly everyone in Valmondois had known Mr. Brennan. While most of the Royal party went to one of the cars for the drive to the church ahead of the procession, Angilia walked to the gates and thanked everyone for honoring Mr. Brennan. Eric smiled as he watched his daughter, the future Queen, lead them in prayer. She had such strength and compassion that constantly amazed and inspired him.

Angilia rejoined her father and Matthew for the procession to the church. The three of them, as the ranking members of the Royal Family, formed the cortege to accompany Mr. Brennan's coffin to the church for the funeral service and burial. When the bells of Christ Church Valmondois rang from the tall bell tower, signaling the beginning of the procession, six soldiers pulled the gun carriage through the palace gates and onto the street beyond. Eric, Angilia, and Matthew slowly walked behind the carriage for the short journey to the church.

Silently, and without any formal planning, the hundreds of people on the mall followed the procession, becoming part of the cortege. Several minutes later, the gun carriage stopped in front of the church, and Matthew stepped forward to join the other pallbearers in carrying Mr. Brennan's coffin to the altar. Eric and Angilia walked behind the coffin until it was placed upon its bier in front of the altar. They all went to their seats in the pews, where they remained standing with the congregation as the choir sang Mr. Brennan's favorite hymn, "Take My Hand, Precious Lord."

Reverend Hutchins, like most people who filled the church to capacity that day, had known Arthur Brennan all of his life. Mr. Brennan had been a lifelong member of the church's congregation, and everyone who met him adored him. The Reverend's sermon that day echoed the truths that Mr. Brennan stated on his last day, that he now lived eternally in Heaven, reunited with his loving family and his friends.

After his sermon, Reverend Hutchins bowed, and Angilia squeezed her father's and husband's hands as she stood and walked to the pulpit to offer the eulogy. "All of us here today are blessed to have known Mr. Brennan. He graced my life and the lives of my loved ones for four and one half years. I told Mr. Brennan several times how grateful I was that God had aligned circumstances so that we met on my 16th birthday. What a glorious gift I received that day as our friendship began. While we worked on his memoir, he often commented that his life, although long, was quite unremarkable. He was too humble to believe me when I told him the exact opposite was true.

"Mr. Brennan's life is remarkable not because of its length, but because of his character, love, and faith. I know how privileged I was to listen to his stories and memories as we drafted his memoir. That he witnessed history in his 100 years is obvious. What he took from that history is not, until you read his words and hear his life lessons as he so charmingly told them to me.

"Mr. Brennan's love for nature, for the world, was with him from his earliest years. We often sat either in the palace garden or his garden, enjoying our tea and conversation, and he would suddenly remark upon the splendors of God's creations. He saw God's hand upon everything, from the lowliest worm to a soaring eagle. One of my favorite stories in his memoir is his earliest memory of seeing a beautiful, colorful butterfly and grabbing for it as his mother held him. He never lost that childlike wonder with which he viewed the world, despite the pain he did endure.

"Like Job, Mr. Brennan suffered many losses and tragedies during his life, and he never once blamed God for his pain and grief. His son's helicopter was shot down during the Korean War, and his body was not found and returned home for more than 10 years. Mr. Brennan did not even know during those years whether his son Adam survived the attack or not. He and his wife Charlotte never blamed God, though, for Adam's death. Charlotte died at home one day while Mr. Brennan was at the hospital volunteering. He found her when he returned home. She was the love of his life, and he adored her. We just learned on Saturday that his daughter Amelia is dead, which no one knew until then. Mr. Brennan had not heard from her in almost 40 years and always wondered why, but he never questioned or doubted God. Now he—and we—know why. Before he died, Mr. Brennan rejoiced in his impending reunion with his family, and I know they will never feel heartache or pain again.

"On my wedding day, Mr. Brennan told me that he did not fear death or the afterlife. He even giggled and said he looked forward to his eternal life with glee. We do not often hear people say such things. Death to most people is cloaked in grief and sadness, even fear, not joy and peace. Mr. Brennan's attitude is not just exemplary but admirable. His faith and trust in God guided his every moment. Yes, I will miss our regular visits, but I too know that when I die, I will see him again, and we can enjoy our talks for eternity. Rather than mourn and feel sadness for Mr. Brennan, we should follow his example and rejoice with him. He is in his eternal home now.

"I want to close with Mr. Brennan's favorite scripture, John 6:24. *'Verily, verily, I say unto you, He that heareth my word, and believeth on him that sent me, hath everlasting life, and shall not come into condemnation; but is passed from death into life.'"*

Angilia sat at the piano to play and sing a hymn at Mr. Brennan's request. The previous year, during one of their visits, he had asked her if she would please sing Charlotte's favorite hymn at his funeral. She smiled as she sang "In the Garden" for her friend, knowing he, Charlotte, Adam, and Amelia were listening and smiling.

After she finished, Reverend Hutchins offered the closing prayer, and moments later he led the pallbearers who carried the coffin through the side door into the church cemetery for the burial. Eric, Angilia, and the Royal party followed, and the rest of the congregation walked out the front church door and onto the side street that faced the cemetery. Patrick had visited Eric after he sent the Royal Proclamation and suggested that the perfect cemetery plot for Mr. Brennan was the one next to Patrick's grave. Eric remembered how much Mr. Brennan enjoyed seeing Patrick at the wedding reception, and he agreed with Patrick. When Eric shared Patrick's idea with Angilia, she was elated.

Now they stood as Mr. Brennan's coffin was lowered into its grave, and Angilia smiled as she recollected him calling Uncle Patrick a little scamp. This was the perfect resting place for Mr. Brennan's body. Angilia laid a bouquet of yellow roses on the coffin while it slowly lowered, and she blew a kiss to her friend as Eric tossed a handful of dirt onto the coffin. Reverend Hutchins prayed, and hundreds of people on the streets surrounding the church and cemetery bowed their heads.

Angilia smiled and placed one white rose on her Uncle Patrick's grave as a token of gratitude and love. Two hours later, after speaking with the people gathered to honor Mr. Brennan, Eric, Angilia, and Matthew slowly walked home together. She kissed each of them, told them she loved them, and smiled.

# CHAPTER 5

"Happy birthday, Daddy!"

Eric smiled as his daughter greeted him, as always, on his birthday. She had walked up behind him as he leafed through some papers on the desk in his sitting room, put her arms around him, and held a wrapped box in her hands. "What is this I see?" he asked, always thrilled by the annual early-morning birthday gifts she gave to him.

"Open it and see," she teased. He took the box from her hands and turned to face her as he untied the blue ribbon and pulled away the wrapping paper. The heavy box perplexed him, and he removed the lid and unfolded the tissue paper to see a very old book.

Eric very carefully lifted it from the box and turned to the title page, which was written in French. He translated the title page aloud, and looked at Angilia in utter surprise. "<u>The Divine Right of Kings: My Belief and Philosophy</u> by Christophe Martineau, King de Valdavia, published 1375. Angilia, where did you find this? I've only heard rumors of this book's existence, but no one I know of has ever seen a copy. This is remarkable."

"I hope you don't mind, but I had to read it, too. Matthew and I came across some really out-of-the-way shops in Scotland, and I found this in one of the shops in Ayrshire. I had to get it for you. I remember your telling me about it, what little was known, and you said you wished you could read it.  Now you can," she smiled at her father.

"Yes, and I will truly treasure and preserve this for all future generations.  I can't believe I'm holding this book.  You read it?  Does Christophe write what I suspect he does?"  Eric had speculated during one of his visits to Oxford, while Angilia taught there, that Christophe did not agree with the Divine Right of Kings theory, which states that monarchs are not subject to earthly authority in any way.  Given what Eric knew of his ancestors and the history of Valdavia, he could not fathom any of his predecessors believing that.

"Yes, it does.  Christophe believes as you and I do, that the monarch is ordained by God but that this does not exempt him—or her—from earthly sanction.  You embody that more than anyone, Daddy.  Christophe understood that despite everything, his life and his family were blessed.  He never took God's blessings for granted.  Neither do you."

Eric carefully returned the book to its box as he felt tears choking him.  He cleared his throat and looked down at his awe-inspiring daughter.  Her love for him overwhelmed him with its depth and breadth.  He pulled her into a hug, kissed the top of her head, and thanked God for the greatest gift, his beautiful daughter Angilia.

§§§§

That evening, Matthew and Angilia corralled Mitchell, Katherine, Alejandro, Juanita, Eduardo, Daniel, Susan, and Bonnie. They sent them ahead to the location of Eric's surprise party. Matthew and Angilia stayed behind until after Eric and Roger left. Roger had scheduled a formal dinner in Eric's calendar so as not to spoil the surprise Angilia had planned for Eric's birthday.

When Eric came to tell them he was leaving, he was surprised to see them dressed more formally.  When he asked where they were going, Angilia simply said, "Oh, we thought we'd go out to dinner while you're at your event."  She kissed his cheek.  "Have a wonderful time, Daddy."

As soon as his car pulled out, they got in Matthew's car and left, taking a shortcut to beat Eric and Roger. They arrived with minutes to spare, and they found everything was ready for Eric's surprise party. Mitchell sipped a scotch while he welcomed his son and daughter-in-law. "I don't think Eric will suspect a surprise party when Roger directs him here," Mitchell smiled, referring to the country club at his favorite golf course. He knew that Eric rarely came to the country club.

Mitchell was proved right when they heard Eric and Roger outside the closed doors. Eric opened the door to shouts of "Happy birthday" and streamers floating through the air. Eric put his hands on his hips, bowed his head, and laughed. "You finally got me. I never suspected anything. Someone had a lot of accomplices in pulling this off, didn't she?" he asked and looked at Angilia with a smile.

Angilia had reserved the country club for the evening, so they had complete privacy for Eric's birthday celebration. As they sat at the large table enjoying their dinner, they shared their own birthday memories. "I once asked Angilia if she remembered her first Christmas, and boy does she. I know she remembers the day she was born, so I won't even ask her about her first birthday," Katherine giggled. "What about everyone else? Who wants to tell us the earliest birthday you remember?"

"I remember my fifth birthday party," Matthew volunteered. "Mom and Dad invited everyone in my first grade class at school. They even rented a pony for the kids to ride. My other birthdays were different, because the school changed my rank after first grade, and my classmates were much older than I was." Angilia smiled, knowing that Matthew had been promoted to high school the following year and had completed the requirements in one year. Then he earned his college degree and entered medical school, from which he had graduated at the age of 13. She knew how he felt not having the usual childhood memories, but neither of them resented or regretted anything.

Finally it was Eric's turn, and he shared his memories of his fourth birthday party. "Patrick was 11 months old, and he wanted all of the presents, so I had to let him rip them open for me. He claimed one of them for himself, though, so Mother bought me a replacement the next day. I remember that. The cake was the big deal, though. It was a chocolate cake with strawberry icing, my favorite. Father lit the candles and I stood on a chair to blow them out. Just after I did, Patrick crawled across the table and dove into the cake. What a mess," Eric laughed as he looked at Angilia.

"The birthday that means the most to me, though, was 20 years ago when I turned 42. Like Patrick was on my fourth birthday, Angilia was 11 months old. We visited Mother and spent most of the day with her in her home. She had been ill for a long while, which is why she couldn't go to the hospital the day Angilia was born. So we went to her that day. Mother rang her maid, who brought up a tea cart with a birthday cake—chocolate with strawberry icing—and tea.

"We enjoyed the cake and tea as we chatted, while Angilia sat on the bed beside Mother. I noticed that Angilia listened to us intently, as if she understood everything we said, and I bet she did. I think I've told everyone that Angilia could walk by then. She slid off of Mother's bed and walked around to me. I kept talking with Mother, but I put my hand on Angilia's back. I placed my plate on the tea cart and when I turned and smiled down at Angilia, I got the most wonderful birthday present."

Eric smiled at Angilia, and she returned his smile. "Happy birthday, Daddy. I love you," Angilia said as she stared into his turquoise eyes and saw tears forming in them.

"My baby said those exact words to me that afternoon in Mother's room. I thought my heart would burst that day it was so full of love and joy. Mother was so startled that she dropped her tea cup. I picked Angilia up in a hug, and when she heard Mother moan, she giggled. She reached for Mother, so I lifted her onto Mother's lap. '*I love you, Grandmother*,' Angilia told her. Poor Mother nearly fainted. I treasure that memory," Eric concluded.

The story did not shock anyone at that point, for they were well aware of Angilia's exceptionality by then. Still, Matthew stared at his wife in reverence, never taking anything about her for granted.

He knew how very special Angilia was, more than ever, and with every new discovery, Matthew loved her more, as did Eric.

§§§§§

"Welcome, and thank you all for coming to our special dedication and celebration in honor of Valdavia's favorite music teacher, Hilda Yost. Most of us grew up knowing her as an enthusiastic, energetic teacher. We are most honored to have with us two very distinguished guests who came to know Miss Yost four years ago. Please join me in welcoming Their Royal Highnesses The Duc and Duchesse de Valmondois," announced Mr. Gruder, the long-serving principal of King Stefan Middle School.

Angilia and Matthew walked onto the stage to a standing ovation, and they waved to everyone. Angilia smiled when she noticed students past and present, as well as colleagues, of Miss Yost. She was pleased that so many people remembered Miss Yost with fondness. "Thank you for such a kind welcome," Angilia said. "Matthew and I are truly honored to be here for the formal dedication ceremony."

"We certainly are. I can honestly say that the week I volunteered in Miss Yost's music class four years ago was tremendous fun. Her energy and love for her job were contagious. She brought a smile to everyone who met her, and judging by the packed room, she made quite a lot of people very happy," Matthew added.

"She certainly did, Your Royal Highness," Mr. Gruder agreed, and he led Matthew and Angilia to a red-draped plaque to the left of the auditorium stage. Turning his attention to the audience, Mr. Gruder said, "Their Royal Highnesses will now officially dedicate the auditorium."

Angilia and Matthew jointly pulled the gold cord and opened the red curtain to reveal the plaque, which Angilia read aloud. "'The Hilda Yost Auditorium, Dedicated in Honor of Her 62 Years Of Steadfast Service, 3 December 2016.'" Everyone in the auditorium stood and applauded, for despite her often-derided curriculum, most everyone did like Miss Yost.

"Thank you all for your generous support of our commemoration of Miss Yost. We have an extra special treat to extend this celebration of Miss Yost, which Her Royal Highness organized with glee," Mr. Gruder announced as he walked to the edge of the stage.

"I truly did, and I am so pleased to introduce to you the self-titled Miss Yost Commemorative Choir," Angilia stated as the stage curtain rose to reveal Valdavian students of all ages on risers. Matthew walked to the back of the risers and stood in the middle of the top riser, joining the students. Angilia sat at the piano, and she asked Matthew and the students if they were ready. They all smiled and said they were.

Roger could not help but cringe slightly when the oh-so-haunting melody filled the auditorium. He watched as the students and Matthew sang the repetitive lyrics of "The More We Get Together" and performed Miss Yost's (in)famous hand movements. He noticed that Juanita sobbed, and he recalled how fond she had been of Miss Yost. He also remembered how lovely Miss Yost's voice was when she sang harmony on Angilia's recording of "Love Was Born on Christmas Day." Angilia beamed at the students, and Roger noticed how much they all seemed to truly enjoy performing the song.

Two years had passed since Miss Yost's death, and Roger admitted to himself that he did enjoy the performance. Eric smiled at him, and he returned the smile. The two of them did have fun in music class, that was true. Roger had tried to hide behind the taller Eric, although Miss Yost had forever coaxed her so-called shy boy out, much to his chagrin. Still, looking back from the age of 64, he realized how much he missed those simpler times.

When the performance concluded, Roger was the first to stand and applaud, much to Angilia's delight. He winked at her, and she acknowledged his gesture with a nod. She smiled at Matthew and then at her father, knowing that Miss Yost's shadow would loom large over Valmondois for many years to come.

§§§§

Angilia sat curled on a sofa in the sitting room, between her father and her husband.  She looked at each of them and smiled, her contentment unparalleled.  Angilia felt only love, peace, and joy as she wrote the final entry in her 2016 diary while the last hour of the year ticked away:

*31 December 2016*

*What an amazing year 2016 has been from its first day to its last. We began the year with dear Mr. Brennan's 100th birthday.  Daddy and I will never forget how happy and thrilled he was to have his milestone birthday at the Palais—he always called the palace by its French name.  He was the only person outside of our family and those friends who live here to know about my engagement to Matthew.  That utterly thrilled him! We arranged it so that Mr. Brennan could watch Bonnie set up and take our official engagement pictures, too, and I asked Bonnie to print and frame copies of them for Mr. Brennan as his birthday gift from me and Matthew.  We even signed the pictures to him, which seemed to make him very happy.  We so love him.*

*Our engagement was announced on my birthday, which made for a very busy, albeit a very emotional and loving day.  That day everything fell into place. God's destiny for me and Matthew was on course, and we both knew that.  We were so happy that day, and I got to reveal my gorgeous engagement ring to everyone outside the palace.  Matthew placed Mommy's emerald and citrine engagement ring on my finger, and I will never forget that moment as we stood in the chapel.  Love filled me and surrounded me.*

*That is how I felt on our wedding day.  Matthew and I just had to marry on Mommy's and Daddy's anniversary.  There was never any other date. That day was also Mother's Day, and I felt Mommy with me all day.  I felt her soul and her love.  Never has one day been as true and right and perfect as that day, 26 June 2016.  Our month-long honeymoon in Scotland could not have been any more emotional than it was.  Our love was so deep and strong, and it has only continued to grow deeper and stronger with each passing day.  I love and trust Matthew with my life, my soul, and my heart.  He is my one and only.*

*When we returned from Scotland, though, we faced the death of our dear Mr. Brennan.  For four years, he was a loyal and loving friend.  Sharing his death was not sad, really, but rather a very religious and loving experience that I will never forget.  For four years, I tried in vain to locate his daughter Amelia so that they could be together again before he died.  I found out why I never found her when Amelia appeared as her father's Spirit Guide on 30 July. Amelia had already died, and she is the one who made his last moments so beautiful. She came to take her father home to Heaven! I am honored to have shared that day with Mr. Brennan, truly honored.*

*We also honored Miss Yost, almost two years after her death, with the renaming of the King Stefan Middle School auditorium. She is thrilled, I know. Miss Yost lived for her teaching, and she so enjoyed what she did. Few people have that passion into their 80s, and Miss Yost certainly did. She told me once that she would teach her music classes until she died, and that is what she did. Miss Yost died at the age of 82 after she returned home from the school one afternoon.*

*My precious father celebrated his 62<sup>nd</sup> birthday last month. Everyone comments on how Daddy does not look his age. I'm not one hundred percent sure what a 62-year-old man should look like, since there is no set formula for that, but I understand what they mean. Daddy looks pretty much the same as he did when I first saw him the day Uncle Patrick died, 19 July 1977, 39 years ago. Daddy was 22 then. His hair was longer and he did not have the close-shaven beard and mustache, and there is a bit of grey in his raven hair now. Otherwise, he looks the same to me. He says the same thing to me, that I have not changed at all. He says I have looked the same since I was 11. We do not control how we look for the most part; God does. We are how and who God predestined us to be.*

*Uncle Patrick! What an amazing public splash my darling uncle made this year! I have some old magazine articles about him from the 1970s, and he was one major teen heartthrob! He still is! Posters of Uncle Patrick were huge sellers this year—of course I bought them for the family archives. Imagine my great-grandchildren admiring their charming great-grand uncle! Patrick got a huge kick out of that when I showed him the posters. His fame and status never caused an ego. He is sweet, charming, goofy, spontaneous, and handsome. He is also forever 19. Of course he is a teen idol!*

*Dear God, Thank you for gifting us this blessed year. I pray that you keep my family and friends in your loving embrace as another year dawns. Please direct me down the path you desire me to follow, and please reprimand me when I do anything against your will or that displeases you. I love you, I love my family, I love my friends, and I love Valdavia. Thank you for your continued love and blessings. Amen.*

# CHAPTER 6

Angilia stretched and opened her eyes to see Matthew smiling at her, just as the sun began its ascent. "Happy birthday, darling," he said and pulled her into a kiss. "I love you, Angilia, my dear." Matthew reached behind him, picked up a red rose hidden there, and offered it to his wife.

Angilia smiled and breathed in the fragrant scent of the rose. "Thank you, Matthew. I love you." She lay on her stomach and gently brushed the rose across his bare chest. "We have an important morning ahead. Are you ready?"

"I suppose. It feels a bit odd to do the whole portrait thing. I haven't done much yet to warrant this," he replied.

"Sure you have. You volunteer at the hospital. You're on their Board of Directors. You're the Patron of the AAV. You are organizing your first foundation. That's a lot, actually, in five months, Matthew."

"You left out my most important accomplishment," he said with a wink. "I married you." She giggled and lay across his chest.

Several minutes later, Angilia sighed and said, "I'm going to shower and dress. Breakfast will be ready in a little while. Come on," she tugged his arm. Matthew moaned, but he followed her to their huge bathroom. A second shower had been installed during their honeymoon the previous July, and they each had their own showers. They showered simultaneously, and she blow-dried her hair as he shaved.

He kissed her cheek when he finished, and went to his wardrobe to dress. She soon entered her wardrobe and dressed. As she sat at her vanity styling her long hair, Matthew stepped in, assisted her, and kissed her again before he went downstairs for coffee. He met Eric in the foyer, and told him Angilia was nearly ready. Matthew knew that Eric and Angilia gave one another early-morning gifts on their birthdays.

Eric rushed back to his suite, grabbed his birthday gift for her, and knocked on her suite door. Angilia greeted him there with a smile. "Good morning, Daddy. I'm just heading downstairs."

"Happy birthday, my beautiful daughter Angilia," he said with a huge smile and a kiss on her forehead. He handed her a wrapped box. "We'll go down in a bit. Open it."

Angilia noticed the letter tucked under the ribbon, and she felt tears sting her eyes. His letters always made her emotional. She told him she would read it later, when she was alone. Inside the box she saw a small black book with no text on the cover. She looked puzzled, and when Eric told her to look inside the book, she wondered what rarity he had found for her.

She gasped when she saw a faded quill pen signature on the inside front cover, with the year 1863 written underneath. Angilia stared at the signature in near shock. She began crying, and Eric looked at her in concern. "Angel, what's wrong? What is it?" She shook her head and leaned against him crying, but forced herself to stop a moment later.

"This is such a wonderful gift, Daddy. Did Matthew tell you?"

"Tell me what? I've known your passion for history since you were a young girl. When this went up for auction, I knew I had to get it for you. I remember how fond you always seemed of President Lincoln, so I knew you'd cherish this diary," Eric told her.

"I do, Daddy. I want to tell you something," Angilia said, took his hand, and led him to the sofa in her sitting room. She shared the story of her and Matthew meeting Abraham Lincoln in the Unborn Children Sphere, much to Eric's astonishment.

"Angilia, how remarkable. But how bittersweet for you, baby. He seemed to know his fate, and so did you. That's a lot to carry inside for centuries." Eric pulled her close. "No wonder you were drawn to Lincoln when you were very young. You seemed to have some special connection to him then, which I never understood. Everything really does make sense now. I never meant to upset you, sweetheart."

Angilia smiled. "You didn't. You never could. It's just another emotional reaction of mine. I can hardly wait to read this, Daddy. Thank you," she said and kissed his cheek.

"You are very welcome, Angel. We best go down to breakfast now," he smiled, and they took the elevator together to the first floor.

§§§§

At 11:00 that morning, Eric, Angilia, Matthew and the rest of the Royal Family and their close friends arrived at the Musée National de Valdavia. As she had five years earlier for the unveiling of Angilia's first official portrait, the Director, Muriel Laperen, curtseyed as she greeted them at the main entrance. She chatted with them for a few moments, and then escorted them into the Royal Portrait Gallery.

The room was filled to capacity, and everyone present had purchased €50 tickets to attend the unveiling. One hundred percent of the ticket proceeds were split evenly between Angilia's Learning for Life foundation and Matthew's Patronage, The Athletic Association of Valdavia. Eric, Angilia, and Matthew stood in front of the draped portraits, while the rest of the Royal party sat in the reserved front row.

Ms. Laperen welcomed everyone. "Five years ago, we gathered for the unveiling of Her Royal Highness' first portrait, which hangs behind me next to His Majesty's portrait. Today, we add new portraits to this historic gallery. The second portrait of Her Royal Highness was painted by renowned portraitist Gustav Minier. The first portrait of His Royal Highness was painted by Simon Thorne. Both artists were selected by Their Royal Highnesses, and the portraits done at the request of the Musée to commemorate not

143

only the Royal Wedding but Her Royal Highness' 21st birthday. Both Mr. Minier and Mr. Thorne are with us today. Gentlemen," Ms. Laperen stated, allowing the two artists to stand for the acknowledgement and applause of the audience.

Next, Ms. Laperen introduced Eric, who approached the podium to a rousing standing ovation. Matthew saw Angilia's delighted smile and felt her happily nudge him. She always enjoyed peoples' love and appreciation for her father, and her happiness genuinely made Matthew happy.

"Thank you all for such a wonderful welcome on this very special day. The portraits of my daughter and son-in-law are truly magnificent, and I know everyone will enjoy them from this day forward. We all extend our sincere gratitude to Mr. Minier and Mr. Thorne for their lifelike portraits of Angilia and Matthew. Without further ado, Angilia will unveil the portrait of her husband," Eric smiled when Angilia stepped to the portrait.

She pulled the gold cord to open the large red velvet curtain and reveal Matthew's portrait. His portrait hung next to the portrait of Marisol that Angilia had painted and donated to the museum in late 2012. The audience stood, cheering the Duc's portrait. For the portrait, Matthew wore dark grey trousers, a white shirt, and a blue suede vest, with black leather loafers. He stood casually in the palace sitting room, leaning against a shelf of books, his hands in his pockets. Angilia thought it captured Matthew perfectly, merging his formal and informal sides in a modern version of a country gentleman's portrait. No one knew that the glint in his eyes was due to her standing nearby as she watched the portrait session.

Eric returned to the podium after the applause finally ended. A man in the audience shouted Angilia's name, much to everyone's amusement. "All right, you'll see her, I promise," Eric giggled. "Matthew, go ahead and unveil your wife's portrait." Matthew smiled broadly as he opened the red velvet curtain to reveal Angilia's portrait. Everyone gasped at the sight, and once more stood, this time in shouts of admiration. Angilia wore a classic strapless ball gown in soft pink, with a silk pink flower at the waist. Around her throat gleamed a pearl choker. Her long blonde hair was pulled back simply. Prominent on her left hand were her wedding and engagement rings.  She posed near the piano in the music room, its gold décor mimicking her glow.

Everyone requested that Eric, Angilia, and Matthew pose with the portraits, and they did so.  Guests and press photographers snapped hundreds of pictures as the trio smiled and chatted and glanced up at the portraits.  Matthew could barely stop looking at Angilia, which thrilled the photographers.  Matthew and Angilia were still newlyweds, and their wedding had been the most-watched Royal wedding in history.  People everywhere adored the Duc and Duchesse de Valmondois.

After nearly 30 minutes, Ms. Laperen stepped to the podium and reclaimed the audience's attention.  "Ladies and gentlemen, thank you all for such an enthusiastic reaction to Their Royal Highness' portraits.  I knew when I first saw them that the portraits would enamor everyone, and they have.  We are honored to house these beautiful portraits in the Royal Portrait Gallery.

"This gallery contains so much history, from Valdavia's first monarch to its future monarch.  Every consort is also represented here.  Our history and our heritage remain so very important to all of us.  We add to that heritage today, not just with the portraits of Their Royal Highnesses but with a portrait of one of the most cherished and popular members of the Royal Family.  Your Majesty," Ms. Laperen said with a curtsey and offered the podium to Eric again.

"Thank you, Ms. Laperen.  I am so deeply honored to unveil this next portrait.  As you know, today is my daughter Angilia's birthday.  Hers is not the only January birthday in my family, though.  In three days, on Friday, January 6, we commemorate the anniversary of my brother Patrick's birth.  Patrick was born 59 years ago on January 6, 1958.  Angilia surprised me on Christmas 2016 with the portrait which now hangs here, alongside her new portrait."

Eric walked to the curtained portrait, pulled the gold cord, and revealed the most extraordinary portrait of his brother. Patrick's dark tousled hair, his steel blue eyes that shone with both tenderness and mischief, and that famous slanted Elvis smile stunned everyone with their aliveness.  Eric hugged Angilia and walked back to the podium. "Ladies and gentlemen, my brother, His Royal Highness Prince Patrick de Valdavia as seen through his adoring niece's eyes," Eric proudly announced as the room exploded with roaring cheers, screams, and applause. "My brother's portrait is finally where it belongs and deserves to be, with his family's portraits."

SSSSS

That afternoon, everyone kissed Angilia and wished her well, and then Matthew drove them through the palace gates and to downtown Valmondois. Hundreds of people greeted them as they pulled out, and the couple waved excitedly, huge smiles illuminating their faces. Everyone in Valdavia knew where their Princess Consort was going that day and why.

When Matthew and Angilia arrived at the Valmondois Bureau de Permis de Conduire, crowds awaited their arrival, much to Angilia's surprise. All Valdavians took their written test and driving test on their 21$^{st}$ birthdays. Angilia's grandfather had changed the age from 17 to 21 in 1965, and 21 remained the legal driving age ever since.

So it was that his granddaughter registered for the written and driving tests on her 21$^{st}$ birthday. Angilia refused offers to cut in line ahead of others, and she and Matthew sat patiently in the waiting area until her number was called. Angilia completed the written test in a matter of minutes and handed it to the clerk for scoring. He smiled and told her she had received a perfect score. Next, he tested her vision and informed her of what she already knew. Her eyesight was perfect.

Finally, the driving instructor bowed and greeted her, and asked if she had a car to use for the driving test. She held the keys to Matthew's car, and her husband walked her to the car and kissed her before her test began. The crowds outside the bureau cheered and whistled, which made her giggle and Matthew blush. Angilia turned the key in the ignition, and soon she drove away and around a corner.

Matthew waited with the crowds on the sidewalk, wanting to see her triumphant return. Matthew and Eric had given her driving lessons on the palace grounds and then the mall before guiding her on the streets of Valmondois. Several months of lessons and real-world driving with one or both of them had made her relaxed and comfortable at the wheel of a car. She had driven Matthew's midsized car, a larger Rolls Royce, and even her father's compact Aston Martin. Matthew knew she would ace the driving test.

He realized Angilia was almost done when he heard cheers at the stoplight two blocks away. Passers-by saw her when she stopped at the red light. She did not let them distract her, though, and she kept her attention on the lights and the other cars. Matthew stepped to the edge of the curb and watched her drive the final block and parallel park near him. The driving instructor wrote on the paper attached to his clipboard, while she turned off the engine and sat waiting for any instructions or comments.

After a few minutes, he indicated that she could get out of the car. He motioned for her to follow him back into the bureau building, and she dutifully did so, with Matthew joining her. Inside, her instructor handed his clipboard to the clerk and then bowed to her again. "Congratulations, Your Royal Highness. The clerk will prepare your driving license." Everyone inside clapped and congratulated Angilia, and she thanked them.

Angilia posed for her license picture and signed the card which bore her vital information. The clerk affixed the picture and official seal, stamped the card, and handed her the license. Matthew snapped a phone picture quickly and sent it to Eric. She playfully swatted his arm and jangled his car keys as she got into the driver's seat of Matthew's car for the drive home. People took dozens of pictures of her as she pulled onto the street and turned toward the palace.

People on the mall cheered when they saw Angilia driving toward the palace gates for the first time. Even the guard at the gate smiled when he saw her drive through the open gate. She laughed when she noticed her father recording her first official drive, and she parked the car near the front entrance. Eric aimed the camera into the car and told her to show her license. She giggled but did so.

To appease the happy requests of those gathered on the mall, Angilia stood and held up her driver's license for them to see. More pictures were snapped of the happy occasion, and with a smile, she said she needed to park the car in the garage. Eric jumped into the back seat and kept recording her over her shoulder. She parked the car, and still smiled as she, Eric, and Matthew walked onto the patio.

"Happy birthday!" everyone shouted, which completely surprised her. Her friends were all there for a true surprise party. Everyone wanted to see her new license, so she passed it around while everyone congratulated her. Mitchell smiled as he thought how much love and happiness filled the palace. He hugged Angilia, realizing that the fifth anniversary of the shooting was just over two months away.

§§§§§

"Angilia!" Matthew's frantic scream startled Angilia out of her sleep.

She sat up and shook him awake. "Matthew? I'm right here, darling. Are you all right?"

Matthew struggled to orient himself, and he glanced around their room breathing heavily. Angilia held him, worried and scared. "Matthew, should I call your father?" He shook his head just as Eric knocked on their bedroom door.

"What's wrong? May I come in?"

"Yes, Daddy, please. I'm not sure what happened." Eric stepped in and saw Matthew sitting up, drenched in sweat, terror evident on his face. Angilia looked at her father, her fear-laden face seeking his help.

"Matthew, did you have a nightmare?" Eric asked as he sat on the edge of the bed near his son-in-law. Matthew looked at Angilia, scanning her body, and Eric knew what had happened. Angilia suddenly knew, too.

"Oh, Matthew. I'm all right, dear. I'm all right." She put her hands on his cheeks and forced him to look at her face. "See? I'm right here, in our room with you. Everything is fine, Matthew."

Matthew appeared to wake from a trance, and he pulled her close to him. Angilia felt his heart rate gradually return to normal, and she gently rubbed his back. "I'm sorry. It was a nightmare, the worst nightmare. It all just came flooding back in a movie that played in my head, and I couldn't turn it off. I couldn't make it stop."

"I know, Matthew. It happened to me almost every night until he killed himself," Eric confessed. Eric noticed Angilia's panicked, pained expression. "It hasn't happened to me since then, though, because the nightmare really did die with him. I knew that Angilia was safe after that. There was no more danger or threat." Eric held his daughter's hand and smiled at her.

"It ended for me immediately, too. I know you both saw how I changed as soon as he died. The threats were over, Daddy was safe, and everything just evaporated at that moment. The fears and nightmares stayed with me most of my life, holding me hostage. I wrote in my diary after his suicide that I was finally free."

"I thought I was, too," Matthew sadly said. "I'm not sure why this happened now."

"Matthew, you carried a heavy weight through all of that. You never left that hospital room for her entire stay except to go to the therapy room with her. You showered and ate and slept there. Doctors don't do that. You did. I knew how you felt almost right away.

"I saw it happen to her. You dealt with the effects of what happened to her. I remember sitting in that small exam room, covered in my baby's blood, terrified of what he had done to her and what you would tell me." Eric looked into Angilia's eyes. "You gave me strength, Angel. You risked your life for me. You fought for me. Despite the pain and the fear, you stayed strong for me." Eric looked into Matthew's eyes. "You gave her security and love, even if she never saw it as love then. You made her feel safe. That was so important, Matthew, more than you knew. More than I knew. She needed you to be her doctor, because she knew you and she trusted you. After all of the years of torture and mistreatment, she needed kindness and compassion. We couldn't have come through this without each other."

Matthew smiled and nodded his head. Eric hugged him, their bond formed because of the woman they both loved. They simultaneously pulled Angilia into the hug. She closed her eyes while she held onto her father and her husband. "Dear God, Thank you for your love and protection. You made sure our destinies were fulfilled. You kept Daddy and me safe when our lives were in jeopardy, and you brought Matthew back into my life when I needed him most. You, God, turned the darkness and fear into love and joy. We know that in our hearts. Thank you. Amen."

Eric and Matthew echoed her Amen, and she squeezed Matthew's hand in reassurance. "Thank you both," Matthew sighed. "Somehow the fear took hold of me again, and I let it get to me. I know not to, but I slipped. I'm all right now, really."

Eric smiled, patted Matthew's shoulder, and stood. "Try to get some sleep before the day really begins." He leaned down and kissed Angilia's cheek and waved as he left their suite. Matthew smiled as he reclined onto the soft pillows, and Angilia leaned over him for a kiss. He held her close, fell into a peaceful sleep, and let go of the horrors he had faced five years to the day earlier.

§§§§

Hours later, after they showered and dressed, Matthew and Angilia went to the first floor together. Everyone knew the significance of the date, although no one was somber. In fact, Angilia felt so light and happy that she pulled aside Matthew and Eric before they entered the dining room.

"Daddy, do you have anything important scheduled for today?" When he told her he did not, she said she had an idea. "Can we all go away for the day? I thought we could drive to the countryside for a picnic and a day of fun and friendship, just a day away from the work and duty. Can we?"

Eric's smile broadened. "That sounds wonderful, Angel. What do you think, Matthew?"

"This will be nice for all of us. Everyone's so busy all the time. We should get away for a relaxing day together."

While Antoine served the breakfast, Eric proposed Angilia's idea to his family and friends. All of them excitedly chatted about the excursion, planning the menu, and Antoine smiled and made mental note of what he needed to prepare and pack. He scurried back to the kitchen to begin preparing the food, while everyone at the table tossed out thoughts for games and other activities they could do.

By 9:00 they were all comfortably seated in Eric's largest car, with Mike at the wheel and Tony in the front passenger seat. Angilia sat between her father and Matthew, and they smiled happily as others pointed out sights along the drive and talked to each other. By 11:00, Eric told Mike to pull off the highway and down a barely-visible gravel road to a lush, green field seemingly miles from the rest of the world. Angilia gasped at the beauty, and she hurried her father out of the car.

"This is absolutely perfect, Daddy. Isn't it, Matthew?" She grabbed his hand and scurried from tree to stone to flower in childlike wonder. Blankets were spread on the ground, and some of them sat enjoying the fresh air and quiet, although several people almost immediately set up a horseshoe game nearby. Juanita and Katherine enjoyed a stroll amongst the flowers and trees.

Angilia lay back on the blanket and unexpectedly pointed to a cloud slowly drifting through the sky. "Doesn't it look like a fluffy bunny?" she asked. Eric and Matthew joined her in finding shapes within the clouds. Tony and Mike stared at the trio in amazement, recalling the picnic five years earlier when Angilia had done the same thing.

After several minutes, Eric leaned up on his elbow and asked Angilia and Matthew if they wanted to go for a walk before lunch. The three of them followed a footpath through the trees, while Susan turned on the radio back at the lunch site. After 30 minutes, Eric, Angilia, and Matthew giggled as they emerged from the trees and returned to the picnic area. Eric heard a song start playing, and he spontaneously grabbed Angilia's hand and began dancing with her. Most everyone smiled and enjoyed watching them dance to Abba's "Dancing Queen," one of Patrick's favorite 1970s songs—the same song Eric and Angilia had danced to exactly five years earlier, after their walk, moments before they were shot.

Tony instinctively reached a hand inside his jacket to grab his gun from its shoulder holster. Mike placed his hand on Tony's arm and smiled at him. Quietly, Mike said, "They're okay. They're safe. You killed that monster." Tony took a deep breath, smiled, and watched Eric and Angilia hug as they laughed and chatted with Matthew. This dance did indeed end differently.

A moment later, they all sat on the blankets while Matthew said grace, and then they filled their plates. The love, happiness, and serenity that surrounded them on March 7, 2017 pushed the nightmare of March 7, 2012 from their minds and hearts. That tragic day had made their faith and their love stronger and had joined Angilia and Matthew, and their families, for eternity.

§§§§§

"Their Royal Highnesses The Duc and Duchesse de Valmondois have just arrived at the Gathered Leaves bookstore for the signing of their first book," Winston Lohr reported for the afternoon news from outside the bookstore. "They are greeting some of the several hundred or more people lined up to purchase the book and have the Duc and Duchesse autograph their copies. The line has grown steadily since early this morning, and by now it stretches more than three city blocks.

"Demand for <u>The Little Angel</u> is strong, with online sales indicating that the book will soon hit the top of the bestseller lists around the world. Her Royal Highness wrote this charming story of a little boy who lives, plays, and does most everything a little boy typically does, all the while never revealing his real identity as an angel. How others learn his identity is quite surprising, actually. When she finished writing, she asked His Royal Highness to illustrate the story.

"His Majesty is the one who encouraged them to send the story and the art to a publisher, and now they are preparing for their first joint book signing.  The Duchesse has published several articles and books over the years, most notably before today, her collaboration on Arthur Brennan's autobiography.  She has even illustrated some of her books in the past.  Most people know that the Duc took up art when he became the Duchesse's personal physician, and how fitting that they join their talents on <u>The Little Angel</u>," Winston concluded his broadcast.

§§§§

Angilia and Matthew stepped off of Eric's private plane to the sight of thousands of people waiting to see them.  Angilia and Matthew walked toward the wire fence for an impromptu meet-and-greet, quickly followed by Susan, Daniel, and Mike.  One hour later, they arrived at their hotel in Midtown Manhattan to another crowd of well-wishers.  After greeting them for several minutes, Angilia and Matthew entered The Benjamin.

Soon they relaxed in the VIP suite.  They ordered lunch, and the five of them dined while they discussed the agenda for their three-day stay.  Angilia and Matthew had a book signing that evening in Times Square, one the following day in Queens, and a final signing on Wednesday morning.  They would leave New York City soon after the Wednesday, May 11 signing.  This was a whirlwind tour, covering four major cities around the world in two weeks.  Angilia was familiar with that from her days of touring with Tom Greenfield.

"Just get sleep when you can," she advised them, especially Matthew.  "Take advantage of our nights and the flights.  Get sleep during the flights so you don't suffer too much from desynchronosis."

"What?" Susan asked, her growing fear evident on her face.

Matthew laughed and translated the medical term.  "Jetlag."

"Right," confirmed Angilia.  "Our flight from here to Tokyo is approximately 13 hours, so we can all get some sleep then.  We'll need it," she told them.  "We even have time to rest before tonight's

153

event.  We have to be at the bookstore at 5:30, so we have at least four hours before we have to leave," she added as she looked at her watch.

Susan settled in the second bedroom of Angilia's and Matthew's suite, while Mike and Daniel went to their VIP suite next door.  Matthew smiled and led his wife to the large, soft bed.  He had vowed to take care of her, and that included making sure she had enough sleep and that she ate properly.  Angilia had a tendency to overwork, forget meals, and exhaust herself.  He made sure that did not happen.

On schedule, Mike and Susan accompanied the Royal couple to the bookstore.  They were greeted, as usual, by a very large crowd, to whom they smiled and waved as they entered.  The signing began at 6:00 and was well-orchestrated and steady.  Angilia and Matthew briefly spoke to each person as they signed copies of <u>The Little Angel</u>.  Four hours later, the manager locked the entrance to the store and the last line of patrons had their books autographed.

By the time they finished, Angilia and Matthew had signed 6,000 copies of the book.  Matthew flexed his cramped fingers and smiled.  They signed one last copy for the manager, thanked him, and returned to their suite, ready for sleep.

After their well-deserved sleep, refreshing showers, and breakfast, Angilia and Matthew prepared for their midmorning book signing.  Mike drove them and Daniel, and they arrived at 10:30 to yet another large group of screaming fans.  Matthew kept his arm around Angilia as they greeted everyone, much to the photographers' glee.

The signing began at 11:00, with a nonstop line of people waiting to meet the Duc and Duchesse and have their copies of the book autographed.  Several people asked to have their pictures taken with the Royal couple, which Angilia and Matthew always obliged.  A few fans became quite emotional when they met Angilia, and she spent a few extra moments comforting them.

Matthew smiled when several people asked if Angilia would sign their copies of <u>Heart-Glow</u> or <u>Love's Legacy</u> as well as the book.  A few people brought copies of her earlier books, including the limited edition reproduction of her handmade book <u>The Gift of You</u> and Mr. Brennan's memoir.  Matthew squeezed her hand and smiled at her.

She soon beamed when a man asked Matthew to autograph an article he had published years earlier in a major medical journal.  Matthew was taken by surprise, even more so when the man told Matthew that he was in medical school due to Matthew's influence.  Matthew had never been told that before.  "Thank you.  What area are you going into?" Matthew asked him.

"I want to be a cardiologist, too.  I begin my internship in the fall at Beth Israel Deaconess Medical Center.  I'm really looking forward to working with the other doctors and helping the patients."

"That's fabulous," Matthew smiled.  "Congratulations.  I wish you the best, I really do," he added and shook the man's hand.  Those nearby who heard the conversation applauded.  News photographers requested pictures of Matthew with the medical student, and the two men stood side by side for a few photographs.

By the time the signing ended at 3:00, Matthew and Angilia had signed over 8,000 copies of their book.  They posed for pictures with the bookstore staff, thanked them, and returned to their suite happy but exhausted.  Angilia curled up in an overstuffed chair and soon fell asleep.

Matthew covered her with a blanket and gently kissed her cheek.  He stood staring at her for several moments.  "My sleeping beauty," he softly said.  Susan smiled and went to her room, closing the door behind her to give them privacy.  Daniel likewise went with Mike to their suite, smiles lighting their faces as well.

The Wednesday morning book signing was very similar to the first two.  The signing occurred at one of Manhattan's oldest independent bookstores.  They left the store at noon, and Mike drove them to the airport, where Susan and Daniel had taken the luggage during the signing.  By 1:00, their airplane was on its way to Tokyo, Japan for their four-day stay.

Angilia was serious about the sleep and the jetlag, for they arrived in Tokyo at 3:00 on the afternoon of Thursday, May 12.

Tokyo was 12 hours ahead of New York. "I feel like I've entered a time warp," Matthew groaned. Thankfully, their first event was a book signing that evening, which gave them a few hours to acclimate themselves. Or so they thought.

As they disembarked from the plane, looking much fresher than they felt, they were stunned to see—and hear—several thousand screaming people gathered outside the airport fence and thousands more crowded in the airport building. People tried to grab for Angilia, forcing Daniel and Matthew to surround her. Mike quickly escorted Angilia and Matthew into a private manager's office where they awaited a backup of police officers to help protect the Royal couple and manage the massive crowds. Angilia offered to greet them, but Mike, Matthew, Susan, and Daniel refused to let her. The risks were too great that she or someone else could be hurt in a stampede or similar frenzy. Fans had knocked down sections of the fence outside and were trying to force themselves into the already crowded airport building.

Two hours later, they arrived at their hotel and were surrounded by police as they entered and were escorted to their suite. The hotel manager had never experienced thousands of fans rushing into the hotel lobby and screaming for a celebrity. Matthew looked out of their suite window and marveled in horror at the sight of several thousand people—mostly young women who had long hair and bangs similar to Angilia's—running toward the hotel screaming Angilia's name.

"So much for resting before the signing," Daniel said. "You two are going to be exhausted when it ends."

"Are you sure you should still go?" Susan asked. "Mike's right. That's a lot of people, and someone could get hurt in a mad rush."

"I'm not so sure it is a wise idea," Matthew agreed as he continued to watch the crowds below. "Traffic is all but stalled out there. I'm not sure how we'll even get out of here, let alone to the bookstore."

"Everything will be fine. This used to happen all the time when Tom, the guys, and I were on tour. Tom's popularity was off the charts. All it takes is a meet-and-greet with them. Maybe we can go down and talk to them, sign things, and just give them some attention. Tom always did that, and it was amazing to watch how people reacted to him. It's the same for Daddy, too. It always has been," Angilia explained and joined Matthew at the window.

"Neither Tom nor Eric are here. This isn't about them, Angilia. It's about you. These people want you, and I get that they're excited to see you, but their adrenaline is too high. They are too pumped, and if they charge at you, something terrible will happen. I'm not letting you take that chance," Matthew firmly told her.

"Matthew is right. You cannot go out there. They may not intend to hurt you, but they will. They will pull, push, grab, claw, and knock you around. It's just too dangerous. I doubt an army could get you through that crowd. There's no way you or any of us are going to a bookstore anytime soon." Mike took control of the situation.

"Susan, call the bookstore and tell them we are forced to cancel. If things calm down, we might be able to reschedule, but that is not guaranteed. Angilia's safety comes first. Daniel, call the local police and explain the situation. Tell them we need at least one dozen officers sent to the hotel to guard Angilia's suite and this floor. I am calling the hotel manager and having him restrict all access to this floor."

Angilia looked at Matthew in despair, ready to protest, and he cut her off. "It's too dangerous, darling. Nothing is worth your getting hurt. Let's just relax and ride this out. We'll see what things are like tomorrow before we make any more decisions." He took hold of her arm, led her to the sofa, and held her against him.

Mike hung up his cell phone just as Daniel informed them that 12 police officers were on the way. Mike added that no one was allowed on the floor and that the manager posted staff members at the elevators and staircases until the officers arrived. Susan explained that the bookstore manager already knew of the mob, as the news was reporting the situation live. He was understanding and sympathetic.

Angilia sadly sighed just as her cell phone rang with Eric's distinctive ring tone. "Oh, no. Daddy knows," she said as Susan handed her the phone. "Hi, Daddy. I love you. So does Matthew." Several seconds later she added, "I'm fine, really. We decided not to do the book signing this evening, so we're staying in the hotel suite." She looked desperately at Mike while she listened to her father. "I promise you, I'm fine. Here, talk to Mike. He's right here in the room with us," she said and handed her phone to Mike.

He explained the situation to Eric, listened for a moment, and answered with, "Absolutely, we will." He returned the phone to Angilia, who listened to Eric tell her what he had ordered Mike to organize and arrange.

"All right. I have never disobeyed you or argued with you. We'll do what you think is best. I'll call you soon, Daddy. I think everyone is feeling the effects of the jetlag. We'll just go to bed and get some sleep for a while. I love you, Daddy."

Angilia sighed and told Matthew, Daniel, and Susan that Eric wanted them to cancel the Japanese engagements and return home as soon as they could safely get to the airport. She had never cancelled a concert or a book signing before. "I just hate letting people down. It's not fair to them."

Matthew held her close and kissed her cheek. "I know, darling, but given the situation we really don't have a choice. Even if you don't get hurt, someone will. Someone will be knocked down and stampeded or run over by a car. Something tragic is bound to happen with this many overly-excited fans out there. You're right. Let's just try to get some sleep."

Mike insisted they all stay in the suite to not only provide a bit more security and safety for one another but so they could remain together should they need to leave quickly and suddenly for any reason. Angilia and Matthew used the bedroom, Susan the pull-out bed in the living room, Daniel the sofa, and Mike a chair he placed where he could guard the door and watch the windows simultaneously.

Angilia lay awake for hours, listening to the thousands of people screaming her name. She quietly walked to the window and peered out at the scene below of police pushing the people away from the hotel, even arresting those who fought back or tried to enter the hotel. She could not comprehend what was happening and why.

Matthew heard her sobbing and went to her. "Darling, you didn't do anything wrong. This is not your fault, Angilia. Sometimes peoples' emotions get out of control. Their love for you and excitement to see you just grew to epidemic proportions. It happens to superstars, and you, my darling wife, are a superstar. This must be what it was like for Elvis and the Beatles. I know your fans don't mean you any harm, but this many hyper-emotional people can cause harm. I read that Elvis' mother watched hordes of fans rip her son's clothes off, scratch and bruise him, bang him up, and it horrified her. If that happened to you, I would be horrified, and so would your father especially. That's why he wants us to return home."

"I know, Matthew. I just never imagined or thought anything like this would happen. I don't understand any of it. It's just a children's book."

"Angilia, this isn't about the book. This is about you. They are reacting to you, the person you are, the magnificent woman you are, the whole package. It's not just one part of you or one thing you've done. You are a huge star. Did you never realize that before?" Matthew turned her to face him. "Of course you didn't, and that is what I mean by the person you are. There is no arrogance or superiority in you ever, despite your rank, position, title, and achievements. You are humble, gracious, talented, generous, and, I might add, extremely beautiful," he said and bent his head to kiss her.

They returned to bed, where Matthew reached for her and pulled her to him. Angilia lay across his chest, comforted by the gentle, rhythmic beating of his heart. He kissed the top of her head and tenderly rubbed her back, soothing her to sleep finally. He stared at the ceiling for a long while, still hearing the screaming mass of people outside as he felt her warm breath against his skin.

Matthew was roused out of sleep by Mike knocking on the bedroom door. He opened his eyes to sunlight peeking around the edges of the curtains. He did not remember falling asleep, but he had. Angilia woke up, too, and asked what was wrong. Mike said he wanted to talk with them, so they put on their robes and sleepily walked into the living room.

"The local police have a great plan to get us safely out of the hotel and to the airport. They will land a helicopter on the helipad on the roof, and you two will be totally surrounded by two dozen police officers as we make our way to the helicopter. Once we are on board, we are safe. More officers will be at the airport to engulf you for the walk from the copter to the plane. I've already talked to Eric about this plan, and he feels it's the best way to get you out of here without getting close to the crowds down there."

Susan and Daniel were already dressed and busily making sure everything was packed and ready. Angilia's and Matthew's half-awake brains subsumed what Mike said. "When do we leave?" Angilia asked. Mike told them the helicopter would land in one hour and that everyone had to be ready to leave the hotel by then. She grabbed clean clothes from her suitcases and went for a quick shower. When she finished, Matthew did the same, and soon everything was locked in the suitcases and prepared for takeoff.

Finally, Daniel, Susan, and two hotel concierges carried the suitcases to the helicopter. Mike stayed close to Angilia and Matthew as 24 police officers surrounded the trio and guided them to the roof. When the Royal couple was safely aboard, the helicopter was locked and flew them to the airport. Everyone on the street below noticed and began running after the helicopter. Angilia was horrified, afraid people would be hit by cars or trampled. She realized that Mike and Matthew had been correct the day before. This was very dangerous.

She did not begin to relax even after the airplane was in the air headed back to Valmondois. The stress of the previous day wore on her, and she began to cry. Matthew carried her to the private bedroom in the back of the plane and laid her on the bed. She wrapped her arms across her chest, and he remembered that crying was still painful for her.  He ran to the overnight case he kept close, removed his medical bag, and quickly returned to the bedroom.

Susan was sent to find out what was wrong, and she sat next to Angilia while Matthew explained and gave Angilia a small dose of morphine for the pain.  The flight to Valmondois lasted nine and one half hours, so Matthew told Susan that he would stay with Angilia so they could get some more sleep.  Susan explained this to Mike and Daniel, and their brows furrowed.  If anything at all happened to Angilia, how would they tell Eric?

They never needed to, because 45 minutes before their plane was scheduled to land, Angilia woke up and smiled at her husband.  He smiled, too, and kissed her.  She sat up, smoothed her hair and dress, and they returned to the seats up front.  She assured everyone she was fine, and now that she was almost home, she was.

When Matthew and Mike helped her down the plane steps, she visibly relaxed.  Eric rushed to her, pulled her into a hug, and they all headed to the palace, relieved, hungry, and tired.  She actually fell asleep against her father as soon as they settled in the car, and his heart ached for what she had been through.  Susan whispered that she would help Angilia change and tuck her in bed.  Matthew agreed that sleep was the best cure to ease her troubled mind and heart.

Angilia awoke on Friday morning refreshed and relaxed.  During breakfast, they discussed whether to continue the book tour dates in London and Paris.  Angilia did not want to disappoint more people, so Eric agreed they could go so long as extra security officers accompanied them and guarded them at each public event.  Mike coordinated the security team, Susan and Daniel prepared the luggage, and they left for the 90 minute flight to London the next day.

Their three days in London were similar to those in New York City, and of course several fans were quite exuberant.  However, the news of the Tokyo cancellation made many people more aware of their behavior toward Angilia and Matthew, and the Royal couple actually felt very welcome and safe during their three days.  During their signings, they autographed a total of close to

20,000 books, pushing their first public collaboration onto the top of several bestseller lists as predicted.

Angilia called her father to reassure him while they flew from London to Paris, where they were cheered and applauded upon their arrival. The French people, in general, felt protective of Eric and Angilia, and now Matthew, since the first Valdavian King had been French himself. Besides, Angilia's albums and performances were always hugely popular in France, and she was beloved in her own right.

Long lines greeted them at all four bookstores they visited during their three-day stay, and this time they were asked by several patrons to also sign copies of wedding pictures, CDs, books, and articles. They gladly did so, and posed with fans for pictures. After the fourth and final signing, Angilia and Matthew cuddled and rested on the sofa in their hotel suite.

"Darling, what do you say we enjoy our last night in Paris? Instead of eating in our room, wouldn't it be nice to go to a Paris restaurant for dinner tonight? We can enjoy the city and some relatively alone time," Matthew suggested.

"I think that seems just dreamy, Matthew. We've barely had time to do much of anything these two weeks. Dinner out will be nice," she smiled.

"Good. We have reservations at the Ladurée for 8:00 tonight," Matthew giggled.

Matthew and Angilia left with Mike and the security team at Eric's insistence. When Matthew cleared the extra night with his father-in-law, Eric agreed so long as they were well protected. Eric did not mind them having a night in Paris for themselves, but he adamantly reinforced that the security must be with them at all times as a precaution. Matthew agreed.

Security sat at the tables surrounding their table, which meant no one interrupted their alone time, as usually happened regardless of where they were. They actually treasured the chance to be truly undisturbed as they ate and talked and held hands. Matthew had arranged a surprise treat for their desert, something reserved for lunch and Sunday tea.  Angilia's smile lit the room when the maître d'hotel served the restaurant's famous Fraisier Ladurée.  "This looks scrumptious," Angilia sighed.  "And it's my favorite color," she giggled, referring to the pink icing.

After dinner, Matthew and Angilia held hands and slowly walked along the Paris streets.  When a clock chimed midnight, they kissed and began the walk back to their hotel.  Matthew carried her over the threshold of their room, which made her laugh.  "We are still newlyweds," he justified.  "And I love carrying you.  I love you," he said as he placed her on the bed and leaned down to kiss her soft pink lips.

Matthew pulled her shoes off of her feet and tossed them on the floor.  He carelessly removed his suit jacket, tie, and shoes, unbuttoned his shirt, and bent to kiss her again.  "I love kissing you, darling.  I love holding you.  I love everything about you," he mumbled as he unbuckled his belt and slipped it off.  He lay next to her, tracing the curve of her shoulder with a finger and kissing her.

Angilia ruffled his dark blond hair, giggled in joy when he whispered he loved her, and looked deep into his soul.  "I love you, Matthew."  She kissed him, he caressed her, they whispered sweet sentiments to one another, and they embraced.

They awoke to sunbeams shining on them, both still attired in the now-rumpled clothes from the night before.  They had fallen asleep after what Matthew laughingly called their make-out session.  They ordered breakfast and ate in bed, feeding one another fresh strawberries.  They kissed, tasting the fresh juice of the fruit on each other's lips.  They lay holding each other for a couple of hours before they showered, changed, and flew home to Valmondois.

§§§§

Matthew turned over and opened his eyes before sunrise, and he beamed at the sight of Angilia lying on her back smiling at him.  He leaned across her, kissed her lips, and then said, "Happy anniversary, my darling."

"Happy anniversary, Matthew.  Our first year was just wonderful, my dear."

"Yes, and we have so many more years ahead. I love you so," he softly said as he rested his head on her chest and heard her heart beating. "You are my dream come true, Angilia, in every way." Matthew kissed her neck, then her shoulder, and finally the top of her thoracotomy scar, which was vertical down the center of her chest and had allowed him to cut her sternum apart, access her heart, remove the near-fatal bullet, and repair her aorta. "I am so grateful you are here with me, my love. My life would be wretched and meaningless without you."

Angilia saw the tears in his amber eyes, and she held him close while she kissed him. "Oh, Matthew, I am grateful we are together, too. That scar reminds me of how God brought you back into my life, as well as of how well you took care of me. That scar bound us eternally before we ever thought we would marry."

Matthew giggled. "Oh, I thought we would, darling. I loved you immediately, and I did think it. In the ambulance, as I prepped you for the surgery, I begged God not to take you. I had just seen you, found you, and I told him you would be my wife and he couldn't take you. He already knew all of that, of course, but I just kept praying." He leaned up, his face sad. "When your heart stopped, I was terrified. I've never been as terrified. I fought like I've never fought. I kept praying and fighting. I refused to let you go. I couldn't let you go. I loved you far too much already."

Matthew kissed her lips, and she placed her hands on his sides and caressed his skin. Matthew moaned, feeling his love for his wife fill his entire being, and he slid her red slinky gown down her body, as she slightly arched her back, and tossed it on the floor. He gently traced the thoracotomy scar with a finger while he kicked off his pajamas. Angilia reached up and kissed his lips as their bodies and souls came together in a tender expression of their deep, abiding love.

# CHAPTER 7

"His Majesty and Their Royal Highnesses depart on Sunday afternoon for a two-month United States tour, the largest tour ever undertaken by a King of Valdavia," Franklin Sydney reported during the Friday evening news. "The tour begins in Los Angeles, California on April 2 and ends in Indianapolis, Indiana on May 31. Anticipation is intense, as Her Royal Highness' superstardom continues to increase. Angilia fever, as it is called, appears to be a global epidemic, and in fact caused the Duc and Duchesse to cancel their Tokyo book signings last year. Security will understandably be heightened during the tour to avoid such incidents. His Majesty and Their Royal Highnesses depart the United States on the evening of May 31, and we are told in a statement from the Palais that they plan to resume their duties in Valdavia the following Monday morning."

§§§§§

Angilia dressed in blue jeans, a white shirt, and new pink cowgirl boots that Matthew had given her on her 22nd birthday that January. She wanted to spend most of Saturday with her beloved palomino Starlight. Joseph helped her with the saddle, and soon she was walking him around the paddock for his warm-up. Before she led Starlight out of the paddock for a run, she asked Joseph to get Midnight ready and warmed up, because Matthew would join her soon.

Matthew and Midnight caught up with Angilia and Starlight several acres from the stable, where Matthew saw Starlight trotting—not running—with Angilia. Angilia reigned in Starlight when she saw them, knowing her husband was still not completely comfortable on a horse. She leaned close to Matthew and met him in a kiss, which made Midnight rear up on his hind feet in excitement. Matthew looked scared, and Angilia grabbed Midnight's reigns and scolded him gently. "You know better, Midnight. Matthew isn't used to that yet."

"Yet? I don't think I'll ever be used to that," he moaned.

Angilia giggled and said, "There's nothing to it as long as you know how to lead and control the horse." She then proceeded to gently pull Starlight's reigns and guide him to stand on his hind legs. Starlight neighed in delight, Angilia smiled, and Matthew nearly fell off of Midnight in fear while reaching for her.

"Angilia! Don't you ever do that again," he nearly yelled at her. "You nearly got yourself killed and darn near gave me a heart attack."

"Oh, Matthew, I'm not in any danger with Starlight. We trust each other too much. He never has and never will hurt me. Come on," she said, turned Starlight, and galloped away. Matthew muttered under his breath and prodded Midnight into a run to catch up to them. He knew very well what she was doing, and he did not appreciate it at all.

When he did catch up, he was out of breath, and Starlight was standing under a grove of trees calmly waiting for him. "That wasn't funny, Angilia. I told you I don't trust this horse yet, and you knew I would come after you. You forced me to make him run. How could you?"

"I'm sorry, but Midnight is gentle, too. Daddy wouldn't have him if he weren't. Just don't let any horse know you're scared, because that makes the horse nervous. Let's take Midnight back to the paddock and ride Starlight together," she suggested. They did, and Matthew sat behind Angilia on the saddle, his arms firmly around his wife.

Starlight alternated between walking, trotting, and galloping them across the many acres of the palace grounds. When Matthew thought they were done, she bypassed the stable, sped by their parents who sat on the patio, and galloped onto the courtyard, where several dozen people were gathered outside the gates on the mall. They were thrilled to see Angilia and Starlight, and the horse seemed to enjoy all of the attention he received.

After a long while, Angilia thanked everyone and said she needed to get Starlight back to the stable. As she neared the patio, Matthew begged to be let off, and she laughingly obliged. Eric, Mitchell, and Katherine smiled and laughed as they watched Matthew wobble dizzily to the table, where he collapsed in a chair. "I may never ride a horse again," he mumbled as he drank a whole glass of lemonade in one gulp.

§§§§

After Sunday church, everyone returned to the palace to spend the day together. Juanita, Alejandro, Mitchell, Katherine, and Eduardo would not see Eric, Angilia, and Matthew in person for two months. Roger laughed and reminded everyone that they would see plenty of the Royal trio on television, the Internet, in newspapers, and in magazines. Katherine sobbed, which flustered Matthew. He had no idea how to calm her.

"It's almost lunch time. Matthew, why don't we take them to lunch? Just the seven of us, since we won't be here to do that sort of thing for a while," Angilia suggested. Matthew agreed, and Katherine flung herself against Angilia in tearful gratitude. Angilia kissed her father before they left, and soon Mike drove them to Angilia's favorite Italian restaurant for a relaxing, joyous lunch together.

Angilia noticed Katherine looking at her, and she smiled at her mother-in-law. "I'm sorry, dear. I don't mean to stare," she apologized to Angilia. "It's just amazing, don't you think so?" she asked Mitchell.

"Isn't what amazing?" he asked, having no idea what she meant.

"We've known Angilia for six years now, since she was 16. She's 22 now. She hasn't changed one iota, not one bit at all. How is that possible?  I've looked at the photos, too, and Eric is right. She has not changed since she was 11.  Her body has matured, of course, but her face has not changed at all.  How is that possible?"

"Good genes," Mitchell offered, while he continued to eat.

"She's an angel," Matthew softly said while he looked at his wife, his eyes once again displaying that love-struck look Mitchell had first noticed six years earlier as Matthew stood at the foot of Angilia's hospital bed watching her sleep and breathe.

Katherine saw the looks of love between her son and Angilia, and she began weeping again.  Juanita did, too.  "Yes, and her outer beauty reflects her inner beauty," Juanita sobbed.  Angilia hugged her grandmother and told her she loved Abuela, soothing her tears.  "She is as God made her.  We all are.  Oh, yes, we can change how we look with plastic surgery and so on, but for most people that is unnecessary."

"I agree," said Katherine.  "Unless there is a serious reason or need for plastic surgery, I do not find it necessary either.  God did not make unattractive people.  This is all about self-esteem, isn't it, Mitchell?  Matthew?"

"To a large degree, yes," Mitchell agreed with his wife. Matthew agreed, too, stating that a lot of one's body image was dictated by the media.

"It's actually ironic this topic came up," Angilia mentioned. "I've been working on a proposal for a new foundation focused on self-esteem, self-awareness, and self-love to help people discover their unique strengths, intelligence, and beauty.  The trend toward body modification as a quick-fix solution does not work, because it does not address the underlying issues.  Katherine, I would be honored if you would join the foundation board."

"What a fabulous way to help people.  I'd be honored to work with you, dear."

"Wonderful.  Thank you, Katherine.  When we return from the tour, you and I can work on the proposal more and present that to the community leaders to elicit more support and board members.  My goal is to take the curriculum on which I'm working into the schools, all grades and ages, and have professionals train the teachers so that all students learn to value themselves and not fall victim to this negative trend," Angilia explained.

"You never stop working, do you?" Eduardo asked with a smile, knowing the answer.

"No, she doesn't.  I try to make her stop when she's been at it for hours, but she never really stops, I don't think.  Her brain never shuts downs completely," Matthew replied with a smile and a kiss for his inspiring wife.  "My wife is such an amazing woman."

§§§§

Carol released the United States of America Tour Agenda moments after the Royal airplane began its 12-hour flight to Los Angeles.  Eric, Angilia, Matthew, Susan, Roger, Mike, and Tony discussed the agenda en route, realizing that they would remain busy throughout the two months but that time for meals and rest had been factored into the schedule to alleviate stress and exhaustion as much as possible:

Los Angeles, California:  April 2 – April 6, 2018

Chicago, Illinois:  April 7 – April 11, 2018

St. Louis, Missouri:  April 12 – April 18, 2018

San Antonio, Texas:  April 19 – April 25, 2018

Louisville, Kentucky:  April 26 – May 3, 2018

New York City, New York:  May 4 – May 10, 2018

Boston, Massachusetts:  May 11 – May 14, 2018

Nashville, Tennessee:  May 15 – May 19, 2018

Memphis, Tennessee:  May 20 – May 25, 2018

Indianapolis, Indiana:  May 26 – May 31, 2018

They discussed the public events, the transportation, the benefit concerts, as well as the so-called private time.  Eric had been on Royal tours previously, and he advised everyone that the schedules were packed, usually due to meeting members of the public who attended each event.  Walkabouts were a known favorite of Angilia's, and her father and husband warned her to not tire herself on the long tour.

Angilia smiled, kissed their cheeks, but reminded them, "I went through this with Tom a lot.  We were lucky if we were in the same city for two nights.  Usually we traveled crisscross throughout the country from one city to another, sometimes performing in the same states weeks apart.  That was a bit hectic.  A week or so in each state seems tame compared to a rock star's tour schedule."

"Maybe so, Angel, but rest and food are crucial to maintain your health and stamina on this tour.  The first tour I went on was with Father and Mother when I was 10.  We went to Australia, and spent four weeks there.  We were constantly doing something, whether an official event, meeting people, talking to the press, attending galas, you name it.  There might be one official event scheduled for a day, yet you end up spending most of the day caught up in a walkabout talking with people.  I enjoy that, too, but within reason.  No more six-hour walkabouts for you, Angilia.  Is that clear?"  Eric and Matthew remained firm on the issue, and she understood why and agreed.  Eric made sure that Susan, Roger, Daniel, Mike, and Tony understood as well.

Mike reassured them that the security team was well aware of the official agenda and would make sure that everyone was well protected.  "Tony and I have also warned them to make sure that Angilia does not overtax herself.  Every security officer is on high alert to cut short walkabouts or meet-and-greets after a reasonable time period.  We are all here to prevent the mass hysteria that happened in Tokyo, as well.  I'm telling everyone up front that if there is any hint of anything similar, the three of you will be surrounded and taken to safety."

"Thank you, Mike, Tony," Eric said.  "I know my security demands may seem strict," he continued and looked at his daughter, "but no one's safety is worth a few minutes greeting people."

Angilia assured him she understood.  "Why don't we try to get some sleep so that we are fresh and alert when our plane lands?" Everyone agreed, and it seemed like mere minutes had passed when Susan and Daniel awoke them so they could freshen and change clothes.

§§§§

Two hours later, the Royal plane landed at Los Angeles International Airport, and the crowds awaiting their arrival burst into screams when Eric, Angilia, and Matthew appeared.  The Mayor of Los Angeles welcomed them and then happily joined them on a brief walkabout to greet as many well-wishers as they could. Angilia's arms quickly filled with flowers and stuffed animals, and Susan took them and placed them in the plane.  Mike, Tony, and two dozen security officers stayed close to them, and after one hour, the Royal party, Mike, and Tony joined the Mayor in his limousine for the drive to the Mayor's home for lunch.  Eric, Angilia, and Matthew attended a gala fundraising dinner with the Mayor that evening and returned to his home after midnight.

The next morning, Angilia joined James Whitmore, Allison Jeffree, Russell Quarie, and Stephen Battingstone at a news conference to discuss the new film <u>Joan and Ralph: Victorious Love</u>. James Whitmore portrayed Sir Ralph de Monthermer, second husband of King Edward I's daughter Joan, who was portrayed by Allison Jeffree.  Russell Quarie portrayed King Edward I, and Stephen Battingstone directed the film from the script written by Joan's 19th great-granddaughter Angilia DeBruce Martineau Taylor.

News leaked before that evening's premiere that Angilia also wrote and performed the film's theme song, and despite several requests by press reporters for her to sing the song, she declined. "Today I want to focus on James, Allison, and Russell, who brought Ralph, Joan, and Edward to life brilliantly and triumphantly.  Their performances capture the essences of the real people perfectly, leaving myth and speculation aside.  Stephen understood the souls and motivations of these three people so well that he brought the story to fruition just as I had envisioned.  I am thrilled and honored to have contributed even a small part to this project," Angilia beamed.

"Her Royal Highness is the one who brought this story and these people to life. Her empathy, compassion, and love give a depth and strength to the script that I seriously doubt anyone else could have accomplished," James stated.

"I agree," added Allison. "I did some research when Her Royal Highness contacted me, and so little is in the public domain regarding Joan that I feared I would have to create a real person from scratch and imagination. Usually when I portray a real person, I have reams of information and references, but not so for Joan. Somehow, Her Royal Highness uncovered quite a lot of documents and information about Joan and Ralph during her genealogical research over the years that she came to know these two people almost intimately. That made my job as an actor much easier."

By early afternoon, the press conference ended, and Angilia thanked James, Allison, Russell, and Stephen, promising she would see them early that evening at the gala premiere of the film. Eric and Matthew had watched the press conference, and they congratulated her while they left the studio and went to the Mayor's home for lunch and rest before the excitement and activity surrounding the premiere.

That evening, the Mayor, Eric, Matthew, Roger, Daniel, and the male security officers headed by Mike and Tony, dressed in classic black tuxedos for the film premiere. Susan wore a long evening dress, styled her blonde hair in a chignon, and then helped the star of the evening with her French braid that was entwined with pearls. Angilia chose a custom made pink and gold silk gown in a modern version of Joan's medieval style, a long dress with a train, flowing sleeves, and square neckline. For a fun twist on the browband tiara that Joan wore, Angilia added a gold extender to one of her gold and pink sapphire chokers to adapt it into a tiara similar to those Joan had worn.

When the limousine pulled up at the red carpet outside the theatre, everyone fought for the first glimpse of Angilia. Security exited first, followed by the Mayor and then Eric, who received enormous cheers and demands for pictures. Eric smiled and motioned for them to wait. Matthew assisted his wife, and when she stepped out, everyone gasped and then screamed. She looked like a walking reincarnation of Joan, with strikingly similar features and long blonde hair. She, Matthew, and Eric accommodated the photographers and fans, posing for pictures as they slowly made their way across the red carpet.

Angilia soon saw James, Allison, Russell, and Stephen, and she motioned for them to join her, Matthew, Eric, and the Mayor. Questions and flash bulbs bombarded them, and the eight of them—Eric, Angilia, Matthew, the Mayor, James, Allison, Russell, and Stephen—handled the press and the fans with grace, poise, and kindness. Without the press coverage and the fans' support, the film would garner little attention, they knew. Angilia's involvement certainly generated far more interest than most films earned, and for that everyone was grateful. Angilia's proceeds were split equally between her Learning for Life Foundation and her soon-to-be-launched Light Within Foundation on which she would collaborate with Katherine.

Eric, Matthew, Susan, Roger, and Daniel had not read the script or seen the film, and as they watched, they were filled with wonder. The dialogue, the internal thoughts expressed through secret letters and diary entries, and the emotions captured therein revealed how very much Angilia did truly know and understand her ancestors. Eric even dabbed away a few tears during the film, as did many people seated in the theatre. When the film ended, James, Allison, Russell, and Stephen were applauded and stood from their seats in the Royal box, where they sat as Angilia's guests. To her surprise, James took Angilia's hand and encouraged her to stand with them. When she did, the audience rose in a standing ovation and gave her their unanimous approval.

The next morning, the newspapers and trade publications headlined the premiere, and Angilia's picture graced every one. She was now a mammoth superstar, having forged her path through music, books, academia, and now script writing. Her literary agent was already fielding offers from film producers, actors, and studios for her to write scripts for them. Rather than focus on the accolades, though, she directed the breakfast conversation toward the benefit concert she and Eric would perform that evening.

Her band and Sam joined them in the early afternoon to get the set list so that they could do the sound and light checks. Eric and Angilia would arrive one hour before start time. Eric insisted on several security officers going with them, the fear of a mob scene always in the forefront of his mind. The news reports he had watched live from Tokyo had terrified him. He refused to ever again allow any risk when his daughter was involved.

So it was that Mike, Tony, and 10 other officers rode in one of the Mayor's limousines with Eric and Angilia that evening. They arrived at the Hollywood Bowl at their scheduled time of 7:00 and entered through the private door at the rear. Sam greeted them and showed them to their private dressing rooms, although they said they wouldn't really need them. They all congregated in what was designated Angilia's dressing room, which was already filled with red roses from her celebrity friends. She smiled while she read the cards and showed them to her father. She tucked the cards in her guitar case, intending to send her friends notes of thanks the next morning.

The Mayor introduced Angilia and Eric at 8:00 sharp, and reminded everyone that the proceeds of the concert went to the Starlight Children's Foundation—Global Office. Eric and Angilia selected the charity for its tireless work with sick children and their families. Angilia noticed several of her performer friends in the audience, and she knew without being told that they had donated far more than their ticket prices to the Foundation. In fact, the concert was a rousing success, so much so that many attendees gave additional donations to the Foundation representatives who were in attendance. The total raised from that one concert was an astounding $20,245,000.

The press reported that number with glee the next morning, along with the Royals' agenda for their final day in Los Angeles. The Royal party spent the day at Disney Land with some of the Starlight Children's Foundation children and their families. Eric, Angilia, and Matthew paid, from their personal funds, for the families to join them for a day of fun at the park. Eric, Angilia, Matthew, Roger, Daniel, and Susan took the children on rides, bought them treats, and watched the puppet shows with them. All of them truly enjoyed their heartfelt day.

When their plane took off and headed toward Chicago that evening, Angilia unleashed her emotions.  Matthew held her as she cried, which in turn made Susan cry.  Finally, she fell asleep against Matthew, and he carried her to the private bedroom in the rear of the plane.  Eric sighed heavily, knowing that many of their official engagements would be just as or more emotional for all of them, particularly Angilia.  Her gentle, kind heart had a difficult time dealing with others' suffering, Eric knew, and she would struggle through many of their engagements on this tour.

§§§§

As usual, the Royal trio arrived at Chicago's O'Hare Airport to a large crowd of fans waiting to greet them.  After a one hour walkabout, the Mayor of Chicago escorted the Royal party to the main event of the afternoon.  At Lincoln Park, they were welcomed by thousands of Chicagoans, as well as people from several other states.  Angilia immediately went to a group of school children who held up a sign they had made to welcome her, Matthew, and Eric.  She thrilled them by autographing the sign so that they could display it in their classroom.  She noticed an elderly veteran, in full uniform, who sat in a wheelchair.  He reminded her of dear Mr. Brennan, and she spent several moments talking with him.

Finally, the Mayor announced their reason for visiting the park.  "Ladies, gentlemen, and children, I am deeply honored to welcome His Majesty and Their Royal Highnesses to our city, Chicago, Illinois.  That they chose our city to be among the 10 cities they visit fills me with gratitude and pride.  Today, His Majesty, the Duchesse, and the Duc will plant trees commemorating their visit.  For generations to follow, Chicagoans will admire the beauty and shade of these three trees when they visit Lincoln Park.  The plaques on display at each tree will also remind visitors to Lincoln Park of our esteemed guests and their generosity."

The mayor handed Eric a gold shovel so that he could remove a ceremonial heap of dirt prior to the planting of his tree, a sturdy oak.  Cameras flashed and people cheered when the King of Valdavia added his shovel-full of dirt to the pile nearby.  When the tree was planted, Eric was asked to pose next to it for several press photographers.

The process was repeated by Matthew, who was also handed a gold shovel. His tree was a maple, and he, too was asked to pose beside it for press pictures. He shrugged his shoulders and teasingly asked if he should hug the tree, much to everyone's amusement. Angilia dared him to, so he did, although his cheeks turned red when several pictures of the moment were taken.

Finally, Angilia was handed a gold shovel and removed some dirt from the hole already dug for her tree. Hers was a magnolia tree with pink blossoms, which Matthew commented was the ideal tree for Angilia. She admired the blossoms, and as she lowered a branch to smell their fragrance, press photographers got their pictures without having to request them.

When the tree planting ceremony was complete, Eric, Matthew, and Angilia agreed to spend a couple of hours mingling with people in the park. Angilia talked with more children, as well as with several teachers who had brought their students on a rare Saturday field trip. One class had made a large card for her, with a poem they had written inside. Eric, meanwhile, was surrounded by veterans and business leaders, all interested in his ideas on improving the economy. Valdavia, after all, was internationally known for its nonexistent poverty. In their brief time, Eric was able to provide them some valuable tips and advice. Matthew was asked for his ideas on the health care system in the United States, and he tactfully addressed peoples' concerns.

Finally, they were driven to their hotel, where they settled into their respective suites. Eric, Angilia, and Matthew ordered dinner from room service and dined together in Eric's suite. Susan ate alone in her suite, and then enjoyed a long, hot bubble bath. Roger and Daniel decided to go to a local restaurant for dinner. Security ate dinner in their shared suites, while two guards stood constantly at the doors to the Royal Family's suites.

Angilia and Matthew went to their suite after midnight, took quick showers, and then wrote in their diaries before cuddling in bed. Their alarm woke them at 6:00, and they showered, dressed for the morning church service, and were joined at 7:00 in their suite by Eric, Susan, Daniel, and Roger. Roger ordered breakfast for them, which was soon delivered and served.  Eric said grace and they joined hands and bowed their heads.

They enjoyed one another's company in the relaxed atmosphere and privacy.  When they and six security officers arrived at the First United Methodist Church at the Chicago Temple for the 8:30 worship service, they were warmly greeted by the Senior Pastor.  They refused special seats, and enjoyed the service from near the back of the pews.  After the service, they spoke with the parishioners for nearly two hours before Eric noticed that Angilia lifted her right foot off of the ground for several minutes at a time; her knee hurt.  He thanked everyone for welcoming them to their church, and soon they were in the car deciding on a restaurant for lunch.

The next afternoon, Sam and the band once more joined Eric and Angilia for a benefit concert at Millennium Park.  The nearly three-hour set brought the sell-out crowd to its feet several times, required four curtain calls, and raised $1,749,253 for a cause close to their hearts—helping children who had been abused, neglected, or abandoned by their parents.  One hundred percent of the amount raised was presented to the Chief Executive Officer of SOS Children's Villages Illinois.  Two of the children who were placed with foster families through SOS accompanied the CEO to the stage.  A young boy kissed Angilia's cheek and gave her one dozen red roses.  A little girl hugged Eric and handed him a lapel pin of the SOS logo.  Angilia quietly slipped a personal check in the amount of €500,000 into the surprised CEO's hand.

Angilia held the roses close to her during the ride to the hotel and kept them on the nightstand while she cried herself to sleep in Matthew's arms.  He had anticipated this reaction, for she felt others' suffering far more deeply than she felt her own.  Matthew silently prayed, asking God to soothe Angilia's pain.  She so wanted everyone's life to be as love-filled and joyous as hers, yet she had not yet come to accept that this was an impossible goal even for an angel who was a Princess.

The next day, Eric, Angilia, and Matthew visited the Art Institute of Chicago in the morning, where they mingled with other visitors and staff for a couple of hours.  At 11:00, an official ceremony began.  A painting of Matthew's, which he had been asked to donate, was unveiled.  Angilia charmed everyone by taking pictures of her husband and his painting with her cell phone camera.

"Thank you all for attending today," Matthew said to the large crowd.  "I am deeply honored and humbled to have one of my paintings displayed in the Art Institute of Chicago, along with so many astounding works by incredibly talented artists.  I never imagined this happening, and I am proud that this is the first museum to display one of my paintings.  Thank you."

Matthew was the center of attention, much to Angilia's immense delight.  She held her father's arm in her elation, her huge smile warming his heart.  While press reporters and photographers surrounded Matthew, she drank in every detail, wanting to capture it in words in her diary entry for that day.  In several years, their son would read about this momentous occasion, as would their grandchildren and great-grandchildren.

Eric, Angilia, and Matthew, along with Susan, Roger, Mike, Tony, and six other security officers, ate lunch at a nearby restaurant before driving to The Museum of Science and Industry for their afternoon engagement.  They were given a tour of the museum, during which they joined a group children in some hands-on activities.  Angilia was asked to autograph the dinosaur puppet she helped one young boy complete.  Eric and Matthew smiled as they watched her interact with the children, and both thought she would be an incredible mother in the foreseeable future.

Eric, Angilia, and Matthew were there to officially open a new exhibit focused on the castles of Scotland.  Everyone knew that Angilia had provided vital information about Turnberry Castle and Robert the Bruce's life there to the historians and artisans who recreated the castles in scale models for the exhibits, along with slides and films.  She even recorded the audio guide for the Turnberry Castle display.  Several teachers had brought their classes to the opening of the exhibit, and Angilia was once more engulfed in a sea of children as they peppered her with questions.  She patiently answered each question, including one asked by a first-grader: "How does it feel to be a real princess and live in a real castle?"

"I love my life and my family very much.  I am very blessed to be given the life and the family I have.  Can you guess my most favorite thing about my job?"  The little girl shook her head.  "I truly adore meeting you, all of you, as well as children everywhere I go.  You make me so happy, you really do."  The little girl suddenly burst into tears and flung herself against Angilia, who knelt down to hug and comfort her.  Eric smiled in happiness, yet again appreciating how much his daughter and heir—the future Queen of Valdavia—cared about people and put their needs above her own.  He also knew how deeply such moments affected her sensitive soul.

The following day, their last in Illinois, was perhaps the most emotional thus far for Angilia.  The Royal party arrived in Springfield early that morning to begin their day in the Land of Lincoln.  First on their agenda was a tour of The Lincoln-Herndon Law Offices on the corner of 6th and Adams Streets.  Angilia smiled upon seeing the recreation of Abraham Lincoln's organized chaos upon the desk and table.  She pictured him sitting stooped over legal briefs, just as his tall frame had stooped over the book of poems so long ago.

Next, the Royal party received a guided tour of the only home Lincoln ever owned, where he and his family lived from 1844 until his election moved them to Washington, D.C. in 1861.  Tears welled in her eyes as she walked through his home.  She leaned against Matthew when they entered the bedroom Abraham and Mary had shared.  Mary's love for and subsequent intense grief for her husband never failed to touch Angilia.  Robert Todd Lincoln's room also affected her, for she well understood Robert's admiration of his father.  Tad's bed made her smile; he was such an active boy, much like Uncle Patrick.  Willie's space, though, made her heart ache, for he died at the age of 11 soon after the family moved into the White House.  She well knew how much Abraham had grieved Willie, but as she quietly said to him while she stood there, the grief ended when the family reunited in Heaven.

Angilia knew what followed their lunch, and she asked if she could have a few minutes alone to pray.  She stood on the front porch, bowed her head, and thanked God for allowing her to meet this extraordinary, brave man in the Unborn Children Sphere.  She also asked for strength and courage to uphold Abraham's wish that she never think of him with sadness.

Angilia nibbled at her lunch, and neither Eric nor Matthew forced the issue. They knew that the day was both joyous and poignant for her. She was the only living person who had met President Lincoln—or at least the only one who remembered the meeting, Matthew thought. Matthew commented to her that he wished he did remember, more for Angilia's sake than his. She kissed his cheek in gratitude.

Matthew and Mike walked to a nearby flower shop with Angilia, where she bought one dozen blue tulips—Lincoln's favorite flower in his favorite color. She asked the florist to tie them with a blue ribbon. Angilia wrote a message on a card which she nestled into the flowers. She also bought four white roses. Matthew held her hand in the car, and put his arm around her when they stepped out and were greeted by a soldier in dress uniform. Sergeant Connors walked alongside Angilia to the President's tomb and escorted the Royal party inside. Matthew felt his wife breathe deeply, and he pulled her a bit closer.

Angilia paused in front of a large statue of Lincoln seated in a chair. She smiled as she recalled his gentle face. "He was so much grander than this often cruel world. His soul was too huge and compassionate. He knew he would suffer and pay the ultimate price for upholding his beliefs and doing what was right and best. He knew, and yet he faced his destiny with courage. '*Now he belongs to the ages*,'" she softly quoted Edwin M. Stanton, Lincoln's friend and Secretary of War. Sergeant Connors smiled, knowing what the Duchesse would see in moments.

When she nodded that she was ready, Sergeant Connors linked his arm with hers and walked with her down a marble corridor and into the room where Abraham, Mary, Eddie, Willie, and Tad were buried. Angilia stopped at Mary's crypt first, stared at the name and dates for several minutes, and then bowed her head in prayer. She bent to place a white rose beneath the crypt, and then stepped to the crypt which contained the bodies of sons Eddie and Willie. Dear, sweet, beloved Willie. Tears fell from her eyes as she gingerly touched his carved name. Eric put his arms around her, himself empathizing with the President's pain upon young Willie's death. He and Angilia prayed together, and she handed one white rose to her father. Together, they placed the roses for Eddie and Willie. The third of the four Lincoln sons buried there was Tad, and she likewise stood before his crypt in prayer before laying a white rose beneath his crypt.

Angilia took a deep breath and reached for Matthew's hand. She turned, saw Lincoln's sarcophagus, and felt her admiration and love for this man swell in her chest. She, Matthew, and Eric stood before the massive sarcophagus, and the rest of the Royal party stood behind them. Everyone felt the solemnity of the occasion, and they, too, bowed their heads when Angilia softly spoke a prayer. "Dear God, Thank you for blessing the world with the character, conviction, and courage of Abraham Lincoln. Few people do so much for the good and betterment of all people, good that changed the world forever. Despite the naysayers and the threats, Abraham never turned his back on what was right. He placed others before himself and stood strong in his beliefs. For that, he was murdered and taken from the world. We know that he resides with you, God, and with his family, for all eternity. His suffering ended long ago, and that knowledge gives me such comfort. I stand before the resting place of his earthly remains today so thankful for his life and so grateful for his gifts to me. I think of Abraham as he wanted, with love and tenderness. Amen." Matthew squeezed her hand, amazed at her fortitude and strength. He continued to hold her hand while she knelt and propped the blue tulips against the sarcophagus.

Sergeant Connors saluted the President's sarcophagus. "Your Royal Highness, you quoted Mr. Stanton earlier. Have you seen photographs of this tomb before?" Angilia told him she had not, and he smiled at her. "Look above the sarcophagus. Engraved there is Mr. Stanton's tribute to President Lincoln." Angilia caught her breath when she saw the very words she had spoken engraved into the black marble between two gold laurel wreaths. "I will leave you alone here for a while," he told her as he bowed and left the tomb.

Almost one hour later, Eric and Matthew stepped out with Angilia between them and the rest of their party following. Sergeant

Connors greeted them once more and introduced them to the President of the Lincoln Memorial Association. She spoke with the Royal party for a long while as they stood outside the tomb. "Your Royal Highness, we are so honored to welcome you here today. Your respect and love for President Lincoln inspires so many people. So very many people around the world admire, respect, and love Abraham Lincoln, yet few seem to have the almost personal connection that you have with him. I am pleased to offer to you this certificate naming you a lifetime member of the Lincoln Memorial Association and an honorary member of our Board." She handed the certificate to Angilia, who smiled and thanked her for the distinction.

"I am the one who is truly honored to accept this. Abraham Lincoln remains a very integral and special person in my life, and I will do whatever I can to help the Association. Thank you." Angilia felt a waft of warm air blow by her, ruffling her hair. She knew it was Abraham's spirit letting her know that he, too, remembered their long-ago meeting. He had come to thank her for her visit.

§§§§

The Royal superstars arrived in St. Louis, Missouri on Thursday, April 12 to a very rousing welcome. Their first scheduled event was a tour of the famous Gateway Arch, during which the Mayor joined them. Thousands of fans gathered to see and to greet Eric, Angilia, and Matthew, and the trio mingled with people for two hours before the Mayor escorted them to a lunch at his office.

The highlight of the week for most people, particularly Eric, occurred the following day. At the lovely Jewel Box—the St. Louis Floral Conservatory—they received a tour and then the world debut of a new hybrid rose. The variegated pink and white rose was a surprise to them. "It reminds me of my wedding dress," Angilia enthused.

The horticulturist who developed the rose bowed in delight. "Your Royal Highnesses, Your Majesty, we at the Jewel Box are deeply honored to present the crown jewel in our conservatory, the Angilia Rose." Everyone gasped while press photographers took hundreds of pictures of the rose, asking Angilia to pose with her namesake flower. Eric, Angilia, and Matthew were given Angilia Rose bushes, which Eric said would have a place of honor on the palace grounds.

Matthew was honored on Saturday with another painting donated, this time to the St. Louis Art Museum. The painting was inspired by his wife, depicting a young girl who looked like Angilia riding a golden horse over white fluffy clouds. She wore a long white dress which billowed in the wind, as did her long hair and the horse's mane and tail. Angel Angilia. While no one outside the Royal party took Matthew's portrayal of Angilia literally, everyone was charmed that the Duc saw his wife as an angel.

The next day began with morning services at St. Louis Abbey, during which the Royal Family relished the camaraderie and warmth of the congregation. They enjoyed lunch at a nearby diner and then went to Forest Park for the ceremonial tree plantings. They spent most of the afternoon in the park mingling with everyone.

Academics filled Monday and Tuesday. On Monday, they went to Washington University in St. Louis, where the Royal trio visited three different classes simultaneously. Eric went to a government class, spoke to the students, and answered their questions about creating laws, running an entire country, and most of all how he maintained Valdavia's nonexistent poverty levels. Matthew visited a pre-med science class, and walked around the laboratory, talked with students, helped them with their work, and answered their questions about medical school, internships, and trauma patients. Angilia chose to attend a literature class, and she was thrilled by the poem on the day's agenda: Shelley's "Ode to the West Wind." She was asked to give the lecture, which surprised her, but she gladly did so, realizing as she did that part of her did miss teaching. Students peppered her with questions about the poem and even about her own writing. When she, Eric, and Matthew reconvened at the end of the visit, they excitedly shared their experiences, even through a late lunch.

Tuesday, the three of them went to Clay Elementary School in Hyde Park. Throughout the day, they visited seven different classrooms and ate lunch with teachers and students in the school cafeteria. "You know, this is my very first school lunch," Angilia giggled. Eric laughed, too, telling her that was one experience she was better off without. At each classroom, Angilia read to students, while Eric told them about his job, and Matthew shared what it was like going from a very private life to a very public life.

Their time in St. Louis concluded with a benefit concert at The Sheldon concert hall. Eric and Angilia chose the Guardian Angel Settlement Association as the beneficiary of the concert proceeds. Guardian Angel's programs to assist those struggling with poverty touched their hearts. Guardian Angel received a total of $2,592,348, which earned Eric and Angilia the eternal love and gratitude of thousands of people.

§§§§

The Royal party arrived in San Antonio, Texas the following day, Thursday, April 19. Their seven days there were busy, from the usual tree plantings in Crockett Park, a day-long visit to the San Antonio Children's Museum, a day split between the San Antonio Missions National Historic Park and The Alamo, church at All Saints Anglican Church of San Antonio, and a day-long appearance at Central Library of San Antonio Public Library, where they donated books and held a book signing. The proceeds of the book signing were donated to the San Antonio Library Foundation.

The benefit concert Tuesday evening at Majestic Theatre was standing room only. After seven curtain calls, the manager announced that $3,167,903 was donated to Morgan's Wonderland. Angilia felt blessed by and grateful for everyone's generosity. She chose Morgan's Wonderland because it resonated with her so deeply. The amusement park was designed specifically for people of all ages who have cognitive and physical needs.

In fact, their final day in San Antonio was spent at Morgan's Wonderland. Every member of the Royal party joined park patrons on the specially-designed rides. Angilia thrilled at the smiles and laughter of those who rode the carousel with her. She appreciated that wheelchairs could be strapped into custom seats so that everyone could enjoy the pleasure of a carousel ride. The day was joyous and, yes, enlightening for all of them. The everyday tasks that so many people took for granted were impossible for most of those with whom they spent the day.  The Royal party members truly realized how blessed they were.

§§§§

The next city on the Royal Tour was Louisville, Kentucky.  Eric's, Angilia's, and Matthew's first task was the tree planting in Cherokee Park, where photographers begged in vain for Matthew and Angilia to pose for pictures on Lover's Lane.  The next day, they went to the Kentucky Museum of Art and Craft, where Eric, Angilia, and Matthew joined local artisans and made one-of-a-kind pieces of art and donated them to be sold in the gift shop.  They sold immediately, at $2500 each, which supported the Museum's programs.

The benefit concert on Saturday, April 28 at The Kentucky Center was another sell-out event.  A total of $6,439,721 was raised for the charity of choice, Blessings in a Backpack.  The organization's work to make sure that all students enrolled in the free lunch program have weekend lunches touched Eric's and Angilia's compassionate souls.  She noticed some of her famous friends in the audience and knew they had donated far more than their ticket prices, as had several attendees.  During Sunday morning service at Fern Creek Christian Church, Angilia once more thanked God for his abundant blessings.

The last day of April found the Royal trio at the Speed Art Museum for a tour.  Matthew and Angilia joined a group of elementary school students who were on a field trip and involved in a hands-on activity.  The Duc and Duchesse admired the children's pictures and were asked to draw their own pictures, too.  To their surprise, they were asked to sign and donate their drawings to the museum. They gladly did so, even though they had not expected the request.

The next two days, Angilia knew, would be the most emotionally draining for her.  During breakfast on Tuesday, she prayed for strength.  "Daddy, Matthew, today and tomorrow will be very difficult for me.  I've asked God to give me strength and

185

courage, but I need your help, too." Eric pulled her close and told her that he and Matthew would remain beside her and support her.

She needed their support as they visited patients at the University of Louisville Hospital that morning. Several terminally ill patients were buoyed by the visits and asked Angilia to pray for and with them. Angilia clasped Matthew's hand each time she bowed her head to offer prayers for each patient who asked. The patients knew they were dying, and were trying to alleviate their fears and anxieties. Angilia spoke with them about the glories of Heaven and eternal life, which brought smiles to many patients.

When they left the hospital, Eric and Matthew insisted she eat lunch. She needed fortitude and stamina to endure the afternoon at the Kosair Children's Hospital. They met children whose conditions were not critical or life-threatening first, for which Eric was relieved. Angilia smiled through the visits, even playing board games or dolls with many of the children. One girl was drawing pictures with her crayons, so Angilia and Matthew joined her and drew pictures. She asked if she could keep their drawings, and they personally autographed them for her.

Angilia asked everyone to pray with her before they were taken to meet the terminally-ill children. Eric and Matthew held her hands as they were introduced to a dark-haired, brown-eyed girl dying of leukemia. "Hello, King Eric. My name is Mary," the girl smiled. Angilia felt her father tremble and tense. She knew how much Mary reminded him of his cherished Marisol. She put her arm around his waist, giving him needed support and strength. This time, Eric sat and talked with Mary, read to her, and at her request prayed with her. Angilia's heart ached for her beloved father, as the unexpected confrontation with his memories punched him to the core.

Finally, their emotionally exhausting visit ended and they quietly returned to their hotel. Matthew understood when Angilia explained that she needed to be alone with her father. She changed into slacks and t-shirt, knocked on the door which joined their two suites, and greeted him with a hug when he opened the door. They spent the entire evening alone talking about Marisol. For the first time, Eric shared his pain with his daughter.

"I've told you before that we all knew Marisol's leukemia was very aggressive and would eventually take her from us. I watched her as she came to accept that in her heart. You were with her by then, and you were her life's purpose. She said that every day. I watched her write that letter to you, the one she stuck in that book of poems she asked me to give to you. Until I read it aloud to you, I never knew what she wrote. She was strong, spiritually and mentally.

"She did not want to die and leave us, but she accepted that she would. We all had to accept that. It wasn't actually her death that hurt me the most, Angilia. Her years of pain and torture hurt me far more, because there was nothing I could do to stop her suffering. Nothing. I had to stay strong for her and hold her as she cried and writhed in pain.

"So many times I went to the chapel or locked myself in my office and just cried. I never wanted to burden Marisol with my pain, when her own pain was incomprehensibly wretched. I couldn't do that to her. I stayed beside her the last week, never leaving her side. I held her as we lay in that hospital bed. She was dying. I knew it. So did Abuelo, Abuela, and Mother. Marisol knew.

"That last day, October 23, 1995, Abuela, Abuelo, and Mother visited, but they said their good-byes and left us alone together. I lay beside Marisol, my arms around her, and I kissed her. She smiled, though her brown eyes were filled with pain and exhaustion. She told me she loved me, and she lifted her hand to stroke my cheek, as she often did. She kissed my lips and smiled weakly. "Tell Angilia that I love her more than life," she said. I promised her I would, and I kissed her and then held her close to me. I felt her stop breathing. Moments later, I no longer felt her heart beating against me. Marisol died in my arms.

"The machines were immediately activated, and I heard your heartbeat on the monitor. You were so alive, just as Marisol wanted. She never wanted her death to end your life, Angilia. Never. She lived and she fought for you. I love her so very much, Angilia. So very much."

Angilia held her father as he cried, never truly knowing how difficult and painful her mother's illness had been for him. The sorrow in his eyes and his voice stabbed her heart. She cried with him. They prayed together, and then held one another as they leaned back on the couch. When Matthew went to tell them dinner was ready, he found them asleep on the couch, still holding one another, Eric's head on her shoulder. Matthew's heart broke when he noticed that they had been crying. He got a blanket, covered them, and softly kissed his Angilia.

Thankfully, the next day was not filled with the expected somberness. Rather, their day at the Robley Rex VA Medical Center proved joyful. Angilia, Eric, and Matthew were impressed with the prevailing positive attitudes of those who had made major sacrifices for their country and fellow Americans.

The following day, their last in Louisville, was far more carefree. They spent half of Thursday at Churchill Downs. The world-famous Kentucky Derby was in three days, and trainers worked with their horses. Angilia enjoyed meeting the horses, and she was even allowed to ride a stallion around the race track. Matthew and Eric took several pictures of her, as did press photographers.

§§§§§

After a relaxing dinner and sleep on the plane, the Royal party arrived at the sixth city on the morning of Friday, May 4. New York City's residents welcomed them enthusiastically, beginning with the ceremonial tree plantings in Central Park. On Saturday, they toured both the Statue of Liberty and Ellis Island. Sunday's church service at the historic St. Patrick's Cathedral soothed their souls after the heartrending week. On Monday, Matthew donated a painting to the Metropolitan Museum of Art. Tuesday's event was a tour of Juilliard School of Performing Arts, during which Angilia offered praise and advice to many music students. One student asked her to sing a song he had written, and she happily did so. The next day, they went to two schools, Public School 67 and Dream Charter School, where they read to and spoke with the students. On their last evening, Thursday, May 10, Eric's and Angilia's benefit concert took place at Carnegie Hall. The Children's Aid Society received the $12,642,913 proceeds.

$$\$\$\$\$\$$

Their four-day visit to Boston, Massachusetts proved as poignant as they anticipated. The fifth anniversary of the Boston Marathon bombings had recently occurred and was at the forefront of everyone's mind and heart. Near the location of the bombings, Eric, Angilia, and Matthew placed wreaths and prayed. Nearby, they planted three trees and were greeted by victims of the bombings, their families, and hundreds of grateful Bostonians. They all knew that 100 percent of the Saturday concert proceeds went into a fund established by Eric, Angilia, and Matthew. The concert at the Boston Opera House raised $15,784,351 for the fund, which would be used to assist the victims of the bombings and their families. Five years later, some still faced medical bills and treatments as well as other financial needs. Angilia led the congregation in a prayer for all Bostonians during service at the Old North Church. On their final day, they met and spent time with patients at both Boston Children's Hospital and Massachusetts General Hospital.

$$\$\$\$\$\$$

The overwhelming emotions of the past several days affected everyone. Eric slept throughout the night, as did Angilia and Matthew; all were drained and exhausted. Their plane departed early the next morning for Nashville, Tennessee. After greeting well-wishers at the airport, they were driven to The Parthenon, where they toured the art museum there and planted commemorative trees nearby. The second day the trio visited Vanderbilt University to meet with some classes, and then the Vanderbilt University Medical Center and its level I trauma center.

On day three, they received a tour of the Country Music Hall of Fame and Museum, during which Angilia—at the Museum's request—donated the first stage outfit she wore when she was six years old and performed with Tom Greenfield. She posed for several pictures next to the display and signed autographs for several dozen fans who came for the momentous event. Eric became noticeably teary-eyed when he looked at the small outfit on display next to one of Tom's stage outfits.  How very young yet mature his little girl had been in 2002.

Their benefit concert the following evening at the Tennessee Performing Arts Center was another standing-room-only sell-out. Angilia, Eric, and Matthew selected Vanderbilt Children's Hospital as recipient of the concert's $8,974,109 proceeds.  The hospital's work with ill children and their families touched them deeply.

Eric and Angilia performed a second time in Nashville on Saturday night at the iconic Grand Ole Opry.  Angilia had performed there several times with Tom, and she recalled those performances as she and her father sang their solo and duet songs. The Opry audience was enthusiastic and excited to welcome Angilia back and Eric for the first time.  They received six curtain calls before they sincerely thanked everyone and prepared for their early morning departure.

§§§§§

The Royal party dressed for Sunday morning church on the plane, since they were driven from the airport to Mason Temple in Memphis, Tennessee.  Angilia had requested that church, for Dr. Martin Luther King, Jr. made his famous "I've Been to the Mountaintop" sermon there on April 3, 1968—the day before his assassination.  She left the service with a full heart and peace.

On Monday, the Royal Family toured the Civil Rights Museum, including the Lorraine Motel where Dr. King was killed. Angilia placed one dozen yellow roses outside Dr. King's motel room, near the place where he fell.  Other tourists greeted the Valdavian King, Duchesse, and Duc at the Museum, and they talked for quite a while about Dr. King and his work.  "Dr. King, like President Lincoln, is American yet belongs to the world and to history.  Both are much loved and revered in Valdavia.  Their influence is stronger than ever," Angilia mentioned.

They ate dinner at a nearby restaurant and Tuesday morning breakfast in their hotel rooms.  Angilia, Sam, and the band met up at the world-renowned Sun Studios on Beale Street.  Fans were selected through raffle tickets to form a small audience inside the studio to watch Angilia and the band perform live in the place where

Rock and Roll originated. Eric and Matthew had prime seats, of course, and as they cheered with the rest of the audience, the performance was videotaped for the Sun Studio web site.

After the performance, Angilia and Eric signed copies of their CDs for fans. Matthew found himself taking pictures of people with his wife and father-in-law, which he enjoyed doing. Four hours later, they finished and went for a late lunch at a Beale Street diner. Angilia then insisted that her father buy a classic pink and black shirt at Lansky Brothers shop; he needed it for their Friday night concert, she smiled. She somehow convinced Matthew that a pink shirt suited him perfectly, although he had never worn anything pink before. "Elvis did, and he looked amazing," she winked.

Wednesday was spent at the Memphis Rock N' Soul Museum, where another of Angilia's stage outfits made its debut. A mannequin displayed a white ruffled dress Angilia wore the first time she performed in Memphis with Tom. She was 10 at the time, still so very young, as most fans seemed to realize simultaneously. Angilia always seemed so poised and mature for her age that people tended to forget how young she was when her music career began. Also in the display case was an autographed copy of her first CD recorded when she was six years old. She had written all but one of the songs on the album; the twelfth song was an older of Tom's songs, the one he had first heard her singing when he walked by the palace that fateful day when they met and began working together.

Matthew wore his new pink shirt on Thursday, which delighted Angilia and made Eric bite back his giggle. Mike drove everyone to Graceland that morning, where they spent most of the day touring the mansion, grounds, airplane, and car museum. They were greeted by the CEO of Elvis Presley Enterprises and given a tour by him. Angilia and Eric were instantly recognized by fans on the tour, and both became a hotbed of attention.

Angilia sobbed when they watched home movies of Elvis with his mother and later with his daughter. Despite the unprecedented fame he experienced, Elvis remained devoted to family, God, and home. His video performance of "If I Can

Dream" affected her, especially after Sunday's and Monday's emphasis on Dr. King.

Angilia enjoyed meeting the horses and petting them, especially the golden palomino that descended from Elvis' much-loved Rising Sun.  The horse trainer welcomed her and mentioned that the horses needed their exercise soon.  She invited Angilia to ride the palomino for a while, which thrilled her.

The most poignant moment came when they entered the beautiful Meditation Garden, where the Presley family members were buried.  Susan handed Angilia the white roses for the graves of Elvis' parents and grandmother, and the marker for his twin brother.  On Elvis' grave she placed one dozen blue carnations, his birth month flower in his favorite color.  She bowed her head in prayer, and dozens of fans did likewise as they gathered around her.

Elvis' private airplane outshone Eric's private planes, with the velvet décor and solid gold fixtures in the private suite bathroom.  "Wow, we need to update your planes, man.  You're a rock star now, you know.  You need to travel like one," Roger teased his friend.

At the car museum, Angilia squealed with glee when she finally saw the famous 1955 pink Cadillac.  She was asked to pose near it for pictures, and Eric and Matthew took plenty of pictures.  "I have to get a pink car," she said, which made her father and husband smile.

They enjoyed their day at Graceland.  Elvis inspired the choice of beneficiary for the Friday night concert proceeds—St. Jude Children's Research Hospital, one of his charities.  Eric's and Angilia's concert at The Orpheum, where Elvis had performed, drew a sell-out crowd that included many singers and actors.  St. Jude's received a total of $18,673,277 between ticket proceeds and donations.  The press declared that the real-life Princess did the King of Rock and Roll proud.

§§§§

The Royal airplane landed at Indianapolis International Airport in Indiana on the morning of Saturday, May 26 for the final six days of the United States Tour. Eric, Angilia, and Matthew were greeted not only by screaming Hoosiers, but by those who came to see the Indianapolis 500. After greeting well-wishers for nearly two hours, they went to the Hall of Fame Museum in Speedway.

At the Museum, they saw race cars, drivers' suits, and sundry mementoes from the 500 race's auspicious 107 year history. Several former winners of the Indianapolis 500 race came and talked with the Royal Family. One of them encouraged Angilia to sit in the number 14 car that won the 1977 race with A. J. Foyt at the helm, making Foyt the first four-time winner of the prestigious race.

Everyone looked forward to the next day's race. Eric, Angilia, and Matthew attended early morning church services and then changed clothes for the day at the Indianapolis Motor Speedway. Angilia sang a flawless a cappella rendition of the national anthem, "The Star-Spangled Banner," which brought many in the stands to tears. Eric drove the pace car which officially began the race, much to everyone's excitement. His handsome, youthful looks never went unnoticed. The Royal party enjoyed the race tremendously, despite the tense moments and accidents.

Eric, Angilia, and Matthew also enjoyed Monday's ceremonial tree plantings in Christian Park, which was attended not only by the usual crowd but by the teachers, staff, and students of the adjacent public school. After the tree plantings, they mingled with well-wishers for an hour and then went into Christian Park School 82, an elementary school, where they visited several classrooms. Angilia always adored meeting children. She read to them, Matthew drew with them, and Eric told them what it meant to be a real King.

They spent Tuesday morning with visitors at the Indianapolis Children's Museum, where they observed the 26.5 feet tall water clock mark the hour. That afternoon, they went to exhibits at The Eiteljog Museum of American Indians and Western Art, sitting in on several with school groups.

Children remained the focus on Wednesday evening, for the selected charity for the concert proceeds was Camptown, which builds confidence, hope, and character through nature programs and outdoor adventures. Angilia's and Eric's concert at The Murat Theatre drew another sell-out, standing-room-only crowd and raised a total of $2,559,361 for Camptown. After a two-hour autograph session following the concert, they spent several minutes with Sam and the band. "Thank you all for your support and friendship. You know I love you each," Angilia said as she hugged and kissed the five men. They commented how much this reminded them of their tours with Tom and promised to visit Valmondois soon.

Eric, Angilia, and Matthew flew home to Valmondois, arriving on Friday, June 1. When they stepped off the plane, they were greeted by their friends and neighbors, which elated them tremendously. Katherine, Mitchell, Eduardo, Alejandro, and Juanita stood by a Rolls Royce awaiting them, and Angilia rushed to her beloved grandparents as Eric smiled. "Oh, I've missed you so very much, Abuelo and Abuela. I love you both."

$$\mathcal{SSSS}$$

Angilia kissed her grandfather's cheek as he sat reading on the sitting room balcony. "I love you, Abuelo. Did you know that?" she smilingly asked him.

He smiled, pulled her onto his lap, and said, "I did, mi nieta. I have always known. I hope you know how much I love you, Angel," he said and kissed her cheek.

"I do. Abuelo, everyone else is off doing their own thing. Would you like to go to the museum with me for the morning? I want to look at the family portraits," she said, her head tilted in that engaging way she had which charmed everyone.

"I can never say no to you, mi nieta. Are you going to drive me in that new pink car of yours?" he winked. She giggled and said she was, and soon she parked her very familiar car at the museum. Eric did buy her a vintage pink car, much to her utter glee. Angilia held her grandfather's arm and they slowly walked into the museum and approached the Royal Portrait Gallery.

When they entered, Alejandro's family and friends shouted "Happy birthday!" He had rarely been so surprised.

"You didn't really think we'd forget your birthday, did you, Abuelo?" Angilia teased him and reached up to kiss his cheek.

"I did wonder, to tell the truth," he admitted. "You all really did surprise me. But why here, at the museum?"

Muriel Laperen stepped forward and curtseyed to Alejandro. "Mr. Martínez, I am deeply honored to welcome you today for our special gift to you and to Valdavia. Would you like to join your family in the front of the room?"

Angilia and Alejandro followed Ms. Laperen to the Royal Family near the podium, where Eric truly surprised his father-in-law. "Papa, everyone is gathered to celebrate your birthday, your 90th birthday, on this lovely August 30. We even have cake and presents waiting for you," Eric motioned toward a table nearby. "I am so very proud to ask Eduardo to unveil this wondrous portrait, which our precious Angilia worked on in secret, as she is often wont to do. Eduardo, please do the honors."

Eduardo beamed and pulled the gold cord to reveal a portrait of Alejandro. Everyone cheered, happy to see this charming, beloved gentleman's image in the Royal Portrait Gallery, where portraits of his daughter, son-in-law, and granddaughter hung. Juanita cried and hugged her husband for several moments. Katherine found the tears contagious, for she, too, sobbed and leaned against Mitchell.

"I am speechless," Alejandro finally said. "This is something I never expected." He turned and hugged Angilia. "Mi nieta bonita, you are truly remarkable and loving. I am not so sure I deserve this, but it fills my heart with love to know that you did this for me. I like that I am near my Marisol in the museum, my most precious Angel. We will remain together for all time."

# CHAPTER 8

"Welcome to the first Board of Directors meeting for the Light Within Foundation," Angilia said to the 12 men and women gathered in a conference room at the office Angilia had leased to house the foundation. "As you know, our mission focuses on helping people overcome their self-esteem and confidence issues so that they do not develop or persist with negative body image problems. This affects people of both genders and of all ages.

"One way to help people change their mindsets is through one-on-one collaboration via targeted curriculum. Waiting until high school is too late, as studies demonstrate, because by then peoples' body image is clearly defined in their own minds. Teenagers in particular need help, because many of them enter high school loathing themselves and the way they look, and this begins during pre-puberty for many of them.

"Our curriculum trains all teachers so that they become better able to proactively work with students who have negative self or body images. Teachers will be trained to help all students in all classes identify, target, and build upon their strengths. Focusing on the positives rather than the negatives helps students build self-esteem and confidence. Several recent studies prove that students with self-esteem and confidence have positive body images.

"Our goal is to forge their positive mindset while not emphasizing body image itself. Students—all people—need to feel accepted and valued as they are, not for what they could be. That focuses on the shortcomings and leads to a negative mindset. The more we, as community leaders, maintain a focus on our own and others' strengths and value, the more we can prevent body image issues and the resulting mental and physical conditions."

Angilia and Katherine presented the curriculum to the Board members, even having them role play as students so they could effectively understand the full benefits of implementing the program through Valdavian schools. When they were asked how the teacher training would be funded, Angilia and Katherine presented their grant proposals. "We feel that several educational foundations as well as companies connected to the beauty and fashion industries would make ideal sponsors for the training. The modeling industry, for example, has worked diligently in recent years to counteract negative body image," Katherine explained. "We have also been pre-approved for a €2 million grant from The Eating Disorder Treatment Center in Paris, France to pay for teacher training."

"We are quite impressed," Randolph Putnam stated. "I, for one, think it is high time someone kicked this beast to the curb," he added, referring to the body image issue. He glanced around the table at his fellow business leaders. "I know we all have associates with financial strength. What do you say we contact them for donations?" Everyone agreed, and Angilia felt elated.

"Thank you all. With the €2 million grant, we will schedule the first training session and have at least one teacher from every school district to attend the initial training. Most of them can become certified to train teachers in their districts, as well. We are already making strong progress toward implementing the curriculum," Angilia stated.

"Yes, we are," Katherine added. "At next month's meeting, we will update all of you on the training and discuss plans for community outreach and education programs, as well."

After the meeting, Angilia and Katherine drove to the coffee shop near the mall for lunch. "You deserve a rest, my dear. You worked so hard for months on the curriculum, grants, and research. I am so very proud of you, Angilia. Your father is right. You are amazing, and you will be one hard-working, benevolent Queen."

Katherine smiled and leaned over to kiss her daughter-in-law's cheek. She, Mitchell, and Matthew were blessed to have her and Eric in their family.

§§§§

"Welcome to our special coverage of Nicole Taulbert's wedding to William Alexander. Three years ago, the world looked forward to Princess Consort Angilia's romantic wedding. Among her bridesmaids was her friend Nicole, whom she met through her work with Christ on Campus. Today, Her Royal Highness supports her friend as Matron of Honor," Franklin Sydney commented on the afternoon of Saturday, February 24, 2019.

"Yes, she does, Franklin," Laurie Dougray confirmed. "The wedding guests have arrived and are awaiting the bridal party's arrival next, followed by Nicole and her father. Among the guests in the church are His Majesty and the Duc de Valmondois. The groom and his best man, his brother Stephen, just arrived and nervously wave to the crowds gathered across from the church before they enter the church. We have just received word that the Rolls Royce carrying the bridesmaids and groomsmen has left the palace, where they prepared for the ceremony."

"Yes, and since the drive is short, we will get our first glimpse of Her Royal Highness in moments. The wedding reception is to be held in the palace, we understand. The Rolls Royce has arrived, and the groomsmen have stepped out and are assisting the bridesmaids. The bridesmaid's dresses are ballet length in a teal green color with draped necklines," Franklin announced.

"They are lovely, Franklin. Scott Ransdale takes Her Royal Highness's hand as she steps from the car. People gathered outside the church are cheering her appearance. She is wearing a full-length version of the dress, her hair in its signature herringbone braid style. She is stunning."

"Yes, she is, Laurie. The Princess Consort has crossed the street to speak to the well-wishers there. She seems to indicate that the bride will arrive soon. Now she returns to the church, and she makes sure the bridal party is inside and ready for Nicole's procession soon."

"Speaking of the bride, the Rolls Royce bearing Nicole and Mr. Taulbert has just arrived. Everyone is applauding the bride, and she turns to wave as she exits and takes her father's arm. Her white, sleeveless gown is bustled and adorned with rhinestones around the waist. Nicole is truly a beautiful bride. Look at that radiant smile as she turns to wave before she and her father enter the church," Laurie sighed.

"Indeed. What a glorious day for everyone involved. We understand that the service is expected to last approximately one hour. We will continue our coverage at that time, allowing everyone to see the newlyweds, bridal party, and guests as they depart the church," Franklin informed viewers.

Inside, Angilia straightened Nicole's train and veil and made sure the bridesmaids and groomsmen were organized. Angilia smiled in happiness for her friend as she followed Nicole and Mr. Taulbert down the aisle. Nicole was the first of her COC friends to marry, and she was ecstatic for Nicole and William. Her friends had given her so much over the past seven years that she was honored to do whatever she could for them. Supporting Nicole on her wedding day filled her heart with love and joy. The young ladies hugged during the register signing, knowing that no matter what happened and where life took them that their friendship was eternal.

Angilia beamed as William and Nicole drove to the palace in a Rolls Royce convertible, thrilled to share the day of love with her dear friends. The reception in the palace ballroom was emotional, humorous, and memorable. William danced with Angilia, and Matthew danced with Nicole. Matthew also asked Darlene for a dance, grateful that she had outgrown her fainting spells whenever she was within a five-mile radius of Eric.

Angilia offered the toast to the newlyweds and showered them with rose petals before they were driven to their hotel room for the night. Nicole and William were flying to the Bahamas for their honeymoon, leaving early the next morning. As Angilia slipped out of the matron of honor gown, she smiled happily at the thought that their lives really were perfectly blessed. Angilia fell into a calm sleep that night, her head on Matthew's chest.

§§§§§

*7 March 2019*

*Today Daddy learns the last of my revelations. Matthew and I have been married for almost three years, and I am at what I am certain is the halfway mark to the most miraculous, momentous moment of my life. My purpose for living is the birth of my and Matthew's son. Our son. Yes, I know we will have one child, a boy. I know his name. I know what he looks like. I know him. Today I share that with Daddy.*

§§§§§

Angilia entered the office she shared with her father and checked his schedule for the day. Eric had a meeting in mid-afternoon but nothing until then. She smiled and waited for him patiently, knowing he always had a morning brief with Roger before he began his work. When he came in, he bent to kiss her cheek. "You are already at work. You are always busy," he said as he sat at his desk.

"I do have something very important I need to do this morning," she told him. "I need to talk with you for a while. I know you don't have any official appointments, but are you busy?"

Eric looked at her intense eyes. "No, Angilia. What is it? Is something wrong? Have you spoken to Matthew?" Seven years after the shooting, he worried that perhaps she suffered residual effects from her wounds.

Angilia smiled and reassured him. "Nothing is wrong. I need to tell you something though. I'll talk with Matthew about it when the time is right." Eric's brow furrowed. She saw the concern on his face and in his eyes, and she reached for his hands. "I'm fine, Daddy, really. It's nothing like that, I promise. I have something very important and life-changing to share with you." She stood and gently pulled him to his feet. "Come with me?"

Eric nodded, never sure what his daughter would reveal at such moments. They took the elevator to the third floor in silence, and she looked up at him as she led him to Patrick's suite. She closed the door and led him to Patrick's sofa. She saw the questions on her father's face.

"Seven years ago I shared my past with you. You read about my life in the Unborn Children Sphere and the Angels Choir. You now know I did not write everything about the Unborn Children Sphere in that diary. Some things were too emotional to write there, like meeting Abraham Lincoln. I told Matthew on our honeymoon, and I told you when you gave me Abraham's diary," Angilia reminded him.

"I know, Angel. Mr. Brennan and Matthew wanted you to write your memoir so everyone will know the truth about Heaven and death. I know you're working on that. Is that what you want to talk to me about?"

"In a way, yes. There is one experience I have never shared with anyone. I want to share it with you, Daddy. I did write it down and I did draw a picture, just like I drew Matthew's picture in my diary when I was five. I never included this in the diary, though. I am not exactly sure why I didn't, except that I remember thinking that if someone found out it could devastate everything."

Eric's face flashed fear, and Angilia grabbed his hands. They both knew it was the seventh anniversary of the shooting. "I'm sorry, Daddy, but I never wanted that doctor to know anything. I'm glad in retrospect that I hid this, though, because it could have given him more incentive to kill me and alter the future. I'm not afraid of death, but I didn't want to leave you and I did not want to destroy another's life."

"Destroy another's life? Whose life, Angilia? Who else was in danger, baby? I don't understand," Eric said, visibly shaken.

Angilia went to Patrick's desk and picked up her 2016 diary. She handed it to her father and told him to read the January 3 entry. He looked both confused and fearful. "My engagement day, yes. I wrote something that night that references what I need to show you and tell you," she explained.

Eric read her words, gasping when she wrote about her future son. Eric reread the entry and stared at her. "Your future son?  If Jamieson had killed you, your son would never be born.  Is he about to be born?  Angilia?  Are you trying to tell me that you're pregnant?"

Angilia giggled and kissed her father's cheek.  "No, not yet.  Probably in a couple of years.  That's when I am quite certain it will happen anyway."

"What?  I don't understand, Angilia.  How do you know that you'll get pregnant in two years?"

She smiled and reminded him, "The same way you knew when Mommy would get pregnant with me.  God let me know, but not how he let you know about me.  He sent my soul to you.  I learned about my son in a different manner.  God must have approved, or he wouldn't have let it happen.  It's all tucked away in Uncle Patrick's secret hiding place."

Eric looked completely befuddled by then.  "Secret hiding place?  What secret hiding place?  Patrick never mentioned it."

Angilia laughed.  "Of course not.  If he had, it wouldn't have remained secret, Daddy.  When I wrote it all down and drew the picture of my son, I sealed it all in an envelope and put it in the secret hiding place.  I want you to read it and see it, Daddy.  Will you?"

"Of course, Angel.  Nothing should surprise me anymore, but this certainly has.  I never expected to learn about my grandson years before his birth," Eric confessed and then watched Angilia walk to a floorboard near Patrick's desk. Eric watched her kneel and touch an invisible latch, and then saw a section of the floorboard open.  Angilia reached her hand in and pulled out a large manila envelope.  She brushed the dust from it, walked back to the sofa, sat beside her father, and handed him the envelope.

Eric looked at her in amazement, and she nodded.  He opened the flap with his finger, took a deep breath, and pulled several pages from inside. Just as he had read her diary detailing her time in the Unborn Children Sphere and the Angels Choir—where she had known Matthew, her great-grandfather, and Patrick—Eric read about his grandson, his unborn grandson.

*17 November 2001*

*Daddy, someday you will read my diary about my life in the Unborn Children Sphere and the Angels Choir. You will know that I met a boy named Matthew in the Unborn Children Sphere, a boy who loves art and who was my best friend. I never forgot him. I never will. You know that Great-grandfather was my teacher in the Angels Choir and that he helped me learn about and prepare for my purpose there. You know that my purpose was to be Uncle Patrick's Spirit Guide, and I pray that the memory of that day no longer causes you pain. It shouldn't. Uncle Patrick is still around, Daddy, and someday you will see him, too. I know that. Seeing you the day I came to escort Uncle Patrick to Heaven remains the one most earthshattering experience for me. I loved you at first sight, Daddy. I hope you know that, too.*

*I met someone else in the Unborn Children Sphere who changed my life before I saw you, though. I will never forget him. I never could. Someday I will see him again, I know that. So will you. I know that, too.*

*Once when I walked down the winding staircase from my and Matthew's tower, I instantly saw a man across the room. He saw me at the same moment. Our eyes locked. I felt odd, like I had to go to him, like I was compelled to walk across the room to him. He drew me to him as if he had lassoed and pulled me to him.*

*There is no age in the Unborn Children Sphere. Everyone takes on the physical manifestation of what they will look like on earth, although everyone appears to be what we know as different ages. Some of the unborn children I met there appear to be five years old, while others appear to be in their 20s or 30s. It's different for everyone. I asked Michael about that once, when I was in the Angels Choir, and he told me that some people in the Unborn Children Sphere parallel the ages they will be on earth during major events in their lives.*

*Maybe that is why I call the person I met a man, not a boy. He appeared to be in his 40s perhaps, like some of the diplomats who visit who are in that age range. That means something major will happen in his life during that time. I wonder what it will be. I honestly have no idea, although I wonder if we will witness that event, Daddy. It's within possibility.*

*I walked to the man and felt so startled when I looked at him and into his eyes. His eyes amazed me. His eyes looked like my eyes. No one else I met in the Unborn Children Sphere had eyes that resembled mine. There were quite a lot of people there with blue eyes, but no one else with turquoise eyes. I never saw anyone else with these eyes until I came for Uncle Patrick and saw you, Daddy. I have your eyes. So does the man I met in the Unborn Children Sphere.*

*He smiled at me, and I felt strange. I can now describe how I felt. My heart fluttered. It did so again when he pulled me into a hug and held me tight for a long while. Something about him seemed so familiar, warm, and honest. I loved him at that moment. That seems odd, I know, since I had just seen him for the first time and had not spoken with him yet. I loved him instantly. I don't know how else to explain how I felt, and I hope that makes sense.*

*He finally spoke, as he still held me to him. He was much taller than I was, but he held me close to him and said, "I love you so very much. I never thought I would see you until my birth. You are all I imagined you to be."*

*I looked up at him, and I am sure my face betrayed my confusion. He took my hand and led me to a settee away from everyone else, where we could talk alone. He smiled and held my hands. "You do not know who I am, do you, Angilia?" He knew my name, and my heart fluttered again when he said my name. I felt as though I recognized him, even though I had never seen him before. I knew I loved him.*

*"I'm not sure. I feel as if we have known each other forever, and yet I have never seen you before. I do love you, I know that," I told him.*

*He smiled at me and pulled me close to him again. "I love you, too, so very much. We will know each other for all time. We met here, but we will meet again on earth in the future. You and I are meant to be together, part of the same soul." He looked into my eyes, and suddenly I knew. I knew who he is, who he will always be.*

*He nodded as he looked deep into my eyes, into my soul's depth. I placed my hand over his cheek and it was as if an electric shock went through my whole being. "I do know you," I whispered. "You are my son, my only child."*

*"Yes. You are my mother. I am your son. You know me. I know you. You are my mother Angilia. I am your son Eric. You love me. I love you. That is how it is and will be for all eternity. We are meant to share a soul. We are meant to be mother and son. God placed us together, and thus it will always be. I love you. Carry that with you while you await my arrival."*

*I nodded, and we hugged.  He kissed my cheek, and I kissed his cheek. We sat together for what seemed like a long time.  I never saw him again, for it seemed not long after that meeting with Eric that Michael came to take me to the Angels Choir.  I somehow feel I will give birth to him in my mid-20s.*

*I never forgot Eric.  How could I?  I never told anyone about him, though.  This is the first I have mentioned him at all.  Just as I drew Matthew so that others can see my best friend as I did, I drew my son Eric.  This drawing shows him just as he looked when I met him in the Unborn Children Sphere, straight from my detailed memory, straight from my heart.*

Eric processed what his little girl had written on his 47th birthday.  He believed her.  How could he not?  He turned to the drawing of his future grandson and could not breathe.  He stared at a face so very like his own it stunned him.  Not only did his grandson share his name, he physically resembled him.  Angilia's son Eric had the same raven black hair, the same nose, the same chiseled cheeks, and the exact same turquoise eyes.  Eric stared at his grandson Eric's face and felt his own heart swell with instant love, just as Angilia's had.

She had told him she was certain she would become pregnant in two years.  2021.  He would meet his grandson in two years.  Tears filled his eyes.  Eric looked at his beautiful daughter Angilia, now 23 years old but appearing just as she had when he first saw her on July 19, 1977.  He smiled at her through his tears and pulled her close to him in a hug that spoke far more than mere words ever could.  His grandson was correct: they shared a soul and would love one another for all eternity.  The sheer beauty and miracle of that surged through his veins as Eric kissed Angilia's cheek and offered a silent prayer of thanksgiving.

§§§§

"I'll be home later today," Eric reminded Angilia as he kissed her cheek and picked up his briefcase before driving to a board meeting.  She smiled and heard him skip down the stairs.  For as long as she recalled, that sound stirred her heart.  She had always recognized the sound of her father's footsteps.

Angilia checked her calendar for the day, May 15, and found no meetings scheduled.  That meant she could write some more grant proposals for the Light Within Foundation. The school board wanted to begin implementation of the curriculum in the fall, so Angilia needed to schedule the rest of the teacher training sessions as soon as possible.

Eric texted her right before the board meeting began, a short, sweet "I love you" to which she likewise responded. Her smile radiated her happiness. Roger noticed her smile when he tapped on the open office door holding a stack of mail. He placed Eric's mail on his desk, stepped over to her desk, and smiled down at her.

"Someone is very happy," Roger commented. "Your dad just arrived at the meeting," Roger said, knowing how Eric always called or texted his daughter before meetings. Angilia smiled up and nodded. "Well, here's your mail," he said, and she reached to take it from Roger's hand. Roger grabbed her hand tightly, his smile suddenly gone. Angilia's smile vanished, too, as Roger stumbled and reached for her.

Angilia stood and put her arms around him, and she felt him struggling to breathe. Quickly, she loosened his tie, unbuttoned his collar, and picked up her phone. "Matthew, please hurry to the office," she said in a voice full of fear. Matthew grabbed his medical bag, screamed at Daniel to call Mitchell immediately, and ran to Angilia's office. What had happened to her? He was terrified.

Matthew ran in breathless, to see Angilia holding Roger. Matthew put his arms around Roger and helped him to the sofa, removed his tie, and unbuttoned his shirt. Matthew did not have to ask any questions, for he instantly recognized the symptoms. "Angilia, in my bag is a bottle of nitroglycerin pills. Get one out for me now," Matthew instructed his wife, who quickly did so. Matthew placed the pill between Roger's cheek and gum. "Don't chew it or swallow it, Roger. Let it dissolve. All right?" Roger nodded, and his face registered his intense fear. Matthew patted his arm and reassured him.

Mitchell ran in at that moment and said he had called an ambulance, which arrived a moment later. He, too, had feared something had happened to Angilia. Matthew listened to Roger's heart, took his blood pressure, and as the nitroglycerin entered his blood stream, Roger's heart rate and blood pressure began to stabilize. Matthew and Mitchell lifted Roger onto the gurney and went down the elevator and in the ambulance with Roger.

Daniel, Susan, and Carol watched in stunned silence as their friend was rushed to the hospital. Daniel was pale, Carol was praying, and Susan was numb. What had happened? Would Roger survive? Would he be all right? Questions swirled through their brains, and they stood immobile in the hallway.

Angilia picked up her phone and called her father, who knew she would not call him during a meeting unless something had happened. "Daddy, you need to go to the hospital. Roger was taken there. Thank God that Matthew was here. I think Roger had a heart attack. I'll tell you what I know when you get there. I'm leaving now, Daddy." She grabbed her keys and arrived at the hospital in minutes. She waited near the entrance for her father, who rushed in with fear and panic on his face.

Angilia described what had happened, and then explained, "Matthew gave Roger a nitroglycerin tablet, which I know is used for heart attacks. Matthew did say that Roger's heart rate and blood pressure began to stabilize as the drug entered his blood stream. Daddy, Roger is so scared, and I just keep thanking God that Matthew hadn't left for the morning." Eric hugged her and then asked a nurse where Roger Rocard was. She led them to a waiting area in the cardiac unit, where Matthew and Mitchell had taken Roger for tests and treatment.

Soon, after they rallied themselves, Susan, Daniel, and Carol arrived. An hour later, Eduardo joined them. "Everyone is worried, so they sent me to get an update on Roger. Any news yet?" Angilia told him no, but she knew that Matthew would conduct several tests to confirm a heart attack and to gauge the severity of the effects. Roger's friends sat quietly for another two hours before Mitchell came to talk with them.

"Roger did have a minor heart attack. There is no heart damage, which is excellent news. Matthew ran several tests already, and he will run more over the next few days. He's keeping Roger here for several days.  Roger is stable, and he's calm now.  He should be all right and able to resume his usual activities within reason.  Matthew will talk with Roger and all of you about that soon.  As Rogers's friends, you need to help him and encourage him, because anyone who suffers a heart attack must make lifestyle changes.

"Roger is very scared, which is understandable.  He's going to need everyone's reassurance, love, and support.  Eric, I'll take you in to see him now," Mitchell said, and then put his hand on Angilia's cheek.  "He wants to see you, too, so I'll take you back when your father leaves."  Angilia nodded and squeezed her father's hand.

Thirty minutes later, Eric returned and hugged Angilia while he explained that Roger was scared but doing well considering what he had been through.  Mitchell put his arm around Angilia and took her to Roger's private room in the cardiac intensive care unit.  Matthew smiled at her and nodded as if to say that Roger was going to be all right.

Angilia smiled at Roger and bent to kiss his cheek.  He put his arms around her and held her close for several moments.  He whispered in her ear.  "Pray for me, Princess."  Angilia nodded, smiled, and sat in the chair next to Roger's bed.  She held his hand as she bowed her head and said a soft-spoken prayer.

"Dear God, Please protect and heal Roger.  Hold him in your loving embrace always, and comfort him.  We all love him, as do you.  Let him feel your love for him.  Remind him how special and important he is to all of us as a true friend.  Help us, his friends, help and support him.  Thank you, God.  Amen."  Roger squeezed her hand and smiled at her, and she could see the fear in his eyes.

Angilia sat with Roger for a short while, until Matthew said it was time for Roger to get some sleep.  She kissed Roger's cheek and whispered an "I love you" in his ear before she left.  Matthew told her that he would stay at the hospital, and she nodded.  Roger needed Matthew, someone he knew and trusted, which Angilia understood more than anyone else ever could.

§§§§

Two weeks after his minor heart attack, Roger was back home in the palace, learning to exercise more, eat healthier, and change other behaviors which would make his heart stronger. He slightly grumbled at first, but he knew it was all for the best.

One morning after a cardio workout, Roger showered, dressed, and sought Angilia. He found her in her sitting room and tapped on her door. She smiled up from her desk and was a bit surprised when he closed her door. "Angilia, I need to talk to you. Please." She nodded and sat on the sofa with him.

Roger sat, his head bowed, for several minutes before he spoke. "Angilia, I am so terrified. I don't want to die. Death terrifies me. When it happened, when I had the heart attack, I thought I was dying, and I was so scared. Help me. Please help me."

Angilia reached for Roger's hands and held them in hers. Tears slid down his cheeks as she bowed her head and prayed. Before she could speak again, he asked her questions she had never anticipated. "How did you deal with it? You actually died twice the day you were shot. What did that feel like? What did dying feel like?"

"I'm not afraid to die, Roger. I know Heaven, I saw Heaven, and I lived in Heaven. I know where souls go when people die, and I saw those people alive and free and gloriously happy in Heaven. The thing about that day is that I could not leave Daddy yet. He was in too much danger, and I was the only one who knew and could protect him. I stayed focused on him. I had to.

"I felt the bullet tear into my heart, and I knew it would probably kill me. But I looked down and saw Daddy trying to stand up. If he had, he would have been killed. I had to protect him. That's all I thought. I remember hearing Tony say that the gunman was dead, but I knew Jamieson would just hire another assassin.

"I tried to fight it. I tried to stay with Daddy. I felt the blood leaving my body, though, and I could barely move. I could barely breathe. I knew I was dying, and all I thought was that no one would be there to protect Daddy. That's all I felt, not the pain. I was terrified for him, not for me. I felt my heart stop beating and everything go dark. I begged God to protect Daddy, to save Daddy. Then I was alive again, and I knew I would have to fight to stay with him and protect him.

"I felt everything during the surgery, too. I've never told that to anyone, not to Daddy or to Matthew. After Matthew began the surgery, I regained consciousness, but I couldn't move, I couldn't talk, I couldn't open my eyes. I felt everything, though. I heard everything. I heard a man come in twice during surgery and tell Matthew that Daddy wanted an update. The second time, he said that Daddy was terrified and distraught. I heard him say that, and I remember trying to move, trying to get up and run to Daddy. I was scared for Daddy then. I felt my heart stop again, and my last thought was that I had caused my father's death. I couldn't protect him anymore. That's when Mommy came and brought me back to life again.

"I know now that the man I heard was Dr. Taylor. I wasn't scared to actually die. I was terrified that if I did die that I couldn't protect my father. Yes, it hurt. It hurt an awful lot, Roger, but I didn't care about that. All I cared about was Daddy. And I know I am meant to have a child, so I have to live at least until my child is born. If I had died then, my child would have never lived, and Daddy's life would have been in danger. I don't care about my own death at all, really."

"Oh, God, Angilia," Roger nearly retched. "You felt everything? Oh, Princess. Matthew told me I'm all right, and here I am whining about all of this. Dear God, Angilia, I don't know what to say, sweetheart. How terrifying. How did you survive all of that? Where did you find the strength?"

"I had to survive, Roger, for Daddy and for my child. I had to. I fought for them. They are my strength and purpose."

"I don't know what to say. You really are amazing. But how can anyone not have some fear of death? I know what you've said about Heaven and all of that, but when you died, weren't you at all scared of leaving your life here? And the pain. I was in so much pain, and it seemed to consume me. That's all I could feel. How could you not feel the pain?"

"I did feel the pain. I felt everything. But my fears for Daddy were stronger than anything else. I had a dual purpose, to save Daddy and someday give birth to my child. When I died both times that day, I returned to Heaven. It's so beautiful and peaceful there, and I knew I was safe and healed there. But I knew Daddy was in grave danger, immediate danger. I had to return for him and for my child. I had to. If Daddy were safe and my child already born, I would have stayed in Heaven, Roger.

"Heaven truly is the only place in existence where fear, pain, and sadness do not exist. Everyone who dies and is welcomed into Heaven continues to live. They look as they did on earth. You saw Patrick die in 1977. You saw him, heard him, and touched him at my wedding reception in 2016. He's the same Patrick, right?"

Roger nodded as he recalled Patrick's surprise appearance at Angilia's wedding three years earlier. Angilia smiled at Roger and said, "I know who can help you. Uncle Patrick, please come to us. We need you." Roger looked at Angilia as if she had lost her mind. Angilia felt Patrick manifest between her and Roger on the sofa, and she saw Roger's face turn pale when Patrick appeared out of thin air.

"Hi, Roger. I think I can help you, buddy. I was afraid of dying, too, once. What would it feel like? What would happen to me after I died? Those are your real questions, right?" Patrick asked Roger in his familiar voice.

"Patrick? You look the same as you did, as you did, you know." Roger could not say the words.

"I look the same as I did the day I died. I know, Roger. I always will. Kinda trippy, I suppose, but like Little One said, everyone looks the same in Heaven as they did on earth. I'm still me. I just live in Heaven, not on earth. That's all that really changed, Roger." Patrick smiled at his friend and pulled Roger to him in a hug.

"So, yeah, those are the big questions for me, Patrick. I know it's wrong to be this scared, but I am. I get that Angilia had to fight to protect her father, but it's different for me. There is no one in my life really. I don't have anyone to fight for," Roger sadly said.

"Roger, you have friends who love you, you dolt," Patrick said. "Anyway, my death was pretty quick. I felt the boat capsize and a moment of indescribable pain. The boat landed on top of me and threw me against rocks under the water. It felt like I had been ripped in two. It hurt so very much, but only for a moment. Then it was over. Then I was standing with Little One beside my dead body. I saw you and Eric, but neither of you saw me.

"When I saw Angilia and knew she was taking me to Heaven, I felt more happiness than I can describe. Roger, the pain, the fear, the doubt all disappeared the second I died. Honestly. Poof. What happened to me after I died? Little One led me into Heaven, Roger. We were in the Angels Choir, but all of Heaven is full of light and peace. I could not stop smiling, right Little One?" Angilia smiled, nodded, and leaned her head against her uncle's shoulder. "Death has been a hoot, actually. I mean, I live in the most loving place, like this huge commune where everyone loves everyone else, and they sing these happy songs all the time. Plus, I can come to earth and visit all of you. It's a riot, Roger."

Roger took a deep breath and sat quietly for a few minutes. Suddenly, he burst into laughter. "No wonder Mr. Brennan was tickled to meet you. You are as goofy as ever. You still talk like a disco-era teenager, Patrick. I mean, here I am almost 68 and you are still 19. That is pretty trippy. Did you just describe Heaven as a hippie commune? Really? I just had a vision of angels joining hands and singing "Kumbaya" in a circle." Roger was silent another moment. "The pain didn't last long?"

Patrick shook his head. "No. I'm glad it happened when it did and how it did."

"What?" Roger asked, stunned by Patrick's comment.

"Sure. If I hadn't died when and how I did, God's plan would have been thrown off course. My death allowed Eric and Angilia to meet each other 19 years before her birth, just like he told you all a few years ago. I am the one who brought them together, Roger. Well, actually my death brought them together. That's pretty darn cool." Patrick smiled and hugged his niece to him as she giggled.

Roger stared at them, both alive and vibrant. Any stranger who saw them at that moment would never know that Patrick was dead. That was clear to Roger. Patrick did not look or act dead. Patrick talked, looked, and acted like Patrick had always talked, looked, and acted. He even wore the same blue jeans and red hoodie he was wearing when he died.

"Roger?" Angilia looked at her father's best friend and reached for his hand. "You were beside Daddy when I was born. You were one of the first people I saw and met after my birth. You really are very special to me. I do love you, Roger. Never doubt how much we all love you."

A tear slid from Roger's eye and he grabbed Patrick in a bear hug. After a moment, Roger pulled Angilia into the hug, and the three of them cried and laughed. As they huddled together, Patrick prayed. "Dear God, Thank you for every blessing you have given to me, especially the gifts of my family and friends. I know all of us will stay together for eternity. What a blast we will have, too, you know that. You do know that, right? Of course you do. You know everything. I can't wait to show Roger around and watch his eyes bug from his head. His eyes always bug from his head," Patrick said, and Angilia playfully smacked his arm. "I really can't wait to see Roger and Daniel in their angel outfits, man. That will be so cool. We are gonna party forever when we are all there together. Okay, maybe not forever. We'll chill together, too, sometimes. All play and no work, I know the drill. Seriously, please just keep my family and friends safe and healthy until it's time for us to set up house in Heaven. Thanks, man. Amen."

"What kind of prayer was that?" Roger asked, while Angilia could not help but giggle. "Wait a minute. What angel outfit? You're not wearing an angel outfit."

Patrick doubled over, his arms around his stomach, and laughed. "A tunic. You know, like the ancient Greeks and Romans wore."

"Oh, no. I don't think so, Patrick," Roger said.

"We'll see," Patrick still laughed as he disappeared from view. "See ya! Love you, Little One! You too, buddy!"

"I love you, Uncle Patrick," Angilia said and waved at her uncle.

"If he thinks I'm spending eternity looking like an extra from <u>Animal House</u>, he's crazy," Roger yelled. They heard Patrick's giggle. Roger smiled at Angilia and hugged her close. "Thank you, Princess." She kissed his cheek, and he went to her door with a smile. "At least I have something to look forward to, huh?" He looked up and pointed a finger toward Heaven. "So does Patrick." Roger winked at her and whistled as he skipped up the stairs to his office.

§§§§

"Mommy! Mommy! Look at the angel!" Those walking to church that morning could not help but hear a young girl suddenly shout excitedly and then see her point toward Angilia. Eric, Matthew, Juanita, Alejandro, Eduardo, Mitchell, Katherine, Susan, Daniel, Roger, and Mike all looked at Angilia, not knowing what they expected to see. To them, Angilia appeared as always, although they all knew of her past in Heaven and that she was an angel.

The Royal party began walking again, while the girl's mother gently tugged on her arm in an attempt to quiet her. The girl persisted, however. "Don't you see her wings? She has large pink wings." No one else saw anything out of the ordinary, although Matthew slid his hand to Angilia's back to feel for wings. The mother bent and quietly told her daughter to stop.

The little girl pulled away from her mother, ran to Angilia, and grabbed her. "You can help my Mommy. I know you can." She turned to her mother. "Mommy, the angel can help you." The little girl held Angilia's hands and looked up at her with pleading eyes. "My baby brother died, and Mommy has been sad since then. She's still not over it. I know you're an angel. I see your angel wings and halo. Please help my mom. Please."

Angilia walked over to the woman and took hold of her hand. At that second, the woman trembled and nearly collapsed. Her hand covered her mouth, and she gasped, "It's true." She, too, saw the truth about Angilia. She saw the wings and mystical glow.

215

Angilia helped the woman onto a nearby bench and turned to her family and friends. "You go on to church. I'll join you later." Eric and Matthew stood motionless, and Mike said he would stay with Angilia. "No, we'll be fine. Please go on ahead." Her smile convinced them, albeit reluctantly, and they slowly walked into the church.

Before Angilia could say anything, the woman began crying as she held onto Angilia. "Why did my baby die? Why? He was seven months old. I had him long enough to love him and start to dream about his future. Then he was just taken away forever. I will never hear him talk. What would his first word have been? When would he have taken his first step? What would he grow up to become? How many grandchildren would he give me? I'll never know any of that. Nothing. Why did I have him if it was for only seven months? That's so mean, you know. Give him to me long enough for me to fall in love with him, and then just take him away. Why?"

The woman's heartbreak cut through Angilia. She held the crying woman for several minutes, gently rubbing her back. "I know my words don't mean much, but I am so very sorry. I can only try to understand your pain, and I won't pretend to know what you have been through. But I can tell you the truth. Your little boy is not gone forever. Tommy is not dead."

The woman gasped and sat up straight. "How do you know his name? Is this some kind of cruel trick?"

Angilia shook her head and tenderly placed her hand on the woman's cheek. "No, Sarah. I am an angel. Natalie is correct," she said and smiled down at the young girl. "Before I was born, I lived in Heaven. I met people who had died on earth, but who then entered Heaven to live for all eternity in peace and happiness." Angilia shared more of what she knew about death, eternal life, and Heaven.

Sarah stared at Angilia, her wide eyes showing both hope and fear. "You really are an angel. But how do you know about Tommy?"

"I can see him, Sarah.  He is happy and healthy.  He has green eyes that sparkle, dark brown hair, and a big smile.  Tommy is fine, Sarah, and he needs you to know that.  He can hear you when you talk to him.  He says you talk to him a lot."

"She does," Natalie said.  "Mommy cries a lot, especially at night.  That's when she talks to Tommy."

"Sarah, he doesn't want you to cry anymore.  He doesn't want you to be sad about him.  He wants you to know that he is fine.  Where Tommy is, there is no darkness, pain, or fear.  All he knows in Heaven is light and love."

"I know that's what people preach and all of that.  How can I believe it about my baby boy?  He's dead and cold.  That's what I felt when I held him the last time.  Nothing.  Just a cold, dead body."  Sarah was crying again.  Angilia knew how to convince her.

"Sarah, have you ever heard of my uncle, my father's brother, Prince Patrick?"

Sarah nodded, but asked, "What does he have to do with Tommy?"

"My Uncle Patrick was 19 when he died in a boating accident on July 19, 1977.  That was just over 42 years ago.  Uncle Patrick is not dead, though.  His soul lives.  He visits me often."  Angilia removed a picture from her wallet and showed it to Sarah and Natalie.  It was Patrick's high school senior picture with "Class of 1976" embossed in gold in the lower right corner.

"I know about your uncle, and I'm sorry, but I still don't understand what this has to do with my Tommy," Sarah stated.

"He's cute," Natalie said as she stared at Patrick's picture.

"Thank you, Natalie."  The little girl's face lit up, while Sarah's turned pale.  Her brain fought to comprehend the truth.  She held up the picture and looked from it to the young man sitting next to Angilia.

"It is you," Sarah finally admitted.  "How can you look the same?  Aren't you about 60 years old?"

Patrick smiled. "I would be 61 years old if I hadn't died in 1977. I've looked the same since the day I died. So I guess I'm forever 19."

"But I can see you and hear you. You look real."

"I am real. I'm still the same person I always was. I just don't live on earth anymore. For 42 years, I've lived in Heaven. That's where Tommy is, Sarah. He's still alive, and he's still Tommy. He just doesn't live here anymore. You and Natalie will be with him again someday, I promise. When you die and your soul enters Heaven, you and Tommy will be together forever. For all time. He will never leave you again, Sarah."

"I don't understand how you can look like you. Your body died. How can you still have the same body?" Sarah asked, struggling to accept everything she saw and heard.

"My body is dead, Sarah. It was buried in the cemetery," Patrick said and pointed toward the church cemetery. "As soon as I died, my soul left my body. My soul took on a spiritual manifestation of my physical body, which looks just like I did on earth. Tommy looks like he did the last time you saw him, Sarah. He is a happy, healthy, seven-month-old baby boy. He hasn't changed at all."

"Sarah, I told you I can see Tommy. Right now, he is playing with his favorite toy. It's a stuffed horse with a red bridle. The horse is brown with white spots, and it has a brown yarn mane and tale. The hooves are black."

"Mommy, that's the horse we bought for Tommy before he was born! Remember? You let me pick it out at the toy store," Natalie excitedly said. "Tommy has one in Heaven!"

Sarah looked down at her daughter Natalie's happy face. Natalie believed. Natalie saw the real Angilia before she did. Angilia's dead uncle was sitting with and talking to them. It all had to be true. It had to.

"Thank you. Thank you both." Sarah hugged Angilia and then Patrick. "No one would believe me if I told them I met two angels," she suddenly giggled.  "I'm sorry.  I've kept you too long.  You were on the way to church," she apologized to Angilia.

"Why don't you and Natalie come with us?" Angilia asked.

"We couldn't.  We're not dressed for church.  Besides, I haven't been to church in years," Sarah said as she looked down at her jeans and t-shirt.

"God doesn't care.  He looks at your heart, not your clothes.  Please come."  Angilia took Sarah's hand and linked her other arm through Patrick's.  Natalie jumped for joy and held onto Patrick's other hand, much to Angilia's delight.  The four of them entered the church near the end of Reverend Hutchins' sermon, and he nodded to welcome them.  Eric had explained that Angilia would arrive late.

Parishioners smiled and nodded to welcome Angilia and her friends.  Many recognized Patrick as the handsome man who had been photographed dancing with Angilia at her wedding reception three years earlier.  Only some of those in the Royal party recognized him as Prince Patrick.

Patrick sat between his brother and his niece, while Sarah and Natalie sat between Angilia and Matthew.  They all stood with the rest of the congregation to sing the hymn "If We Never Meet Again (This Side of Heaven)."  Angilia smiled at Sarah, knowing how true the lyrics were and how timely they were for Sarah.

Eric smiled at his brother, dapper in his dark suit and tie.  Whatever had occurred outside, Eric knew that God had used Patrick and Angilia to help Sarah.  Eric knew that she had not been walking near the church at that moment by mere coincidence.  The little girl had seen the real Angilia, because God knew that Angilia would soothe Sarah's troubled heart.

*14 July 2019*

*Sarah and Natalie unexpectedly entered my life this morning.  Natalie instantly recognized me, not as Angilia, but as an angel.  She saw my wings, which no one else has seen before.  When Natalie pleaded for me to help her mother, I had to.  God wanted me to.  Dear Uncle Patrick came at the perfect moment, when I showed his 1976 high school picture to Sarah and Natalie.*

*Sarah knew that Uncle Patrick had died, so her seeing and talking with him really touched and opened her heart. God allowed me to see her baby boy, so when I described his favorite toy, she knew the truth. Thank you, God.*

*I am writing my memoir, as I promised Matthew and Mr. Brennan I would. I had intended the book to be private, only for family, but I now see that Matthew and Mr. Brennan were right. If my truth, my life, can touch and change someone else's heart, then I am doing God's will. Not only did today's encounter help Sarah and Natalie, it helped me. God enabled Sarah and Natalie to accept death as the gateway to eternal life. God showed me that my life can help others. I will, therefore, share my true story with the world and do what God directs me to do. There is a purpose for my life, for my past in Heaven and my memories of that, and God has shown me that. Thank you, God.*

§§§§§

"Happy birthday, my magnificent father!" Eric smiled at Angilia as she stood in his suite doorway. He held his arms open for a hug, and she went to him, put her arms around him, and leaned up to kiss his cheek. "I love you so very much, Daddy, always and forever."

"Oh, my beautiful daughter Angilia, I do love you. You, my little girl, are the most miraculous and precious gift I will ever receive."

"Oh, Daddy. I thank God for you every morning and every night. I am so incredibly blessed to be your daughter."

Eric felt tears stinging his eyes, and he pulled her close and kissed the top of her head.

Angilia smiled up at him. "I'm not the only one who loves you. Have you looked outside yet, Daddy?" He shook his head. "The mall is filled with people who want to wish you a happy birthday," she smiled as she handed him a wrapped gift. "Happy birthday."

"Your gifts always touch my soul, Angel," Eric said, and removed the lid to see another of her one-of-a-kind handmade books. Eric's tears slid from his eyes when he looked at the cover.

A watercolor painting of him and Marisol sparkled underneath the title: <u>First Love Never Dies</u>. Their daughter captured their love in every word and painting that filled the small book.

Eric turned back to her inscription inside the front cover and reread her heartfelt message. *Dearest Daddy, Your love for and devotion to Mommy fills my heart and soul with love, warmth, and gratitude. Your courage and strength awe, inspire, and teach me more than you can know. I love you, I love Mommy, and I thank God for both of you. Your eternal love created me and gave me life. With my eternal love, Your Angilia xoxo*

§§§§

"Welcome to the Musée National de Valdavia on this beautiful Saturday," Muriel Laperen greeted the standing-room-only audience in the Royal Portrait Gallery. "Today we honor His Majesty on his 65th birthday with the unveiling of a new portrait. Fifteen years have passed since the last portrait of His Majesty was unveiled, which you can see over my left shoulder.

"I do anticipate a grand reception to this most recent portrait," Ms. Laperen teased. "The artist who painted this portrait knows His Majesty well, better than anyone else, in fact. I would like to invite Her Royal Highness Princess Consort Angilia, Duchesse de Valmondois to officially unveil her portrait of her father, His Majesty King Eric de Valdavia."

Angilia stepped to the red-curtained portrait, pulled the gold cord, and uncovered a stunningly lifelike portrait of her father. In the portrait, Eric wore a black sweater, grey wool slacks, and black oxford shoes. He leaned against a white and gold sitting room wall in his familiar casual stance, with his hands in his pockets and his legs crossed. His breathtaking turquoise eyes glistened and his dimpled smile lit his face. Angilia captured the man she so dearly loved, her father.

The audience jumped to their feet in rapturous cheers and applause. The people of Valdavia loved and admired King Eric tremendously. They noticed that Angilia's portrait of Eric hung beside her portrait of Patrick, a symbolic and intentional placement. Angilia felt it appropriate that her father and her uncle remain together in the museum as they did for eternity.

# CHAPTER 9

On January 3, 2020, Angilia's 24th birthday, the Royal Family and their friends gathered at the Musée National de Valdavia for another auspicious occasion. This time they congregated in the main gallery, where a new display would momentarily be unveiled to the public. The museum was crowded, and as everyone mingled before the official program, most people wished Angilia a happy birthday. Matthew beamed at his beautiful wife as she was surrounded by fans and well-wishers. He looked forward to her reaction to his surprise.

At 11:00, Muriel Laperen welcomed everyone. "All of us at the museum are ecstatic about the newest acquisitions to our art collection. Twelve paintings by His Royal Highness The Duc de Valmondois officially join the museum's collection today. Our deepest gratitude extends to His Royal Highness for donating his paintings to the museum. When we approached him with the proposal to purchase some of his works, His Royal Highness donated 12 paintings of our choosing with the suggestion that we donate the funds to his charities. We were more than pleased to do so, and as you know, the total proceeds of today's tickets go to The Athletic Association of Valdavia.

"When you have the chance to view and to study His Royal Highness' work, we are certain you will be as impressed with his talent, point of view, and style as all of us are. At least one of these paintings is deeply important to His Royal Highness, if I may be so bold in stating. That painting is the nucleus of the display, as I am sure you will understand when you see the subject. I am honored to welcome His Majesty to unveil the museum's Duc de Valmondois Collection."

Eric hugged Matthew and Angilia before he walked to the wall which contained Matthew's dozen paintings. The wall was covered by large red velvet drapes, which Eric opened by pulling the gold cord. In large gold letters along the top of the wall gleamed the title "His Royal Highness The Duc de Valmondois Collection." The 12 paintings were framed and hung on the wall, 11 of them surrounding what Ms. Laperen and Matthew considered the cornerstone piece of the collection.

Everyone burst into applause, straining to see each work as soon as Eric revealed the paintings. None of Matthew's family had seen that central painting until now, and Eric looked at it in pleasant amazement. Juanita and Alejandro smiled as tears formed in their eyes. Katherine, Mitchell, and Eduardo stared in wonder, as did Susan, Daniel, and Bonnie. Roger smiled, knowing that Matthew's painting truly captured Angilia as no other ever had. Angilia looked at Matthew, her eyes seeming to besiege him with questions. He smiled and kissed her cheek just as Ms. Laperen introduced him to the podium.

"Thank you, ladies and gentlemen, for coming today and for your generous donations to The Athletic Association of Valdavia. I never expected any of my works to be on display, but I am honored that Ms. Laperen and the museum staff feel my work is worthy enough to be included in their impressive collection. These 12 paintings span the past seven years, since I moved to Valmondois.

"You will recognize the landscapes from various locations throughout Valdavia. Many of you probably recognize the horses in one of the paintings as my wife's beloved Starlight and my father-in-law's stallion Midnight. Two of the paintings are entirely from my imagination," Matthew commented, referring to two paintings of unrecognizable places and people.

"The central painting is an artistic portrait of my wife, yes. This is how I and others see Angilia," Matthew smiled, referencing Mr. Brennan and Natalie, who both saw Angilia as the angel she was. Matthew's painting depicted Angilia, in a flowing white gown, standing amidst trees and wildflowers while birds, butterflies, rabbits, and deer encompassed her. A deer nuzzled her arm, a rabbit stood up at her feet, a bird perched on her finger, and butterflies flitted around her. Large pink angel wings protruded from between her shoulder blades and a glow emanated from within her, surrounding her in a halo. "Angilia is my angel, our angel, and knowing her as I do, this is actually an accurate depiction of Angilia. More than any other painting I have ever done, I am most fond of this one," Matthew admitted with radiant smile and eyes. "I will also say that Angilia's memoir is published in early April, and when you read her life story, you will agree with my vision of her in this painting," he teased.

§§§§

Angilia kissed Matthew's cheek and sat up. He turned and smiled at her through half-open eyes. "Sorry I woke you. I'm going to Patrick's room to write some songs. I'll see you at breakfast," she whispered as she put on her robe.

"Okay. Want to hear them. What time is it?"

"1:00." Matthew moaned and turned onto his stomach. Angilia smiled and quietly walked to the east wing, into her uncle's suite, and closed Patrick's door behind her. She picked up the tablet, pen, and guitar she kept there and sat on the floor. Soon she had one song completed.

By 3:00, Angilia felt frustrated. She had the music and half of the lyrics of the second song written, and for the first time she was stuck. The rest of the lyrics would not come to her. She leaned against Patrick's sofa to support her in standing up, and then walked onto his balcony. She hoped the fresh air would clear her head and help her find the words she needed.

"Hey, Little One! Another new song? Let me hear it."

Angilia hugged her uncle and held him close. "I love you so, Uncle Patrick."

"Hey, what's wrong?"

"Oh, it's not important.  I'm trying to finish a song, but nothing I come up with or try is right."

"It will come to you.  May I read what you have?"  Angilia nodded and Patrick bent, picked up the tablet of paper, held it, and walked in a circle as he read.  Suddenly he tossed the tablet onto the sofa and ran to another secret hiding place.  He removed the painting from the wall and ripped a hole in the paper on the back.  He reached in and grabbed a spiral-bound notebook.  Angilia smiled as she watched him, wondering how many secret hiding places he actually had.

Patrick quickly flipped through the pages, back and forth, until he found the one he sought.  He scanned the page, nodded, and rushed back to his niece.  He handed her the notebook, and Angilia read the page, her face revealing her bewilderment.  She looked at Patrick, who stood smiling down at her, and grabbed him in another hug.

Angilia sat on the floor again, picked up her guitar, and sang the song all the way through, alternating her lyrics with Patrick's words.  She did not have to change any of the words or the melody.  The song was complete!  "It works?" Patrick asked her.

"Of course it works.  We wrote almost the same thing, male and female perspectives of the same theme, 47 years apart.  This is incredible.  You completed the song, Uncle Patrick!  Thank you!"  Angilia leaned over and kissed his cheek.

"You need to record it," he said with a smile.

Angilia shook her head, though.  "I can't, not solo anyway.  This song demands a man and a woman for the two points of view.  This is a male-female duet."

"Then you and Eric record it."

Angilia nodded.  "I want to hear what it sounds like with both voices.  It's far too early to wake Daddy.  Sing it with me."

Patrick giggled. "I've never really sung before. I don't know if I can." She looked at him, her eyes pleading, and he shrugged. "Okay, why not? What can it hurt?"

Angilia played the music on her guitar again and they sang the song as intended, Patrick singing his lines and Angilia singing hers, their voices harmonizing on certain key lines. When they finished, Angilia's eyes twinkled and she asked him to help her stand. She grabbed the papers from the floor, then his hand, and said, "Come with me."

"Where are we going?" he asked her as she headed toward the elevator.

"The recording studio," she said, and before she knew what happened, Patrick whisked them to the basement. "Thank you," she giggled. He watched her turn on the lights and the recoding console, then set the controls, and activate the recorder. Sam had taught her how to set up the equipment for her self-made demos. She pulled two stools to either side of the microphone and adjusted the mic between them. She told Patrick to sit across from her, while she plugged in her acoustic guitar and sat down.

"What are we doing?"

"We are recording the two songs," Angilia told him.

"We are? He'll be up soon. You don't need me."

"Uncle Patrick, please. I do need you. Just sing with me."

"Okay, but what if my voice doesn't record? I mean, I'm not human and all. I've never tried to do anything like this."

"I'm sure it will be fine. There's a first time for everything. Let's do this one first," she said and handed him the sheet music she'd written a few hours earlier. "You come in at the second verse and sing the rest of the song with me." He asked her to sing it once so he could hear it and get a feel for it, and she did.

"Who is this about? Is it who I think it is?" Patrick asked her. "I remember this. I was nine when I saw the stories on the news and in the magazines. She was too famous too soon, I think.

She seemed too caught up in the whole rock and roll lifestyle. She didn't seem all that comfortable with herself at all. So sad."

"Yes, it's about her. I was in the Unborn Children Sphere when it happened, and Michael came to get me. He said God wanted me to talk with the woman before she stood in front of God for her judgment. We know that God sees, knows, and understands everything. He knew what the woman told me. She did regret the choices she made, but she was reacting to the pain she held within her. She'd held onto the pain most of her life. I don't think she was ever really happy or at peace when she was alive. God understood that. I do not believe that God condemned her for those choices. Why would he have her talk with me first if he already knew he would not accept her into Heaven?"

"Yeah. I can see why he chose you to talk with her and help her open up. You are very compassionate and nonjudgmental, even if you don't agree with someone's choice or behavior. You made her feel safe and loved, Angilia. She must have been a scared little girl inside, and you made her feel safe and loved, just like you did with Sarah that day. Let's do this," Patrick said, and soon the song was recorded.

A few moments later, Angilia nodded and began playing the chords to their song. Within minutes, it, too, was recorded, and Angilia already knew in her heart that the two songs were perfect. She had never heard her Uncle Patrick sing, despite meeting him 43 years earlier. His voice was young, sweet, honest, emotive, and tender. She loved his voice.

Angilia walked to the recording booth and played the two songs. "These are perfect. You are perfect. Everyone needs to hear you and your words, Uncle Patrick. We need to release these songs as is, with no changes at all."

Patrick giggled. "Our words do belong together. It's almost uncanny how alike our words are, so many years apart. They're meant to be together. But what will people think if you tell them you recorded with me?"

"I don't care what people think, Uncle Patrick. It doesn't matter. Matthew already painted me as an angel and donated that portrait to the museum.  Everyone has probably seen it by now. Besides, my memoir comes out next month, so everyone will know the truth about us anyway.  Right?"

"Right.  Okay, let's do this.  You're right, there's a first time for everything.  I wonder if an angel has ever recorded songs before," Patrick said, but then realized the answer and laughed.  He hugged his niece.  "Of course she has.  You, Little One!  You are an angel and a recording star!"

§§§§§

By 6:30, Angilia was drying her hair when Matthew stumbled from the bed, kissed her, and stepped into his shower.  She was dressed and already downstairs when he finished and found a note taped to the mirror telling him she loved him and would see him at breakfast.  Matthew smiled, shaved, dressed, and all but ran downstairs.  He pulled his wife into an embrace and kissed her.  "I need coffee.  How can you look so fresh and awake?  You've been up half the night."

"You were up half the night?  Why?" Eric asked and kissed his daughter's cheek.

"Oh, I had a couple of songs to write.  Daddy, do you have a few minutes after breakfast?  I want you to hear them."

"Absolutely, Angel.  I can't wait," Eric smiled while everyone entered the dining room and took seats at the table.  Eric led grace, Antoine served breakfast, and the family and friends talked, smiled, and enjoyed the beautiful mid-March Monday morning.  Matthew sat next to Angilia, and Eric noticed how he barely ate but stared at Angilia with his too-familiar love-struck expression.  Eduardo noticed, too, and he smiled at Eric.  Nearly four years after their wedding, Matthew was still quite besotted with his wife, which charmed everyone.

After breakfast, the chatting continued as everyone began the work week.  Roger, Susan, and Daniel went to their offices on the fourth floor, while Eduardo drove his parents in a four-seated buggy to the gazebo for a relaxing morning outdoors.  Katherine and Mitchell went for a stroll through the gardens.  Matthew went to get his art supplies and paint outdoors for a while.  Eric smiled at Angilia and took the elevator to the basement with her.

"So you wrote two new songs overnight, huh?  I get to be the first to hear them?"

Angilia hugged him and confessed, "Not this time, Daddy. Someone's already heard them.  But you are the second person to hear them," she winked and walked into the control booth.

"Who else was up and about to hear them?"

"You'll know soon enough," Angilia teased.  She pushed the play button, and Eric listened to her sing the first verse of the song she had written about the female singer who had died in 1967. Angilia watched her father, and saw his face register surprised recognition when he suddenly heard his brother's voice join hers. He smiled as tears filled his eyes.  A lone tear slid down his cheek when the second song began and he heard Patrick's solo voice gently open the song.

Angilia held her father's hands and smiled up at him.  Eric pulled her close into a hug and kissed the top of her head.  He listened to the beautiful duet, his brother's and daughter's voices so sweet together.  When the songs ended, Angilia told him the details from the early hours of the morning and how everything came together in perfect destiny.

At that moment, Roger came down, looking for Eric to sign some papers.  Eric quickly signed them, and said, "Roger, round up everyone and ask them to come down here and listen to Angilia's two new songs."  Roger nodded and began calling and texting everybody, telling them to report to the recording studio.  Eric knew that Roger and Daniel would recognize Patrick's voice and get a kick out of hearing the songs.

Fifteen minutes later, after everyone was seated, Eric smiled and promised, "You will be totally awe-struck by these two songs." Angilia played the audio from the very beginning, including Patrick's conversation with her about his doubts over his voice even recording and his thoughts about the first song's subject.  Roger and Daniel did indeed recognize Patrick's voice immediately, and they looked at one another and then at Angilia. Daniel was stunned, although Roger expected pretty much anything from his buddy at that point. Nothing Patrick did truly surprised him anymore.

Matthew, like Roger, was caught by surprise, but also expected anything from Patrick. Why wouldn't Patrick sing with his niece? Patrick seemed to do darn near everything anyway. Susan, Alejandro, Juanita, Eduardo, Katherine, and Mitchell realized who was on the tape with Angilia only after she called him Uncle Patrick, and their faces revealed their confusion and surprise.

People sat quietly, listening to the two voices talking and singing together. Everyone speculated about the subject of the first song, although Eduardo figured it out first. "Sounds like Pearl McGee's story to me," Eduardo said. "I was 10 when she died of a drug overdose, and I remember the magazine stories, too. People at school talked about it a lot. We all listened to her albums and stuff, but I wasn't that into the whole psychedelic scene, so I didn't follow her closely. But I know what happened. Is it her, or can you tell us?"

Angilia nodded her head. "Yes, it's her. There are so many things and people I'm just starting to talk about or write about now that the book is coming out. I feel freer to do so now. This song was in me for so very long, and now was the time to finally write it. That song took about 15 minutes to write down. It came easily and quickly.

"The second song didn't. I had the music and half of the lyrics, and I just got stuck for the first time. That never happened to me before, but it happened for a reason. Uncle Patrick had already written the rest of the lyrics when he was 15. He pulled an old notebook of his from one of his hiding places, and when he showed me these words, I knew the song was complete. It was meant to be as it is, a collaboration between the two of us. I knew he had to sing it with me. I would sing it with him or no one."

"Play them both again, please, Angilia?" Daniel asked. Roger smiled at his friend and echoed the request. Angilia played the two songs again. Eric, Roger, and Daniel knew what a blessing they received from Patrick.  His words and his voice filled them with peace and contentment.

As the first song still played, Sam arrived suddenly and quite unexpectedly.  He stood in the doorway listening, his mouth agape and his hands on his hips.  When he heard the second song, he doubled over, the purity, beauty, and innocence almost literally knocking him off of his feet.  As soon as the songs ended, he launched into an outburst of thoughts and feelings.

"When did you do this?  Why didn't you call me?  Now I know why I came here.  Something woke me up in the middle of the night and told me I had to come here right away.  I got on the first flight I could, and here I am.  I walk in to hear this!  I've never heard anyone like this.  Never.  Who is he?  Where is he?  How soon can you get him here?"

Angilia giggled, went to Sam, and hugged him.  She walked with him to the control booth and asked him to sit in his usual seat there.  He sat in amazement while she told him the detailed version of everything that had occurred since 1:00 that morning.  Sam looked at Eric.  "Your brother?  The one who died at 19?  He sings, too?"  Eric smiled and nodded.  "I don't know why that surprises me.  Of course he does."

Most people looked at Sam in bewilderment.  That Patrick sang surprised him?  That Patrick recorded songs with Angilia 43 years after his death did not surprise him?  Sam looked around the room at the suddenly quiet, stunned group.  "What?  Oh, I got an advanced copy of Angilia's memoir so I could be prepared for the media storm that's going to hit when it's released next month.  I know all about everything," he said nonchalantly.

Sam turned his attention back to Angilia and took out his handheld computer.  "I love these, darling.  I love everything about them, especially his voice.  Patrick's voice is not technically perfect, but boy is it sensitive, true, and charming.  He is the next big teen idol.  I need to get these two songs set up on the web site ASAP for sale and download.  I need to call Dave Rodan at the radio station and have him debut these worldwide tomorrow morning.  Angilia, you will do the show with Dave tomorrow morning.  Say whatever you are comfortable saying about them and about Patrick. It's not like people won't know soon anyway, since it's all in your book. I need to arrange for their release elsewhere as soon as that can be set up. Lots to do, Angilia. Are you ready for the storm?"

Angilia looked at Sam, then at Eric, and finally at Matthew. She had not expected things to move quite so quickly. Sam would handle most of it, though. "Sure."

"I want to hear this from the beginning," Sam suddenly said, and when he heard the conversation between Patrick and Angilia, he beamed. "Dang, I wish we could get him on air. He's made for this, especially television. Can we?" he asked and looked up at Angilia. "How do we arrange that? Who do we contact?"

"Who do you contact? Oh, Sam, who do you think?" Angilia asked with a giggle.

"Then you get on that. I don't think I can handle that part of it. We won't show him yet, though. People will fall in love with that voice first, and then, bam, we'll bring him out and let people see him for themselves. Can I meet him before that?"

"Yes. I'll see what we can do, Sam," Angilia promised him.

"Great. I just want to listen to this again," he said and played "Our Dreams" once more. As stunned as many of those in the recording studio felt, they could not deny the beauty and charm in the lyrics and the voices.

*Our Dreams*

*(Patrick) When I was a boy I dreamed of an angel*

*Who would take away all my doubts and fears*

*And soothe my soul so I could face my death*

*With courage and strength throughout all the years.*

*She'd come from Heaven in a golden halo*

*And bring me love, peace, and joy forever.*

*She'd bring me sunshine and laughter every day.*

*On my golden horse I'd ride her away*

*(Both) For an eternity of love and beauty.*


*(Angilia) When I was a girl I dreamed of a prince*

*Who would banish demons that tortured me*

*And threatened my world and those I so loved.*

*He'd be my protector and hear my plea.*

*He'd charge down from Heaven on his golden horse*

*And bring me love, peace, and joy forever.*

*He'd bring me sunshine and laughter every day.*

*On his golden horse he'd ride me away*

*(Both) For an eternity of love and beauty.*


*(Angilia) My dream came true, there are no longer demons.*

*(Patrick) And I don't have any lasting doubts and fears.*

*(Angilia) Wherever we are we'll stay together.*

*(Patrick) Our hearts and souls entwine through all the years.*

*(Both) And now we ride on our golden horse*

*We both have love, peace, and joy forever.*

*(Angilia) You are my prince and my shining knight.*

*(Patrick) You are my angel and my saving light,*

*(Both) For an eternity of love and beauty.*

§§§§§

"Welcome to a very special show for this Tuesday, March 17, 2020.  Happy St. Patrick's Day.  I'm Dave Rodan, your music man, and we have a very special guest with us for the world debut of two new songs that will totally blow you away.  I heard these for the first time about an hour ago, before we went on air, and all I can say is wow!  Turn the volume up and be prepared, that's all I can say.  All I have to do is introduce my guest for you to know that you have a special treat in store.  Welcome to the studio, Your Royal Highness Princess Consort Angilia, Duchesse de Valmondois."

"Thank you for allowing me to come on such short notice, Dave.  It's been a while since I've joined you here," Angilia replied.

"It has, but we will more than make up for that this morning.  You have two new songs out, and I understand that they are available for purchase and download on your website beginning today, and soon elsewhere."

"That's right.  Sam Burton, my tireless manager and producer, worked with his team to have the digital downloads and shopping carts set up by this morning.  The two songs go live at 8:00 this morning.  Sam is working to get them available at all online venues as soon as possible, as well," Angilia confirmed.  "One hundred percent of the proceeds go to The Athletic Association of Valdavia, which was Patrick's favorite patronage, and is now my husband Matthew's patronage."

"When did you write these songs?  When did you record them?"

Angilia repeated the story of her very early morning songwriting session and her struggle in completing the second song.  She explained that her uncle had written the remainder of the song, the stanzas that completed it perfectly, when he was 15 in 1973.  "We recorded the two songs as soon as the second song was written, in our basement recording studio.  It was just the two of us, my uncle and me.  We played the songs for my father and then the rest of our family and friends.  Sam arrived that morning, he heard them, and here we are," Angilia commented.

"The first song seems to be about someone else, another singer. What inspired that song, if I may ask?"

"Her life and her death are filled with sadness, because I don't think she was ever truly happy during her lifetime. I don't think she ever felt loved or appreciated, at least in her mind. To compensate for that, she made some regrettable choices. Ultimately, her true story reminds us to show love to those around us, to let them know that they are loved and appreciated. Without love, anyone is subject to similar emotional turmoil. So, while her story is sad, it does contain hope. We can all prevent this from happening to anyone else if we just take some time each day to show our love to those around us," Angilia said without naming the subject publicly.

"You said that your uncle wrote part of the second song when he was 15, which was 47 years ago," Dave said, doing some quick math in his head. "You wrote your lyrics just a few hours ago basically. How did you manage to merge the two divergent pieces so smoothly into one song, given that nearly half a century separates them?"

"I didn't have to change anything, Dave. Patrick's words are used just as he wrote them. When I saw his words written in his notebook, I was admittedly stunned that we each wrote basically the same thing 47 years apart. His words were meant for this song. They fit perfectly without any tweaking at all, not even of the music. If you look at the lyrics, you will see that my lines and Patrick's lines share the same meter and rhyme scheme, as well as the same theme. Some lines are even identical. I knew as soon as I read his words that he completed the song," Angilia expounded with a smile.

"You didn't change anything? Not even one word?"

"No, not at all. What people hear is our individually-written words flowing together seamlessly to complete the story told in the song. I wrote half of the lyrics and the music, and Patrick gave the song the rest of the lyrics it needed. From the first moment it came together, I knew this song was destined to be a true collaboration between Patrick and me. It is, in every way," Angilia stated with firm conviction in her voice.

"I heard the two songs earlier, as I said, and I had to listen to that one twice. Listeners, we are going to debut both songs, and when you hear them you will indeed feel as blown away and amazed as I was. We will play "Little Girl Lost" first, and then move right into "Our Dreams," the song Her Royal Highness co-wrote with her uncle, His Royal Highness Prince Patrick. Before we debut the songs, please tell everyone listening who your duet partner is, please, Your Royal Highness." Dave anticipated the response her answer would receive, especially after people heard the songs and Patrick's voice.

"My Uncle Patrick recorded these two songs with me."

Throughout Valdavia and on syndicates that carried Dave's radio program around the world, listeners stared at their radios in befuddlement. How could Angilia record new songs with her dead uncle? Most people knew about splicing techniques where one singer's voice was merged into the recording to duet with an existing track done by someone else, such as the famous duet of many years earlier by Natalie Cole with her father Nat "King" Cole. How could Angilia have done that, though, if she had just written the songs?

Those and other questions were quickly forgotten, though, when people heard the two voices harmonizing on "Little Girl Lost." People were charmed and did fall in love with the sweet voice they heard. However, when "Our Dreams" began and listeners heard Patrick's solo verses, they were, as Dave promised, blown away. The radio station phone lines received so many calls that the telephone system could not handle the volume and the lines went dead. The email inboxes quickly filled to capacity and caused subsequent messages to bounce.

Dave took a few calls live on air when the songs ended, and Angilia agreed to answer some questions and respond to comments. The first caller said she remembered her uncle. "We graduated high school together, and Patrick was always silly and even rather quiet in school. I got the feeling he didn't like school a lot. We all thought he was the most handsome boy in school, but he was oblivious to all of us. He was far more interested in his boats. I don't know how you managed to do this, but I just want to thank you for this. You have brought back many lovely memories," the woman told Angilia, while Eric listened in the palace sitting room with Roger and smiled.

No one seemed to figure out the technicalities of how Angilia recorded with her dead uncle, but the overwhelming consensus was that the two songs were lyrically and vocally the most heart-searing, beautiful duets anyone had heard.

By 5:00 that afternoon, Sam met with Angilia and Eric in the palace sitting room. "These two songs have already gone gold just from the purchases on your web site, Angilia. I think we do need to do some more media, just because the public response is unprecedented. Is it at all possible to set something up for television? I don't know how all of this works when one of the singers lives in Heaven," Sam confessed, as he sipped coffee. "What will work?"

"We might be able to, but not yet. Michael wants us to hold off on that until after the book. Once people read about Patrick and understand that truth, then we can probably arrange something," Angilia told him.

"Michael, the head angel?" Sam asked, and Angilia nodded in answer. "Okay, what about in print? Anything?"

"Probably," Angilia said while she texted someone. "We need to discuss it a bit more, but a magazine article will be okay." At that moment Eduardo appeared and asked what she wanted.

"Come in, Uncle Eduardo. Sam wants us to do a print interview, and the only person I trust to do this is you. Will you?"

Eduardo was stunned. "Me? I haven't written anything like this in so long, I'm sure I am rusty." Angilia, Eric, and Sam ignored his protestations and excuses. "If you don't conduct the interview and Bonnie doesn't take the pictures, then I'm not doing it. Neither is Patrick. Right, Uncle Patrick?"

"Right," he said. He had not manifested, so they could only hear him. Eduardo stood up in shock at hearing a disembodied voice. "It's okay, it's just me. We have something really cool in common. We're both Angilia's only uncles, man!"

Eduardo slowly sat down, wondering if he were hallucinating. "Right," he finally said, shaking his head to clear his brain.

"Will you, Uncle Eduardo?"

He looked at his precious niece, the girl who had engineered his freedom eight years earlier, and nodded. "For you, I will do anything, my Angel, especially after that wonderful surprise party and birthday gift you gave me yesterday afternoon. Hearing your new songs was the perfect start to my birthday, it really was. The book you made for me takes my breath away, Angilia," he said and hugged her, referring to an illustrated biography of him she had made as his 63$^{rd}$ birthday present. "Patrick is right. Being your uncle is very cool."

§§§§

Over the following two days, Eduardo interviewed Angilia about her upcoming memoir and the two duets with Patrick. In detail, she explained how the two songs came into existence and how her (dead) uncle recorded them with her. Without giving away any so-called big reveals in the book, Angilia explained and clarified the questions she was most asked. The one most asked question was how a man who died in 1977 could record newly-written songs with Angilia. The second most asked question she received was whether Matthew's portrayal of her as an angel was fantasy or reality. His comments at the gallery opening teased and confounded people.

Throughout the two-day interview, Bonnie took dozens of pictures, and followed uncle and niece around the palace and its grounds as they chatted comfortably. Eduardo carried an audio recorder and a notebook. He made notes about what he would add to the article in addition to the standard questions and answers. Eduardo would expand upon what he considered essential and offer commentary as well as first-hand knowledge and confirmation to the piece.

On Thursday afternoon, Eduardo and Angilia sat in the music room talking, while Bonnie snapped pictures. Suddenly, Angilia felt Patrick's familiar warmth and smiled at him as he

239

manifested beside her on the sofa. "Hello, Uncle Patrick. Uncle Eduardo is writing an article about our songs and the book."

"Yeah, I know. I've been listening. I just wanted to drop in and say hi to everyone. Hi!"

Angilia giggled and hugged her perpetually-youthful uncle. "Uncle Patrick, I love you. You remember Uncle Eduardo from my wedding. Uncle Eduardo, this is Uncle Patrick."

Eduardo recalled the handsome stranger who had danced with Angilia, and he remembered seeing Patrick in church that Sunday with the mother and daughter. He had never even suspected that the young man was Eric's teenaged brother. Eduardo reached over and shook Patrick's hand, quite surprised that the hand felt human. Bonnie snapped pictures quickly, capturing the moment more for Angilia than for use in the magazine.

Eduardo included Patrick in the interview, as well, since he was half of the duo. Eduardo asked Patrick what had inspired his stanzas in 1973, so long before Angilia wrote her matching lyrics. "Well, I turned 15 that January, and it was around that time that I started feeling all of this fear and doubt about my death. I just had this gnawing feeling that I wouldn't live long, that I wouldn't get married and have any children. I was afraid I would die without anyone to carry on my legacy. I was afraid no one would remember me or that what I did when I was alive wouldn't matter. I think that's why AAV was so important to me, because I could do something valuable that mattered to me and to other people. It all kinda started swimming in my head around that time."

"That's what you wrote in "My Purpose," Uncle Patrick. Those fears and questions came out in that poem. Until I read your stanzas of "Our Dreams," I had no idea it was all inside of you for so long, though." Angilia held her uncle's hand in both of hers, and felt tears fill her eyes.

"Yeah, but it's all okay. You know why, Little One. You are my legacy. You live for me. I wasn't even talking about songs when I said that the first time. But you do carry my legacy, my torch. You've kept me alive on earth." Patrick smiled at Angilia and gently brushed a tear from her cheek.

"Patrick, in your stanzas, you wrote that you dreamed of an angel. Why did you use that noun in 1973?" Eduardo asked.

Patrick sat for a moment, seeming unsure of the answer himself. "I don't know really. There were plenty of other two-syllable words that would have fit—woman, lover, girlfriend, maiden, lady, princess—but angel is what I wrote in the first draft by instinct. I remember sitting in that huge chair in my room just writing quickly in the notebook. I knew what I wanted to say basically, and I just let it come out of me and onto paper. If you look at the page, you'll see a few places where I scratched out some words and replaced them with better words. But angel just seemed right. It felt right. And the whole thing was like a dream, so it did fit. If I was to dream the perfect girl to help me, she would be an angel. I didn't have to dream her, though. She did come to me, and she did save me. She erased all of my doubts and fears."

"You mean a real angel came to you, Patrick?" Eduardo asked, already knowing the answer.

"Yeah, sure. When I died, she came to me. My niece Angilia came to me 19 years before she was born. She came to me from Heaven, and that's where she took me after I died. She took away the fears and the doubts and replaced them with peace and joy and love. She really did. Angilia is the angel I dreamed about," Patrick said while he smiled at his niece. "Angilia is an angel in every sense of the word, literally and symbolically. You know that, Eduardo."

"I do, Patrick. Angilia saved me and Bonnie and the other hostages. She is our angel, too. She did what no one else had been able to do. Angilia arranged our freedom. She gave us back our lives," Eduardo said as tears choked him. He noticed Bonnie wiping tears, too, and he motioned for her to join him on the sofa. The four of them sat in silence for a few moments.

Suddenly Bonnie smiled. "I want to take a picture of the three of you together. Get close together." Eduardo moved to sit next to Angilia, placing her between her two uncles. Bonnie took several pictures as the three of them moved and giggled, smiled and hugged. She pulled the pictures up on her computer and showed them to Eduardo, Angilia, and Patrick.  They all agreed that their collective favorite should be used in the magazine.

The May 2020 issue of <u>Music Beat</u> monthly hit the newsstands on Monday, March 30 and sold out in record numbers throughout Valdavia, France, Italy, Spain, England, Scotland, Wales, Ireland, and Germany where it was published.  A special edition was published in North America and the East to meet worldwide demand.  Until talk began spreading, no one knew that Patrick was in any way involved with the interview, but his participation and picture created global interest and buzz.

His status as a teen idol had been officially reinstated as soon as the two songs were released.  When people, especially teenagers, saw his picture in the magazine, the demand for all things Patrick created an industry of Patrick souvenirs.  His pictures appeared on lunch boxes, t-shirts, backpacks, notebooks, socks, handheld computer cases, and even postage stamps.  One high-end collectible doll company even manufactured a Prince Patrick doll which became their best selling product in their 25 year history.  The president of the company, Robert Geppetto, sent a Prince Patrick doll to Angilia as a gift that year with a personal letter explaining that 50 percent of the doll's profits were donated to the AAV.

The same day <u>Music Beat</u> was released, Sam rushed to the palace, overwhelmed and thrilled simultaneously.  "Angilia, people can't get enough of you and Patrick.  Listen, I know the book is coming out in a few days and you have the book tour starting.  In the next few days, we have to do something if we can.  I can schedule a concert if you and Patrick can be there to perform.  What do you think?"

"I can, but I don't know about Patrick.  We have to talk it over with Michael, you know," Angilia answered.

"Michael says it's fine, really he does," Patrick assured them as he suddenly manifested.  "He says it's close to the book's release and we have the official blessing.  I'll be there, she'll make sure of that," Patrick promised with his characteristic giggle.

§§§§

Sam managed to book a concert for Saturday, April 4, 2020 at downtown Valmondois' largest venue, the Gateway Arena. Tickets went on sale March 30 and sold out all 25,000 seats within three hours. Despite the lack of planning time, several hundred fans flew from all parts of the world for the double billing of Angilia and Prince Patrick. Speculation was still rampant as to whether Patrick would appear in some sort of hologram form. Wasn't that how the photograph of Angilia, Eduardo, and Patrick had been created? Regardless of how it was done, people longed to see and hear this concert.

People crowded the mall outside the palace all morning, hoping against hope to see Angilia before the concert. "Hey, Little One. I'm ready when you need me. What's going on?"

"They want to see you," Matthew said from a chair in the music room, where he and Angilia were relaxing.

"Oh, okay. Come on! Let's say hi to everyone!" Patrick led Angilia to a small balcony facing the mall, and Matthew called Mike and Tony to the music room when the frantic screams of lovesick fans nearly shook the palace foundation. Mike and Tony rushed in just as Eric, Roger, and Eduardo ran in to find out what happened. They all stood in stunned silence for a moment, never expecting such a public spectacle before the concert. Sam arrived at the palace and bolted from his car when he looked up and saw Patrick and Angilia waving to several hundred frantic fans.

When Sam breathlessly ran into the music room, his frown turned into a smile. "You know, I was going to put a halt to this immediately. I hadn't wanted him to be seen before the show. But this is actually wonderful! Brilliant, in fact. Everyone here sees him with Angilia, and they are over the moon in ecstasy right now. Their idol is right in front of them. This is going to build the anticipation before the show. Speaking of which, we have to get to the arena soon." Sam called his two megastars back into the room and told them to get ready.

Within the hour, Sam, Mike, Tony, and six other security officers left for the drive to the arena with Angilia and Patrick. Mike and Tony demanded that the dark windows remain closed to protect

Angilia and Patrick from a rush of fans. Soon they were inside the arena with the band, who met Patrick for the first time. They, too, had read Angilia's book and accepted everything she wrote as truth. They knew her far too well to ever doubt her.

The concert began in two hours, so Angilia, Patrick, Tim, Greg, Joe, and John did the sound and light checks for 45 minutes. One hour before show time, the audience was let in, and the excited voices and shouts could be heard from the dressing rooms backstage. Eric, Matthew, and the rest of the Royal party arrived via the VIP entrance and greeted the band and everyone else.

Matthew smiled as he watched Angilia, and when she turned from talking with Sam, she smiled back and hugged her husband. Eric watched his little brother toss a small rubber ball into the air and catch it, something Patrick had often done as a boy. If he had not seen Patrick die, even Eric would doubt that the teenager he watched at that moment was actually dead.

Patrick smiled at his brother, as if sensing Eric's thoughts, and threw the ball to him. Eric caught it and smiled back. Patrick leapt from the counter where he sat and lunged at Eric in a huge hug. "You should join us, Eric. You would really send everyone over the edge if you made a surprise appearance at the end."

Eric smiled, but shook his head and said the moment belonged to Patrick and Angilia. "That's actually brilliant! Why didn't I think of that?" Sam suddenly enthused. "Eric, you will join your daughter and brother for the last song. Just make it a trio instead of a duet. Can you imagine the reaction when you walk out? Oh, man, this is going to be the concert to top all other concerts."

Angilia smiled and said, "You already know the song, Daddy. Sam can text you with a three-song warning so you can leave the box and come down." Angilia handed her father a copy of the sheet music for the last song she and Patrick had on their set list, and Eric smiled.

"Are you sure?" Eric asked her and Patrick. They both beamed and hugged him, telling him they would never accept a refusal from him. "Okay, then, I'll come down. You know, this will be the first time Patrick and I have sung together."

§§§§

At 5:00 Angilia was introduced, and the curtain rose to reveal her center front with her four-member band behind her. Angilia began playing the opening chords of the late 1960s song "Get Together," and Patrick's voice joined hers on the chorus. He bounded on stage, and as Angilia knew they would, the audience jumped to their feet in delirious euphoria. He and Angilia could barely hear one another over the shouts, screams, and cheers of the audience.

This continued throughout most of the concert, as they sang duets of 1960s and 1970s songs that Patrick had selected: "Put a Little Love in Your Heart," "Mr. Tambourine Man," "Turn, Turn, Turn," ""What the World Needs Now," "Where Have All the Flowers Gone?," "San Francisco (Be Sure to Wear Flowers in Your Hair)," and "Catch the Wind." When Patrick took the lead vocals for the first time, on an interpretation of "Run to Me," the audience became miraculously quiet so that they could hear him. His lead vocals were peppered throughout the set and included "Ruby Tuesday," "Wildfire," and a song Eric remembered his brother playing a lot during the spring of 1977, "That's Rock 'n' Roll."

Near the end of the concert, Angilia's guitar chords sent the audience into rousing cheers again when they instantly recognized "Little Girl Lost." Ten minutes after it ended and she encouraged them to stop screaming, Angilia promised the audience, "This is the song you've been waiting for." She played the opening notes of "Our Dreams," and girls began crying and reaching for Patrick. To older members of the audience the reaction reminded them of Donny Osmond or David Cassidy concerts in the 1970s. Patrick really was a bona fide teen idol.

Finally, Angilia glanced at stage left, turned to her band, and nodded. Eric was ready to join her and Patrick. Tim Hanley's electric guitar kicked off the familiar melody of the huge 1972 Elvis hit "Burning Love," the song Patrick selected to close the show. He wanted to do at least one legitimate rock song. She had planned all along to sing harmony, so Patrick began singing, while Eric sang with him and ran on stage.

Everyone in the arena jumped to their feet yet again and screamed, cheered, and charged to the stage. The sight and sound of Eric and Patrick together did exactly what Sam predicted. Peoples' reactions seemed to explode and literally rock the arena. Their demand for more could not go ignored, so Angilia, Patrick, and Eric quickly decided on two more songs to sing together.

They closed the concert with impromptu trio versions of two songs which they felt best expressed the overriding message they hoped to impart. The first was "My Sweet Lord," and the final song they performed was an energetic and heartfelt rendering of "Spirit in the Sky." Angilia, Patrick, and Eric bowed, thanked everyone, and waved to the audience for several minutes. Finally, they walked backstage, where Sam grabbed them in a collective hug and said they had exceeded even his expectations.

The concert led news stories that night and Sunday morning and filled trade publications and news magazine for several weeks to follow. One respected music critic proclaimed Patrick's instant stardom a miracle and lauded the young Prince as "a gentle, expressive singer who touches the soul of the listener." In fact, Patrick caused a near riot Sunday morning by walking to church with his family and friends. His existence as an angel was out in the open now, and when Angilia's memoir was released in three days people would know everything about him, her, and Eric. Their lives would forever change, and they knew that their story and truth would affect and change others' lives as well. Everything they did was sanctioned and sanctified by God.

§§§§

Angilia, Sam, and 12 security officers arrived at Gathered Leaves bookstore at 9:30 on the morning of April 8, 2020. Her memoir, <u>My Life In Heaven and Earth</u>, was officially released that day, and most retailers had opened at midnight to meet public demand for the book. Fans who had purchased the book earlier stayed in line to have her autograph their copies. When she arrived and greeted the people lined up, she noticed that many were already reading her memoir.

Angilia was scheduled to discuss the book and answer questions prior to the signing.  People had been given numbered tickets when they bought books or arrived to stand in line, so that they would have an assigned order for the autograph line.  Sam made sure everything was ready for Angilia, including a stool so that she could sit at the podium if she needed.  Since she would be at the bookstore for several hours, he made sure she had plenty of water and that a lunch break was included in her schedule.

At 10:00, people entered the bookstore and took seats in the largest area of the store, where Angilia would talk with them about her autobiography.  Marian Templeton, the bookstore owner, introduced Angilia, who was greeted with a standing ovation. "Thank you for coming and for your interest in my story.  I was encouraged to write my earliest memories and experiences in 2012 when Mr. Arthur Brennan saw the truth about me.  Four years later, when Matthew and I were in Scotland, he, too, told me that I needed to write my life story.  I had intended to write this book for my family only.  Last year, though, a not-so-chance encounter with a lovely mother and daughter convinced me to make the book public.

"Natalie, who was six years old at the time, saw me as I really am one Sunday morning.  She wanted me to talk with her mother Sarah, and since that pivotal moment opens the book, I won't spoil it and reveal too many details.  Suffice it to say that Sarah and Natalie were not there that morning by happenstance.  God placed them in my life for a reason, to show me that my story can make a difference.  In fact, Sarah and Natalie are here today," Angilia said with a smile as she encouraged them to stand for recognition.

"The most important statement I can make is that I wrote my true story.  I cannot claim to know anyone else's story except my own.  Everything I wrote in these 12 chapters is true for me.  I even rushed to write a postscript about the recent duets with my beloved Uncle Patrick.  That experience is detailed in the postscript, but I will tell you that his involvement was not coincidental, either.  What turned into the song "Our Dreams" began easily enough, but after I wrote my lines, I just could not finish.  Patrick manifested for a visit and retrieved an old notebook of his that contained his lines.  He had already written the other half of the song in 1973.  Our words were meant to fuse together.  Patrick was destined to do this.

"In fact, his involvement is ordained and blessed.  If Patrick were still physically alive, he would be 62 years old.  He died in 1977, which means he is perpetually 19 years old.  My father saw his brother on Christmas Day 2012, for the first time since the day of Patrick's death.  One of the first things my father said to me was that Patrick looked just the same as he had on July 19, 1977.  Sarah said the same thing last year when Patrick manifested to join our conversation.

"The arching truth in the book is that people do not die.  Their bodies die, but their souls never die.  Souls are eternal.  Uncle Patrick has not changed at all since his physical death.  He officially lives in Heaven.  His residence changed.  He didn't change.  Angels exist among us.  Rarely do they manifest, though.  Patrick does, probably so that people can see him for themselves and believe the truth.  So many people know my uncle or know about him.  Seeing him on stage with me or walking to church with his family shows people that his essence, his soul, still lives.

"Eternal life is quite a difficult abstract concept for most people.  The idea that time never ends is alien to humans, because we live by the clock.  Time does not exist in Heaven.  Realize, though, that when you die, your soul will spend eternity in the most gloriously beautiful place surrounded by your loved ones who have already died.  That is our reward for living a godly life on earth.  I can tell you with honesty and first-hand knowledge that you do not want to be anywhere else for all time than Heaven.  I know some people refer to Valdavia as a Utopia, but the real Utopia, the only Utopia, is Heaven.

"When I was in the Unborn Children Sphere and the Angels Choir prior to my birth, everyone except my Uncle Patrick told me that I would never remember anything about either place or what happened to me there. Patrick is the only one who told me I would.  I do.  I remember everything and everyone quite vividly.  This memory of mine that got people talking about me years ago, this hyperthymesia, is a gift from God.  God wanted me to remember everything.  His purpose for me and my differentness led me to this book, this memoir, in which I reveal everything about my life before, during, and after my birth. My goal is to try my best to fulfill his will and calling. I hope as you read the book you at least accept it as my truth."

For the next hour, Angilia answered questions about Michael the Archangel, her meeting with God to get Patrick out of trouble, being a Spirit Guide, going from Heaven to earth, and her drawings of Matthew, the Unborn Children Sphere, and the Angels Choir. People were fascinated by her life, and many had already read several chapters since midnight. Sarah and Natalie were even asked about their talk with Angilia and Patrick and what it felt like talking with two angels. Many in the audience asked Angilia to pose for pictures with Sarah and Natalie, which she gladly did.

In fact, the first copies of the book she autographed were for Sarah and Natalie. Gathered Leaves had ordered 12,000 copies, the most they could order due to global demand, and all 12,000 copies sold before Angilia's signing was scheduled to end. She talked with people over the remaining 90 minutes and reminded everyone about the publisher's web site for the book, which included a discussion forum. "I promise to get on as often as I can and answer questions," she said as everyone applauded her and clutched their beautiful new books.

While Angilia and Sam prepared to leave and return to the palace, they were approached by a man they instantly recognized from television. "Your Royal Highness, I am pleased to meet you. I bought your book at midnight and have already finished reading it. What a fascinating, elucidating memoir. I would like to invite you and Prince Patrick as guests on my show. If it helps to persuade you, I will donate your appearance payments to Learning for Life," Walter Catscombe said in his famously serious voice.

Angilia thanked him, and Sam said it sounded like a great opportunity. "I trust tomorrow is clear for Their Royal Highnesses. I have already rented the downtown theatre for the day so the show can broadcast from there. Angilia and Patrick will be my guests for the entire two hours. I'm hoping you will perform your two hit songs, as well. Do we have a deal?"

Angilia was stunned. "I have to check with Patrick so we can clear this with Michael. May I be excused for a moment so I can contact Patrick?"

"No need, Little One," Patrick suddenly said as he manifested between her and Sam. "Michael said it's okay. You let me know when to show up, Little One, and I'll be there."

Walter's eyes were huge and his mouth was open in his astonishment. "Can you do that tomorrow? I'll introduce Angilia, and she will come on stage and take her seat near me. Then she will call you and you can—what's the word?" he asked as he quickly flipped through the book. "Manifest. You can manifest when your niece calls you. That will be amazing."

Patrick giggled. "Sure, I can do that. It's not hard. That's how I always appear to Little One or Eric."

"Super. I will see you both at the theatre tomorrow morning at 9:00. Sam and I will go for some coffee and settle the contracts. Thank you both," Walter smiled and took Sam's arm to lead him away. Mike and Tony shook their heads, aghast at Catscombe's directness and presumptiveness.

§§§§§

Sam, Mike, Tony and six guards drove Angilia and Patrick to the downtown theatre, where the two megastars were greeted by several hundred screaming fans. Security surrounded Angilia as she entered the VIP entrance. Patrick simply changed into spirit form until he was inside, then giggled as he manifested again. "That was fun," Patrick enthused.

Walter Catscombe greeted them, whisked them into the green room, and pointed out the coffee, juice, fruit, and pastries. He was so insistent that Angilia accepted a glass of orange juice and a few strawberries. "Patrick? What would you prefer?" Walter asked the young man who sat unmoving on the sofa beside his niece.

"Nothing, thank you. I'm fine."

"You had a hearty breakfast, I take it?" Walter smiled with a blindingly white row of teeth.

"No. I don't eat," Patrick simply replied.

"You don't eat?"

"No, of course not. Angels don't need to eat. I haven't eaten since the morning of July 19, 1977," Patrick said as he pulled the ball from his hoodie pocket and tossed it in the air and caught it.

"I love it. I just love it. We have to include this in the show. People will eat this up. Pardon the pun," Walter said. "You are perfect, just perfect." He turned to Sam and the security team. "This boy is a natural. This is going to be the highest-rated show I have ever hosted. Brilliant." He let out a loud "Yes!" when he left the room.

"Wow. Whatever. We're here on God's behalf, not for his ratings," Patrick said, still tossing and catching the ball.

Angilia smiled. "Include that in your comments, too, when you magically appear." Patrick giggled and hugged his niece.

Patrick did say just that when Angilia introduced her uncle and he manifested beside her on the sofa. Walter Catscombe appeared flustered by the unexpected, unscheduled reference to God, but when the audience cheered in agreement and support, the host smiled and knew he had a winner indeed. Handsome looks, boyish charm, talent, Christian faith, and the fact that he was a prince and an honest to goodness angel—how could this not become the ratings coupe of a lifetime?

Walter was, in fact, impressed by Angilia's memoir, and he was quite familiar with her multi-faceted career. He realized that her Christian faith was strong, as well as a major influence on her life. He knew he had to respect that on the show or face the world's wrath. He asked her questions about when she started writing songs and why, as well as from where she got her ideas and inspiration.

"I wrote my first song when I was four, a sophomoric song about an old brown clock that my Great-grandfather kept in his suite. It ticked loudly. My ideas come from my life and the people, places, and things that somehow affect me. That ranges from something as simple as a clock to something as complex as facing death."

"You write in the book that you have never been afraid of death. What do you mean that facing death is complex?" Walter asked Angilia.

"I'm not afraid of death. There is nothing to fear. However, had I died eight years ago, my predestined life would have halted and thrown so many other parts of God's plan off course. For example, I knew I would marry and have a child. Had I died at the age of 16, my child would never have lived. Two lives would have ended at that moment. I never want to jeopardize my child's life. My child is my sole purpose for living," Angilia explained.

"That is a very selfless perspective, Your Royal Highness. Patrick, the poem you wrote when you were 16, the one Angilia set to music and recorded with her father, speaks to your fears of death. You wrote something similar in the poem, that you feared dying young with no children. Was your point of view similar to your niece's at that age?"

"No, because I was more focused on myself, actually. My thoughts were selfish really. I wondered what would happen to my legacy and my memory after I died. I sensed I would die young, which did happen, but I was afraid of what would happen to me. I now know how wrong that is, but like Angilia told me when she found my poem, lots of people feel that at some point. Will I make a difference? Will people remember me? Pretty common questions, I guess," Patrick said in his openly honest way.

"How is it that you are here today, Patrick? Angilia's book has generated a lot of talk about angels and Heaven, and many people do believe in angels. Still, no one has experienced an angelic encounter in this fashion before, where the angel manifests and is for all intents and purposes human. What prompted you to go public?" Walter asked the 62-year-old teenaged Prince.

"Angilia, actually. There are people who saw her as the angel she is, with her angel wings and halo actually. Those who saw the real Angilia were changed and affected deeply by the experiences. Michael sent me down to join Angilia one day last year when Angilia was talking with Sarah, a mother whose baby had died. I manifested, and because Sarah knew about me and yet saw and heard me, she believed that souls never die. I still look, talk, and act as I did in 1977. I always will. The trippy thing is that if my body hadn't died, I'd be 62 years old now. But because my body is dead, my soul is forever 19. Souls never age or die. Angilia is my angel and my inspiration," Patrick said and put his arm around his niece.

Walter asked Patrick what his instant superstardom felt like. "I'm pleased that people respond to what Angilia and I do, I really am. Michael signed off on all of this, because he and God knew it would reach people and make them see the same thing Sarah saw, that physical death is never the end. The soul lives forever. The purpose behind all of this really is part of our serving God," Patrick explained.

"I knew once Michael approved of my memoir that Patrick's giving me his stanzas to complete "Our Dreams" was ordained. That was meant to happen. Patrick's visibility is analogous to the Apostle Thomas, who doubted Jesus' resurrection until he saw and touched the risen Jesus. When people see, hear, and touch Patrick, they believe that he is real even though his body died 43 years ago," Angilia added with a smile for her uncle.

For the following hour, Angilia and Patrick answered questions from audience members. One woman introduced herself as Alexandra and said she graduated high school with Patrick. "I spoke to you live on the radio, Princess Angilia," she reminded them of her call to Dave Rodan's program. "Patrick, you signed my yearbook in June 1976. Is it possible for you to sign it again?" Walter beckoned Alexandra to the stage and had her show Patrick's yearbook picture on camera. Everyone saw that he looked exactly the same. Patrick took a pen from Walter and signed a new message alongside his 1976 message: *"Dear Alexandra, Keep the faith! Love, Peace, and Joy, Patrick* ☺ *"* Patrick kissed his former classmate's cheek when he returned the yearbook. "He's real all right," Alexandra excitedly proclaimed as she left the stage and returned to her seat.

They closed the Walter Catscombe Show by singing their two songs, just as they had recorded them—their voices accompanied by Angilia's guitar. They charmed and put everyone under their spell. The two of them agreed to sign copies of Angilia's memoir for everyone in the audience. That two-hour edition of Walter's show did indeed break ratings records and generate quite a lot more talk about angels and Heaven and eternal life.

§§§§§

Eric, Matthew, Roger, Susan, Daniel, and Sam traveled with Angilia on her book tour, as did Mike, Tony, and two dozen security officers. Her first engagement took her to the New York Public Library location at Fifth Avenue and 42nd Street. As she had done at Gathered Leaves, Angilia spoke about key moments and themes in the memoir, answered questions, and signed copies of her book. One member of the audience approached her at the end of the signing and introduced himself as Father Andrew Lord of the St. Patrick Catholic Church.

"Your Royal Highness, I have read your memoir four times, and am enthralled by your truth and peace. I realize this is very short notice, but our entire congregation has read or is reading your life story, and we would so like to ask if you might speak to us about your life in Heaven. Our church is located in Jamestown," Father Lord said rather apprehensively and apologetically.

Angilia thanked him, asked Sam and Susan to check her schedule, and chatted with him for several moments. Sam finally confirmed that if they managed to visit the church the following afternoon they could maintain their schedule. Father Lord quickly printed driving directions from a library computer, gave them all his business card, said he would call his church members immediately with the time of her visit, and kissed Angilia's hands.

Sure enough, the following day, April 17, proved busy. Angilia's previously-scheduled talk at a large Manhattan bookstore lasted most of the morning, ending in time for a quick lunch before they drove to Father Lord's church. He greeted the Royal party and led them inside, where the pews were filled to capacity. Everyone began talking excitedly when they saw Angilia, and she smiled as she followed Father Lord to the front of the church.  People quickly made room for the King, Duc, and members of the Royal party.

Each member of the congregation held a copy of <u>My Life In Heaven and Earth</u>, anxious to hear from the angel herself.  None of them had met an angel or had an angelic encounter before.  They sat engrossed in Angilia's words, her anecdotes, and her experiences.  When Angilia spoke of her purpose for being an angel and staying in the Angels Choir, one woman raised her hand to ask, "Would it be possible to meet your uncle, too?  We would love to hear from him what it is like being an angel in Heaven."

Angilia smiled and said, "Uncle Patrick, the parishioners of St. Patrick Catholic Church would like to talk with you about Heaven."  Each member of the church sat in quiet anticipation, and when Patrick suddenly manifested, some of them fell to their knees in prayer while others jumped to their feet in praise.

"Hey, everyone, it's just me," Patrick giggled.  "Cool name for the church, though.  I hope I can live up to my namesake saint and do God's work and will as well as he did."

Patrick's mere presence alone convinced them that he and Angilia were indeed angels on earth doing God's work.  They were praised as modern-day apostles, even saints, by many who saw and heard them throughout the four-week book tour.  Several churches invited Angilia to Sunday services and asked her to speak to the congregations.  She gladly did so, often with Patrick's assistance, as Eric, Matthew, Roger, Susan, Daniel, Sam, Mike, Tony, and the other security officers watched in love, admiration, and gratitude.

The Royal party arrived home in Valmondois on May 11 to a veritable parade.  Angilia was never more surprised—or touched.  Valdavians had followed Angilia's book tour and knew how she—and Patrick—had touched countless hearts and souls over the past four weeks.  To them, their future Queen was already a saint for her compassion, her tireless work, her generosity, her faith, and now for her work on behalf of God.  Their devotion to Angilia grew to epic proportions henceforth.

§§§§

Angilia returned from her COC meeting on June 3, and entered the office she shared with her father. "Hello, Daddy," she said and went to hug him and kiss his cheek.

"Hello my beautiful daughter Angilia," he smiled as he pulled her onto his lap. "You are incredible, Angel. You always have been, but now you are genuinely touching hearts and changing lives. I watch you do this evangelistic work so effortlessly and honestly, and I am blown away by you each time. I always knew you were ordained by God, baby, but now the whole world knows, too. I am so honored and humbled to be your father, Angilia. I love you so very much." Eric closed his eyes and hugged his daughter close.

"Oh, Daddy, you give me far too much credit. The credit goes to God and to you. Both of you are my inspiration, my strength, and the source of my knowledge. Without both of you, I would never exist. I am so grateful to God for blessing me with you. I love you more than life, Daddy." Eric held her, and tears slid down his cheeks. He, more than anyone, knew the deep truth in her declaration of love.

§§§§§

One month later, Angilia and Katherine took Juanita to the coffee shop for tea and camaraderie for a couple of hours. The three of them sat at Angilia's favorite table chatting, laughing, and enjoying the fresh air and sunshine. The lemon tea and Juanita's favorite anise cookies proved sweet and relaxing.

Juanita suddenly hugged her granddaughter. "I am so happy to spend some time with you, mi nieta. This year has been quite a frantic and busy one for you, Angilia. I do not know how you have crammed so very much into six months. You never seem to stop. You never fail to amaze me."

"Abuela, I love you. I'm sorry I haven't been here much of the year to spend time with you and Abuelo. I love you both so very much. I hope you know that. I never expected any of this to happen, Abuela. God put the pieces together and showed me the path I must follow, so I have done the best I can to honor and obey him. I always knew there was a reason I am the way I am, though, and now I know that reason. God is using me and Patrick to do his bidding on earth, and we are both humbled and honored to do so. You have all been so understanding and patient with me through all of this," Angilia said, taking Juanita's and Katherine's hands in hers.

"Oh, mi nieta, we love you and we are so honored and grateful to be your grandparents. Knowing you blesses us every moment, you must know that. We always saw God's hand on you, just because you were so unlike anyone else, so advanced and talented. None of this truly surprises us, but it does fill our hearts with love and joy," Juanita said and kissed her granddaughter.

"Mitchell and I feel the same way, Angilia," Katherine added and kissed Angilia's hand. "You are so very special, and the love, happiness, and peace you bring to Matthew touches my heart so much, my dear. We can see the love between the two of you every moment. I must say, some of this did take us by surprise, especially seeing your uncle, but it really shouldn't have. We know how special you are, Angilia."

"You two are going to make me cry. I do love you both. Before we have teary-eyed pictures of us all over the press, let's head home, okay?" Angilia had a very special reason for wanting to take her beloved grandmother home soon. She and Katherine helped Juanita into Angilia's pink car and soon she drove into the palace garage and helped Abuela walk to the patio.

"Happy birthday!" everyone shouted as they popped streamers into the air.

"Oh, my goodness, I had no idea," Juanita said with a big smile. "I thought tea with Angilia and Katherine was my birthday treat."

Angilia kissed her grandmother and said, "You don't think we'd ever settle for just lemon tea on your birthday, do you? You deserve so much more, Abuela."

Alejandro kissed his wife of 72 years, a tender moment that brought smiles and tears to everyone present. Everyone kissed Juanita and wished her a very happy 90th birthday. Eduardo cried as he held both of his parents close to him, grateful and blessed to be with them and to have them with him.

Everyone sat on the patio while they relished having the entire circle of family and friends together. Their love and joy filled the universe and their hearts that day while they talked, laughed, hugged, sang, and prayed.

Soon, Eric surprised everyone by telling them to freshen up and get in his Rolls Royce. Twenty minutes later, the car arrived at the Musée National de Valdavia, and the Royal party was welcomed into the Royal Portrait Gallery for a private unveiling. As he had on Alejandro's 90th birthday, Eric spoke from the podium.

"I am so very honored to introduce the latest portrait to our family's gallery. I look around at the faces of all who have come before and those we have known. There is one face missing, however, and that is soon to be corrected. My daughter somehow managed to paint another portrait for the museum during one of the most amazing years of her very young life. Eduardo, please do the honors and unveil the gallery's newest portrait."

Eduardo beamed when he pulled the gold cord to reveal a beautiful portrait of his mother, which Angilia asked be placed above her portrait of her mother, Marisol. Juanita turned and leaned against Alejandro in tears—"Happy tears," she managed to reassure them. She reached for her granddaughter and kissed her cheeks multiple times in her happiness.

"Mi nieta, you sat there as I talked about all the many things you have done in just six months this year, and you never let on once. How do you do all of this? Oh, never mind, mi nieta. You are the light of my life. I love you, Angilia. You make me look so much better than I truly look," Juanita said to a muttering of giggles and protests. "I am so happy to join the family here, and to be close to my Alejandro and my Marisol. You make my heart so very happy, my precious Angel, so very happy."

# CHAPTER 10

"Happy birthday, my Angilia," Matthew said when he opened his eyes and saw his beautiful wife watching him. Matthew put his arms around her waist and pulled her to him. "I love you so," he whispered and kissed her passionately. "Oh, how I love you."

"I love you, darling," Angilia replied and leaned across him. "Our engagement was announced five years ago, Matthew. What a happy, glorious, wonderful five years we have shared."

"I know. I never imagined I could be so very happy. You made me believe in happily ever after, my love. We will be happy for all time."

"We will." She pulled the pendant from under her gown and Matthew gently held it as they looked again at the miraculous view of Eric, Marisol, Angilia, and Matthew together in Heaven. "Matthew, I love you and our life together. If we are this happy now, on earth, imagine how very happy we shall be for all eternity in Heaven." A tear slid from Matthew's eye and he held his wife close, knowing beyond any doubt that she spoke the truth.

§§§§

"Happy birthday, my beautiful daughter Angilia," Eric said with a smile as he leaned in her suite doorway.

Angilia stood from her desk chair, where she was writing in her diary, and hugged her father. "I love you, my magnificent father."

Eric cleared his throat, feeling tears forming, and handed her a wrapped box. She felt tears in her throat when she saw his birthday letter to her under the pink ribbon. She placed the letter on her desk, untied the ribbon, and removed the box lid. Nestled in protective foam she saw a music box unlike any other she had ever seen. "Oh, Daddy, this is truly beautiful! I don't know what to say. Thank you." Angilia kissed her father's cheek while she held the music box in her hands.

"The idea came to me several months ago, and I had a master music box artisan in Germany create this. I described what I wanted, and sent him several of your wedding pictures and the music to your piano piece for Matthew on your wedding day. He made it just the way I saw it in my head. You and Matthew on your wedding day, waltzing to the piece you wrote just for him." Eric turned the key and they watched the miniature sculptures of Angilia and Matthew come together in a waltz as the melody of "Love's True Blessing" played. The gold base was adorned with pearls, garnets, and blue sapphires. "I'm glad you like it, Angel."

"Like it? Oh, Daddy, I love you, and this is such a treasure for all time. Your love created me and everything you do for me. I cherish this, because it, too, is made from your love. Your love is everything to me, Daddy."

§§§§

*3 January 2021*

*My Beautiful Daughter Angilia:*

*Happy 25th birthday, my wondrous, angelic daughter. The past year filled my heart and my soul with such love, admiration, and joy as you shared your truth with the world. God truly ordained you, my little girl, which I always knew. Your obedience to God is inspiring. I am more humbled, though, by your courage to follow God's path for you. Not many people would have the courage to face the world as you do. You placed your whole self in the open and let God use you to evangelize for him. I love and respect you so very much, Angilia.*

*Thank you so much for bringing Patrick back to me eight years ago and opening the door for God's plan to happen. The two of you amaze and awe me. My daughter and my brother! Seeing the two of you out there, fearless, steadfast, and loyal to God taught me so very much about faith, conviction, courage, and strength. Even when faced with naysayers and disbelievers, you never faltered or wavered. You kept marching, both of you, at the head of God's army. I remember when I visited you at Oxford just before your graduation. Even then, surrounded by praise and accolades, you pondered why God made you as he did. Now we know, Angilia. He always knew that you would spread his message to the world, both you and Patrick. This must be the reason Patrick remained in the Angels Choir—his important mission.*

*Angilia, five years ago we shared your engagement to Matthew with the world. This year we celebrate your 5th anniversary. I have never forgotten what you shared with me two years ago. We will also celebrate the birth of your son Eric this year, my beautiful daughter Angilia! What a blessing and treasure you are to me every second of my life. I love you so incredibly much, Angilia. So much. Words fail me. My feelings cannot be captured in mere words. Every day I love you more than I did the day before.*

*My Eternal Love,*

*Daddy*

§§§§§

Unable to sleep, Angilia turned onto her right side and placed her left hand over Matthew's heart. He forced his eyes open and smiled at her. "I'm sorry I woke you, darling," she whispered.

Matthew shook his head and turned onto his left side, facing her, and put his right hand on her side. "No. I'd rather have the real you than the dream you. You filled my dreams tonight, Angilia. You have filled my dreams for nearly nine years." Matthew kissed her. "What time is it?" he suddenly asked. He lifted his head and looked at the clock on the bedside table near Angilia.

"Happy Valentine's Day, my Angilia," Matthew smiled. He kissed her pink lips passionately, and simultaneously turned her onto her back. He sat on his knees, quickly removed his pajamas, and helped her onto her knees. Matthew slid her white silk gown over her head and dropped it on the floor beside the bed. He looked into her hypnotic turquoise eyes and kissed her again, pulled her to him, and lay down with her.

"I love you, Matthew.  You are my first and only love," she softly said into his ear.  "Today is our day, my love," she mysteriously said, and then she pulled his head closer and kissed his lips.  Her hands gently stroked his back as their bodies merged and they felt their love more intensely and purely than ever.  As they had vowed on their wedding day, they loved one another completely—heart, soul, and body.

At the moment Matthew moaned in ecstasy, Angilia's hands tightened, and she gasped.  "Matthew," she barely whispered.  He looked at her in fear, afraid he had hurt her.  She smiled at him, placed her hand on his cheek, though, and kissed him.  "Matthew, let's shower and get dressed so we can have plenty of time before church.  I need to share something very important with you."

"What?  Now?  Are you all right?"

She kissed him, stood up, and promised him she was fine.  She reached for his hand and pulled him to the showers behind her.  He knew that whatever she told him would stun him.  Whenever she said she had something important to tell him, she always stunned him.

Forty minutes later, she took him to Uncle Patrick's suite, sat him on the sofa, and went to the secret hiding place in the floorboard, just as she had done two years earlier.  She removed the same manila envelope and held it as she sat beside her husband.  "Matthew, do you remember in Scotland when you asked about the people I met in the Unborn Children Sphere?"

"Of course, I do.  I couldn't forget any of that if I tried to."

"I told you about Abraham Lincoln that day, and last year when I wrote that song, I told you all about meeting Pearl McGee.  There are others, as you know, but there is one I have never told you about before.  Today, I want to share him with you, Matthew."

Angilia removed the pages from the envelope and handed them to Matthew.  He read about his son in the early morning light, his brain and his heart racing. When he finished reading, he looked at her colored pencil drawing and stared at the face in breathless wonder, just as Eric had done. Matthew felt his eyes fill with tears, and he knew with certainty that he looked at the face of his unborn son. Still holding the pages, Matthew bent over, his head on his knees, and cried unabashedly for a long while.

Suddenly, he sat up, looked at his wife, and clutched her in an embrace. Angilia held him while he continued to cry on her shoulder. Finally, his sobs ended, and he said, "Oh, Angilia, you could never give me a greater miracle than this."

"Actually, I can, Matthew dear. I am pregnant with Eric. I felt him enter me earlier. I felt him. That's why I gasped, darling. I wasn't in pain. I felt our son enter me. He is with us, Matthew."

Matthew stared at her, his heart now throbbing against his sternum. His amber eyes glowed, his mouth formed a smile, and he felt love as he had never felt love before. "Angilia?"

She nodded her head. "I felt him, Matthew. Now I know what Daddy felt when my soul entered his heart on Christmas Day 1994. Eric's soul entered me, and he has begun his life on earth with us."

Matthew kissed his wife and held her close to him. He placed his hand on her tiny stomach and said, "I love you so much, Angilia and Eric."

§§§§

Matthew smiled at Eric when they met in the dining room that morning to get coffee. "You're happy today, Matthew."

"I am, more than I could ever say. Angilia wants to talk with you before breakfast. She's in Patrick's sitting room," Matthew told his father-in-law. Eric gulped his coffee and whistled as he skipped up the stairs to the third floor. Matthew smiled still, knowing the news would make Eric happier than ever. Matthew also thought how energetic, healthy, and youthful Eric was at 66. He would need that energy later that year when he became a grandfather!

Angilia heard her father's familiar footsteps and smiled. Just as he reached Patrick's door, she stood and held her arms open for a hug. Eric smiled, walked to her, and hugged her close.

"What is this for, Angel? You and Matthew are quite happy today."

"We are, Daddy. I have something wonderful to share with you. In your birthday letter to me last month, you wrote that we will celebrate the birth of my son Eric this year. We will, Daddy. I felt him come to me. I felt his soul enter me, early this morning, and I know he is with me. Your grandson will be born in nine months, Daddy."

Although he still held onto Angilia's arms, Eric's knees grew weak, and she grabbed him tighter. "Angilia? Oh, baby," he said and pulled her closer. Just as Matthew had, Eric cried the happiest tears of his life. "I love you, my beautiful daughter Angilia."

§§§§

Eric, Matthew, and Angilia decided not to tell anyone else about her pregnancy so early. It was far too soon, so they agreed to wait until her second trimester, the fourth week of May, to break the joyous news to their family and friends. Despite their unprecedented happiness, they carried out their work each day as usual. Several times each week, in the privacy of their bedroom, Matthew examined Angilia and checked her heart rate, pulse, and breathing. Six weeks after she knew she was pregnant, Matthew found her heart rate fairly normal.

During those six weeks, she attended Light Within board meetings, COC meetings at the high school, fundraising events for Learning for Life, talks about her book at Valdavian churches, and AAV fundraisers with Matthew. She snacked on more fruit throughout the day, and her friends and family presumed that Matthew had finally convinced her to eat more often to maintain her stamina.

Every morning, Eric greeted her when she left her suite for breakfast. One bright, sunny mid-April morning, he hugged her as usual, kissed her forehead, and walked to the elevator with her.

Before they reached the end of the hall, Angilia stopped walking and clutched her father's arm tightly. Eric turned, and his smile instantly vanished.

"Daddy," she gasped, her other hand over her heart. Eric picked her up and rushed to her room shouting for Matthew, who had just begun to dress after his shower. Just as Eric carefully placed Angilia on the bed, Matthew ran from his wardrobe with his shirt unbuttoned and his hair damp.

Matthew grabbed the medical bag he kept near the bed and quickly put on his stethoscope, listened to her heart, and felt his own heart sink. Her heart rate was extremely fast, dangerously fast. Eric listened in horror as Matthew called an ambulance. "We need to get to the hospital immediately. I need to check her heart," Matthew explained, trying to keep his panic and fear from his voice so he did not alarm Angilia and make her condition worse.

"Eric?" Angilia's wispy-voiced question stabbed her father's heart. His daughter was ill, and her son was the one she cared most about. When Marisol's leukemia worsened, her first question and concern was about Angilia. *Dear God, Please protect my daughter and my grandson. Keep them both safe and healthy. Please, God, stay with them and protect them both. Thank you. Amen* Eric silently prayed as the medics arrived with the gurney and Matthew lifted her onto it and buckled her in place.

Eduardo and Daniel noticed before Juanita and Alejandro did, and both understood her frantic expression. She wanted them to keep her grandparents from seeing her wheeled to the ambulance. She did not want the shock of this to make them ill. Mitchell ran up just they placed her in the elevator, his own face full of fear. Roger dropped his coffee cup to the marble foyer floor when he saw her pale, in pain, and afraid. Susan stood numb behind him and suddenly fainted to the floor.

They all knew her heart had suffered severe damage nine years earlier, and they feared residual effects. Roger ran to his car and followed the ambulance to the hospital. Angilia had been there for him, and he had to be there for her, as well as for Eric. Eric kissed her before Matthew quickly took her to the cardiac unit for tests and evaluation.  Roger arrived at that moment, when Eric was left alone and scared.  Eric stood unmoving, his head lowered.  When Roger walked to his side, he heard Eric praying, and he, too, bowed his head and prayed.

"Eric, hey, I'm here," Patrick suddenly said and put his arms around his brother.  Eric held onto Patrick, trying to keep his fear at bay.  "She'll be all right, I promise.  She will.  It's not her time to leave here.  She has a lot more to do, Eric."  Patrick placed his hands on Eric's face and forced his brother to look at him.  "Her most important task is to give birth to her son."

"They will be all right?  You know that?"

"Yes, Eric.  God is not ready for Angilia yet.  His plans for her are not over by far.  He heard your prayer, and he sent me to tell you that she and her son will be all right.  It might be rough, but they will be okay, I promise you," Patrick declared.

Roger remembered Angilia saying she had to stay alive so that her child could be born.  No wonder she looked so scared.  She was not afraid for herself; she was afraid for her son.  Roger, too, put his arm around Eric, and the three men stood in solidarity until they were joined by Mitchell, Daniel, Susan, and Katherine.  Several hours later, Matthew emerged and said she was stable.

"Her heart rate was dangerously fast when I checked her, which is why I demanded she come here.  She suffered the most severe form of cardiac dysrhythmia, called tachyarrhythmia.  A normal adult heart rate is 100 beats per minute.  When you carried her into the bedroom, her heart rate was more than double that.  I did lots of tests, and found a few concerns that we addressed that returned her heart rate close to normal for her.

"She's had an irregular heartbeat since the shooting, but this was extreme.  Her potassium and magnesium were extremely low, so we quickly gave her large doses of those to raise their levels almost immediately.  I also gave her an IV of adenosine, which is an anti-inflammatory heart block that forced her heart to stop its erratic quivering and beat normally.  I need to keep her here for a few days so we can monitor her and keep her on the adenosine.

"Angilia will have to take it easy and slow down her work load for a while to avoid a recurrence. Another episode could cause permanent heart damage or worse, I will tell all of you that. I've already talked with her about all of this, and she knows it's the best for her. We won't get any pouting or arguments from her. But that means refusing lots of public engagements for the foreseeable future. By the end of the year, she should be back to normal." Eric knew what Matthew meant: Angilia would give birth to her son sometime in November, and the strain on her heart would be greatly reduced.

"Eric, come with me. She wants to see you and let you see that she's okay. Patrick, come with us," Matthew said, his arms around Eric and Patrick. He opened Angilia's hospital room door and the three men walked in. As soon as she saw her father and her uncle, she beamed and reached for them.

Eric hugged her, kissed her nose, and thanked God for protecting her and little Eric. He saw pain in her eyes, though, and felt pangs of fear. Patrick patted his back and reminded his brother, "Hey, she's not going anywhere anytime soon. Neither is Eric. Okay?" Eric smiled and nodded at his brother and his daughter.

"Daddy, we're fine, really. Matthew told me everything, and I understand. I will do what I need to in order to protect me and Eric. I promise."

Matthew pulled a chair to the other side of Angilia's bed, sat, and motioned for Eric to sit, too. "There is something I need to tell you, darling. This is very early in the pregnancy, and already the effects are causing dangerous heart strain. As the pregnancy advances and Eric grows, that strain will increase. You both have to be monitored closely until his birth. I've already told all of you that a recurrence of tachyarrhythmia is very risky and dangerous. I have to be blunt. Another episode could prove fatal.

"You must greatly reduce your work during the pregnancy, Angilia, for both of you. The pregnancy is a blessing, but it's making your heart work far too hard. I am your husband and your cardiologist. As both, I have to tell you that you can never risk another pregnancy, Angilia. You just can't." Matthew held her hand in both of his, lifted it to his mouth and kissed her hand as tears trickled from his eyes.

"I know, Matthew. Daddy, Matthew, when you read about Eric, didn't you notice something?" she asked them, their stunned brains unable to recall anything that would have been a red flag. "When I realized who Eric is, I told him I know he is my only child. I've always known I will have one child, our son Eric. That is God's plan for me. He must have known all of this, that more than one pregnancy would jeopardize the baby and me. He is gifting us with Eric, and our son will bless us immensely. I've always known Eric will be my only child."

"Oh, Angilia," Matthew said and placed his head on her lap. She stroked his hair and reached for her father with her other arm. "You are so strong and wise, darling. I love you," Matthew cried.

"I love you, too, Angel. Your strength and courage never fail to amaze and humble me, baby," Eric said and kissed her cheek. "You are so much like your mother in that regard. I see so much of Marisol's strength and courage in you, my beautiful daughter Angilia."

§§§§§

Matthew kept his word and monitored Angilia's heart rate three times each day and tested her potassium and magnesium levels every week. Each day she thanked God for protecting her son Eric. She felt him slowly growing and knew that everything was well and right.

Just before the end of her first trimester, she wrote in her diary while Matthew showered:

*21 May 2021*

*Dearest Mommy,*

*I love you so much. I feel your soul with me always. I feel your love. I know you feel mine.*

*You know that I am a mother, too, and that my son grows in me. I have so much I want to tell you, but not on paper. I want to visit you today and spend some time with you.*

*Happy Birthday, Mommy*

*xoxo*

After lunch, Angilia made a bouquet of flowers, tied it with a green bow, and joined her father in the foyer. He put his arm around her, and they walked to the church. Inside, he unlocked the Royal vault and turned on the light. Angilia smiled as they walked to Marisol's tomb. Eric smiled, knowing it was Marisol's 70th birthday.

Father and daughter bowed their heads in prayer, and then Eric softly said, "I love you, Marisol. You are the love of my life, my eternal life. You bless my life every day, my love. You continue to inspire me. Every day I feel and see our love alive in our beautiful daughter Angilia. And now our baby girl is having her baby boy, Marisol. Our lives and our love live in our daughter and our grandson Eric. We are so blessed. I love you." Eric bent his head and prayed again, and then he smiled and kissed Angilia. "I'm going to spend some time in the cemetery, Angel."

Eric left her alone with Marisol; he knew she wanted to talk to her mother. He sat on the marble bench near Patrick's and Mr. Brennan's graves, where he could spend some quiet time with his thoughts and prayers. He loved his wife dearly, and he knew he would be with her again someday. Still, he admitted, he missed her. He would miss her until he died and joined her in Heaven.

Angilia lowered her head to pray, thanking God for her parents, Matthew, family, friends, and her precious son Eric. "Happy birthday, Mommy. I love you, you know that and you feel that. How can I ever thank you for the amazing gift of life you fought to give me? I now have an understanding of your intense love, courage, and selflessness, Mommy. Eric is the most important person to me, and I will do anything for his life.

"Oh, Mommy, feeling Eric grow inside of me is truly a miracle. I felt him immediately, and I knew the moment his life began within me, the moment he began his earthly life. I remember so well leaving Daddy and entering you. That is the moment my earthly, human life truly began. Daddy told me he knew the moment you became pregnant. He felt my soul leave him and enter you. Feeling Eric's soul enter me is a sensation unlike any I ever have or ever will again experience.

"I'm sure you know what happened to me, Mommy. I came close to dying last month, and all I could think was that if I did die then Eric would die, too. I never want that to happen. I will not, I cannot, jeopardize his life. I can't. His life is far too precious for me to put myself before him.

"Mommy, I know what you did for me, to save me. I know why. I will do the same for Eric if I have to. I must. You taught me how strong, true, and eternal a mother's love is. I now feel that kind of love for Eric.

"Today is the anniversary of your birth, and Abuela's love for you has never weakened or faltered. It can't. It won't. You are her child for all eternity, just as I am yours and Eric is mine. Thank you for loving me as you do. I love you, and Eric does, too. He will know you, Mommy. You will be part of his life. I love you, Mommy."

Angilia slid the usual slip of paper with "I love you, Mommy" and the date written on it under the plaque on Marisol's tomb. She said a silent prayer of thanksgiving and placed the flowers atop the tomb. She looked around the vault, at the many tombs there. She walked to the tomb of King Christophe, Valdavia's first monarch. "Eric, my son, these are our ancestors, those who forged, shaped, and led this country. Each of them kept their faith in God regardless of their personal pain and heartbreak, just as your grandfather and I do. You will do the same, I know that. Someday, my dear, you will lead Valdavia and be an inspiration to people. You are the country's future. You are my future. You will become King Eric II de Valdavia, my precious son."

Angilia smiled, turned off the light, and locked the vault. She went outside to join her father. She sat beside him on the bench and put her arm around him. "I love you, Daddy."

Eric smiled and held her hand. "I love you, my beautiful daughter Angilia."

They sat quietly for many moments, not needing to say anything. Suddenly, their smiles grew huge as they felt Patrick's warmth surround them. "Hi, Uncle Patrick," Angilia said seconds before he manifested beside her.

"Hey, Little One, Eric. It's lovely here today. And you are lovelier than ever, Little One," Patrick said. He gently pulled her close and kissed her cheek. "I love you."

"I love you, Uncle Patrick," she said and rested her head against his chest.

Eric smiled and placed his hand on Patrick's shoulder. "You know, nine years ago, I sat here and thought how wrong it was that your life on earth was so short, Patrick. It was short. But it was not wrong. It was as it had to be. It took Angilia to break open the wall I'd built within me so that I accepted the truth about you. Nineteen is very young to die, and that means there are things you will never do here. But I look at everything you have done, and I feel such peace within, not sadness."

Patrick sighed but smiled. "Yeah, I know. I'll never marry, have children, and grow old. But it's okay, because I have all of you, Eric, Angilia, and little Eric. I am a grand-uncle," Patrick giggled.

Angilia smiled and hugged her father and uncle. "Yes, you are. Eric is so very blessed to have you both in his life. We love you, both of you."

§§§§

Two days later, after lunch, Eric asked everyone to gather in the sitting room. Angilia and Matthew smiled and entered the room with Eric. Eduardo assisted Alejandro and Juanita. As she watched them, Angilia felt such love for them. Abuelo moved very slowly now and was frail. The glint in his eyes never dimmed, though, and his sly smile was as charming as ever.

Eric sat with them on the sofa, knowing how happy the news would make them. Matthew gently held Angilia and smiled. "We asked all of you to gather here, because we have something very happy to share with you. We know you will be as thrilled as we are," Matthew said.

Angilia smiled up at her husband. "Matthew and I are so blessed. Our son Eric is with us, and he will be born in November."

After a few seconds of stunned silence as everyone registered the news, the room filled with screams, cheers, and tears, lots of tears. Alejandro turned to his son-in-law, tears illuminating his face, and hugged Eric.

"Mi nieta, my dear, come to me," Alejandro said. Eric moved, but Alejandro told him to stay and pulled Angilia onto his lap. Alejandro held her close for many minutes. "I prayed to live long enough to meet my great-grandchild, and God willing I will do so. My precious granddaughter, you are the greatest miracle." Alejandro kissed her. "I love you so."

Juanita hugged her granddaughter next, holding her close. "Yo amor tú, mi nieta. You are so blessed by God, and you bless us. The day your father and mother told us about you is the only day that can ever compare to today, my Angel."

Katherine had immediately grabbed Matthew and smothered him in tears and kisses. For once, she was rendered speechless. Mitchell managed to hug his son while his wife sobbed relentlessly. "I am so happy, son. You know the baby is a boy already? When did you have the ultrasound?"

"We haven't done an ultrasound, Dad. Angilia knows our son, though. She knew the moment she got pregnant."

"How is that possible, Matthew?"

"Oh, Mitchell, really," Katherine said, as if he should already know. "Why wouldn't she? Eric knew the moment Marisol was pregnant with Angilia, and he knew his baby was Angilia. Besides, she is an angel. Of course Angilia knows," she said and turned to hug her daughter-in-law and cry for many more minutes.

Mitchell smiled and hugged his son. "I can't argue with your mother's logic. We all know how unique and ordained Eric and Angilia are." Matthew's eyes sparkled as he smiled broadly and watched his wife.

After Katherine relinquished Angilia, Susan had her several moments of tears and congratulations. "Oh, Angilia, when you were born, I never knew what the next 25 years would bring. Watching you, learning from you, and knowing you all these years have been so amazing, darling. I am so very happy for you."

Daniel squeezed his way to Angilia, hugged her, and kissed her cheek. "I watched your birth, and now you are having a baby. That is so awesome. It makes me feel special to share this with you." Bonnie congratulated her next, echoing Daniel in saying she felt privileged to know them and to share this miracle with them.

Eduardo finally walked to his Angel and held her close to him for a long while. He unashamedly cried, feeling such love and respect for his niece. Through his tears he managed to say, "I love you, Angilia and baby Eric." Angilia kissed his cheek, knowing that every moment of the past nine years was a miracle to Eduardo.

When Eduardo turned to hug Matthew, Roger came to Angilia with a smile. He, too, held her close, and he softly spoke in her ear. "Princess, you are even more remarkable and miraculous than I realized. I saw you last month. I saw you unafraid for yourself, but fighting for your son. You showed me that selfless love and strength you possess. You have taught me so much about love, life, and death. They're all so closely connected. I watched your birth, too, and I saw that indescribable love between you and your father. Of course you know your child. I'd be surprised if you didn't. I can't wait to meet your son Eric. Nice name, by the way," Roger smiled and hugged her close.

§§§§

"Happy anniversary, my Angilia," Matthew said when he woke up and saw Angilia smiling at him.

"Happy anniversary, my love," she replied and kissed him.

273

Matthew leaned down and kissed her stomach, and said, "I love you, Eric, my son."

Angilia smiled through her tears. "Oh, Matthew the past five years have been so full of love, and yet each day our lives are filled with more love. God blesses us so abundantly, Matthew. I love you."

"I love you," Matthew softly replied and held his Angilia against him as the early morning sun filled their bedroom.

# CHAPTER 11

"Happy birthday, beloved Daddy," Angilia said as she joined him on his sitting room balcony early on the morning of November 17, 2021.

Eric smiled and gently hugged her to him. He bowed his head and prayed softly: "Dear God, Thank you for the beautiful, miraculous gift of my Angel. Thank you for the precious gift of my grandson. Your blessings humble and awe me. Amen."

Angilia leaned her head against his shoulder. "Amen. I love you, Daddy." She giggled and added, "We both love you, Daddy. Eric just let me know to add him."

"He's a very active boy," Eric said with a huge smile, referring to his grandson's frequent kicks.

"Yes, he is," Angilia smiled and handed him her birthday present.

Eric kissed her nose and opened the box. Eric cried when he saw her pastel portrait of his grandson, a portrait just for her father. He hugged her again. "How beautiful, Angilia. How incredible to see him as he will be in the future. I can't believe I will actually meet him soon."

"Yes, you will, Daddy, and sooner than you think. Your grandson won't share just your name, but your birthday," Angilia calmly said, much to her father's shock.

"Angilia!  Sit down," he said and guided her to a chair and slowly helped her sit.  He pulled his phone from his pocket and called Matthew.  "Come to my room now.  We have to get Angilia to the hospital."  Eric hung up and felt her pulse.

"Daddy, you didn't tell him why.  He's probably. . . ."

Sure enough, Matthew feared another attack of tachyarrhythmia, dropped his coffee cup on the dining room floor, and ran as fast as he could to the third floor.  He barged in as Angilia was lovingly reprimanding her father, and fell to his knees in front of her.  "Matthew, I'm all right.  I'm in labor.  Eric decided he wants to share Daddy's birthday."

"Really?  Oh, darling," he gushed and hugged her.  "Okay, Dad and I will get everything ready.  Just sit still until I come for you.  I love you."  He kissed her and stood up, excited and happy.

"I love you, too," she replied as he rushed from the room.  Eric sat on the arm of the chair and held her, his heart overflowing with love.  Within 30 minutes, Angilia was wheeled into the King Gerard Hospital, where she had been born on January 3, 1996.  The same obstetrician who had performed Marisol's Caesarian section greeted her, Matthew, Eric, and Mitchell and led them to the Labor and Delivery Department.  Eric and Mitchell kissed and hugged her before Dr. Wakefield and Matthew accompanied her to her private room.  The nurse helped Angilia undress and put on a hospital gown, and then helped her into the bed.

Matthew joined his wife, and as her cardiologist would remain beside her throughout labor, delivery, and her stay.  Dr. Wakefield also came in to check her and get her vital signs.  When the nurse, Debbie, attached the fetal monitors, she and Dr. Wakefield saw that Eric's lungs and heart were normal.  Angilia and Matthew had never wanted any confirmation of the baby's gender, and Dr. Wakefield was reminded of Eric's and Marisol's instinctive knowledge that their baby was a girl.  Dr. Wakefield knew that Angilia's baby was the boy she had known he was all along.

Once Angilia was settled, examined, and checked, Dr. Wakefield allowed Eric and Mitchell into her room.  They all realized that Eric had never experienced the labor and delivery process. Mitchell had been beside Katherine during her entire labor and delivery of Matthew. Matthew had attended a few of his heart patients' deliveries, so he was familiar with the process. Eric had been a father for 25 years, yet Angilia's birth had been quite unusual.

"I guess we both get to experience this for the only time in our lives, Daddy," she softly said with a smile as she held his hand.

"Yes, we do, Angel. I love you, baby."

§§§§

A few hours later, Angilia was in the throes of labor, with Debbie, Dr. Wakefield, and Matthew constantly monitoring her and baby Eric. Mitchell and Eric went to a private waiting room, where they called Katherine and Eduardo. Soon everyone arrived, and Juanita hugged her son-in-law.

"Mi hijo Eric, this is a truly special and blessed day. Your birthday is now your grandson's birthday. He has your name. What a beautiful gift," Juanita said as she looked up at him.

Eric smiled, kissed her cheek, and said, "I know Mamá. Angilia had just given me her birthday gift, and then her water broke. I just pray everything is fine, that she and Eric are safe, and that the delivery is not too long or difficult for her."

Juanita saw the concern in his eyes, as well as the joy. She knew what he feared—another heart complication. "Eric, there is no reason to worry. Our Angilia has not suffered any other difficulties. God will not let something happen to her now."

Eric took a deep breath, nodded his head, and gave her a small smile. Juanita took his arm and guided him to the sofa to sit with her and Alejandro. He sat with his hands folded in his lap and his head bowed for three hours. Juanita patted his back, suddenly feeling him tense. Eric sat straight for a few minutes, breathing deeply, and then stood.

"No," he whispered. "Not Angilia. Not my baby." Before anyone knew what was happening, Eric ran from the room toward his daughter's private labor and delivery room. Mitchell followed, but before he caught up, Eric pounded on her door and screamed, "Angilia! Please stay with me, Angel!"

Mitchell ran to him, reminded of the night of Angilia's emergency surgery when Eric sensed that her heart had stopped. As he held Eric, Mitchell's fear increased. He held Eric firmly, and said, "Eric, you need to stay here. I'll go in and find out how everything's going. All right?" Eric nodded, his face taut and pale.

Thirty minutes later, the door opened. Mitchell reappeared and handed Eric a hospital gown. "Put that on and come in."

Eric entered with Mitchell and saw his little girl, pale and exhausted, propped up in the bed holding her newborn son. Angilia beamed at her father and motioned for him; she patted the bed next to her, and he sat facing her. "Happy birthday, Daddy," she said weakly. "Meet your grandson Eric."

Tears slid from Eric's eyes as he looked at his precious daughter and her small, dark-haired son cuddled against her. He leaned over and kissed Angilia's cheek, placed his forehead against hers, and said, "I love you my beautiful daughter Angilia." He kissed her nose and smiled through his tears. "You are my miracle, Angilia." Eric smiled at his grandson and gently touched the small hand that stuck above the blue blanket that wrapped him. The baby opened his eyes, and Eric inhaled deeply. Even though Eric had seen his grandson's face, seeing those turquoise eyes took his breath away. Baby Eric did have his grandfather's and mother's eyes.

Angilia smiled while she watched her father and her son. "Daddy, God gave us your grandson Eric Matthew Patrick DeBruce Martineau Taylor on your birthday."

Little Eric kicked his legs as if in excitement, and Eric, Matthew, and Mitchell smiled. Angilia handed her son to her father and leaned back into the pillows. At that moment, Matthew slipped on his stethoscope and listened to her heart. Eric looked at them, the concern back on his face. He then noticed the IV in her arm. Something had happened to her. "What's wrong? Tell me." Eric stared at Matthew, his tense face insistent.

Matthew glanced at his father, and Mitchell nodded. "The delivery put too much stress and strain on her heart. I'm monitoring her carefully. I'm going to keep her here a couple of days as a precaution, but she and Eric should go home Friday afternoon," Matthew calmly said.

"What happened? I know something happened. Tell me."

"Eric is fine, Daddy. Isn't he, Dr. Wakefield?" Angilia asked.

"Yes, he is. His heart and lungs are fine, and his weight is healthy."

"Daddy, I'm okay now. I heard you. You brought me back," Angilia said and placed a hand on her father's arm while he held little Eric. She saw the fear on his face and in his eyes. She looked up at Matthew, who suddenly sat down and covered his face with his hands. It all unexpectedly hit him, and his delayed reaction forced Angilia to tell her father what Matthew could not.

"It was just after Eric was born. He was never in any danger, Daddy. Dr. Wakefield and Debbie were taking care of him. I saw him, and I knew he was all right. But it was hard to breathe, and suddenly I felt my heart racing and I could barely move. Then I was with Great-grandfather and Uncle Patrick again. I heard you scream for me right then, and Uncle Patrick shoved me backwards. I opened my eyes and I was back here. It's all right now, Daddy," Angilia said, looked at her father with a weak smile, and squeezed his arm reassuringly.

Still holding his grandson, Eric gently sat beside his daughter and put his arm around her. She rested her head against him, smiled up at him, and put her right hand over his left hand that cradled little Eric. Soon she was asleep, elated but weary. Matthew checked her vital signs and audibly said "Thank God" when the heart monitor showed a relatively normal heart rate.

Eric carefully lifted his right hand from Angilia and held it toward Matthew. He took hold of Eric's hand and felt his father-in-law gently pull him to sit with them. Matthew softly sat beside his wife and tenderly kissed her cheek. "I knew Eric was fine,"

Matthew whispered. "I did not want her to go. I didn't. Right before she closed her eyes, she told me she loves me and Eric. She said to tell you she loves you always. I had just begun defibrillation when we heard you pound on the door and scream for her. She opened her eyes a second after you screamed for her to stay with you."

"Patrick told me that God would not take her yet, but I felt something wrong. I knew she wasn't here. I was never worried about Eric, though. I knew he was fine. He's perfect, isn't he?" Eric asked, his broad smile back. He looked down at his grandson, who looked at him and then moments later fell asleep against his grandfather's chest.

Mitchell sat in a chair beside Eric and patted his shoulder. The two grandfathers smiled at each other, both relieved and ecstatic. "I'll go tell everyone that Eric is here," Mitchell softly said. He also told them everything that had happened to Angilia, which stunned them all. Alejandro stumbled, and Eduardo held his father close against him. "Angilia is sleeping now. Her body is exhausted and weak right now, but her heart rate is stable. Little Eric is fine. He was never in danger. Eric Matthew Patrick was born at 2:13 this afternoon. He is eight pounds, 10 ounces and 20 inches. Prince Eric has dark hair and turquoise eyes just like his other grandfather. In fact, he looks a lot like Eric. He is asleep in Eric's arms right now. When Angilia is awake, you can start to go in and visit her and meet Eric."

§§§§

Mitchell escorted Katherine, Alejandro, Juanita, and Eduardo into Angilia's room at 6:00, after Matthew and Dr. Wakefield examined her and she fed Eric. Katherine and Juanita burst into tears when they saw Angilia holding Eric. Alejandro leaned on Eduardo, frail and weak, and went to his granddaughter and great-grandson. He sat on the bed beside Angilia, hugged her, and wept.

"I love you, Abuelo," Angilia said and kissed his wrinkled, soft cheek. "Abuelo, meet your great-grandson Eric Matthew Patrick." Angilia placed her son in her grandfather's arms.

Katherine took pictures of Angilia, Alejandro, and baby Eric together, capturing the first meeting for all time.

Alejandro kissed his great-grandson, and little Eric giggled. "Abuelo, Eric giggled just like I did when you first kissed me," Angilia smiled. Alejandro's mustache must have tickled little Eric as it had baby Angilia. Alejandro smiled and kissed her cheek.

Katherine hugged her son, kissed Angilia, and sat in a chair beside her daughter-in-law. Eduardo helped his mother to the other side of the bed, where Juanita leaned across Alejandro to kiss her granddaughter. She gently kissed little Eric, and sat in a chair beside her husband. Everyone gave Alejandro and Juanita time with Angilia and Eric, knowing how tiring and stressful the day had been. Alejandro in particular deserved the time, for he had become much weaker over the past few months. Mitchell served as the family doctor, and he knew that at 93 Alejandro was nearing the end of his life. He had advised Eduardo, Katherine, Eric, and Matthew, but had not said anything to Juanita or Angilia.

Mitchell watched Angilia, though, and saw the love and concern in her eyes as she smiled at her beloved grandfather. "Abuelo, you fill me with love. Seeing you hold Eric is such a beautiful sight," Angilia said. Alejandro kissed her again while baby Eric slept in his arms. Forty minutes later when Eric woke up, Alejandro kissed him and gently placed him in his mother's arms.

"I love you, mi nieta. I love you, mi bisnieto. I can never tell you how very happy and blessed you both have made me," Alejandro smiled with tears in his eyes.

Juanita hugged Alejandro and patted his arm. "You go home now and rest," she ordered him. "You can visit again tomorrow."

Eduardo hugged his father, and Mitchell drove Alejandro home and made sure he was doing well and was comfortable. Chef Antoine brought him a salad and a sandwich, and Alejandro enjoyed the fresh air on the patio while he ate. Antoine promised Mitchell he would stay near Alejandro until the family arrived home.

Mitchell returned to Angilia's room to see Eduardo holding Eric and smiling. Juanita stood in her son-in-law's arms happily watching them. Finally, Eduardo kissed his grand-nephew and niece and took his mother home.

Katherine cried again when Angilia handed Eric to her. "Oh, he is wonderful, Angilia and Matthew, just perfect."

"Thank you for being so patient. I know how much you wanted to hold him," Angilia said.

"Oh, dearest girl, your grandparents deserved to see him first. There is plenty of time for me and everyone else to hold him. I won't stay too very long, though. Everyone wants to see you and Eric, too. I remember what it's like after giving birth. It's the most joyous day, but goodness is it exhausting, physically and mentally. You and Eric need to rest tonight. Yes, you do," Katherine said and looked down at her grandson, gently caressing his cheek with her finger.

Katherine knew that Angilia's health was priority, so she held Eric for 30 minutes before handing him to Angilia. "I think he's hungry, my dear. You feed our precious boy and get some rest," Katherine smiled at Angilia, kissed her cheek, and motioned for Eric and Mitchell to follow her.

In the hall, Katherine took charge. "After she feeds Eric, the others can come in and see him and Angilia, but she needs rest. They can see her when she's released and home. On a good day, giving birth is not a fun experience in and of itself. I'll leave, and Mitchell, you need to keep the other visits brief." She kissed Mitchell and Eric, and returned home to sit with Juanita and Alejandro.

After Angilia fed Eric, he fell asleep. Matthew and Dr. Wakefield examined her, and Matthew repeated his mother's assessment that the remaining visits be short so that Angilia, too, could sleep. She appeared happy, tired, and in pain. Matthew refused to compromise his wife's well-being. He kissed her and Eric while his father went to the waiting room.

Mitchell explained the need for a short visit to Susan, Roger, Daniel, and Bonnie, who all agreed.  They stayed long enough to see Eric and let Angilia know how much they love her.  Roger hugged her and whispered, "I love you, Princess.  You are remarkable.  We'll be waiting to welcome you and Eric home."

That night, Angilia fell asleep to the sight of her baby boy sleeping in a crib beside her bed.  Matthew held her as she slept, and every few hours when she woke to feed Eric, he examined her.  He prayed, thanking God for bringing Angilia back to them and for protecting her.  Her heart rate remained stable, although he knew that her heart literally hurt.

When she woke the next morning, Angilia smiled, kissed Matthew, and asked him to hand her Eric.  She kissed her baby boy and said, "I love you, Eric."  She fed him, and then let Matthew hold him while little Eric slept.  When Eric and Mitchell arrived, they smiled and joined their children and grandson.

Angilia greeted them both with kisses and a large, joyous smile.  "I love you all," she said.  "Thank you for loving me and for taking such good care of me and Eric.  We are so very blessed.  Our family is complete."

§§§§

Angilia and little Eric were released from the hospital on Friday, 48 hours after his birth.  Matthew and Eric stood on either side of her as she carried her son.  Roger had alerted them that thousands of people waited outside the hospital and the palace, along with a swarm of photographers.  Mike and Tony walked out of the hospital ahead of the Royal Family, and four security officers followed.

Matthew, Angilia, and Eric paused on the hospital steps for a few moments.  Angilia smiled and waved to everyone, as did Eric and Matthew.  People cheered in utter delight, nearly drowning the photographers' shouts to show the baby's face.  Angilia ignored their demands.  Instead, she waved one last time to those who came to see them.  Matthew and Eric helped her down the stairs and into the Rolls Royce.

The route to the palace was lined with more people, all cheering them.  Angilia, Eric, and Matthew waved to well-wishers until the car pulled into the garage.  Eric stepped out, and Angilia handed little Eric to him while Matthew helped her out of the car.  Eric returned the drowsy baby to her arms, and they all entered the palace to find the staff waiting to greet them.

Angilia smiled, truly touched, and thanked them.  She gently pulled the blanket away from Eric's head so that all of them could see him.  Most of them commented on how much he resembled His Majesty.  They understood not to overtax her, so they congratulated Angilia, Matthew, and Eric and returned to their work.  Antoine asked if she wanted anything, and she asked for a fruit smoothie.

"Let's get you both upstairs now," Matthew said.  He wanted her to stay in bed until the next day and regain her strength.  Eric kissed her and little Eric outside her suite, and Matthew led her to their bedroom.

Angilia smiled and kissed her son when she saw her bassinet beside their bed.  "Welcome home, Eric," she said, and she tenderly laid him in the bassinet.  Matthew put his arms around her and smiled, grateful to be home with his wife and his son.  He kissed her and told her she needed to get in bed, too.  She kissed him and unbuttoned her dress, slipped it off, and pulled on her pajamas.  Matthew helped her in bed, tucked her in, and kissed her.

Antoine knocked on the door, and Matthew thanked him for the fruit drink.  Angilia sipped all of it and snuggled into the pillows.  She had fed Eric right before they left the hospital, so he was asleep.  Matthew moved the bassinet closer to her and sat facing her.  More than 15 minutes later, she smiled and pulled Matthew down to her for a kiss.  "You haven't eaten since breakfast," she told him.  "Go eat lunch.  We'll be fine.  I'll text you or call you if I need anything," she promised, and picked up her phone from the bedside table.  Matthew nodded, told her he loved her, and quietly closed the door behind him.

Angilia watched Eric sleep, more content than she had ever anticipated.  "Uncle Patrick!" she softly said when she felt his familiar warmth.

"Hey, Little One.  I love you," Patrick whispered and bent to hug and kiss her.

"Angilia, my dear, we are so happy for you."

Angilia sat up, tears already sliding down her cheeks, and held out her arms.  "Great-grandfather!  Oh, I love you."

Stefan sat facing her and held her against his chest.  He still wore the robes she had always seen him wear in the Angels Choir.  "I love you, my darling girl," he said as he kissed her cheek.

At that moment, a gentle knock on her bedroom door made their smiles larger.  "Is that my other grandson?" Stefan asked loud enough for him to hear.

Eric opened the door, and his eyes filled with tears.  "Grandfather," he said and joined his grandfather and brother for a hug.  "I love you, Grandfather."

"I love you, my boy," Stefan replied, and hugged Eric to him for several moments.  It had been 57 years since they had seen one another.  "Now, let me see my great-great-grandson," he smiled.

Angilia very gently lifted her son from the bassinet and handed him to Stefan.  "Great-grandfather, meet your great-great-grandson Eric Matthew Patrick DeBruce Martineau Taylor."

Patrick smiled at his brother, pleasantly surprised.  "He has our names, Patrick," Eric said and hugged his brother.

Patrick's smile seemed a mile wide, and he hugged his brother.  He sat beside Angilia on the bed, hugged her, and said, "You didn't tell me.  You only told me his first name, Little One.  This is so cool.  Thank you."  Patrick held her close and softly said into her ear, "I love you so much, Angilia."

Angilia held him tightly to her, and with tears in her eyes said, "I love you more than I can tell you, Uncle Patrick."  She turned and smiled up at Stefan.  "I love you tremendously, Great-grandfather."

Stefan smiled, handed little Eric to Patrick, and sat on Angilia's other side. He held her close to him for a long while, her arms around him and her head against his chest. Patrick smiled and motioned for Eric to sit next to him. The three men sat with Angilia while she slept in Stefan's arms and Patrick held his grand-nephew.

"Look at him," Patrick grinned. "He looks like you," he said to his big brother. Eric put his arm around Patrick. "It wasn't her time, Eric. We weren't going to let her stay with us yet. God knew she would come close, but he wasn't going to let her return until her pre-destined time. She heard you scream for her, and she didn't want to cause you or Matthew any pain. I had to push her soul back. She'll be okay, Eric. She'll be here for quite a long time."

"Thank you, Patrick." Eric smiled and leaned his head against his brother. "You're a natural with babies. I never would have thought I'd see you hold Angilia's son. I never thought I'd see either of you again until I died. When you came to church nine years ago, Patrick, I was stunned, thrilled, and amazed. Now it's so normal and natural to see you and to talk to you. It's like it always was. Grandfather, Angilia loves you so much and told me about her life in the Angels Choir. Seeing you here today, for Angilia, means so much to her and to me."

"I always knew Angilia is very special and unique, but I never knew what she would experience during her life on earth," Stefan said. "I never expected her to remember anything from before her birth. None of us did, not even Michael. Only Patrick knew she would. I have watched you and then Angilia since my death. You are the most extraordinary King of Valdavia in the country's history, Eric. That is clear. Your concern and love for the citizens of Valdavia and the world are strong and vibrant.

"Angilia has always placed others above herself, starting with you. That day she came for Patrick and she saw you, her life changed. I never expected you to see her, though. You were not supposed to see her, but I learned later that God wanted you to. I even remember scolding Patrick for manifesting and buying a teddy bear for Angilia after she brought him to the Angels Choir. But she was inconsolable, and she cried as she held the bear. I could not blame or chastise Patrick for trying to comfort her.

"The two of them bonded immediately, and he always knew her so much better than anyone did. He knew how she felt having to leave you and return to Heaven. He knew that you loved her instantly. The two of them were a delightful pleasure to watch. After her birth, Patrick came to her often," Stefan said with a smile.

Patrick smiled, looked at Angilia, and said, "Yeah, I could never stay away from her for her entire lifetime. Do you remember when you came to her room once and heard her talking, but you didn't see anyone else? It wasn't her imagination, Eric. It was me. You didn't see me sitting on the floor across from her."

Eric giggled and said, "She was three then, I think."

"Yeah. She was the same in every other way except her appearance. She was so little, but we talked about the same stuff and even stuff I didn't really understand. I remember helping her pack some things before she went to Oxford. I was still here, in this room, when you came in and sat with her and tucked her in bed the night before you took her to Oxford. She was crazy smart."

"I know, Patrick. I had no idea how my little girl was off the charts intelligent. All those years before she told me everything, she often said things that didn't make any sense to me, things about clouds, Heaven, death, and angels. And this incredible memory of hers. She always takes my breath away," Eric softly said.

"How do you think I feel?" Patrick giggled. "I'm the dumbest member of the family."

"You are not, Uncle Patrick," Angilia suddenly said. She kissed her Great-grandfather's cheek and sat up. "You are perfect just as you are." She kissed Patrick's cheek, and Stefan snorted.

"You should never tell him that, my dear girl. You do remember how mischievous he is," Stefan drolly stated.

"Hey!" Patrick feigned offense, and the four of them laughed. Little Eric gurgled, which made Patrick say, "Are you going to laugh, too?" Patrick held him and smiled at him, and Eric cooed. Patrick kissed his forehead at the moment Matthew stepped into the room.

Matthew stood, staring at the sight of four generations of the DeBruce Martineau family together.  He instantly recognized Stefan from the portrait above Angilia's desk.  Angilia smiled up at her husband.  "Matthew, meet my Great-grandfather, King Stefan," she said.  Matthew snapped to attention and bowed.

"Come here, young man," Stefan requested, and Matthew walked to him.  Stefan stood and pulled Matthew to him in a hug.  "It is a pleasure to finally meet the man who fills our Angilia's life with love."

Matthew talked with them for a few minutes, and then asked if he could take a picture of the four of them with little Eric.  They began to sit up straight and closer together.  "Why don't we have Bonnie take some pictures?" Eric suggested.  Matthew called Bonnie, who came with her camera, while Angilia said they should sit on the sofa.  Matthew helped Angilia put on her robe, and she sat between Patrick and Stefan holding her son.

Bonnie took several pictures, including one with Matthew joining them.  Angilia displayed the framed pictures on her wall, where they remained for many generations:  the group of all six; Eric and Patrick with little Eric; Patrick holding his grand-nephew; Stefan holding his great-great-grandson; and Eric holding his grandson.  Bonnie also took the first picture of Angilia and Matthew with their son.

During the session, Angilia asked Abuelo, Abuela, Mitchell, Katherine, and Eduardo to join them.  Bonnie took what Angilia called the historic photograph: little Eric with his parents, grandparents, grand-uncles, great-grandparents, and great-great-grandfather.  Bonnie printed a 24 inch by 24 inch copy, which she placed in an antique frame and presented to Angilia and Matthew.  It hung alongside the portraits of Stefan and Eric above her desk.  Prince Eric would treasure the picture for his entire life.

§§§§

Angilia had just finished feeding Eric and was singing to him while she held him as she sat on the sofa in her sitting room. Alejandro smiled as he watched them from her doorway. "Abuelo, come sit with us," Angilia smiled when she saw him there.

Alejandro walked slowly, his shoulders hunched, and kissed her when he sat beside her. "I love you, Abuelo. Do you know how much I love you?" Angilia told him and kissed his flushed cheek.

"I feel your love, mi nieta," Alejandro replied, covering his heart with his hand. "I hope you feel mine, mi nieta."

"I do. I always have. Eric does, too, Abuelo," she giggled when Eric reached for his great-grandfather.

Alejandro smiled with tears in his eyes and carefully took Eric. He kissed Eric's cheek and said, "I love you, sweet Eric. I am so very grateful I lived long enough to meet you." A tear slid down Alejandro's cheek, and he looked at Angilia with an expression that told her he knew he was dying.

Angilia kissed his cheek and held him to her, his head against her shoulder, and she picked up her phone and texted her father, Matthew, and Mitchell. Eric and Matthew ran to her room, while Mitchell spoke with Eduardo, who fought his emotions as he escorted his mother in the elevator. Matthew listened to Alejandro's heart, but Alejandro waved him away and whispered, "It's my time, son. None of that."

Matthew looked at Angilia, and she nodded. Matthew stood, and Eduardo helped his mother onto the sofa next to Alejandro. Juanita put her arms around her husband and great-grandson and kissed Alejandro. "Yo amor tú, mi marido. Yo amor tú." Eduardo patted her arm, and he stood to hug and kiss his father for the last time.

Eric stood behind his father-in-law and put his hands on Alejandro's shoulders. He bent, kissed Alejandro's cheek, and said, "I love you, Papa. You mean the world to me. You welcomed me into your life and your heart the moment Marisol introduced us. You and Mamá won my heart immediately." Eric looked at Matthew and Mitchell with tears in his eyes, and they both nodded, silently telling him it would not be much longer.

Alejandro gasped for each breath and still leaned against Angilia. He glanced at her and gave her a small smile, patted little Eric, and motioned for her to take him. Angilia did, handed Eric to

Matthew, and put her arms around her grandfather. Alejandro's breathing grew more labored, and Juanita sobbed against Eduardo.

A long 20 minutes later, Angilia gasped and smiled as tears fell down her cheeks. "Abuelo, look in front of you," she whispered. Alejandro forced his eyes open and smiled, too. He weakly kissed Angilia's cheek and managed to say, "Mi Marisol."

Angilia kissed her grandfather, smiled up at her father, and said a tear-choked, "It's Mommy. She came for Abuelo." Eric leaned down, put his hand on Angilia's shoulder, and smiled through his tears. Angilia whispered in his ear, "You see her, don't you, Daddy?"

"Yes, baby. Marisol, my love."

"Mommy, I love you," Angilia whispered.

They both saw Marisol smile and hold open her arms. Just as Angilia felt her grandfather die in her arms, she saw his soul manifest and join Marisol. Alejandro smiled and blew a kiss to Angilia, and she blew a kiss to her grandfather and said, "I love you Abuelo. I love you, Mommy."

Alejandro gently nudged Marisol, and she bent to hug and then kiss her daughter. Marisol hugged her husband and kissed his lips. Angilia felt her father tremble at the kiss he had not felt in 26 years. His beloved wife touched his cheek and smiled at him. While Eric cried against Angilia's shoulder, Marisol hugged and kissed her mother and her brother. Juanita and Eduardo felt her, even though they did not see her.

Eric and Angilia did, and they watched Marisol take her father's hand. Alejandro and Marisol slowly vanished into spirit form and went to Heaven. Juanita fell against Eduardo in sobs, and he cried while he held her. Matthew held little Eric in one arm and placed his other hand on Angilia's shoulder. She and Eric smiled through their tears, and she kissed her father's cheek as he put his arms around her. What a miraculous gift they had received.

§§§§§

*6 December 2021*

*Abuelo died this afternoon, and I am honored to have shared this with him and to have been beside him. I was holding him, actually, and I felt him die. I will always miss him, of course I will, but I know that he still lives and that someday I will join him in Heaven. That is the beauty and miracle of death. It is never final.*

*The most beautiful miracle was gifted to me just before Abuelo died. Standing in front of him was his Spirit Guide—Mommy!! Mommy came to escort Abuelo into Heaven! I saw Mommy for the first time today, far sooner than I thought I would. I thought I would have to wait until my death before I saw her in Heaven. I saw her today, though.*

*Mommy is just as beautiful as she was when I saw her in her tomb after my birth. That was her dead body, though. Today I saw her alive, smiling, and shining with love. She bent and kissed me, and I will remember the touch of her soft lips for the rest of my earthly life.*

*Daddy saw her, too!! He loves her so very much, and the fact that he saw her and felt her touches my heart so very deeply. Their love, his devotion to her, and their eternal bond are the truest fairy tale of all. She kissed Daddy, and I can never thank God enough for that precious gift to my father. The look of pure love and joy in his eyes is unforgettable. I love and miss Abuelo and Mommy, but they are together in the most unfathomable beauty. Someday Daddy and I will be with them there, and we will never have to part again.*

*Thank you for your never-ending and amazing blessings, God. xoxo*

§§§§

*6 December 2021*

*What an incredibly emotional and miraculous day for our family. Alejandro left us today, which I had dreaded for some time. I had not told either Juanita or Angilia just how frail he had become, as I did not want to cause them any stress. Angilia knew, though. I saw it in her eyes the day Eric was born. Papa was with her when he began to die, and for that I am actually grateful. For many reasons. Angilia kept Alejandro calm, peaceful, and surrounded by love.*

*I will miss Alejandro, but I know my loss can never compare to Juanita's. They were married more than 73 years. Of course she will grieve his death and miss him. That is normal. I am grateful for their longevity and happiness. I am so grateful for Eduardo's release nine years ago so that he could have those nine years with his father.*

*More than anything, I am so eternally grateful for the miracle you gave to us today, God. My beloved Marisol! I saw her, I felt her! She is just as she was on the day I met her. She kissed me, I kissed her, and it is as though nothing has changed. Oh, God, thank you. I know that the moment I die, Marisol and I will reunite for all eternity. She is the love of my life, my wife, and my best friend. I will never forget the sight of her or the feel of her lips on mine.*

*Angilia. Our beautiful daughter Angilia. She saw her mother! She has always had faith that she would meet her mother in Heaven when she dies. The wonder and love in my daughter's eyes will remain in my heart forever, as well. What a beautiful precious gift you gave to Angilia, God. Thank you for that.*

*Juanita and Eduardo felt her soul, her essence, as well, and they know that Marisol lives and that they will reunite someday. We will all remain together, a family, for all time. Angilia and Patrick are right—facing death is not in itself painful or frightening. How could it be, when my love Marisol—and the rest of my loving family—await me in Heaven?*

*Thank you for your abundant blessings, Dear God. Thank you.*

§§§§

Alejandro was buried in a tomb next to his daughter Marisol's tomb in the Royal Vault on December 8, 2021. Angilia selected the scripture for his tomb's plaque, which read:

Alejandro Martínez Agbulos

30 August 1928

6 December 2021

We took sweet counsel together, and walked unto the house of God in company.

Psalm 55:14

†

Juanita placed a white rose on her husband's chest and said, "I love you, Alejandro. I will miss you, mi marido, until my soul walks into Heaven to join you and mi hermosa Marisol. When that will be, I cannot know, but I will be with you, I know that. Mi nieta showed us the truth of that. With Angel here beside me, I shall not cry sad tears, Alejandro. When I do cry, it is because I know the joy you feel now in Heaven. I will feel that, too, in a few years. Until then, I look forward in anticipation, not backwards in despair. Yo amor tú, Alejandro."

# CHAPTER 12

As they did every year, the Royal Family and friends left for Christ Church Valmondois at 11:30 on Christmas Eve night. Mike drove them, and, Eric, Patrick, Angilia, and Matthew joined Reverend Hutchins in greeting those who came for the midnight service. Everyone was thrilled to see little Eric in his mother's arms, looking angelic himself in an heirloom lawn and lace gown. He was now five weeks old, and he watched everyone and everything with huge turquoise eyes.

The Royal Family followed Reverend Hutchins down the aisle and took their seats in their pew. They remained standing, and the rest of the congregation stood with them, for the invocation which formally opened the Christmas worship service. After Reverend Hutchins' sermon on the spirit of Christmas, Eric stood and walked to the pulpit.

As he had done every Christmas since 1979, Eric recited the Christmas story from Luke, Chapter 2. Patrick and Angilia smiled at one another and watched Eric with love and reverence. Eric smiled at them, recalling that moment exactly nine years earlier when Patrick had manifested. Eric's eyes shone with tears of love and gratitude when he looked at his grandson, watching him from Angilia's arms. What a beautiful sight to see his brother, his daughter, and his grandson together in church on Christmas Day.

When Eric returned to the pew, Patrick patted his shoulder. Angilia handed little Eric to Matthew, took Patrick's hand, and walked to the altar with him. The church musicians played while

Angilia and Patrick sang their hymn of choice, "O Holy Night." Never had the hymn resonated with as much love, honesty, and beauty as it did that night. While they sang, the congregation saw a golden glow surround Patrick and Angilia. The sight and the sound brought tears to many eyes, including their family members'.

When the service concluded one hour later, Eric, Patrick, Angilia with little Eric, and Matthew joined Reverend Hutchins in the traditional greeting line. "Oh, Angilia, never has anything been as beautiful and true as tonight," Nicole said through tears and hugged her friend. William, Nicole's husband, felt the truth and glory of the service, as well, and thanked Patrick for the touching hymn.

Darlene greeted them as she came through the line, hugging Matthew and wishing him a Merry Christmas. She kissed little Eric's forehead and hugged Angilia. "Gosh, Angilia, you are so amazing, you really are. I always thought you were special, but I never knew just how special you are." She whispered, "Your uncle is wow. I had no idea angels look like that." Matthew rolled his eyes when he overheard, hoping Darlene did not collapse when she greeted Patrick next. She kept her poise, barely, when he shook her hand, although she just stared at him with her mouth agape. Patrick knew her history, and he passed her hand to Eric in a grand gesture that made Darlene's face turn bright red. Scott once again, as usual, apologized and helped Darlene from the church.

Angilia smiled at her father, uncle, and husband. Scott and Darlene had started dating a couple of years earlier, and Angilia was happy for them. Besides, who else other than Scott would understand and tolerate Darlene's chronic adoration of King Eric and now Prince Patrick?

The Royal Family thanked Reverend Hutchins and returned home at 2:00 that morning. After good night hugs and kisses, Susan went to help Juanita prepare for bed, while Eric, Matthew, and Patrick helped get little Eric ready for bed, and Angilia changed into her pajamas. She stepped from her wardrobe/changing room and beamed when she saw Eric, Matthew, and Patrick gathered around little Eric's changing table.

Angilia joined them and relished the sight of the three men with little Eric. "I love you all so much. Eric and I are so incredibly blessed to have you in our lives. Every moment is a miracle with each of you, my darling husband, my magnificent father, my perfect uncle, and my precious son." Angilia kissed each of them and hugged them to her collectively.

"Dear God," she prayed, "Thank you for your tremendous blessings. Our lives are so filled with love, joy, peace, and faith because you love us and watch over us, God. Without you, we have nothing of substance. You remain our beacon and our truth. On this day when the world celebrates the birth of your miraculous Son, we thank you for the ultimate sacrifice you made in giving him life and letting him die for us. We understand how great a sacrifice that is, and we thank you eternally for that precious gift. Through you and your Son, Jesus, we have the promise of eternal life. Amen."

Eric, Matthew, and Patrick echoed her Amen, and little Eric gurgled. Angilia giggled through her happy tears and picked him up. "I think someone needs to eat and get some sleep," she said. Eric and Patrick kissed little Eric and Angilia, hugged Matthew, and left the young family for the remainder of the night.

Matthew sat beside his wife as she fed little Eric, and his eyes shone with love at the sight. No one and nothing could ever eclipse the miracles that Angilia and little Eric were and would always be for Matthew. When he had first seen her nine and one half years earlier, he never dared dream that his life would be so rich, full, and blessed.

§§§§

After breakfast, everyone settled in the sitting room, the traditional location of the family Christmas tree, and enjoyed the company, talk, and laughter of their loved ones. Little Eric's first Christmas was warm, cozy, and loving as everyone took turns holding and playing with him. Angilia smiled while she watched Roger talk to and hold little Eric. Roger seemed relaxed and happy, for which she was grateful.

Still smiling, Angilia walked out onto the balcony and took a deep breath. Eric quietly joined her and slipped his arms around her. "This is where it all began for us, Daddy. This is where I first came to you.  I will never forget seeing you again after 17 years in the Angels Choir."  Angilia turned and looked up at him.  "Oh, Daddy, I love you."  Tears slid down her cheeks.

Eric pulled her to him and kissed the top of her head.  "I know, Angel.  I love you.  Christmas Day truly is a blessed and holy day, baby.  I will never forget that sensation when your soul entered my heart.  I felt different inside.  I can't describe the feeling, but I just know that from the second your soul merged with mine, I have been different.  You changed me for all time, Angilia."

"I know what you mean, Daddy, because you changed me forever that first time I saw you.  Uncle Patrick knew it.  He saw it in me.  You consumed me.  You forged me.  I am God's child, and I am your child.  The two of you created and formed me."

"I may never know what I did to deserve you, my beautiful daughter, but I am grateful for you every second," Eric said through the tears choking him.

"You are you, Daddy.  You are the strong, wise, compassionate, righteous man God destined and wanted you to be.  You really are my David," Angilia softly said, smiling and referencing her inaugural 2012 Father's Day sermon.

Eric bowed his head as tears welled in and overflowed his eyes.  Angilia held him as he cried, unable to staunch her own tears.  Their love, though immeasurable, filled their hearts and souls and bound them for eternity.  Patrick watched them, his own soul filled to capacity with love for his family.  As he did, he saw a sunbeam break through the thick clouds and shine on Eric and Angilia, and he smiled.

§§§§

Antoine and his staff set up a lunch buffet in the sitting room, and soon the room buzzed with laughter, chatter, and squeals as their friends arrived.  Scott, Darlene, Shannon, Amy, Amanda, Nicole and William, Billy, Sam, John, Tom, Greg, Joe, Christopher, and Wayne Chambliss gathered for an afternoon of food, love, and joy.  Everyone wanted to wish little Eric a Merry Christmas, and he clapped his hands when Nicole and William handed him a small stuffed bunny.

"He's so sweet, Angilia. May I hold him?" Nicole asked. Angilia smiled and nodded, and Nicole held him cradled in her arms and cooed at him. Little Eric smiled at her, and Nicole smiled up at William.

"Nicole, William, congratulations," Angilia smiled at them and kissed Nicole's cheek and hugged William. They looked as stunned as they felt.

"How did you know?" Nicole quietly asked.

"I see it in your eyes," Angilia said. "When?"

"Next June. Oh, Angilia, I never imagined I could feel so happy," Nicole gushed. "I just hope our baby is as healthy and happy as your Eric. Gosh, he's so handsome. He does look like your father."

Darlene walked to them at that moment and smiled. "He does. Of course he's handsome. I still say your father is the most gorgeous man I have ever seen," Darlene admitted with a blush. She saw William shake his head. "Well, he is. I can't help it if he's so darn good looking. At least I'm not as awkward as I used to be."

"That's true," Nicole smiled.

"Of course, Prince Patrick is incredible, too. Everyone in this family is beautiful. It's almost unfair," Darlene said. "I am so happy for you, Angilia. You have your loving family, a wonderful husband, a beautiful baby, and you are here with all of us." Darlene hugged her friend and when tears threatened her, she excused herself and ran to the powder room.

The other young ladies and Scott circled around them and cooed over little Eric, congratulated Nicole and William, and formed a prayer circle. Nicole said a prayer of thanksgiving, and the friends hugged after they said Amen.

Throughout the afternoon, love was so tangible in the room that Angilia found herself smiling for hours. Everyone gathered on the sofas and chairs to watch "It's a Wonderful Life," and afterward Patrick performed his version of a parlor trick and made his white angel wings appear. Little Eric leaned over and grabbed for the wings, which made everyone giggle.

"Come here, little Eric. I have a special treat for you," Patrick said and held his grand-nephew in his arms. His wings flapped, and Patrick circled around the room, several feet off the floor, much to everyone's delight and amazement.

Patrick smiled down at his niece, and said, "Join us, Little One." Angilia looked at her father, and Eric smiled and shrugged his shoulders. Angilia shrugged her shoulders, as well, and right before their eyes, Angilia's pink angel wings became visible. She slowly flew around the room with her uncle and her son, while their family and friends watched with huge smiles.

"You have to do this for our baby," Nicole said. "How many babies get carried in the air by angels?" Angilia giggled and promised she would.

Juanita smiled as she watched her beloved granddaughter, the angel, waft through the air. Her large pink wings seemed to glow. "Mi nieta, you are the most beautiful angel," Juanita smiled, her hands folded in prayer before her. "Dr. Matthew's portrait of you is so true and perfect."

Angilia alighted in front of her grandmother and hugged her close. "I love you, Abuela. I always knew you suspected all of this, just as Mr. Brennan did. You are quite special, my sweet Abuela."

Juanita hugged Angilia and said, "Alejandro and I always knew how blessed we were with our Marisol and Eduardo, and then Eric and you, mi nieta. Now we have Dr. Matthew and little Eric. We could never dare want more blessings than that. All of you give me such love and pleasure. My heart is so full of love. I never need or want more than that."

§§§§§

That evening, after their friends had left amidst hugs and smiles, Angilia fed little Eric and put him in the bassinet. While

Angilia sat watching him, Susan quietly came in and offered to sit with little Eric for a while. "I don't mind at all, darling. Besides, your grandmother wants to see you in the sitting room when you finish with Eric."

Angilia stood and hugged Susan. "Thank you, Susan. I've known you my entire life. You, Roger, and Daniel were the first people I saw other than Daddy. I love you, Susan. I don't tell you that enough, and I'm sorry."

Susan wiped tears from her eyes. "Oh, foo, it's not like I don't cry enough as it is," Susan laughed. "Honey, you don't have to tell me. I know it. I feel it. And you know, if you hadn't revealed that you are an angel, I'd really wonder about you, you know. You were never like other babies. Now, if this little guy starts calling me Susan tonight, we have to talk," she teased. "He can't inherit your special powers, can he? Or can he?"

"Oh, Susan. I'll never tell," Angilia winked before she went to the sitting room and hugged her grandmother.

"Abuela, I love you," Angilia said and sat beside her grandmother.

"Mi nieta, I love you. I have to give you something before Christmas is over," Juanita said and asked Eduardo to get a present from the tree across the room. He gave it to his mother, and she held it close to her. "Your grandfather loves you. He asked me to give this to you today," she told Angilia and held the wrapped gift toward Angilia.

Angilia smiled at Juanita and Eduardo through her tears and took the package in her hands. She bowed her head in silent prayer for a few moments, dried her eyes, and carefully removed the paper. A book, secured by a flap and tie closure, revealed itself to her. The leather cover was worn and cracked. Before she touched it, Angilia knew it was Abuelo's journal.

"He wanted you, of all people, to have this, Angel. He started this diary when your mother and father became engaged. The day you were born and we visited you in the hospital, that is in here.  Alejandro marked the page with the ribbon.  He wanted you to read that first, mi nieta."

Angilia kissed her grandmother's cheek and blinked away tears while she opened to the bookmarked page and read what her grandfather wrote almost 26 years earlier:

*January 3, 1996*

*My heart does not have words for today.  Mi hermosa Marisol lived her life for today.  She did not live to see today, but she sees from her home in Heaven, I know that.  Eric, dear, strong Eric, what must his heart feel today?  Tomorrow he must bury his one true love and celebrate the birth of their daughter.  That I cannot fathom.  My heart both rejoices and breaks for Eric.*

*Their daughter.  My granddaughter.  She is so tiny and so very beautiful.  She is too perfect to be real, but she is real.  She has her father's eyes and curly blonde hair.  Those eyes look at me in such an unusual way I can't describe really.  It is as if this newborn baby knows everything already.  Or is that the proud grandfather in me boasting?  I doubt that.*

*Angilia Erica Charity, mi nieta.  Her name means Angel.  For many months, I have heard Eric and Marisol call her that, talk to her, sing to her, know her.  There is something about her, something I cannot put my finger on.  This tiny baby looks deep into my soul.  She seems to have what many people call an old soul.  She knows things no baby knows.  I am certain of that.*

*I watched her, this baby who is just hours old, and I saw her seem to glow from within.  Eric has said from the beginning that their daughter is very special, and I start to believe him in earnest now.  Who would believe me?  No one.  They will tell me that every grandfather thinks his grandchild is special.  Perhaps they do.  But mi nieta Angilia is different, I feel it.*

*I cannot say how happy I am.  I look forward to watching Angilia grow up, and then I will see just how very special she really is.  What will she show to me as she grows into a woman?  How much of her life will God allow me to see?  She is just born, and I love her more than I have loved anyone.*

Angilia carefully closed the diary and hugged Abuela close.  "Thank you, Abuela.  This is such a treasure of a gift.  I will read and reread this, and I will read this to little Eric.  He will share this with his children and grandchildren.   Abuelo will never leave us or our hearts."

§§§§

*31 December 2021*

*This year is the most miraculous of my lifetime to date.   My beloved son Eric joined us!   After so long reliving our meeting in the Unborn Children Sphere and praying for his survival during the precarious moments, God blessed us with our handsome, precious son Eric Matthew Patrick DeBruce Martineau Taylor.   Eric was born on Daddy's 67th birthday, 17 November 2021.   What a miracle and gift from God!   We love him more than words can ever impart, but God knows and Eric feels our love, I know that.*

*This year my wonderful Abuelo left us and went to live in Heaven. What a truly blessed experience to share with him and the family.   I know he felt our love surround him in his last moments with us here.   Even more beautiful is that Mommy came as his Spirit Guide, and she kissed Daddy and me.   I can only try to understand what he has felt for 26 years without her earthly presence.   For her to manifest for him and to kiss him is such a miracle itself.   I saw his face, his eyes, and I know how much he treasures that moment. He last kissed his wife moments before her body died, 23 October 1995.   How much I love Mommy and Daddy!   We will all reunite in Heaven someday, we know that.   Until then, we have this precious moment to hold in our memories.*

*A few days ago, Abuela gave me a Christmas gift from Abuelo—his diary dating back to Mommy's and Daddy's engagement.   He wrote the last entry in it a few hours before he died.   Reading it touches my heart so tenderly. He gave me the gift of seeing everything through his eyes.   What a legacy he leaves for future generations!   I love him so very much!   Seeing him leave for Heaven with Mommy fills my soul with such love and peace.*

*The past five years—what loving memories to cherish for my lifetime and to leave as part of my legacy of love for Eric, his children, his grandchildren, and all future generations.   When they read my diaries, they will know how I felt, and they will see my experiences through my eyes.*

*2016, the year I turned 20, was such a momentous year.   Matthew and I shared our engagement, married, basked in our love during our Scottish honeymoon, and fulfilled God's destiny for us.   We also shared Mr. Brennan's death and ascent to Heaven with him.   His daughter was his Spirit Guide, and*

303

*his joy banished any sadness we might have felt at his death.  Sharing death with someone is an absolute blessing and gift.*

*That year, Uncle Patrick returned to the public spotlight, when he and I co-wrote a song that Daddy and I recorded.  Uncle Patrick's words worked a minor miracle themselves in helping to ease peoples' fear of death.  God ordained Uncle Patrick, and the song was just the first of Patrick's public works on behalf of God.  Little did either of us know just what God did have planned for us in the coming years!*

*In 2017, Matthew and I wrote and illustrated a children's book together, and I know now that is was God's way of preparing me—and the world—for his major task awaiting me.  The book is about a little boy, an angel, who lives on earth.  His real identity is unknown for years.  It's no secret where that idea originated!  Matthew and I went on a book tour, which was both fun and somewhat unsettling, since we had to cancel the Tokyo dates due to some overexcited people.*

*Daddy, Matthew, and I spent two months on a tour of the United States in 2018.  We met so many wonderful, kind, and inspiring people.  Daddy of course was the superstar he always is, and he literally won their hearts and admiration.  He is so respected and loved around the world!  On that August 30, Abuelo celebrated his 90th birthday, and his portrait was unveiled in the museum.  He truly deserves to be represented there for all time.*

*Daddy's 65th birthday was 17 November 2019, and a new portrait of him was placed in the museum, next to a portrait of Uncle Patrick that was displayed there in 2017.  How beautiful that these two remarkable, magnificent men's portraits hang side by side in the gallery!  I love them both so incredibly!*

*Also that year, Roger suffered a heart attack, and although he is all right now, it caused his fear of death to surface.  Uncle Patrick came to my room while Roger talked with me, and Patrick really eased Roger's fears and stress.  God truly used Patrick a lot starting that year.*

*That summer, Sarah and Natalie literally walked into my life, and to help convince Sarah that her baby boy was alive in Heaven, Patrick manifested.  Watching him erase Sarah's heartache that day filled me with such peace and warmth.  I knew that day that God has very special plans indeed for my charming Uncle Patrick!*

*Matthew's art pieces were donated to several museums in the United States during our tour, and last year several of his paintings were donated to our museum. Matthew's gallery gains at least one new painting a year! I love him so very much, and seeing him create the art he was meant to create is such a soothing, peaceful feeling. He is doing what he did in the Unborn Children Sphere, and what he was always meant to do! His work is stunning, truly it is.*

*Beloved Abuela celebrated her 90th birthday that July, and her portrait joined Abuelo's in the museum. They should be there as Mommy's parents. It's only fitting and right. The family gallery would be incomplete without their portraits. I've already talked to Matthew. For the 100th anniversary of Abuelo's birth, in 2028, I want Matthew to paint a portrait of Abuelo and Abuela together that will have a place of honor in the gallery. Matthew will more than do my beloved grandparents justice, and I can think of no one else who should paint their portrait than my love, Matthew.*

*2020 was the year of Uncle Patrick! He was a poster boy and teen idol in the 1970s—I have the clippings and vintage posters to prove that. Last year, though, he made a major public comeback! I've already written in detail about all of this in the diary and my book, but Patrick and I co-wrote a song and recorded it and another song. His voice charmed the entire world! Before people saw him, Patrick was a major megastar!*

*God planned this perfectly, for our recordings coincided with the publication of my memoir. I finally wrote and published my true life story. God blessed the recordings and the book, and through them, Patrick and I were able to travel the world on behalf of God. Doing God's work means everything to both of us, and we remain honored and humbled to do whatever God asks or directs us to do. That is the least we can do for all of God's blessings and love.*

*Uncle Patrick—what can I say? I love him. He is my angel, my knight, my prince. He is my most treasured friend.*

*Last year ended in the storm surrounding the recordings with Patrick and my memoir. This year our son Eric joined our lives and filled our hearts. I could have never predicted the past five years, but I would not have anyway. I leave that to God, for he knows best. He planned our lives before our births, and I pray to do his duty and to earn his love. His love, his blessings, and his protection surround us every moment, and for that we remain eternally grateful.*

*A new year looms nearby, waiting to greet us with more adventures, experiences, people, places, and blessings. What will 2022 bring to my precious family?  I do not know, nor do I want to know.  I will accept whatever happens in 2022, regardless of what occurs.  As I know from past experience, God does not cause everything that happens to us.  You know, I just realized that the tenth anniversary of the shooting will be on 7 March 2022.  Someone attempted to alter God's plans for Daddy and me, but God did not let that happen.*

*Instead of letting a godless person interfere with his plans for us, God stepped in and realigned our lives.  Matthew became a cardiac surgeon so that he could save and re-enter my life.  We are now blissfully married, and our precious son Eric is alive and with us!  I trust God completely to lead me, guide me, teach me, and control my life.  If I do not trust him, I am doomed.*

*These past five years taught me more about love.  I always knew and felt love, but never romantic love until Matthew literally ran back into my life.  Yes, I was afraid of what that all meant at first, as I was young and inexperienced.  Matthew, to his immense credit, kept his promise and waited for my heart to mature.  What few people know is that prior to our marriage, Matthew in many ways was as inexperienced as I was.*

*Matthew is my love and my hero.  He never paraded his purity, and despite a lot of mean-spirited comments in the press about the handsome playboy doctor pursuing the chaste princess, he never let it upset him.  It bothered me more than it did him, because I knew their lies.  Matthew had never had a serious girlfriend.  Somewhere in his heart, he knew his destiny, and he waited for me.  What a gift and a blessing my husband gave to me!*

*My entire life is a gift and a blessing!  I know that, and I never want to take one second for granted.  Every moment is a wonder and a joy.  As 2021 ends, I look back with love and peace, while I look forward with love, peace, and faith.  Everything in my life will be according to God's plan—perfect, blessed, and full of love.*

**Sheilah R. Craft** is an English professor, writer, blogger, poet, artist, ardent genealogist, and book lover. Born and raised in the Midwestern United States, Sheilah was born surrounded by a close family—including several educators—books, and animals. She began reading and writing very early, and has published short stories, articles, and poems. <u>Heart-Glow</u>, the first novel in what will be a six-book series, was published in 2012. <u>First Love Never Dies</u> is the second novel in the series.

# Web Site and Exclusive Content

Please visit the companion web site, which contains additional information, pictures, and exclusive features. Those who purchase this book have access to specific password protected content on the web site. To access the exclusive content, please visit Heart-Glow: A Novel at **http://www.heartglownovel.org**

On the protected pages, when prompted for the password, please enter **heartglowcraft16***

www.ingramcontent.com/pod-product-compliance
Lightning Source LLC
Chambersburg PA
CBHW082053090726
47909CB00010B/3018